LILITH'S CASTLE

Gill Alderman was born in Dorset. She is married with two daughters and five grandchildren. She lives with her second husband (a research scientist), six lurchers and three cats in Cobh, on Cork Harbour in Ireland. Until 1984 she worked in micro-electronics research. This is her fourth novel.

Voyager

GILL ALDERMAN

Lilith's Castle

Each page a promise that all
shall be well

HarperCollins*Publishers*

Voyager
An Imprint of HarperCollins*Publishers*
77–85 Fulham Palace Road,
Hammersmith, London w6 8jb

A Paperback Original 1999
1 3 5 7 9 8 6 4 2

A catalogue record for this book
is available from the British Library

ISBN 0 00 648272 4

Typeset in Sabon by
Palimpsest Book Production Limited,
Polmont, Stirlingshire

Printed and bound in Great Britain by
Caledonian International Book Manufacturing Ltd, Glasgow

To Justine and Dorothy
with love.

ACKNOWLEDGEMENTS

The quotation on the title page is from Séan Dunne's poem *Message Home* (from his collection *Against the Storm*, Dolmen Press 1985) and those heading the two parts from the *Dhammapada* and Dante's *Inferno*.

The quotations which head each chapter are from *The Burial Service*, The Book of Common Prayer, (Prologue); *Táin Bó Cuailgne*, Irish anon., twelfth century and earlier, Thomas Kinsella's translation; (adapted from) *The Law of the Jungle*, Rudyard Kipling; (adapted from) *Old Peter's Russian Tales*, Arthur Ransome; *Táin Bó Cuailgne*, Irish anon., twelfth century and earlier, Thomas Kinsella's translation; *Prologue to The Canterbury Tales*, Chaucer, transliteration Nevill Coghill; *The Human Seasons*, John Keats; *Excelsior*, Henry Longfellow; *The Old Wives' Tale*, George Peele; *Native American Song from Omaha*; *A Shropshire Lad*, A.E. Housman; *The Metamorphoses of Ovid*; *Traditional riddle*.

Other quotations are as follows: the Sage, p. 83, quotes from the *Bhagavad-Gita*; Koschei in his Journal, p. 197, from *Helen* by Oscar Wilde; Darklis, p. 133, sings lines from *Drinking* by Abraham Cowley and p. 201, a hymn by Jan Struther; Koschei reads from *Hyperion* by John Keats, p. 213; the Red Horse's rhyme, p. 250, is traditional and Gry's, p. 261, is adapted from a Native American verse; the Shadows sing, p. 273 and p. 281, lines adapted from the hymn by B. Ingemann; Koschei's soul is trapped between two of John Keats's *Sonnets*, p. 383, and the Cathedral Choir sings a line from Psalm 149, p. 353. The Castle of Truth game is loosely based on Keats's *St Agnes' Eve* and all quotations in that section are from his work except, p. 359 a hymn by Jan Struther and, p. 380, *The World's A Bubble* by Francis Bacon. The Old English on p. 291 is from Bede's *Ecclesiastical History*. Aurel's battle cries are from the O.E. poem, *The Fight at Finnsburgh* and *Excelsior* by Longfellow.

Thanks to
Chitu Patel for putting me on the right track in 'India', to Aeschylus and Dante for help with geography and language in Hell and the Palace of Shadows, to John for the late night conversation about memory locations and to Thomas Pike for advice about Ben.

he fleeth as it were a shadow

....

Nandje, Rider of the Red Horse, Father and Imandi to the Ima tribe, lay still beneath the ceremonial blanket which covered him. The bustard feathers woven into it pierced his face with their long barbs and the rawhide strips lay heavier than lead on his throat, part of him and also something separate, deadly and symbolic. The felted horsehair had sucked up his blood and sunk into the rotting craters which were his wounds. He knew himself to be no longer human and a man but as much and little as the earth on which the Horse Herd also trampled, wounding its soft surface with the same lunular pits.

It was ill to be thus trapped underground, within a redundant body whose eyelids were held down with stones, nostrils and lips sewn shut with dried Plains grasses. Nor could he recall the Past, whatever that unlikely concept was, or look into the Future as he had once been able, in life. The Now, terrible, endless, was all: death inescapable, triumphant, eternal.

Aza, the Shaman, lifted the blanket from Nandje's face and observed the dead Imandi's crushed skull and grotesquely distorted face. The skin was drying out and splitting, pulling his twelve-month-old stitching apart. He found an end and pulled the grass strands out, to the last shred and wisp, using his nails where the flesh had tightened round the thread.

'The sleep of death is long,' said Aza 'but there comes a time to awaken.'

He took up the pointed stick he had prepared during the long mourning and thrust it between the lips and teeth of the corpse, down savagely, hard to the base of the throat. It groaned and belched as the gases rose and bubbled from its liquid interior and a terrible stench was hurled into his face. The corpse moths which had been incubated in Nandje's body flew free, a many-winged pied cloud.

'Nay, go peacefully to the Palace of Shadows!' he cried. 'Be wise and kind, as you were with us.'

The final alteration had taken place with the freeing and the flight of Nandje's soul. All that remained was lolling, putrefying matter which Aza might leave alone to complete its metamorphosis, flesh to grass. Tenderly and carefully, for this was the last office he was able to perform for Nandje, he rolled back and folded the death-blanket and carried it with him, up into the light.

THE PATHLESS WAY

Leave the past behind; leave the future behind;
leave the present behind

It is the usual thing for a herd led by a mare
to be strayed and destroyed

....

The night was almost over and the Red Horse walked slowly out of it, pacing steadily over the low hills which lay between Nandje's tomb and his Herd. He had made this nightly journey since the burial, observing how the body he had carried at both easy walk and furious gallop was decaying and what tender care the shaman took over his rituals. Yet, each time he returned to the Herd, he felt at heart less satisfied and more restive. These emotions, he knew, came to him because his understanding was beginning to awake and not from sorrow at the untidy fate of Nandje, nor any fellow-feeling for the fine man he had been.

The horses stood in small constellations, group by group within the universe of the Herd. The stars were fading and dawn about to break. A skein of geese, pointing like an arrow to the far horizon, flew overhead and the Red Horse paused to watch them out of sight. They were flying into the wind and making heavy weather of it, yet the song of their wings was hopeful and eager: they were always moving on from riverhead to marsh, from forest lake to seashore, water their element as his was this grass-grown earth of the Plains. The wind pushed at his back and he moved off, breaking into a canter as he breasted the last hill and saw his mares and young stallions, his filly foals and colts all facing forward, all looking out for him. The Herd neighed a soft welcome, the sound passing from horse to mare, and he returned the greeting joyfully: this part of his life was whole and good. He turned his head toward the village where the Ima slept. The sun always rose beyond it. He waited patiently for its first, arising rays to touch the round roofs of the houses.

Nandje's daughter crawled from her house. It was the only way to enter or leave it, through the low tunnel which was both doorway and defence. She was still in mourning for her father, deeply shocked and deeply grieving; but there were the everyday tasks to do, the chores which kept her headless family comfortable and the wolf, hunger, from the door. Milking was the first each day, a little thin, blue-tinted milk to take from each milch mare. She (as every Ima man and woman must) loved her horses and, equally, her wide, bleak birthplace in the Plains. Her name was Gry and her age, since time is lawless in Malthassa, was perhaps seventeen.

The cold wind blew in Gry's face. She tasted the salt in it and covered her ears against the stories it brought from far away. Nothing could be done while the Salt Wind blew from the furthest corner of the Plains and passed over Garsting on its way to bring down the trees of the forest; and nothing could be done while they were all in mourning.

Her hair had begun to grow again and covered her scalp as the new spring grass does the ground, sparse and short. She knew how ugly she was and had been, shorn thus and stripped of every piece of her silver jewellery. That lay, with her hair and her happiness, in her father's tomb while each new day began heavy and slow and continued unrelieved into night. She lifted her milking-pail and laid it across her shoulder, turned her back on the wind – that was where the Horse Herd would be, facing away from the salt-savour, heads low and ears flattened to diminish the rumours which – now – ears uncovered – she heard fly past her, the brittle voices of the zracne vile shrieking 'Sorrow! Sorrow! Bitter death!' It seemed to Gry that all of Malthassa, from marsh to ocean, from the unknown beyond the Plains to the end of the world at the back of the mountains, had died with her father. She trudged out across the first low hills, her bare feet shrinking from the chilly ground and the skin pail clammy against her neck. All the world was grey and dusky; of late, the birds, cowering in bush and grass, had forgotten their songs and did not take to the air on pliant wing; but the zracne vile, the spirits of the air, tumbled past in the wind, now head first, now blown backwards, hair and limbs awry.

None of the women, save Gry, could see spirits; sometimes her companions looked strangely at her, or whispered tales behind her back, for all that she was Nandje's daughter. But today she had come alone and early to the milking, stealing out before anyone else in the village was awake.

Gry climbed the third hill. Something was keeping pace with her: she sensed its warmth and knew it was not a wolf or any beast to fear. A heath-jack perhaps or a deer strayed from the forest to graze. It moved closer and she saw its outline as the light increased, big, massy, equine. A thrush flew up and sang suddenly, tossing random, joyous notes on high in the instant she recognised the horse and her heavy heart, against all expectation, lifted. The Red Horse: it was he. Lately, over six or seven recent days, he had begun to come to her, stand only feet away and watch her from huge and sympathetic eyes. Once, he had nudged her with his moss-soft nose and shied away; once snatched the sweet grass she shyly offered him. He loomed, a dark bulk in the dawn, and she reached out, awed when her hand at last touched and rested on his smooth hide. He suffered her to walk with him. Then, as the sun rose higher, something marvellous: the Red Horse halted for a moment, turned his head to Gry and rested it against her chest. She, leaning forward, enclosed as much of the great face as she could reach with her free arm; and they walked on, horse and girl, into the midst of the Herd, where the mother-mares were waiting to be milked.

Gry drew a little milk, before the foals fed, from each mare's teats. The white mare named Summer, a rarity in a herd of dun and russet Plains horses, and chief wife of the Red Horse, waited last. Gry stroked her and bent beneath her to milk. When her pail was full to the brim she drank a little of it herself, wiped her mouth on her hand, and set the pail upright on a level piece of ground. The Red Colt was feeding well, the long sticks of his legs splayed and his short tail rotating with pleasure. Gry smiled and heard the Red Horse snort his pleasure. He moved close again; she felt she should hold her breath or repeat one of the shaman's lucky charms aloud. The great horse shivered, nervous as a cricket, and lowered his head still further as if he wanted to kneel before her and beg a favour. She found herself leaning against him, taking comfort from his bulk and warmth and, when he bent his near foreleg, placing her left foot there, above the knee and springing without thought but only instinct upward, turning in the air and settling on his back while she spoke the ritual phrase her father had always used.

'Greeting, Horse. Permit me.'

Gry sat in her forbidden seat, elated and fearful. The reputation of the Horse was all ferocity, virility and fire. No one was able to ride him – except her father, Nandje, who had worshipped the Herd for itself and as a symbol of life, who had loved each individual horse as much as his children; who had died when he was swept from this same, broad back (so wide it pulled the muscles of her groin to straddle him.) The terrified Herd had trampled Nandje into the ground.

No one was allowed to ride the Red Horse; save the new Imandi when he, at last and at the end of the long days of mourning, was chosen. She remembered the trials Nandje had undergone, in the old days when she was a child, to catch and afterwards mount and master the Horse and she looked down on the mane and neck which swept upwards to his pointed, eager ears. In a moment he would bend that neck, throw up his hind feet in a mighty buck and dash her down; then she would see Nandje again, in the place beyond death. But all the Horse did was whinny softly and, shaking a presumptuous fly from his head, settle into his long, smooth stride. Gry breathed more easily and let herself sink into and become a part of the force and balance which made him what he was, the Master of the Herd. It was not as if she could not ride. Horses and their culture were her birthright. Her own mare, Juma, had lingered, heavily in foal, on the margin of the group of milch-horses; lately she had been lent the swift and stubborn Varan who belonged to her eldest brother, and she had many times ridden the lesser stallions and Summer too, before the getting of the Colt. But today there were no reins to be gathered up, none of the usual preparations and practices; just herself, Gry, and the Red Horse. She pulled her skirts into place and rested her hands comfortably on her thighs. How much more easy would she be in loin-cloth and twin aprons, bare-legged and booted like the men!

Her country, the great Plains of Malthassa, was before her and about her, turquoise in the morning light. She could see the blue flag of her people fluttering above Garsting, though the village itself was hidden behind a hill. Three other villages, Sama, Rudring and Efstow were visible, their underground houses grass-grown mounds very like the green hills of the Plains. She looked into the wind, which blew less strongly but was still laden with the bitter salt, and her gaze came to rest on the distant, grassy knoll which was her father's last dwelling place and tomb. Outwardly there was little to distinguish it from the houses of the living.

Nandje's burial-mound had been raised a half-morning's journey from his village. Gry, although she was female and so excluded from funerals, executions and the daily rituals of the Shaman, which belonged to the men, knew that it was dangerous to let the dead stay close by the living, for they may talk to one another or appear in each other's dreams. And she knew that there were strict rules and observances to be obeyed when any man of the Ima visited an ancestor in his house. The first of them was that no woman may enter there.

I am already guilty, sitting up here on the Imandi's Horse – no, riding forward, letting him carry me toward the burial-mound, thought Gry. So there will be only a little more harm if, when we reach it, I get down and walk to the mound – just to see the doorway they must have carried my father through, and to stand there and remember him and say farewell. I am beginning to forget him already: I have thought only of myself and this pleasant morning since I milked the mares –

9

and the milk will be quite safe where it is. The wind will cool it well.

'Well!' echoed the zracne vile, 'Farewell!' and the Red Horse, before she could change her mind or jump down, broke into a ground-eating canter, which carried her swiftly forward across the Plain.

He halted in a hollow below the burial-mound and let Gry slide from his back before lowering his head to graze the sweet, young grasses which the wind, become as gentle as a sleeper's breathing, moved hardly at all. Gry went on tiptoe up the slope of the hollow and knelt outside the entrance to the tomb. Someone had walked there a little while before. The grass showed the prints of large, booted feet leading away and she remembered that the shaman had been living there for a long while, to tend her father's body. There was no door. Doorposts and a lintel of the boulders which littered some parts of the Plains surrounded a dark opening. She peered into the darkness, but could see nothing within. Indeed, the darkness brought back all her sorrow: it was terrible to end in such a dismal place. She closed her eyes to hold back her tears.

'Oh, kind and valorous Rider, wise Imandi,' she began bravely, but could not stop the tears. 'Oh, my father – why did you have to die? I could not even say goodbye because the men took you away and put you in *there*.'

He used to come home at sunset, she remembered, and hang the Horse's bridle on its hook on the east side of the house. Then, after walking round the fireplace to the far side, would sit and wait for her to bring him water to wash in. 'The sun is low,' he always said, 'I am glad to sit by our fire' or, sometimes, 'There is a wonderful smell coming from the pot, Gry – like the thyme your mother used in her cooking. Is it her recipe, my daughter?'

She could almost hear him, so intense were her memories – just behind her as he used to be when seated in the house and she dipping water from the bucket into the copper bowl. She looked round. Nandje stood, with a gentle smile on his face, close by the Red Horse. She knew at once that, though he looked so solidly real, he was without substance, a ghost which could not be touched and could not touch her. He, and all his clothing, looked grey as ashes. With him had come a familiar, long-loved smell, the burnt-sugar odour of his pipe tobacco which floated unseen about him.

'Gry, my daughter,' he said, 'be calm. Do not give way to fear. Aza has released my soul from my body and I must begin my journey to the Palace of Shadows. There is nothing in the mound now but my discarded and useless body surrounded by the offerings of sorrow: that is all. Go in and look at it if you will, but remember me as I was in life – whether at home or abroad with the Herd. Remember me –'

'Father –'

'I cannot stay. Take care of the Horse. Remember me . . .'

Gry stared at the space where Nandje had been. The noise of the Red Horse grazing comforted her: he had behaved as though nothing was amiss so, when she had assured herself that he was content, she turned back to the mound and walked into its dark and cavernous interior. Soon, when her eyes were used to the dimness, she could see. Some light had followed her in, enough to show her the bier of woven willows and her father's remains lying on it. She approached and looked down on them. What he had said was true: she had no need to fear. This racked and ruined body had nothing to do with Nandje. He had become a memory, and this ugly thing was the same as anything from which the soul has gone, a bird lying dead in winter, a heath-jack killed for the pot, meat which has once been a fleet horse. Gry fingered the offerings which lay in a circle round the body: her two plaits, her silver necklaces and bangles; the little vial of her brothers' mingled blood, Garron's best belt and Kiang's finest dagger; the dishes, beakers, arrows, fish-hooks and snares her uncles and aunts had provided; the bag laid there for Nandje to carry these grave-goods to the Palace of Shadows.

Gry walked sunwise round the bier, bent and kissed the dead thing on what was left of its crushed forehead. Nandje's weathered skin was taut and dry, punctured full of the holes from which the corpse-moths had crawled, after feeding on his flesh. His

11

falchion and bow were in his withered hands, gripped more by exposed bone than by vanishing flesh; his hands had been calloused, Gry remembered, from the bowstring and roughened by the Plains wind and the cold. He had been dressed in his best, blue aprons, red boots and gilded belt; they was all shabby, drab and decaying. His two clay pipes and his tobacco pouch were in their places on his belt but – she glanced about, searching – not his dagger with its narrow blade of Pargur steel and bone hilt, and the copper sheath with the horse-head chape. She knew it so well. The dagger had been drawn to cut hide into ropes and sheets, to carve meat, slice apples, open hog nuts; even to stir honey into hot kumiz.

'An Imandi, unlike lesser men with needy families, is always buried with his goods and weapons,' Gry said to herself. 'I know this, though I am a woman. Perhaps the knife was mislaid before the burial rite – but another would have been got. Perhaps a thief has crept in here! I shall ask Aza – except that I can't know the dagger's gone, or I would be a thief myself in Aza's eyes. I'll ask Garron, no – Aunt Jennet. Or look for it myself and bring it back –

'But how will my father do without a knife to cut his shadow-meat?'

She shivered, though it was not cold underground. The death house had become much darker, for the light was fading. Then she saw the Red Horse in the doorway, head and shoulders filling the gap. She smiled and went to him.

'You came for me,' she said. 'Or did you come to see what has become of your Rider?'

The Horse pushed his head against her and she stroked him. She thought she heard her father's voice once more.

'*You* are the Rider.'

She shook her head in dismissal and disbelief.

'We must go, Horse,' she said. 'You to your Herd and I to the milk and my woman's duties. Yet I shall spend this day as I have spent so many, wondering where it is my father has gone – oh, not his poor, broken body, not that, but himself, Nandje who

12

rode you everywhere, who was my father and my mother too, since Lemani died.'

Aza, the Shaman of Garsting, crouched in his hollow. He, alone of the Ima, lived always above ground and knew which way the wind blew and what it told; saw sunrise succeed sunset and the sun crowd the moon from the sky. He had put away the death-blanket and the sharpened stick he had used to release Nandje's soul from his outworn body. The blanket would be used again to cover Garron or Kiang, Battak or Oshac, whoever was chosen Imandi, when his time came; but the stick, that was a mark on the wayward calendar of Malthassan time, and Aza had a bundle of them. He was very old, yet seemed himself to have cheated age in his wrinkled brown skin and mane of white hair. He was old and jealous of the young. He could still run, true enough, but they could walk faster; he could sigh and remember his young manhood, but they were in possession of it, their blood red and their appetites fresh and keen. Nor did Aza feel any softening of his heart towards young women. He had forgotten his first wife, the one who died in childbirth; his second, who had fallen into the flooded River Nargil and his third, the pretty creature who had left him for a horseman. He had outlived his children and his grandchildren and was truly alone upon the earth, but for his talismans and the spirits.

The north wind passed over Aza in his hollow. The shaman kept five spirit-horses, long and fearsome creatures made of ash-poles, skulls, and hides and hair, and he looked up, seeing how the wind moved their skins and brought life to their dried tails and manes. The horses guarded him and there was one to face East and one to face West, one for the South and one for the North; and one to watch the sky. At night, or when he had gone into the breathless trance, Aza spoke with them and learned what they had seen; now they were silent, unless the rattling of their skins against their bones of ash wood was a kind of speech, or a lament for earlier and better days, when they had galloped, eaten the sweet grass and roamed the Plains at will.

Aza had a sixth horse which he had inherited from the old shaman, Voag, when he was called to his seat at Russet Cross. He kept it in a basket. Now, he rose and fetched the basket from where it lay upon a rolled-up prayer flag. Unpegging the lid, he lifted the separate pieces of this horse out of its basket and stable and began to arrange them in an intricate pattern on the ground. He wanted to weave a bridle out of the living grass and to do this, it was necessary to bring the power from the bones of the sixth horse and a hungry sprite from the earth.

'Svarog, see me! he cried, 'Stribog, hear me! Feel me walk upon you, Moist Mother Earth. O, send me a puvush, a goodly puvush lacking nothing but her malice and wanting nothing but food. I will feed her, I will put bread in her mouth and send her back to you uncharmed and unharmed.'

In front of Aza, the ground rippled as if it had become water, and the limbs of the bone horse lying on it clashed together. A small mound grew beneath the grass and, suddenly bursting open, let go a long, grey body thinner than a snake or blind-worm. The puvush reared up and the skeletal horse jumped high to follow her and join her wild dance. It had been strong and fleet before it was killed and remembered how its joints fitted together and how it had run and shied at shadows whenever it desired, and drunk the constant wind; and how its head had been taken from its body and burned in a fire so that it could no longer do any of these things.

'Rest, little Tarpan!' Aza commanded it. 'Your part is finished.' The bones subsided and lay still and Aza knelt beside the dancing puvush to wait until she tired. At last, her head and body bowed and she turned her pinched and greedy face towards him. He was ready and thrust the bread crust he was holding into her open mouth.

'I have you. You are mine,' he said, 'for the time that begins now and the time it takes for this feather to fall to earth. Make me a bridle: I have something to bind.'

Aza's magic skylark's feather rose into the air and swayed there while the puvush, moving faster than the winter wind about the shaman's sky-roofed house, picked a bundle of grass stems, twisted each stalk thrice and wove them into a bridle. The shaman's eyes grew sore and his head dizzied from watching her. It was done, the charm complete; but Aza groaned aloud. The price of this charm was a cupful of blood, to be drawn from his arm before sundown and offered to Mother Earth. The feather fell to earth and he bade the puvush be gone in a gruff voice, testy with fatigue.

It was done. The hooves of the spirit-horses clapped together at the ends of the skin tubes which had been their legs: Aza had his bridle, which he held up, admiring its close weave and counterfeit, bristly bit. He was ready, he, Aza the Shaman, who no longer had any use or affection for women, excepting the Night Mare, and who had seen Gry, Nandje's daughter, an unwed woman, riding like a man (no less!), doing what she should not, and entering where she was forbidden. Therefore the shaman had made his preparations, his defence and attack.

Gry sang. Her sorrow had lifted as the day lengthened. I do not know where Nandje's shadow rests, she thought, but there is no longer any reason to cry because I have spoken with him. Life ends so that death may begin.

The Red Horse followed as she walked him back to his mares and to her pail of milk, which she lifted to her shoulder. Then she patted the Horse with her free hand and watched him wander into the new grass and lower his head to graze, his back toward her, his tail twitching off the flies. She turned in the opposite direction and made for home. The blue flag of her people was flying bravely over Garsting and its colour, brighter than the sky in midsummer, made her think of warmth and the coming Flowering of the Plains. She sang cheerfully of love and marriage:

> 'I long to be married when the red poppies grow
> And the grass whispers "Leal is my darling,"
> It's time to wear yellow and braid up my hair,
> But I need a pair of boots for my wedding –'

It was that time before dusk when the light lingers on the hilltops of the Plains and the hollows in between are awash with violet shadow; it is hard then to judge distance and to keep one's mind from wandering into the dreamworld which rightly belongs to night. Yet Gry, carolling the chorus to her love song, strode through the gloaming and wondered if anyone had missed her. There were few to do so. Her aunts had their own households to care for and their own mares to milk, while she had only a few milch mares and Garron and Kiang, who were both courting and often out teasing their lasses or hunting jacks and partridge to give them. When she got home, she would pour the milk into the kumiz vat and rake away the ashes from the embers on the hearth; she would pile on fresh fuel, knead last night's dough again and set it to bake on the stone; perhaps Garron would come in then, with his keen gaze that was so like her father's and his forest-wood bow. He would sit to unstring and grease it while they talked over the day. Or Kiang would hurry in, bending in the doorway, laughing at some mishap or joke – Gry started and the milk slopped over her neck. The song had already died . . . It was Aza: what could he want? She did not like him, for all he was a holy man. He used to scare her with his auguries and chanting when she was small; she did not nowadays care to be alarmed for nothing. Especially when she had just learned to be whole and happy again.

'It is warm; the grass grows,' she said, conventionally.

'It is warm, my daughter, and warm enough for travelling,' the shaman answered. Gry immediately resented his words and, her face reddening, said stubbornly, 'I am my father's daughter, Aza.'

'This makes you bold. You have been a long time at the milking – a morning and an afternoon to bring the milk of ten mares home to your brothers!'

'My brothers are courting, Aza, and don't care what I do –'

'But I do, Nandje's Daughter – or have you an ambition to be his third son? I saw you by the burial-mound. I saw you and the Red Horse at the burial-mound.'

16

Aza came nearer, detaching himself from the shadows, a wizened spider of a man hung about with the sharp bills of ravens and the curved beaks and talons of hawks which scratched at and tangled with his strings and necklaces of shell and bone, and with the dried faces of the Plains stoats stitched like battle-trophies to his mantle. A monkey's skull was fastened in his wild white hair.

'I saw you astride the Red Horse!'

The shaman leapt forward suddenly and grasped Gry by the arm so that the pail flew from her shoulder and all the milk soared out of it in a great, white arc.

'More than milk will be spilt,' said Aza.

Gry did not move. He terrified her, leering in her face with his thin lips and his black and broken teeth. He smelled of corruption and death and his touch was that of a viper, dry and mean. Slowly, he lifted his left hand, waving it as a snake does its head to mesmerise a heath-jack. He held a bridle, she saw and then, in the blinking of an eye and before she could bestir herself or scream, it was tight on her, its straps chafing her cheeks and brow and its bit, which was thick and full of spines, digging into her lips and tongue . . . she would scream. She tried to open her mouth but the bit, and Aza's hands on the reins, prevented her; a thick, bubbling sound shook her throat. She thought she would be stifled.

'You must be shown to the men. You must explain how you bewitched the Horse,' said the shaman and jerked her forward. Like a stubborn, unbroken horse, she dug her feet into the ground and pulled against the bridle.

'Proud mare!' Aza cried. 'Must I drag you?'

The bit cut into Gry's tongue and the straps grew tighter; but she did not move, only tried to breathe and struggled to stand her ground. Aza jerked the reins again and raised a hand. There was nothing in it but she felt the sting of an invisible whip. She whimpered and, lowering her head, let the shaman lead her.

They came to Garsting village, Gry and the shaman. Evening had

17

already taken possession of it and dulled the grassy house-mounds and the tracks that wound between them to a uniform leaden hue, the colour of concealment and secrecy. The place was blanketed with the acrid smell of smoke from newly-lit fires and the empty drying-racks looked like skeletons. Aza turned towards the Meeting House, where the men of the village met to hold council and drink and smoke their short clay pipes, and Gry, perforce, turned with him. The shaman ducked into the low entrance-tunnel and dragged her in after him.

When they met at the brook with their washing, or for cheese-making or the berry-picking, the women used to talk about this House of Men. None of them had been in it because none of them was allowed; there were many stories:

'The puvushi rise up through the floor and dance on the hearth when the men are drunk.'

'A puvush seduced old Heron, they say!'

'They keep a spirit-bear, chained up. It tells them who will die and who will go to the Fiery Pit and who to the Palace of Shadows.'

'Women aren't allowed there because, once, a girl – Huçul her name was – crept into the House when it was empty and the men out with the Herd. She hid herself behind a vat of kumiz and waited to see what she would see and hear when they returned. Things she would rather not have seen, such as the man from Rudring who had dishonoured her mother. Things she would rather not have heard, such as the name of the man who had killed her father and the name of the bridegroom the men had chosen for her.

'It was dusty in behind the vat and Huçul sneezed. She was discovered at once and done for, because the men rushed up and caught her. They accused her of wishing to be a man and, setting her on one of the wildest stallions, tied her there. Then they all yelled like demons and let the horse go – they watched him gallop off into the deep Plains.'

'What happened next?' Gry had asked that question, while the

18

other women stared at the storyteller and sighed and clucked in sympathy and sorrow.

'When the Herd was rounded up, next spring, Huçul was still astride the horse, which was madder still and had to be killed. (My Konik loosed the arrow.) The girl was dead and wasted and all her clothing had blown to wisps and rags. Only the ropes held, good as they ever were. The men untied them and coiled them up.

'Huçul was buried beside the Nargil in puvush-haunted ground, without rites. Don't walk there at dusk, nor in the early morning! Her fate has made her bitter and she is jealous of young women.'

Aza pulled Gry out of the tunnel and kicked her to make her stand up. The men were in the House. Perhaps Aza had called them together before he captured her. She recognised Battak, Klepper; her brothers; Leal Straightarrow, Oshac.

There was a spirit-bear. Its skin lay on the floor by the fire and Heron, the historian of the Ima, was seated on it.

The House was full of smoke, from the fire and from the pipes of the men who were looking fixedly at her, boring holes in her spirit and consuming her with their eyes.

Heron shifted on the bear's skin and spoke to Aza.

'What have you brought us, Shaman? Is it a young mare from the Far Plains? Is it a horse to break?'

'This?' answered Aza, leading Gry by the head. 'What is this? You are right to ask me, Heron. I have brought it here for the men to consider and, when they have considered it and debated its purpose, to decide what shall be done with it. I shall only tell you that it was once a woman of the Ima.'

Gry stared at the double circle of men as she walked and they stared back, each one letting his gaze rest on her feet, her skirts, her milk-drenched back and shoulders, her untidy head with its shameful binding; and her fettered mouth. She would not look down, though Oshac grimaced at her and Battak made the gesture with his left forefinger which meant 'this woman is not worthy

19

of respect.' Leal sat next to Battak; at last, she turned her head away. He stood up and she watched him out of the corner of her eye, sidelong. He was a little taller and heavier than the rest, but dressed as were they all in the double apron, soft boots, and belt of silver discs, his dark hair clotted with horse-grease mixed with pine-oil and red ochre. She had liked him for his height. It gave him distinction and made him more like a man of the South and less of a squat Plainsman. He had been very close to her father.

'Whatever she has done – or is supposed to have done –' said Leal, glaring angrily at Aza, 'does not gives you the right to lead her like a slave.'

'I know what she did: my knowledge gives me every right,' Aza answered.

'But let her go – she won't dare run away. How can she defend her actions if she cannot speak?'

'For what she has done, there is no defence. But, as you will. Her freedom is over: she can only stand and listen to the debate.' The shaman pulled the end of the rein and the bridle slipped from Gry's head and fell into a rope of plaited grass and then into a bunch of hay which scattered on the floor. Aza bent and gathered it up. He dropped it into the fire, and no one moved, or spoke, until it had flared and burned away. Now, it was time for Aza to leave. He must pay his debt to Mother Earth and he bowed swiftly to Heron and was gone. Gry stood alone before the men.

In the silence, Heron drew deeply on his pipe and Leal, without venturing to look again in Gry's direction, sat down. The smoke from the historian's pipe drifted towards Gry and she smelled its thick sweetness and breathed it in. Nandje, pulling on his pipe, had once told her where the tobacco came from and now, that name rose to the forefront of her mind: Wathen Fields. But Heron was speaking:

Heron's Story: How We Began

In the beginning was Sky and Earth, our Father and Mother. Then came the Stars and Water, the birds, fish and animals, the horse and the Red Horse among them. Aagi, the first Man, was born of a chance union between our moist Mother and the Red Horse; and the first woman, who was made to serve and delight Aagi, came afterwards when Earth fell in love with the bright star-warrior, Bail, whose Sword hangs in the sky on clear nights. She was called Hemmel, which means Earth-star; those mushrooms the women gather at the end of summer and cook in milk are also called hemmel because they shine in the dark like stars.

Aagi and Hemmel lived together under the open sky. She bore Ima, and Panch who went away and bred with the forest folk and so come the Southron peoples. Ima met a fair spirit-bear walking by the River Nargil and so came Orso, the same who went to the Altaish where he bred with dwarves and therefore come the Westrons. It is in memory of Orso and his mother than we honour the Bear. Ketch, the brother of Orso, got Lo, and Cabal who made the first Ima house. There are fifty generations between Cabal and Gutta, the grandfather of Nandje, He Who Bestrode the Red Horse, Nandje the son of Nandje, lately Imandi. Nandje the First married Yuega from Sama village and begat the Rider, he who married gentle Lemani of Rudring, the mother of Garron and Kiang and a host of girl-children who died, except for this Gry.

Heron gestured at Gry with the stem of his pipe.

'This glorious lineage is of no significance,' he said. 'Aza has already told us the woman is no longer one of us.'

'Then you have no right to try her!' Leal shouted from his seat, so passionately that heads turned in his direction.

'She was found on our lands and has committed a crime there,' said Heron.

'Can you prove it?' Konik spoke, for the first time.

'We do not need to prove what the Shaman has declared who sees with the eyes of the night and the wind.'

'But Aza said we would discuss her!'

'Discuss? Is she comely, Leal? Would she be a good mother of sons?'

'I am willing to attempt a proof of that.'

Garron jumped up.

'I did not hear myself bless your forefathers nor give you leave to court my sister!'

Kiang was half a pace behind his brother. Both men moved from their places and stood on the hearth. They laid their hands on their dagger-hilts and waited for Leal to make the first move, ready to fight without the formality of a challenge or the reason of war. Then all the men were on their feet, shouting and shoving each other, every man of them yelling the name of his champion. Leal! Garron! Some were so excited that they shouted for Kiang, who had lately taken his seat in the Meeting House and was scarcely out of boyhood.

Aza, sitting without in the dark, heard the shouts and smiled to himself. The clouds raced in the sky; there were no stars. All was in turmoil; but let him honour his pledge to the earth and complete the ritual he had begun with the bone horse and the puvush. Swiftly he drew his dagger and drove its point into his arm. The blood came, rapid and hot from the vein. He let it flow until it reached the earth; and let it flow still until there was a wet patch of it beside his knee. The zracne vile overcame him, reached into his hazy mind and set his body on the narrow branch which swings between sky and earth. He swayed giddily there with them, looking down on Garsting and seeing the creatures which, though they walk by night, men ignore: the cockroach and the louse, the green slug and the snail which is the puvush's horse, and countless spiders weaving their webs of guile. And while Aza was between heaven and earth, the zracne vile played with his thoughts, tossing them like coloured balls through the air.

At last, the shaman became so light and insubstantial that he floated from the spirit's airy realm and was wafted down to earth, where he lay exhausted in the dirt. He rolled over, and sat up;

he wiped his brow. The night heaved and swam about him like the Ocean which, Voag had taught him, lapped at the edge of the world. The angry voices had not ceased. He staggered, half crawling, through the low doorway of the Meeting House and used the lintel to pull himself upright.

They did not see him, full of their manhood and turmoil. The girl stood silent in the midst of their tumult, exactly where he had left her. Rage possessed Aza, empowered by his blood-sacrifice, a cold and holy rage which differed from the anger of the Ima as does a lawful killing from murder. He pushed his way through the throng, his mantle with its stoats' heads flying and his strings of corpse-gleanings singing the chorus of Retribution, and pulled a burning brand from the fire. Flourishing it, he drove the men back to their seats, a hyena before a herd of cattle. He forced Heron to crouch in a corner and stood on the bear's skin himself, his flaming torch throwing his spidery shadow across the roof.

The shaman spoke scornfully.

'It is the usual thing for a herd led by a mare to be strayed and destroyed. She has you all there, beneath her little thumb, pressed as firmly to the ground with your passion and desires as if you lay with her and the position was reversed! Garron is a man of his word and so is Leal; both of them honourable and strict, master horsemen and great kumiz-drinkers. Garron led the wolf-hunt last winter and it is not so long since Leal went adventuring with the Paladin who came to us out of the storm. You are all horsemen and Ima.

'Yet –' Aza paused to whirl his brand about until the sparks flew. 'And yet, you allow your reason to depart and blow about you as wildly as these fire-imps. You let *her* unman you, in body as in spirit. You bring yourselves as low as she.

'Keep away from her, Ima. Draw back your feet, draw in your horns! – unless you wish to see the devils which dwell in the cold regions she is destined for!

'I will tell you what the woman has done; when you have heard me you will know that there should have been no argument.'

23

Aza let the branch in his hand burn out and smoulder. The smoke from it gathered in a cloud above him; when he had enough for his purpose, he dropped the wood in the fire.

'Look, Ima!' the shaman cried. 'These are her crimes.' He blew into the smoke, which swirled about and formed itself into the semblance of Nandje's burial-mound. The men, staring at it with wide eyes and fear raising the hair on their necks, saw Gry standing there; and saw the woman they knew to be the flesh and blood Gry, Nandje's daughter, stand amazed in the place she had not moved from, the edge of the hearth. The false Gry crouched down and entered the mound.

'And more!' Again, the shaman blew into the smoke which, gathering itself once more into a cloud, grew legs, a head and tail, until it looked like the Red Horse. And, in silent dread, the men of the Ima saw the phantom woman, other-Gry, mount the Horse, sit tall upon his back, sit boldly on him like a man as the Horse moved forward and, passing through the solid wall, left the house.

'Which is the greater crime?' said Aza into the chorus of sighs and groans. 'You cannot tell! You can tell nothing because this woman, this *daughter of foxes, this sister of the wolf*, has stolen the will of the Ima, the hearts of every man of you. She laughs and throws dirt in your eyes while she pretends to be a dutiful sister and to mourn her father as a good daughter should. Let Aza wipe your faces clean: I will free you from your disgrace and send your dignity back to you. The woman deserves to die.'

'N-ooo!' Leal's shout was a cry of pain. 'No. Give her to me and I will take her and myself away, out of this place and land, to whatever – long life in exile or sudden death on the way to it – lies before us.'

'Never!' said Garron and Kiang together.

'Hear me!' cried Battak. 'This is what we must do, and secretly, without the knowledge of the men of Rudring, Sama and Efstow or of the far villages: let us take this instrument of our humiliation to the river and, when we have shaved off what is left of her hair and stoned her into repentance, drown her there – and let her

24

body be left to float downstream as far as Pargur and beyond, to be a warning to light women and Southron sinners.'

'It is my opinion,' Konik said, 'that she should be fastened to the earth, which she has disgraced, and left to her kin, the wandering wolves and the Wolf Mother.'

Oshac said nothing, but got up from his place and walked slowly to the hearth. He stood close to Gry and began to stroke her face.

'She has been weeping!' he said. 'Perhaps she is sorry.' He let his hands wander over her breasts. 'She is a pretty girl, and will soon learn willing. Give her to me for a night and, the next night, she shall be yours, Battak; and then yours, Konik; and yours, Heron, and every man's, even her brothers', for they should share in the shame she has brought on the family. After this, she will be fit only to carry refuse and ashes to the midden.'

At this, Garron cried out and Kiang held him still; but Leal, who seemed able to snatch courage from adversity, jumped up and swiftly made his way to the hearth where he fearlessly pushed Aza aside and took hold of Oshac. The older man grunted.

'You have a bear's grip,' he said. 'Keep it to defend yourself when you are proved wrong.'

Leal did not answer, but flung Oshac aside, so that he lost his footing and fell into the first row of men.

'Answer me this,' Leal said. 'How could Gry ride the Red Horse without his bridle? It is not made of the skin of the great Om Ren, Father of the Forest, for nothing; strong magic is necessary to control the Horse. Aza has scared the wits from you with his illusions. There are other reasons for his ill-use of Garron's sister and they are all to do with the choosing of the next Imandi. For it is no secret that Aza favours Battak and no one but Aza claims to have seen Gry at the tomb and riding the Horse.'

The shaman laughed, and his necklaces chattered their hideous song. On his back, he carried a talking drum, a flat disc of skin and wood shaped like a silfren shell or the face of the full moon. To subdue Leal, he quickly undid the string which held it there and, grasping the drum by the manikin whose

25

outspread limbs made the frame of it, he stroked the taut skin with his nails.

'Aza always tell the truth!' said the drum, 'Aza is a man of honour!'

Like a man who has watched all night, Leal bent his head and let his body droop; and every man sat motionless and listened to the shaman.

'This Gry,' said Aza, making his voice hiss like that of the drum. 'She! This false seductress has forfeited our protection – has been kneeling at the crooked feet of Asmodeus, *kissing* them no doubt; basely kissing others of his nethermost parts, for how else but by sorcery could she tame and ride the Horse?' and the Ima all sighed and nodded their heads in agreement, except for Leal whose head remained bowed.

'Nandje himself could not master the Horse without the Bridle,' Oshac said, amid a chorus of agreement, 'and Leal has condemned the woman out of his own mouth. Stand straight, Brother, and admit your error.'

Leal did not move but only stared at Oshac and Aza as if they, not he, had lost their senses, while the shaman beat his drum and brought the violent sounds of quarrelling from it.

'Many have spoken,' he said, 'but none harshly enough. Your punishments are fit for common criminals, mere transgressors of the Law; for tricksters and adulterers, for thieves and murderers. Have you not heard the wisdom of the ancients? The punishment must fit the crime. This woman has put herself in the place of a man and of her father, the Imandi of the Ima. Let me punish her for you! I will tie her to the strongest of the unbroken stallions and chase him for a day and a night until he tires; then, if the woman is still alive, she shall be put in the mound with her father's soulless body and the ghouls and corpse-moths which tenant it; and the doorway filled with boulders.'

At this, Leal rose like a hurricane and called out with its voice, 'Never! Never! Not until the rivers dry up and the stars fall!' His voice was so strong, so loud that the women of the village stopped whatever they were doing, sewing or cooking, and their

26

children began to wail as Leal's cry went leaping and echoing over them and across the grassland terrifying small creatures and large until it reached the horses which kept watch at the margins of the Herd. These sentinels pricked up their ears and stood ready to signal flight. The mares heard Leal and, turning to their foals, nuzzled a warning; Summer and the Red Colt heard Leal and the Colt danced in alarm as his complaint came at last to the two black-tipped ears of the Red Horse. The great horse turned his head to hear it better; nodded, almost like a man, that long, sagacious head; and cantered forward to join his sentinels.

Then Leal, on the hearth of the Meeting House, called for compassion and justice for Gry and on his friends for aid and support. Seventeen men joined him there; the rest swore to follow Battak, all but Garron and Kiang who were left like abandoned princes between two armies. Each faction began to shout for its leader and Gry, lost in the noise, opened her bruised, sore mouth at last and spoke.

'Nandje came to me,' she said. 'My father told me I might look on his body because his soul was on its way to the Palace of Shadows. He did not chide me for my friendship with the Horse.'

Her voice was so low and full of fear that none but her brothers understood her, and they could not believe their ears. Nor did Gry dare repeat the words which had floated into her head as she and the Horse made ready to leave the mound: 'You are the Rider.'

Heron rounded on her, out of the throng. The rest, in their growing quarrel, had forgotten her, the source of it. The historian, by contrast, had become civil. Though he dominated her, leaning his bulky body too close to her and touching her indelicately with his eyes and thoughts, his voice was gentle and persuasive.

'Not one of them is fit to choose the new Imandi,' he said. 'I must put you in a place of safety and then, by our fathers! we shall discover what your fate is to be.' He took her arm and led her from the House and across the empty ground in the centre of the village where the communal hearth, which was used on feast days and for cooking the horsemeat at slaughtering-season, was deserted and cold, another testament to her alienation. She thought of escape, of flight; but her soul was terrified and had curled itself up like an unborn babe and retreated so far into her body that she could not tell where it was; she was nesh, her limbs addled as if she had a fever; and this weakness, she thought, was the shaman's doing.

Heron, not unkindly, pushed her into the low mound where the dried meat was stored; and came in after her.

'You won't be frightened in the storehouse,' he said. 'The children play here and lovers, too, at midsummer.'

Gry felt obscurely grateful. He wasn't so bad, the old memory-keeper. A man would have been tied outside in the cold and watched from the warm shelter of a house doorway. She knew this and began to think herself lucky, resting at last on the ground. It was dark in the storehouse. She heard Heron rummaging and the sound of a hide being dragged.

'Here is a skin,' he said. 'Put it beneath you, there! Soon, I will bring you water and meat, and tomorrow I will speak for you in the House. I have heard many quarrels and listened to many judgements. It seems to me that your punishment will not be as terrible as that of Huçul.' Again, she heard the sound of horse-leather being moved: it was Heron unbuckling his belt. Where was he, beside her, before? The sun-disks on the belt jingled. 'Oshac's solution is best, for then you will not die or have to leave the Plains, nor exchange them for the fiery wilderness of Hell.'

Gry, in the blackness of her prison, felt his hand on her wrist.

'I have the captive's choice,' she said.

'Then choose wisely! If I am to speak for you, it would help your case to show how willing you are and how meek. Let an experienced man, weighty but wise in his knowledge, be convinced of your remorse.'

His voice came from the darkness directly in front of her; indeed, she could feel, and smell, his breath, which was coming in short gusts like that of an animal which has been running hard.

'It is no choice at all.'

The man fell on her in a rush, all at once, pressing her down on the horse-hide. He was heavy and his calloused hands tore at her skirt and rasped her thighs. She did not dare resist, nor want to; everything the future held was dull and mean. Slavery meant being used. He was merely the first. She felt his thing nudge her. She thought it was huge and swollen like a stallion's; it would hurt. It pushed against her as if it would devour her from the inside out or, at last finding the way, suck out her soul through this, the narrow passage which was meant for her lover and her babies. She tried to think of healing, of wind and water, of small, blue flowers in the grass, of birds in flight; but all she knew was the man, his heaviness, his rank smell. The ground heaved under her: she had heard that was what happened when man entered woman's gates and Heron, with a horrid, passionate gurgle, crashed across her and was still. Astonished, she lifted one hand to touch his face. Was this all? A short struggle and nothing more, no kind words or sweet sensations. Was this the great and wonderful union that the lays told of, the songs celebrated? Like a dead baby in its grave-cloth, Heron's head was wrapped in the horse's hide and one of the long tubes of leather which had once covered its legs was taut about his neck. He did not speak, nor ever speak again.

Gry shivered violently. The quarrel in the Meeting House was still going on. She heard the men shouting insults and challenges, their voices fuelled by kumiz. She lay completely still, under the dead man. Time crawled. Something was sticking to her left hand and she moved it, touched it cautiously with the other. It was the cloth of her skirt and Heron's blood on it – not her own, the blood of her torn maiden's veil, nor his – *stuff*. Those – she felt – were lower down, some on her, some on his cast-aside clothing. This – it felt like blood from a wound. She did not, could not understand, and lay motionless again.

After a time, she convulsed and struggled free, throwing Heron off. The body fell to one side, so much dead meat in the hide wrapping, and she spat on it. She was stiff: cramps in her legs

29

and arms. Eventually she got up, on to her knees, and crawled into the doorway.

The night smelled clean, fresh as flowers; cold as spring water. Out in the open it was spaces, stars, wings, freedom. What was in the dark storehouse behind her she wished to forget, seeing, sensing only this, the changed, new world.

Gry wiped her hands, herself, on a tuft of grass and stood cautiously up. There was no one about, the house-mounds dark, the shouting replaced by drunken laughter all muffled like puvushi chanting underground. The sound was not of this wide, starlit world. She was glad to see the stars and Bail's keen Sword there pointing towards the inhospitable mountains of the Altaish, a pitiless place of ice and snow. Beyond them, as she knew well, the world ended. Far brighter than any other star shone that marvellous light which the Ima called the Guardian of the Herd. It had appeared not long after the stranger Paladin, the wanderer called Parados, had left the Ima and, to Gry, was like a sign from him that all would and should be well. And perhaps it was truly a sign tonight, for it burned ardently and seemed to wait for her, halfway between the rocky ridges of the Altaish and the ragged skyline of the distant Forest. Or perhaps it was a sign that she must seek and find her father, wherever his grey shadow had fled.

A footfall disturbed the grass; she heard it clearly, and another, two, three and four. Not a man. A horse. The Red Horse paced calmly into the village, came close to her and laid his head on her shoulder. His warm lips caressed her neck; then, drawing slightly back, he pricked his ears as she might raise her eyebrows, to ask a question, and raised his foreleg so that she could mount. She heard the voice in her mind:

'Come on! It's time to go.'

His hooves marked the frosty grass, once, twice. Then he was into his stride and they were away, crossing the village grounds, bounding up the first hills. She expected him to carry her into the Herd, but it was nowhere in sight and they were heading into the barren wastelands beyond the pasture-grass. The Swan spread her starry wings above them and Gry bent forward and spread her arms to hold the Horse's shoulders, for it was bitter cold up there on his back. Someone said, 'No hair, no coat!' or perhaps it was a thought. At least his long mane covered up her hands and arms.

Her mother used to carry her in safety, in front before the saddle, so that she could sit straight and believe she was riding alone, stretch forward and embrace the striding warmth of the mare's shoulders or, leaning back, nestle into the fur binding of Lemani's jacket: when they were all young and hopeful, Nandje not yet leader of his people, Lemani a beautiful young woman whose silver and jet jewellery was handed down from the oldest ancestors, perhaps from Hemmel herself; when she had sisters still alive and was herself a child, Garron a little boy, and Kiang an unborn soul in the Palace of Shadows. Those were the days, the Ima at peace with their enemies and with one another, the grass rich, the horses glossy and fat, Nandje himself strong and ardent, but wise. Gry let herself pretend, feeling the white wolf-fur and the cold, hard beads and the sharp-pointed silver stars touch her back. She grew tolerably warm.

The grass flowed like a dark river beneath them, the Horse and herself; but sometimes he made mighty bounds and sideways leaps across streams or into the stretches of gravel that appeared with greater frequency as they neared the wastelands; and always a restlessness or a tensing in her mind preceded these leaps and bounds so that Gry knew she must likewise move back a little way or tense the muscles of her legs to keep her seat on his back. The Horse, it was clear, was trying to confuse anyone who might find and follow his hoofprints.

The low hills of the open country gave way to steeper, rocky hills. Narrow valleys, which the Horse must thread, passed between them; falls of water dropped suddenly, cascading out of the dark; a rustling patch of bushes, which might hide any number of thieves, or lions, appeared on the left. Yet, the Red Horse hardly slowed his pace and, in Gry's mind, nine words constantly jumped and span,

31

'Good. Free. Good Bridle. Free of. It is good to be free of the Bridle.'

In Garsting, Aza, flushed with kumiz and the madness of failed magic, crawled from the Meeting House and squinted at the sky. A flight of cranes passed overhead, marking the ground with their cleft shadows. Aza read what the shadows told him: the Heron is dead. The hoofmarks in the grass told him the rest: the girl has fled with the Horse. He plodded wearily across the village to the storehouse.

It had become a death house during the long night. Aza crouched to examine Heron's throttled, bloodstained body, primming his thin lips briefly, almost smiling when he saw what carnal conquest the historian had been attempting when he died, his scarlet, double apron cast aside but still attached to his unbuckled belt, his unwound loincloth stained with the tinctures of his last, greedy act and with the bright blood which had spurted from the unstoppable fountain of his heart.

'She did not have a dagger – she *found* a dagger? One was lost among the skins, perhaps?'

The shaman puzzled over Heron's death-wound. As to the throttling, it was all too obvious how that had come about: the iron grey horsehide which was still wound tight about Heron's head and neck had come from the stallion, Winter, jealous rival of the Red Horse, fast and cunning, if a mite too weak to usurp the rule of the Horse. Both stallions had favoured the white mare, Summer, but the Horse had won and taken her; now she nursed and nurtured the Red Colt while Winter had died in the last Killing, driven over the precipice of the Rock of SanZu. Leal had skinned him; Garron and Kiang had disembowelled and cut up his carcass; Leal's mother had made him into wholesome food, dried hross, succulent stews, sausages thin and thick, lard – but it had been Heron who spoke the ritual of placation over all the dead horses of the killing-harvest. So.

Aza frowned and struck his forehead with his rattle. None of this explained the heart-wound. None of it made sense. And his head was thick with kumiz-ache, his mouth and tongue parched, longing for a draught of clear river-water.

Heron was dead. Nothing remained of the Ima's long history but a few fragments in the head of Heron's successor, Thrush – who had committed only one third to memory. What was left? Gossip and women's talk; some songs; the Lays, the Tales too – inaccurate fables which praised the ancestors and the deeds of the rare and heroic strangers who strayed into the Plains. Heron was dead. History was dead.

Henceforth, all Ima history would begin with the Red Horse's Flight.

Why had he gone with her?

Aza trembled then, recalling his accusations in the Meeting House: 'this *daughter of foxes, this sister of the wolf*, has stolen the will of the Ima' and 'how else but by sorcery could she tame and ride the Horse?' He had not known fear since he had fought to rid himself of the death-curse of his last wife, and now it visited him, licking the nape of his neck with its long and slimy tongue, laughing and blowing up the skirts of his gown so that he shivered. He wanted to rid himself of it, lie down upon the spirit bear and surrender to the dreams which lived there – he could not. He must discover Revenge, drag her out and parade her before the Ima until they, too, were possessed with her spirit.

Aza closed Heron's eyes and weighted them with stones. That was all he could do: for rites, for burial, the historian must wait; meanwhile, let him haunt whoever and wherever he would. The shaman crawled into the day, uncovered his drum and began to beat it. He pounded it, walking always about the village, hurrying before the crowd as it gathered.

Leal Straightarrow, Garron and Kiang, Nandje's sons, ran in a pack with their supporters:

'Gry is gone!'

'May Mother Earth protect her.'

The men rushed from their beds, or from their drunken slumber in the Meeting House:

'Who is dead?'

33

'The story of the Ima has been murdered.'
The women came from their milking, wild-eyed and wailing:
'Where is the Horse?'
'Search for the Horse! Find our Red Horse!'

For the strength of the Pack is the Wolf,
and the strength of the Wolf is the Pack

···

Night stayed a long time in the wastelands where it was hard for the sun to penetrate the valleys and drive away the shadows which dwelt amongst them. The crags seemed to build themselves up about Gry and the Red Horse, towering high, until they resembled buildings made by men. Nandje had told her how the city men, they of Tanter, Myrah, Pargur, made themselves artificial cliffs and tors from stone, great hollow eyries where men and women ate and slept, made love, gave birth and died. Castles, they were called. So, Gry imagined these fabled people as she rode, lords and ladies, sorceresses and magicians, lovely Nemione, evil Koschei.

Overhanging bushes caught at her clothing. She could duck and dodge them but the shadows, which travelled with them and tormented her because she could not make out what they were, she could not avoid; and, soon, she noticed that the shadows had legs and were running; she saw ears, long, bushy tails and 'Wolves!' she breathed. Wolves, which could catch the birds out of the air and pull down a charging wisent and, easily, a horse, even one as fleet and mighty as this, her saviour.

'But wolves are Good Animals,' murmured the Voice.

It was clear that the wolves were driving the Red Horse. He had lost impetus and his pace had slowed. The wolves knew where they wanted him to go and pushed him on with small rushes and nips at his heels. Gry tucked her feet up, as high as they would go on the undulating back of the Horse. Above and before them, the lowering cliffs and giddy bluffs had joined themselves together to

35

make a castle indeed, an ominous pile of deep, unpierced darkness which loomed huge at the summit of a pile of jagged rock. She was terrified, feeling the Horse tremble too. They were forced on, always on, and upward towards the walls in which, at the last dreadful moment when she believed the wolves would trap and overcome them against the barrier, she saw a doorway – yet it wasn't a doorway, only an arched formation in the rock and the great room beyond was no chamber but an open space, walled in by the rocks and roofed with the dark sky and a welter of glittering stars. This castle had not been built by men.

The wolf pack had fallen behind, dragging itself like a furred train after the Horse; ready, she thought, to run in and dismember them whenever it would with teeth of ivory and jaws of iron, and she crouched lower on his back and bit into a strand of his mane in her fear. He had stopped moving altogether and was bowing his head, cowering before a lone wolf almost as big as he. The wolf pointed its nose in the air and howled, 'Foe, foe, foe!' and the pack answered, 'Woe, woe, woe!', its hundred voices reverberating among the rocks and echoing across the sky, loose and terrible among the cold stars.

'It is their queen,' whispered the Voice and Gry, in the same moment, thought, 'It's the Wolf Mother.'

The great wolf sniffed the air and put out her red tongue. She panted and her tongue lolled over her teeth and moved about her jaw and her thin black lips – 'She's smiling,' Gry said aloud. 'Just like my Juma when I give her sweet grass to eat,' – The tail of the wolf thumped audibly on the ground. 'And they are going to eat us.'

The wolf walked slowly all round the Horse, who had become a horse merely, a poor mesmerised animal stripped of his power; about to die. Again, she circled them and stopped, was approaching, was close, her head level with Gry's knee. Gry shrank back, and felt the wolf's wet tongue lick her foot. She looked into the beast's eyes where a yellow flame flickered in a ring about pupils as dark and deep as wells; soon, when she had enjoyed her triumph, the wolf would pull her by the ankle from her perch.

The wolf continued to lick, smoothly, softly. She backed away and crouched on the ground, her hindquarters high and her tail tucked so far in, it was no longer visible. Her ears shrank; she pulled them tight against her head; she made tiny, puppy-like whining noises.

'She's bowing to you.'

'Oh . . .'

'Say something to her!'

'Good w-wolf,' stammered Gry.

'That's hardly appropriate! She doesn't speak our language.'

'What . . .' said Gry, 'Ah –' and put her hands suddenly to her head, holding them high and confident, like ears. Then she lowered one arm and swung it like a tail. The wolf sprang up, Gry shrank away and, growing bold again, leaned forward, talking with her 'ears' until, at last, the wolf persuaded her with whines and gigantic thumpings of her tail upon the ground, to jump from her last refuge on the back of the Red Horse to the certain peril of the hard and open ground.

Gry glanced behind her fearfully. The wolf pack was still, its two hundred eyes upon her and glowing with desire. Her 'tail' drooped and all the wolves tremulously lowered their tails and shrank into their skins until they looked more terrified than she.

But wolves are treacherous.

'Not to their friends.'

Gry looked at the Red Horse. He stood tall, huge and invincible; *his* ears were up. What did he mean? Meanwhile, the Wolf Mother had crouched down beside her and was delicately sniffing her crotch.

Gry heard the voice in her mind. Its tone was one of amusement and delight:

'Just like a faithful dog!'

'It's you!' she cried and the Red Horse nodded his head.

'It's me.'

'But –'

'Not the time to explain – attend to your hostess. She is not interested in me: I'm just your conveyance.'

37

Gry sniffed the air as close to the tail of the wolf as she dared.

'Her name is Mogia,' said the voice of the Red Horse.

'Mogia?'

'It means Child of the Lightning.'

The big wolf, when she heard her name, leaned against Gry in a friendly manner, wagged her tail and seemed to invite Gry to walk with her. Over the stony ground they paced, backwards and forwards, while Mogia sang to the stars and the Red Horse walked solemnly behind. Soon Gry was singing,

> 'When the bright stars hang clear and still
> The grey wolf comes loping o'er the hill,
> He is hungry, he is strong, it won't be very long
> Before he has hunted and eaten his fill.'

It was a song her mother, Lemani, had taught her, of fifty-two verses and a chorus repeated fifty-five times. In Verse Thirty, events turned against the hungry wolf and he was pursued, surrounded and hacked to death by brave Ima; but this, Verse Two, fitted the time and place and Gry sang it over and over again, her voice lifting as free and high as that of Mogia, the Child of the Lightning.

Mogia, pressing her right side hard, turned her about and led her across the sky-roofed chamber to a great boulder on the top of which was a lesser, but wide, flat stone; and here girl and wolf sat and sang together while the pack howled and the Red Horse kept time by beating his hooves on the ground.

Presently, the wolf stopped howling and lay down, her nose on her front paws. In the court below, the pack followed her example and the head of the Red Horse nodded, as if he too, would sleep. The wolves' eyes closed; some of them snored, or dreamed in their sleep, ears and tails twitching, while the legs of the smallest cubs, which had not yet learned to know motion from stillness, moved continually as they slept. Gry lay close to Mogia, her head pillowed on the soft flank of the wolf.

At dawn, Mogia woke, turned her head and licked the bare arm of the sleeping girl tenderly, as she might one of her own cubs. The Red Horse was awake already, staring out into the new day beyond the Wolf's Castle. Gry, confused, yawned and stretched in her wolfhair bed.

'Yellow dawn – *Good* morning!' The voice of the Horse, sudden and cheerful as a happy thought, woke Gry properly. She was hungry; she was cold – as soon as she moved away from the warm body of the wolf – but, she thought, free and outside, far from the terrible, dark storehouse where Heron had died as he lay on her; very far from the men of her tribe, their Meeting House and their Law; far from her home and every small thing which filled it and her life; a very long way from Leal, whom she had (once upon a time: it was all as distant as a dream or a fairy tale) begun to love. Her dress was torn and bloodstained; she had neither silver nor horsehide on her, no wealth whatsoever.

'It may be a good morning for some,' she said.

The pack had also woken. Several young wolves, whose manes were as yet small and brown in colour, were dragging something across the ground and up, across the jagged rocks towards her. It was a chesol deer, tawny as the Plains grasses when they flowered. A number of other wolves – five, six – followed them; these carried groundapples in their mouths. Raw deer and fresh fruit, this was breakfast, Gry realised, when they had all climbed the rock of the throne and laid their burdens in front of her.

'Wise creatures!' said the Red Horse. 'You have eaten my poor relatives, mixed with quail eggs and wild garlic in your Herdsman's Comfort, Gry; so do not gag at this sacrificial deer. And the groundapple, intelligent choice! You know as well as I do that its juice is as good as fresh water.'

'But I'm cold,' moaned Gry.

The food helped warm her. As she ate, quickly swallowing the pieces of deer-meat which the wolves chewed from the carcass for her and sucking the acid juice from the groundapples, she saw that other yearling wolves had come to the deer and were tearing its skin into long strips and rough triangles. Soon, while the Wolf Mother directed them with little barks and sharp nips in their ears, the young wolves had picked up all the golden pieces of the deerskin and were laying them at her feet. Two were bold enough to drop their gifts in her lap.

Mogia wagged her tail and, cocking her head, gave Gry a lopsided look.

'Warm clothes,' murmured the Red Horse.

Gry gathered up the bloody pieces of hide and, too modest to be a true member of Mogia's pack, retired behind a rock and tried to make a garment from them. When she squatted to evacuate and relieve herself, she found fresh blood on the insides of her thighs – Svarog – Sky! It was her own blood: she should rejoice; she bent forward until her forehead touched the ground and gave thanks to Mother Earth. This blood-cleansing was another freedom, and nothing of Heron had remained inside her long enough to make a luckless, bastard child. Hastily, shivering, unburdened, she tore rags from her skirt and made a pad to soak up the blood. Next, the deerskin strips made footless leggings and, with the help of more rags from her skirt, the triangles could be fashioned into a shorter, thicker overskirt and a small shoulder-cape. She chewed holes for her makeshift cape-strings in the skin, tasting the fat and sinew, spitting out hairs and feeling as gorged as a well-fed wolf. So, dressed at last, she stepped out and showed her new clothes to the pack and the Horse. A cub barked once, quickly silenced by his mother, and the adult wolves howled an acclamation; but, deep inside Gry's head, a low, delighted chuckle started and swelled – the Horse: as if a horse could laugh! Evidently, he could. She listened well – had she not heard that laugh somewhere before? In some place that was friendly, homely? In a place in which her father was alive and lively, Nandje, Son of Nandje, He Who Bestrides the Red Horse, Imandi of the tribe? Nandje's laugh had been raucous, cackling; this, it was gentle, even cautious, in its happiness.

She remembered walking along the main street of the town of Vonta in the Near Altaish where Nandje and Lemani had taken her for the Horse Fair; she had been sucking a greengage lollipop when a boy her age had passed her and grinned, waving his own lollipop

40

in the air, before he blushed and turned away, pretending to look in the window of a toy shop. Something in the display there had amused him and he had laughed aloud, a happy, bubbling sound: it was not that laugh.

That, until now, was the only time she had been out of the Plains.

Gry shook her puzzled head and, making a small fist of her right hand, thumped the Red Horse gently on his neck. In answer, he nuzzled in her breast.

'Horse!' she cried, and thumped again.

'You are beautiful, even now,' came the reply.

'I am as wild as a drunken shaman after a spirit-feast,' said Gry.

'When you find a tarn or lake up in the hills and use it for your mirror – oh, you will! – you will see that I am right. But listen to Mogia. She says that, though you look like a deer, you are almost half a wolf for "eating meat with Us brings the wisdom of wolves, which men call cunning."'

Mogia's Story: Winter Hunger.
Take care. The road to true wisdom is long and hard. I was a cub in the years of Koschei's Winter. Snow covered the Plains and the rivers were ice. Small birds fell dead from the skies and, for a while, we were content to eat them. Then came a day when all the birds were dead. We had eaten the land-animals long before: the deer, the heath-jacks and their kith and kin. The last mouse had been swallowed whole.

My mother called the Pack together and we left the Plains, journeying long and high into the Altaish, where the snow and ice endure for ever. Some of the wolves spoke against her, arguing that if we could not find food in the frozen Plains, what could there be to eat in the mountains? There was a fight – so bad that two wolves were killed in it, and wolves never kill their own: to this, the magician had driven us with his foul heart and fouler weather. The rest of the dissenters left the pack and turned into the forest where, they said, they were certain to find prey. We travelled on.

Soon the way grew grim. Great boulders made of ice reared themselves in front of us and the ice made hard stones of itself in the soft spaces between the pads of our paws so that we had many times to lie down in the cold and chew the ice away before we could walk on. It snowed, sometimes so hard that we lost our way and must, once more, lie in the bitter cold until the storm died and we could see. Four of the old wolves lay in their snowy nests and never got up again. Still my mother led us on, and higher.

We dared venture into the remote, Upper Altaish and here, as my mother well knew, we found great companies of mountain lemmings which, being animals of the cold and the heights, had not died out. We had a great feasting – taking care, by my wise mother's orders, to leave enough of the creatures alive to breed new colonies, which they do most rapidly, in the time it takes for the moon to grow from a claw to an open eye; so we remained in the Altaish until Koschei's power waned and the spring came, living as do men-farmers by taking care of our herds.

'See, my Sisters and Brothers, my Daughters and Sons,' said my sagacious dam, 'the truth of our old saying *For the strength of the Pack is the Wolf, and the strength of the Wolf is the Pack!*

'"But, woman-Gry, wolves' wisdom will not serve you at all the turns,"' said Mogia in the Horse's familiar voice. '"You must consult your own ancients, the shamans at Russet Cross. I will lend you a guide –"'

Mogia broke off her whining in the Red Horse's ear and howled once. A young, grey wolf came running to her side.

'"This is my scout, my dear son Mouse-Catcher! – who loves a succulent mouse so much he hunted nothing else in his infancy, bounding over the long summer grass, high and low, like a heath-jack in his love-madness. Mouse-Catcher knows the salt wilderness. It is one of his hunting grounds. He loves a mouse with a salt savour. Hey! dear Cub,"' and the great wolf licked her son's ears lovingly.

Gry looked up at the Red Horse. He was nodding his head but, this time, she could not tell whether he meant to speak to her or

42

was only ridding himself of the first flies of the morning which, attracted by the meat or by her strange, uncured skin clothing, were beginning to swarm about them.

It is the blood, she thought. Flies love to drink it – and I am stained with it, Heron's, mine, and the chesol deer's. Three have died – there was Heron and the deer; and there would have been a baby if I had not begun to bleed. Poor soul, it must hurry back to the Palace of Shadows and wait for a happier coupling to bring it to Malthassa.

The flies will follow me now and bother the Horse – I have no lemon-root to rub on him and keep the flies away.

She felt Mogia licking her hand and put her sad thoughts away. The Red Horse nudged her and offered his foreleg to help her mount. Mouse-Catcher danced, eager to be off and running hard.

Leal's rage had settled inside him like a hard and indigestible fruit. He had ceased to mull over Aza's accusations or regret his own passion at Gry's fate although it made him an outcast too, and a thief. He was in Garron's house, turning over the household goods, Gry's possessions, her brothers' things – as for Garron and Kiang, they were without somewhere, helplessly watching as Battak and Aza drummed up a pursuit. He would pursue her too, alone – without those loyal seventeen who had pledged him their faith. There was no other way: he must be silent and circumspect like a hunter in the forest. No one must know which way he had truly gone; and he would go, very soon, when he had found what he sought in the house.

In the village, there was anarchy and the men of Rudring had heard of it. It would not be long before they of Eftstow and of Sama also heard and rode to join the throng.

Where was it? He lifted the lid of a chest. It was full to the brim with carefully-folded clothes. He let the lid fall softly.

The women had their opinions, too. He had listened to some of them when he washed, at the river.

'She was foredoomed – a spirit was in her,' one had said – Daia, Konik's daughter.

43

Battak's wife had no sympathy: 'If she had taken one scrap of her father's wisdom to herself, she would be on solid ground. But she was always wayward. If she had liked our company and gone milking with us, she would have kept clear of the Horse and of temptation. What folly to milk alone, when the dew is still on the grass and the puvushi scarce abed!'

'I heard she has a lover in Rudring,' said Oshac's wife maliciously.

He came out from behind the reeds then, naked, just as he was, thinking to shame them. But they had stared at him, bold as hares, and Daia had smiled and flirted up her skirt, pretending its hem was wet. He clearly heard what she whispered to the other women: 'Leal is a horse of a man.'

Where had Nandje kept it? Leal spun slowly on his heels. Ah! Fool that he was. The bridle hung on the wall, in full view. It had been behind him. He lifted it gingerly down, almost expecting it to burn him. Then it was in his grasp and stolen, the Red Horse's bridle – which I shall need, he told himself, when I find Gry and the Horse. It was made of soft Om Ren skin, cut from the hide of the old Forest Ape which the Red Horse himself had killed.

But somewhere in the forest fastness there would be a young Om Ren growing, and his hide would be taken for the Red Colt when the time came.

Leal looked about him, trying to memorise the interior of the house. Here, Gry had cooked and worked, sewing hides into horse-gear and silk and linen into garments for her father and brothers. She had tended the fire on the hearth where the cold, black ashes lay. Earth, an ill season! Time to go. His feet scuffed up the dry soil of the floor and something which had been missed, for all Gry's sweeping, caught on the toe of his boot. It was a single band of silver with a clasp of horn, Gry's ankle-ring. He sighed, remembering her narrow feet and long, grass-stained toes, kissed the silver and tucked it in the folded cloth at his waist.

Then he moved, ducking swiftly out of the house and striding out to the hollow in the Plains where he had left his gear. He caught fleet Tref and the sorrel mare Yarila, saddled Tref and hung the

44

magic bridle from the cantle, under his bow, put a halter on the mare; and was gone from Garsting.

Aza listened to the wind. Stribog, he blew from the north, bringing the thud of hoofbeats and the howling of hungry wolves to the ears of the shaman who breathed in the god through dilated nostrils, filling his lungs. Cold, his body sang, Meat, Salt.

'Russet Cross!' he cried, the words leaping from his open mouth.

'We ride, then,' said Battak gruffly. 'Into the bitterness and the cold.'

'Ay!' Konik shivered. 'Bring a fire-pot, Klepper. We shall need it.'

The men mounted their horses and turned their heads into the wind. They rode slowly at first, rubbing their watering eyes, until the immensity of the Plains and its high and empty sky took hold of them and they urged their horses into a lope and then a gallop, laying out the thin, black line their enemies feared.

Gry expected to see the Altaish, immense, cold heights upon the horizon, as they travelled into the day, herself, the dear Red Horse and the grey wolf, Mouse-Catcher; but the hills before them were low and crimson as blood. The salt wind, blowing in her face, alarmed her, but Mouse-Catcher paused to relish it, wagging his tail as if all was well. The air grew damp and the bothersome flies left her. She put out her tongue and licked salt crystals from her lips.

They were still among rocks, boulders scattered across level pavements of stone whose crevices were home to low, fleshy plants. Mouse-Catcher, by biting their leaves and sucking out the dew inside, showed her that these were almost as good for thirsty travellers as groundapples. There was nothing else fit to eat or drink: the further from Wolf's Castle they journeyed, the saltier the ground became until they were crossing white flats on which the larger crystals lay as thick as frost and glittered as the sun rose higher. Further on, the salt-bearing rock was red or, sometimes, the two kinds of salt lay close together, forming wonderful, twisting patterns. The hills were nearer, seeming homely because, for all their weird colour, they were shaped like the green hills of home.

Again, the wolf sniffed the wind which, whirling over the salt ground, sang with a mournful note. Mouse-Catcher howled with it.

'We must go further,' the Red Horse told Gry.

The wolf and the Red Horse travelled hard, stopping neither to eat nor rest, while Gry slept deeply, so benign was the rocking motion of the Horse. She woke and slipped from his back at evening, while Mouse-Catcher ran among the rocks and found what edible plants he could. Swiftly, they ate and sucked the water from the fleshy leaves.

'. . . and further still,' said the Red Horse, offering a foreleg for Gry to mount by.

When morning came again and the sky was pale as the inside of a new-laid egg, Gry sat tall in her seat and stretched. The salt ground had never altered, continuing to unroll beneath them like the skin of a skewbald horse. The pallor of the horizon was remarkable, dipping down to touch land which wavered like a summer mirage in the Plains. She watched the sun colour the land, marking out the different zones in the rock, russet and stark white; laying a watery tint on the undulant distance. All at once a man appeared, motionless in the landscape. He had one thick, brown leg and one which was thin as a stick of willow. She did not want to meet him.

'Please turn back,' she begged, but the Red Horse gave no sign that he had heard her and kept up his steady pace, following after the wolf. It was the man who began to run, waving the long stick he had been leaning on and which Gry had thought a leg, and followed closely by the large flock of sheep which she had taken for bushes.

'Wolves and sheep don't mix!' said the Red Horse.

Mouse-Catcher turned his head in the direction of the fleeing sheep and gave a deep, appreciative sniff.

'He is an honest wolf and he is hungry – but we must hope he will not follow his instincts,' the Red Horse remarked. 'Are you comfortable up there? It has been a long ride.'

'As if I sat on my mare, Juma,' said Gry. 'I think my legs have stretched to fit your broad back.'

She heard the gentle laugh of the horse again and, again, it puzzled her.

'What is that place?' she asked. 'Is it another plain?'

The voice of the Horse, busily talking like a dream-voice in the very centre of her head, was even and affectionate.

'It is a plain, of sorts,' he said, 'but it is made of water. Men call it the Ocean. It rolls between the worlds, too deep and cold to swim across. It is ruled by the moon, which pulls its waters first one way, then another. Such movement is called a tide; and those rolling hills you see in the water are waves. In a moment – there! – one will arrive and break in pieces on the shore.'

Gry watched the waves surge up the beach.

'The Ocean is like a huge river,' she said. 'River-water also turns to mist when it hits rock.'

'You are a wise woman.'

'I? – I know little beyond the Plains. But *you* are a wise horse. How can a Plains horse, though he is the Horse, know so much?'

'I have heard many tales,' the Horse muttered evasively.

'In Garsting? When Nandje rode you?'

'My ancestors had the wisdom of centaurs.'

'Of sentries?'

'Centaurs. Mythical beasts, half-man, half-horse. You know, Chiron – of course, you would not . . . Come, Gry, muffle your face in the scarf you have made of your seductive skirts, blue as eyebright in the grass! We shall soon be on the shore and the wind will try hard to fill your mouth with grit.'

Obediently, she wrapped her head in the torn cloth. The smell of the sea caught her by the throat, frightening and exciting her. The Horse's hooves drummed on the rippling watermarks and the wind, as he had promised, blew salt sand in her face and filled her eyes with tears.

It was a lonely place. The sands ran on for ever, combed and billowed by the sea and the land curved gently down on left and right; but ahead, where she was being carried, there was nothing but the glinting water with its random spouts and crests of white spray; and that water made roaring, dragging sounds which deafened her and filled her head and senses so that, though he was speaking, she could not hear what the Red Horse said. Strange plants grew in the sand, stiff like trees made of glass, their tiny branches broken. Fresh cloven hoofmarks crisscrossed and surrounded them, for the sheep had been feeding here.

The wind got inside her thin clothing and chilled her to the bone. They forged on, the wolf pushing himself forward with all his might, his fur blowing wildly about him.

'Where are we going?' she cried into the din. 'Over the edge of the world?'

The Horse was shouting too, a whisper in her mind.

'Almost! Look ahead.'

The waves were roaring louder than a thunderstorm. Gry wiped the wind and water from her eyes. It was hard to see. The water tossed up its countless heads. Something stood there, firm in the spray, a giant or a mighty beast of the spume. It reared high and held out stiff limbs. Gry wiped her eyes again.

It was a great tower, stripped of any skin or covering it might once have had, a rusty, metal skeleton many times taller than a forest tree.

'Russet Cross!' the Horse shouted. 'What a structure!'

'Russet Cross?' she echoed, and scarcely heard herself, scarcely believed it. An awful thing, she thought, like the shaman, Aza's, house which was no house but a grassy hollow in between the hills. Or like Wolf's Castle, no castle but stones piled up by the spirits themselves: as this storm-blasted tower, she supposed, had been built and wrecked.

The Red Horse stopped at the water's edge, Mouse-Catcher sheltering, ears down, beneath his belly; both of them gazing at the metal monster.

'Russet Cross,' Gry repeated. 'What is it?'

'A misplaced memory, a meeting place,' the Horse replied. 'The point at which the winds and the waters meet. Where spirits howl together and pass on their voices to those who must hear.'

'Mogia wanted me to come here?'

'She had her good reasons, Gry. The water is not deep at this state of the tide,' said the Horse calmly and, for the first time, Gry heard the wolf's answer, an audible shadow in her mind,

'Deep for me. Terrible for the warm land-She.'

The Horse walked into the water. Gry clung tight, looking down, horrified as each wave rose and threatened to engulf him and her clinging self, and passed them by to be succeeded by another just as great. Nothing was steady now, nothing sure. The good ground had vanished; in its place, the treacherous, moving water.

The wolf, who had remained behind, spoke in his throat, neither whining nor growling: 'Rurr – rrr – rurr!' And, having voiced his opinion, followed them.

They soon reached the nearest limb of the tower. A stairway hung from it, giddily down to touch the water.

'You must climb it, Gry.'

'I can't – Red Horse – I can't. How can you climb stairs?'

'I shall wait here, up to my withers in sea water. Mouse-Catcher will go with you so there is no need for fear.'

'It is high; I can't tell how high!'

'Fear not, trust me. You won't fall – look, there is a rail.'

There it was, a handrail looping and scrolling at the staircase-side, though she had not noticed it before. She reached out and took hold of it. The Horse was warm beneath her. Wasn't she well-used to climbing trees at gathering-time, when the women journeyed across the Plains to pick a harvest of nuts and berries from the trees at the forest-skirt, and mushrooms, toadstools, puvush-cushions, puff-balls and spirit's saddles from inside the forest itself? The stair looked firm. She swung suddenly on to it, climbed two steps and looked down. The Horse was afloat already, solid, glossy, alive in the cold, wet Ocean, his tail fanned out like weed behind him. Mouse-Catcher was swimming too and his ears were up. She tried to be brave.

'Goodbye, dear Horse!' she called.

'Climb, my sweet Gry! I shall soon welcome you back.'

Thirty steps, and she was in translucent cloud, chasing raindrops and rainbows as she climbed. She felt the wolf behind her, hairy, soaking wet, and then his nose against her hand, comforting her. The rust-coloured limbs of the tower bent about and enclosed them as they climbed. Thirty steps more: her head was above the mist, in sunshine. She looked up and saw, flying on the tower-top where two metal beams made a huge, jagged cross, the blue flag of her people, the Ima of the Plains. Its fluttering challenge stirred her heart and she climbed more rapidly, passing through a circular doorway in the floor of a rickety platform. The nose of the wolf touched her hand once more.

A table had been placed there, far above the sea, a table set for a feast. The guests were waiting for her and two stools were empty. She crept forward, wary and reassured by turns for the other feasters were dressed like her, in tattered indigo and skins. The wolf at her side began to moan quietly, in that midway voice: 'Rurr – rrr – rurr.'

The old ones had been sitting a long time, wind-dried and wizened in the eye of the sun, neither on the land nor in water, each one salt as grief and dead as stone.

Gry buried her fingers in Mouse-Catcher's thick mane and looked at the circle of shamans. They were fearsome, shrunken like trophy-heads, preserved but loathsome like the food on their plates, withered plums, black slivers of meat and grey heaps of mulberries. The skulls of some were visible through leathery pates, under wisps of hair; from others, the fingers had dropped and these lay on the table among the dishes. They wore creased robes of balding stuff which had once been good horsehide, and were hung about like Aza with necklaces of birds' skulls, thunderstones, claws and bones; a circlet of wood, which had been a drum, was propped against the foot of one; another had lost its nose although its lips had dried into two hard ridges which were pinched together in disapproval.

Gry curtsied to the dead shamans, while she wailed, 'Oh, my father – protect me!'

The shaman nearest the stair was less cadaverous than the rest: he must be Voag, Aza's master, who had died when Nandje was a boy. To propitiate him, she spoke his name and said, as she might to any one of her people, 'The grass grows!' Immediately the words were out, she clapped her hands over her mouth: what if he should answer with thin words blowing? She listened hard, but no sound issued from Voag's cracked lips and she sighed with relief and bent close to the wolf, putting her own warm lips against his head. She kissed his muzzle and spoke softly in his ear.

'Why am I brought here?'

Mouse-Catcher licked her hand and his voice came to her, a tiny whisper in the terrifying silence: 'Yours is not theirs.'

Gry went a little closer to the old ones. One of them was a woman who must, in life, have been a great beauty. Her skin, even in death, was smooth, though it was blue with tattoos; her head had been shaved and a wig of black horsehair, dressed in a crowd of little plaits, put skew-wise on it and, over that, a tall wooden crown from which hung small figures of horses and deer. She wore SanZu silk under her horsehide and furs and Gry, without thinking what she did, touched the shaman lady's hanging sleeve.

So, she woke the sleeping princess who raised her tattooed arms from where they rested on the table, turned her head to look at Gry with blind, opaque eyes and spoke with the sad voice of the winter wind:

'Who disturbs the Lady Byely?'

Gry fell to her knees and bowed her head.

'Gry, Madam. Only myself, Lady. Gry, Nandje's daughter.'

'Look at me!'

Byely was holding a sharp knife like doom above her. She was too frightened to move and could only stare at the skeletal fingers and the dagger-hilt they gripped, a doubled ring of bone chipped

51

at the top – and with a dark smoke-stain below it running all the way about and down to the steel, Pargur steel.

'That is my father's dagger!' Gry exclaimed.

'Do you need it? Do you demand it?' Byely loosed her hold and let the dagger fall lower between her naked finger-bones.

'It should be with him so that he can cut his spirit meat – yes! – give it me!'

And Byely let the dagger fall altogether, clattering on the rock.

'I can – not . . . harm . . . yooo . . .' she said, and slumped down on her chair and was again a corpse and withered remnant many ages dead.

'Poor lady,' Gry whispered, while her eyes filled with tears and she felt her heart beat strongly in her chest.

'Not poor. Once great, greatest shaman in the world. Past – pastures of Heaven,' sighed Byely.

'Sad lady, you must struggle for your voice.'

'Sad now – go, Gry – know you . . .' Byely, spent by her efforts, fell across a bowl of desiccated plums and mulberries, sundering her frail bones and dispersing her lovely face, brittle as an eggshell, across the table. Mouse-Catcher, who had stood by silently, opened his mouth and whimpered so loudly that Gry swung round. The scabbard which belonged to Nandje's dagger lay on the table in front of Voag whose ruined hand covered it as a spider covers her young.

Touching Byely's sleeve had woken her. What might Voag do, if his sleep were violated?

Nandje, when he put away the dagger, had always been careful to lodge its sharp tip exactly in the chape, the hollow horsehead of shiny cherrywood which protected it. Gry bent, picked up the dagger and felt its edge and tip: still keen. She must have the scabbard as well. Moving stealthily, she tried to pull it free and did not touch the hideous hand. The copper sheath slid forward, once and again, but the hand came with it, keeping tight hold, and the voice of Voag snapped out at her, a scratchy thorn-snared twig.

'Aza sent me this! Why should I give anything to Aza's enemy?'

52

'Because I am the daughter of Nandje, the Rider of the Red Horse, and the Lady Byely gave me his dagger.'

'The vultures stole it from Aza and storm-birds carried it to her, but Aza gave me the scabbard. Why should I part with it?'

'Because it belongs with the dagger.'

'Because, because! What has reason to do with the matter? Nandje is like me now, girl, dead as mutton, blind as a granite boulder. He does not need either: dagger or scabbard.'

'The scabbard protects the blade.'

'Well, well: common sense too from Nandje's daughter who was condemned by the Ima, ravished like a captive, forced to flee –'

'My father's spirit spoke to me.'

'That is – not a bad thing –'

'The Red Horse travels with me.'

'– and, I was about to say before you interrupted, you are a murderess into the bargain.'

'I did not kill Heron!'

'I know you didn't, quick little fool; but Aza thinks you did and so do Battak and Konik, all the men except your brothers, who do not know what to think. And Leal, of course, but he is blinded by love . . . that, in your hand, is what killed Heron: Nandje's dagger, and the grey horsehide which had an old score to settle.'

Gry held the dagger more tightly, moved it about as if she would strike.

'I'm already dead!' Voag shrilled.

'I don't understand . . .' said Gry.

'Are you a magician? Are you a shaman? No? Well, accept what you are told by one who knows. Go away now, go! I shan't give you the scabbard: you don't deserve it. Yet.' His fingers rattled on the table, reaching for her.

'Unless you would like to sit beside me,' he said. 'This is your seat, next to the one that waits for Aza.'

'No!'

The Lady Byely lifted her drooping head with broken fingers and began to collect the shattered fragments of her face from the table-top and put them back in place.

The dagger, useless here where the dead stood up and spoke and the living had no defence against them, was in her hand; Gry gripped it and with her other hand the mane of the grey wolf. They ran together, fleeing unsteadily down the steps. The sound of the sea came up to meet them and, from above, rang down the clatter of bone joining with bone and of angry voices skirling. The stair plunged into deep water and only the heavy body of the wolf, pushing her back, stopped Gry from falling in. The Horse – where was he?

She saw him then, a red island rising and falling with the waves, and she leaned down to grasp his trailing mane and slide on to his back. Mouse-Catcher jumped into the sea and struck out, paddling hard.

'All's well,' said the Red Horse, with a smile in his voice. 'The dead can't harm you. So welcome, Gry. Have you got it?'

'My father's dagger, which should be in his tomb – how did you know?'

'I guessed.'

Her feet trailed in the water, so high had it risen, but she must sit there, watching the bobbing back of the wolf and the mobile ears of the Horse, which signalled his discomfort and the effort he made to bring her safely to the shore; and she must continually look behind, over her shoulder, for a sight of the angry ancients; for she knew better than the Horse, that dead shamans were not as the common dead. But only the thickening clouds appeared behind them, gathering together in a dense wall of fog. She wanted a clear view – they might all come leaping out of the cloud and fall on her; she was certain they had no need ever to swim but could fly and levitate themselves across any obstacle. The water soaked her and the dampness crept upwards until she felt it reach her waist and, rising still, begin to soak her bodice.

The sound of the Horse's hooves, striking rock, woke her. She had been dreaming, or daydreaming, of Leal who was lost to her; and it was no longer day but a grey evening as full of moisture and mists as she felt herself to be, cold and nodding on the wet back of the Horse. Were those lights, low down but sparkling, just there? She blinked, and blinked again. He was cantering now, easily.

'That is the village of Russet Cross. Not to be confused with the tower of rust and bones,' he said cheerily. 'Our shepherd lives there. You must dismount and lead me in and it will be wiser, and more polite, if you take that scarf of yours and lead Mouse-Catcher as well. Shepherds and wolves are never the best of friends.'

Seven low houses, built of rocks from the shore, and a large pen of hurdles in which the sheep were confined, was all the village of Russet Cross. Dogs came barking out to defend it, snapping at Mouse-Catcher as he walked subdued by his leash of blue cloth. In her other hand, Gry held a lock of the Red Horse's mane, to lead him, and she had secured the dagger at her waist so that its hilt, old and damaged as it was, protruded from the skins there and looked workmanlike, not to be trifled with. Doors opened, light spilled, and someone with a tremulous voice called,

'Traveller, wolf or wight?'

'No wight,' Gry answered, 'but a traveller – with her horse – and her wolf.'

In the pen, the sheep had begun a tumult of bleating; in the houses, men began to shout wildly, as if they were drunk or crazy with fear. Gry shrank into herself, remembering the men of the Ima. A single flame detached itself from the blaze of lights in the nearest house and moved rapidly towards them. It was carried by the shepherd and he, as he came up and saw them, the soaking, fur-clad girl, the grey wolf on her left and the great horse walking docilely on her right, dropped to his knees and lifted his torch on high like a greeting or a gift.

'I ran from you this morning,' he said. 'Trouble us no more, I beg you.'

'We won't hurt you, or your sheep. We are gentle creatures.'

'A wolf – gentle!' The man almost laughed.

He was the first living man she had been close to since Heron. He was dark and rough-looking with an untidy beard and wild hair and the smells that rose up from him were meat, smoke, beer and boastful maleness. Gry shivered; yet he was one of her kind, a human animal with two legs to walk on and two arms with proper fingers and thumbs; and that long fifth member – vile, dangerous, inevitable! Her eyes filled with the hot darkness of the storehouse in Garsting and she heard Heron's lustful breaths.

'Come up,' said the Red Horse as if he were a man speaking to a disobedient horse. 'Come out of it, Gry; step away from the shadows of the past.'

'I am only an outcast woman,' she said, hoping to waken the shepherd's sympathy.

He crouched lower. 'Wild Lady!' he said, 'Lady of the Wolves.'

'Make him get up!' she cried to the Horse.

'You can command him. Be a great lady.'

So Gry tried again, imagining herself a person of consequence like Nemione or the Goddess of the Grasses the Ima men sang of, in their spring song.

'Stand up, shepherd. We are not used to waiting for our dinner.'

He got up immediately and began to shout for his fellows who came running, burning brands held high, while the women of the village who were dressed like those of her own in heavy skirts and silver and copper jewellery, gestured towards the lighted doorways from which spilled welcoming smells of meat and new-baked bread. The men helped her down and led the Horse away – in the direction of the sheep-pen. Hearing him sigh 'O, for a jug of wine, a loaf of bread and Thou, dear Gry,' she thought he mocked her and, standing uncertainly in the middle of the excited crowd of women, tried to sleek down her unruly scrub of hair.

Mouse-Catcher did not try to follow the Horse or herself, but lay down where he was, and curled into a ball, nose between paws, thick tail over all. Gry tied his leash to the leg of a slaughtering-bench, and was ashamed to restrain him.

She woke early and did not know where she was nor, for an instant, who. The mat beneath her was pliant and warm – wool, she remembered and, reaching about in the darkness, found the objects the shepherds had given her, presents of a rare and costly

56

kind. Gry, I am, Gry alone, she thought. I have no place here, nor anywhere. She listened: the shepherdesses in whose hut she had been entertained were all asleep, breathing softly as lambswool clouds in a summer sky, and there was another sound of breathing, deeper, familiar, kind. The Red Horse was close by.

Gry rose from the warm bed and, pausing only to gather her gifts into her skirt, crept from the house. The sky above the distant Altaish was the colour of butter and she could see the Horse waiting by the porch. He had evidently grown tired of his confinement in the sheep-pen and leapt out. She ran to him and kissed him on the nose. The wolf, Mouse-Catcher, rose like a shadow from the place where he had lain down and licked her hand. Some brave person had thrown him meat in the night, she guessed, for a much-licked and gnawed bone was lying beside him. She untied the leash and freed him, putting the torn, blue cloth it to its proper use as the scarf about her neck.

'Is it time to go?' she asked the Red Horse.

'It certainly is! The Altaish are no closer – indeed, they seem to be further away.'

'Is that where we are going?'

'Not immediately. Mount, Gry, and let us be gone or the shepherds will interrupt our journey with their fuss and ceremony.'

'They were kind to me. They gave me lots of presents.'

'They were hospitable, but you are neither the Wolf Lady nor Goddess of the Grasses. They would beggar themselves feasting you.'

'I *am* Nandje's daughter.' Gry spoke uncertainly as, burdened by the gifts it seemed she had no right to, she clambered on to the Horse's back.

'I am well aware of that!' He tossed his head and broke into a swift trot before she was settled. The present she had liked best, the multicoloured string of beads, dropped from her bundled skirt and fell behind. She looked back for an instant, full of regret for the pretty necklace; but the Horse would not stop, she knew that. His head and his limbs were full of purpose and soon he broke into a canter.

The wolf ran before them as they travelled in the dawnlight beside the sea. The watery plain was green now and raw and tossed its uncountable heads impatiently. A shoal of ripples escaped the waves and ran on to the beach. Gry, soothed by the rocking motion, gazed out to sea, surprised to see neither mist nor rusty tower. Instead, a strange object moved over the water, almost at the horizon, a floating house or a waggon maybe, pale in colour and glistening like a polished catamountain's claw. It flew along parallel to the shore and Gry, seeing how inexorably it sped, grew alarmed and called out to the Horse, 'Faster!'

The Horse laughed softly and plunged to a halt.

'Watch, and learn!' he said.

The thing in the sea had huge black awnings above it which flew out from a pole and had many ropes attached. The waves, flying faster than the strongest wind, were broken into white and scattered fragments by its tapering, buoyant body and a multitude of sea birds followed it, mewing and shrieking in their own mournful language.

The Horse, facing out to sea, considered, while Gry trembled on his back and the wolf raised the mane on his neck and all along his back and held his ears stiffly out, listening.

'You are right to be terrified; and I am wary and ready to flee, my Gry,' the Horse said. 'It is a ship, although there are no ships upon the seas of Malthassa. That is the one and only: Hespyne, the Ship of the Dead, which never sails close to the land unless someone is dying, and never lowers her anchor unless there are fresh corpses lying in their graves. Hespyne comes for the souls of the dead and carries them far away, to the Palace of Shadows.'

'Then I will soon see my father!'

'She has not come for us. Maybe a shepherd has died this morning, or the hermit of Worldsend who dwells on the island there, beyond the marshes. But we must flee or the Wanderer, Jan Pelerin, who captains the ship, may hear us and draw us to him in a net of spells.' At once, the Red Horse bounded into a gallop, Mouse-Catcher speeding beside him, and there was nothing for

Gry to do but bend low and hide her fear in his whipping mane while she clung to his pounding shoulders.

Her skin smelled of the sea. She put out her tongue and touched it to her arm: salt! Yet the raw-meat-and-blood smell had evaporated and her odd and daggletail skin garments were as fresh as good, cured furs.

'Are you cold?' asked the Red Horse.

'Not cold, but very thirsty. My skin is as salty as meat in winter.'

'Be patient for a little longer. Soon, we will come to Pimbilmere, where you shall drink, and bathe if you will. Listen, while I carry you deep inland. This is why your skin is salt: it is the same phenomenon you know in the Plains, the Salt Wind; but all the air by Russet Cross is salt and the sea itself is salt – a good place for a leathery old shaman to preserve his mortal remains!'

'Or hers,' said Gry. 'There was a she-shaman on Russet Cross, tall and stately. Her skin was covered all over with blue tattoos.'

'That is the Lady Byely.'

The Red Horse's Story: The History of the Lady Byely
Byely was the daughter of a long-ago king of the Ima, when your people lived in cities which rose up like the hills of the Plains and are buried now beneath them. She was a Music-Maker and a Beauty, crossed in love, before she became a shaman. Her tears were salt and they have preserved her as much as the wind and the sea.

Byely played a lute made of the shell of an ocean-turtle. She strummed its seven strings with a hind-toe of the beast and sang to it, small plaintive melodies which told of forsaken lovers and maids who drowned themselves or hurled their lovesick bodies from tower-tops when the moon was on the wane. The courtiers, especially the ladies, said she was melancholy herself, but they listened in silence to the songs and, afterwards, applauded.

'My songs are sorrowful because they have water in them,' Byely told them. 'Salt water, of the sea. My turtle,' she patted the polished shell, 'swam in it, breathed it, swallowed it, heard

59

it. The Ocean is in him and of him. Listen!' And she played a rippling chord.

When Byely grew to marriageable age, she was taken out of the city to meet Scutho, the Shaman of the Plains. First, she was put up on her horse – a mare like your Juma, round and not very tall; red-roan too, her dapples scattered on her coat like bird-cherries in the grass. Her name was Martlet. Now, although Byely (being a princess) was used to being treated with ceremony, she had always mounted Martlet without help and, soon as horse and reins were properly gathered, galloped off with the young women who were her companions, the daughters of great herdsmen and traders. They were like a bunch of fillies themselves, playing in the strong, spring sunlight while they raced each other and the cloud shadows in the Plains.

Byely was told to rein Martlet in and go sedately after her father in the procession. It passed along Chance Street where the gaming-tables were set up in the shade and where pipes of good, Wathen Fields tobacco could be bought, even in those far-off days, and out by Slate Gate, on which the Ima hung the heads of their enemies. Just then, a company of horsemen passed by, the young men boasting and shouting, Plains partridges, heath-jacks and strings of quail slung across their horses' necks; the older men were smiling like good schoolmasters. There was a youth in their midst, short-haired and dressed all in green; not a Plainsman, not one of the Ima though he was mounted on a russet Ima horse. He smiled at Byely, who turned her head to look after him.

'Who is that?' she asked; but no one would answer her in the solemnity of the procession. Only the wind breathed 'Haf!' and, not knowing the name of the youth, she named him after this gusty sound, 'Haf! Haf . . .'

Byely spent fourteen days with Scutho, the Shaman of the Plains and fourteen more with the College of Shamans in Rudring. When the new moon rose, she was a shaman herself and must not ride out with her friends but, laying aside her turtle-shell oude and her jewellery, put on the skins and fox-fur robe of her calling and submit to the barber, who shaved her head to make way for the headdress of rowan-wood and wig of horsetail plaits she must wear. Her body was tattooed, even to the corners of her eyes and the beautiful bow of her upper lip. For everything a shaman does and wears has a significance beyond this world of Malthassa.

As for her mare, Martlet: she had been killed and eaten at the initiation ceremony.

'What it is to be the daughter of a great man,' said Byely to herself, 'promised to the four winds and the moon from birth. I cannot shirk my destiny, but what man will look at me now? Certainly not Haf. I will have to marry Scutho, who is kind enough when in his proper body – though he's as ugly as a wolverine with his filed teeth and his dirty, ridged nails.' And she went on foot from the city and far beyond, until she found Scutho lying in the summer grasses in a trance. She woke him with a kiss and he turned to her and gave her his wolverine smile. And so, in a little while, they had mated as the beasts do and he had run off to his hut while she sat amongst the broken grass stems and salted the eye-bright flowers with her tears. The flowers closed tight and so they have ever after when the Salt Wind blows.

The moon rose and Byely stared up at her.

'Now you are both shaman and wife,' said the moon. 'Never forget which is the greater calling.'

Having no instrument with which to celebrate her sorrow, Byely picked up two stones and beat them together. She sang of her lost love and, in the morning, began to make a healing song. When the sun began his slow decline towards afternoon, she collected herbs and went among the poorest herders to cure them of their ailments. She cured many and the people revered her. Once, they say, she brought a stillborn baby to life and she was sovereign at horse-medicine and horse-lore.

One blazing summer's day, Byely sat outside Scutho's hut to wait for the cool of the evening. Horsemen were travelling in the Plains: she could see the dust rising and, soon, riders grew out of it and approached her. Dismayed, she saw the youth she had named Haf in their midst.

Scutho was inside the house, preparing spells, and so she must

61

greet the travellers herself. They dismounted and sat in a circle while the servant-boy brought them kumiz and bread and cheese.

'Who is that?' Scutho called from within.

'Only a party of herders,' she replied, and sat down with the visitors. Haf was sitting in the next place. She looked at him and loved him, still more; and he, looking beneath her tattoos, saw her beauty and loved her.

'Who is that beside you?' called Scutho from within.

'Only a poor herdsman who has a pox to be cured,' she replied.

It grew dark and the travellers lay down to sleep. Haf and Byely rose from the circle, to be private with each other beyond the nearest hill.

'Who has broken the circle?' called Scutho from within.

'Only the servant-boy and a maid of the herders,' she replied.

Scutho and the travellers found Byely and Haf next morning. Their throats had been bitten out.

'It is not safe to sleep away from the house,' the shaman said. 'Every herder knows how far and keen the wolverine roams. Help me raise a mound to cover my wife, for she was once a princess. But let the stranger lie where he is and may the rats and vultures feed well; for he stole Byely from me.'

'Poor lady,' said Gry. Her tears fell like rain on the Horse's shoulders and, when she had shed enough of them to make her feel cheerful, she dried her face on his mane and sat up. The wolf carried his tail high and happy and Gry's posture on the Red Horse's wide back was easy and relaxed. They ran through a green landscape where bushes laden with catkins and blossom grew and the sun shone in a blue sky. Skylarks rose from the ground, ascending specks against the sky. She heard their song flood down and fill the open lands through which they rode, and she smiled. The shepherds' gift of sparkstones danced a lively jig in their bag, which hung round her neck, and she had tied their beautiful blouse about her waist until she could find the time and the place to wear it. It was yellow like the day

62

and made of Flaxberry silk bound with ribbon as juicily red as mulberries.

'I shall put it on when I have bathed in Pimbilmere, whatever that is and wherever that may be, for I would follow Mouse-Catcher anywhere; and I would ride my beloved Red Horse to the edge of the world,' Gry said to herself.

The Horse was silent, pounding along. Soon Gry found herself singing the song Lemani had learned from the tobacco traders:

'Oh, soldier, soldier, won't you marry me,
With your falchion, pipe and drum?
Oh no, sweet maid, I cannot marry you. . .'

'For I have no coat to put on – I know it well,' the Red Horse interrupted, 'but a horse can only nei-hei-heigh! – carol on, little Rider. My heart is singing with you.'

The lake called Pimbilmere stretched left and right before them, an open eye in the heathland. Birch trees huddled together in small stands or hung over the water, dipping long, silver fingers. The mere was bordered by a bright margin of green grass and a line of clean sand.

The three companions were delighted. Mouse-Catcher jumped over the heather-clumps, disturbing the mice and voles which were hiding in them and living up to his name. Gry, longing to drink the water and to cleanse herself, slid down from the Red Horse's back and ran to the shore. As for the Horse, he flexed his lips in the shape of a smile, shook out his mane and the aches in his neck, lay down and rolled his weariness away.

'The grass looks fresh and good,' he said. 'I am hungry! – and perhaps Mouse-Catcher will bring you a heath-jack for supper.'

The wolf's hunting had already taken him out of sight and, soon, the Horse was a red shape in the distance as his grazing led him along the shore. Gry stood at the water's edge, shyly lowered her dress and overskirt to the ground and stepped out of them. She unwound her leggings and, leaving them where they

63

fell, walked into the water. It was warm from the sun, clear over a sandy floor from which sparkling grains swirled up as she trod. She undid the strings of her cape and threw it ashore. The mere received her like a lover; she lay down in it and swam, drinking the water and ducking her head. Time slowed as she floated there, content. Her bleeding had stopped: they must have been travelling seven days, but months and seasons did not always follow each other, Herding after Birthmoon, Summer before Leaf-fall, in the Plains and, now that she had left, they were altogether out of order. She knew left from right and right from wrong but, if anyone had asked, she would have told him that at Russet Cross it had been springtime while, here, it was a fine day in autumn.

The sun dried her as she sat by the water, clothing to hand in case the Horse or the Wolf should appear.

'I am not like Byely,' she thought, studying her lean, brown body. 'What man will look at me?'

When she was dry, she dressed in her old rags and slowly put on the beautiful blouse, buttoning it carefully and turning about to admire her reflection in the evening-shadowed mere. Next, she collected dry heather roots and dead wood from a birch-clump and made a fire with her sparkstones. The smoke smelled sweet and woke her hunger: all she needed now was meat – and there, in the lengthening shadows, came Mouse-Catcher, a fat heath-jack in his jaws. The Red Horse was following close behind. He carried some twigs in his mouth which, when he dropped them by her, she saw had blueberries on them. She ate the fruit hungrily while she skinned and cut up the heath-jack and set it over fire on a skewer of tough heather-stem.

'That is a splendid garment for a poor nomad,' said the Red Horse, looking at her with his great, umber eyes.

'It is better than my old dress!'

'It turns you into a princess. Dear Gry, if I were . . .' She waited, full of guilt and melancholy, for him to finish his speech, but all he did was strike the ground impatiently with one of his forefeet and mutter, 'A horse! A damned horse!'

'That is a good knife,' he said, after a while.

64

'My father used it all the time – for every kind of task. But it should have gone with him and not to the Lady. If I could, I would lay it on his body in the mound –'

'Only you cannot return to the Plains. Not yet. Perhaps you will find a way, as we travel, of telling him that you have it and take good care of it. Surely the rabbit is cooked? It smells delicious! If I were not a horse, I'd eat with you.'

'But you are a horse, the Horse. I am glad of it.' She patted his neck and turned away, to her meal of roasted meat.

They crowded together in the firelight, the Horse, the wolf and Gry who was busily tying and folding her old bodice into a carrying-bag. When it was done to her satisfaction and she had made a strap for it from her scarf, she wrapped the remains of the heath-jack in grass and put it in her bag.

'Breakfast – maybe dinner as well.'

'After sleep. So – Goodnight, Gry.'

'Goodnight, Red Horse and Mouse-Catcher. Sleep tight.'

The wolf answered her, his voice more certain than before, 'Starshine on you, small She,' as she lay down between him and the Horse and pillowed her head on her arms.

She slept at once, her breathing light and relaxed. The Horse, keeping the first watch, looked fondly at her and, a thought from his mysterious and mystical past floating light as thistledown into his head and, spiny as a thistle, sticking there, wrinkled the velvet of his nose and shook his great head to dislodge it:

'They were all as false as fool's gold, my great Loves.' He snorted. 'It is better to be the Horse.'

The stars came out and Bail's sword was mirrored in Pimbilmere. The great guardian-star shone in his solitude over by the Altaish, and the air, as the night deepened, grew cold. Gry stirred, curling tight against the Horse. She was dreaming of a knight like those in the old Lays of her people, not Bail but one who was beautiful to look upon and who was gentle and brave, gallant and bold; so, she passed from dreaming to deep sleep as the night-animals of the heathland hunted or were hunted, living out their short and furious lives. In the mid-night, the wolf woke and took over the watch while the Red Horse closed his eyes to sleep and was powerless to prevent the alternative story he could resist by day from capturing his mind:

I, Koschei the Deathless, Traveller Extraordinary, Onetime Archmage and Prince of Malthassa, now Magister Arcanum, write this sitting at the cedarwood table in the small white temple with the gilded roof which is the satellite of my Memory Palace locked in unreachable Malthassa. It is a fair room and I can see the pink siris and the smaller Tree of Heaven from my seat. Beyond, in the 'real' world (as some say) it is a Holy Day, the day for the propitiation of the great Naga or cobra snake, and the people have laid food and water at the round doorways of the snakes' houses. My Lady smiles and says nothing; she has kept her human form since we first met on the slopes of the Rock at Solutré; she has been Helen for two whole world-years who once was Helen Lacey, supreme gypsy-witch; who was Silk Leni, Lèni le Soie; Ellen Love, the Bride of the Loathly Worm and Helena, Grand Duchess of Galicia with Beskiden, schemer, stealer of hearts, drinker of young mens' and maidens' blood; who once, in the Golden Age, belonged to Menelaus, was stolen by Paris and taken to be the glory and the bane of Troy! Who is Lamia, snake and woman, viper and pythoness, beauty of the jewelled far-seeing eyes and banded coat, sin-scarlet, bitter-orange, deathly black . . .

Oh, Mistress of Mortality, Identity and Age! How gladly I travel with her, knowing Wrecker of my heart, dark shadow of my older Love, the fair, inviolate Nemione, whose brown body and lustrous witch's hair, whose forked tongue and pitch-mirk eyes are the counter of Nemione's fair pallor and golden showers, soft corals and sapphires set in pearl. Parados loved her as well as I, that's sure and she has left him to his fate to go with me.

Q What difference for her, since I inhabit his discarded body, which works hard for me, by day and by night?

A My mind, controller, not his. My intent, vicious, not his. My way, devious, not his.

But I have, with Parados's body, his fount of brute energy! And something of his hopefulness, I think, a residue he left behind when he condemned himself to exile from himself! Mine's the better deal – new life, new landfalls and horizons, new mistress; and the same misspelt name, Koschei, which he – or I – trawled from the infinite world of the imagination, collective memory, universe of tales.

Here they think it is a gypsy name and that is what they take me for, one of themselves, dark-skinned from the hot sun of this land, a Rom colourful and canny.

Our lives are simple, Helen's and mine. Our angel-haired son left us a while ago in a cold country, in winter, the snows and the mountains calling him – he drove away in the wheeled firebird to whatever dissolute or physically punishing pastime best amuses him and we travel on. Our conveyance now is a creaking cart with a canvas tilt for the rains or worldly privacy; once it was painted in gold and red and black and decorated with suns and moons. A few streaks, weather-ravaged, of this old coat remain, for we fashioned it together (one starlit night in the Yellow Desert) out of the material of her vardo, her gypsy caravan. From the skewbald horse we made a brown and white ox to draw it. We love and laugh and live as gypsies, the last of the true vagrants, and tell fortunes when we are asked. Helen reads hands while I pretend to scry in my little prism – I found it lying in Limbo beside Parados's abandoned body. It is a useless, shiny bauble now, the only souvenir I have of Malthassa, its compound, magnifying eye fixed firmly on the last thing it saw, the dove-woman Paloma flying (in her second apotheosis at my, or should I say 'the cruel hawk's' talons?) into Malthassa's sun.

My divine Helen, for her rich clients, uses her magic Cup, the King's Goblet upon whose surface passes not only What is Gone but What Will Be, here on Earth. It is not hers, this wondrous Cup, but stolen like my body – and I think we are both scented by an ambitious pursuit for I have seen (one dawn in the Shalimar Mountains) an eagle fly up hastily from the rock beside our camping-place and (in the hot afternoon when the red dust rises over the Thar) a camel wake from deep sleep to stare after me.

We have wandered through the warm, wine-loving countries which crowd around the shores of the Mediterranean Sea; we have crossed the driest deserts and the highest mountains to reach this, our temporary

home. Its people, who are god-fearing and industrious, call it Sind;
but we belong to a smaller nation, my Lady's Tribe of Romanies which
history, legend and themselves name the Gypsies of the Gypsies, the
Dom, whom Firdusi called the Luri and others, the Zott. They crowd
about and protect us with their noise and numbers while we make our
grail-less, idyllic odyssey.

All too soon, the stars waned and dawn came. Gry woke suddenly,
for Mouse-Catcher with eyes wide open and ears erect was sitting
by her, a great furry watchdog waiting for the sun to shine; but
the Horse snorted in his sleep and pricked his ears as if he were
listening to another's tale.

Go into the forest till you come to a fallen tree;
then turn to your left and follow your nose.

....

'I must show you my tail,' Mouse-Catcher said to Gry. 'The Red
Horse will be pack-leader of you as before-me. What-men-call
Pimbilmere is the last place of my wolf-mother.'

Gry looked into his yellow eyes in case she were dreaming still.
Inside the small, contained world of her head she had heard the
wolf's voice clearly. It was a voice which travelled quickly up
and down an inhuman scale and was full of yelps and soft
growlings.

'She says, leap quickly beneath the trees. Run there. A tree fell
down –'

'And then – what will we find?' Gry interrupted.

'New animal-country? I never smelled it. Never jumped
Pimbilmere in my cub-days. But now. Dear She, Mogia says
again, do not howl to the samovile.'

'I am not afraid of spirits!'

'But do not yap to the birch-people. They know brother-spirits
in the shadow castle.'

The wolf looked about him and sniffed the air. He pointed his
nose at the sky, which was high and grey with heavy clouds flying
fast toward the country they had come from, and gave a queer
little howl.

'I know your smell. Until breath stops,' he said, came closer
and thrust his muzzle under her hand so that she had to lift it and
stroke him. For a short time, he was still while she smoothed his
heavy ruff of hair and wished he would stay. Then he lifted his

69

tail high and bounded away from her across the heather clumps. He did not pause or look back and soon was hidden by the purple stems and the gaunt yellow grasses which grew amongst them.

Gry stood up to stretch and taste the wind. It blew steadily and smelled of wet earth and toadstools. The Red Horse stirred, lifted his head and shook it. His hairy lips wobbled as he snorted and blew the sleep from his nostrils and eyes.

'So Mouse-Catcher has gone home to the Pack,' he said. 'A wolf is uneasy when he is away from his kin.'

Gry stared at him as he rose, forelegs first. He was so very big and his tail so long and mane so thick: all horse; magnificent now, and when he guarded and chivvied his mares, when he mounted them in season, when he fought the lesser stallions. He was splendid as when Nandje used to ride him on feast-days or at the horse-gatherings, his red coat hidden beneath ceremonial trappings of spotted catamount skins, the tails hanging down all around him and bouncing as he galloped.

Yet –

You don't *sound* like a horse, she thought, remembering how the wolf had howled and yowled his words and the peculiar way he had of fitting them together, so that you had to guess at his meaning; while the Horse spoke well, like a village elder or a travelling teller of tales.

She ate one of the legs of the heath-jack Mouse-Catcher had killed, chewing the tough meat reflectively and sucking the grease from the bones. Then she packed her belongings into her bag, and walked a last time on Pimbilmere's sandy shore. She drank its water thirstily. The sounds she made when she walked and drank seemed to her loud and rudely human: she had neither the speed and elegance of the horse nor the courage and stamina of the wolf although, like Mouse-Catcher, she wanted to go home. The wind had nothing now to tell her and merely stirred the reeds and ruffled the expanse of water which was grey and cheerless like the sky. She hurried back to the Horse.

Gry, riding between the blackened, wintry stems of sloe and gorse, had lost her look of sturdy fortitude, shrinking in the chill immensity to a fragile, brown elf. Even the Red Horse looked smaller.

'These melancholy lands are called Birkenfrith by the heath-cutters who live alone in their most secret dells,' he told her as they passed from the heather in amongst the birch trees where, to avoid being swept to the ground, she had to lie full length along his back.

Golden leaves brushed her head and she looked up at the tree spirits' feet, appearing no more substantial than they, who were green of hue and whose tangled skeins of hair hung down like spiders' webs. She felt the transcendent power of the birches themselves. The spirits stared back with huge, shining eyes whose pupils were as luminous as moonlit pools, and gestured at her with spiky fingers like broken twigs. Some had young clinging to their backs, two or three chattering imps which lunged outwards from precarious holds to bite off crisp leaves and nibble them with long black teeth. The older samovile had grey skins like their trees and thin, silver hair. Their faces were wrinkled and lichen-hung.

As the Red Horse and his small burden passed the samovile called out to him and shook the branches till they groaned and the trees cast their dying leaves to the ground where they lay and drifted in trains of gold and ochre. Their song passed from mouth to mouth and from tree to tree:

Red Horse come not near!
Horse run mad, Horse afear'd!
Leave our birch frith wild and weird,
To your pastures, to your Herd!
Away!
Be gone!

'Keep your horny hooves away from us, Old Nag!' they screeched and danced wildly on the tossing branches.

But the Horse walked stolidly on, looking neither to right nor left. Some of the vile dropped leaves on him; and these covered Gry in a rustling blanket. Only her eyes and the tip of her nose showed. Fragments of birch-song filled her ears and ran about in her mind with alluring images of sun and snow, of the slow drop of falling leaves and of new, yellow growth thrust forth in spring. There came a muttering and commotion in the branches above her and a gust of wind as the vile blew the leaves away and soothed her with warm draughts of air. Suddenly the Horse gathered his legs beneath him and jumped a fallen tree trunk. Some of the spirits were holding a wake over it and tending it by straightening its crushed boughs and brushing the soil from the broken toes of its torn-up roots. They bowed to Gry.

'Turn to your left, little brown woman!' they cried. 'Follow your nose.'

Wishing to thank them she opened her mouth and whispered, 'You are kind folk –' and bit her tongue as she remembered Mouse-Catcher's words: 'Do not yap to the birch-people. They know brother-spirits in the shadow-castle.' He meant 'You must never speak to the birch-vile unless you want to find yourself with the dead.'

The birches grew more sparsely; tall chestnuts whose arrow-shaped leaves were blowing away on the wind succeeded them. Gry saw no vile but sensed them close by, hiding in hollow trunks or lying high where the tapering branches waved at the sky and whispered sparse songs. Once, a stony-faced puvush looked out from a hole in the ground; once, a blue and white jay flew chattering above them. She sent a thought to the Red Horse:

'Is this the Forest?'

'Yes,' he answered. 'The Forest-margin at the least, safe enough for woodcutters and foresters by day. This must be Deneholt where the young River Shu runs; it is brother to the Sigla and, like him, a tributary of the great River Lytha.'

'My father often spoke of the Lytha – though he had never seen it! And Leal too, who had not seen it either.'

'Near Pargur it is so wide you cannot see the far bank.'

'Shall we go far enough to find it?'

'Perhaps, little Gry, perhaps – but the Shu, as you will see, is more like your own Nargil, shallow, fit to drink and easy to cross unless it is in spate.'

'Battak threatened to drown me in the Nargil.'

'Battak is a hard and tormented man – and no river is without danger.'

'They say the Nargil flows into the Lytha . . .'

'All rivers flow into the Lytha; all the river-water flows into the Ocean.'

'You will fall into the Shu, Horse!'

'Then hold fast, Gry! Perhaps I will have to wade.'

From her high seat on his back, Gry saw how steeply the river bank swept down to water's edge. The Horse went cautiously, slipping and sliding on the dead leaves until he reached the shallows. Here, he stopped to sniff the air and to drink. The far bank was hidden in vegetation except for a narrow beach littered with mossy stones and for this, he struck out the water creeping to his knees and, near the middle, swirling as far as his belly. He stood still and looked down into the water.

'I am a handsome fellow, Gry, am I not?' he said, as he admired his reflection. 'The nivashi think so. I can see one there, by the big boulder. She has the haunches of a high-bred mare and a smile like the Lady Nemione's. Her eyes are white opals.'

Gry was afraid. He sounded less and less like her dear Red Horse; but perhaps he was bewitched and a nivasha *had* got hold of his soul. She sat very still to listen for its thin, ululating cry; and heard nothing. A fly buzzed in her face and she waited until it had flown away. Then, like the whine of a gnat on a still summer's night, she heard the soul of the Horse. 'Help!' it was crying. 'Help me!'

The Horse, while she listened, had lowered his head and now stood with his mouth in the water and his eyes on the hurrying ripples which flashed silver and green as they eddied about him.

Gry kicked him hard, as if he were an ordinary horse. She clicked her tongue and whistled to him; and he stayed where he was, frozen and immobile in the middle of the River Shu.

'I am not afraid of you, nivashi!' she said, and slid into the water. It came to her waist but she surged regardless through it until she reached the beach on the far side, where she wrung out her skirts as best she could. The Horse had spoken of foresters and woodcutters; such men would have ropes or might know of a shaman who could break the enchantment. Before she set off, she called out to the Red Horse but, dull and motionless as the stones themselves, he did not look up.

The brambles and thorns above her looked impenetrable so Gry walked along the beach. The river bent twice, to the right and the left; the shore became sandy and low. She climbed a bank and stepped at once into a grassy glade. Five hens and a splendid cockerel were feeding there, close to a gypsy bender-tent which stood like a small, multicoloured hillock in the exact centre of the clearing; for the bender, though clearly made of willow sticks and green-fir branches, was finished with a roof of chequered cloth, red, yellow and blue. So soon! Gry rejoiced. A gypsy forester: I never thought of that! The bender reminded her of the shelters the Ima put up when they were herding far out on the Plains and she hurried to it, while the chickens clucked and pecked contentedly at some corn-grains scattered in the grass.

She could not see the door. 'Hello!' she called. 'Is anyone at home?'

No one answered her, but there was a loud rattle. The bender moved suddenly, jumping up on seven-toed feet of willow twigs and settling as quickly on the ground, while Gry rubbed her eyes and shook her head in disbelief. At least, she thought, she had found the door, there, arched and low in front of her. Again, it reminded her of home and she knelt and peered in.

She called again, 'Are you inside?'

No sound came from the dark interior though a chaffinch in a treetop trilled, dipped his wings and flew off. She saw a three-legged stool on a hearthstone, bent her back and crawled forward. There was no entrance tunnel: you were either out or in, and she was within. Her eyes grew used to the dimness. She saw a bedplace made of cut bracken, a blanket of the tri-coloured cloth lying across it, and a small chest for clothes and possessions. There was also the stool, very low like the ones at home. She sat down on it to look about her. Curious – it almost seemed as if the place was growing lighter – and bigger. A rustle in the hearth

74

made her jump. The sticks had fallen together and a small flame leapt up. Soon the fire was burning brightly and the kettle began to sing, while her wet clothes steamed faster than the kettle and in a moment were bone dry.

In the far wall was an archway tall enough for her to walk through and there, beyond it, was a high and airy bedroom equipped with every luxury from cushion-littered bed to silk carpets and cut-glass bottles of lotions and perfume. She pulled the stopper from one and put a dab of golden liquid on her wrists. It smelled of waxy cactus-blooms and far-off, spicy desert sands. She saw them as she breathed it in, enchanted. Beyond the bedroom was a transparent, six-sided tent with an empty bath sunk in the floor. She touched the walls and marvelled at their hardness; knelt to examine the pictures of deer and huntsmen with which the bath was lined. Water began to flow from the mouth of a stone snake coiled on the bath's rim: Gry backed away and bumped into the glass wall. Outside was a garden in which herbs and sunflowers grew against a picket fence and bees made constant journeys to and fro between a row of wallflowers and a straw bee-skep. But there was no door into the garden and neither grassy glade nor forest trees beyond the fence. The view was wide and inspiring: of a flower-starred meadow amongst high mountains capped with snow and divided, one stone face from another, by shiny ribbons of falling water.

Gry ran back the way she had come. The fire burned merrily on the central hearth, but the doorway had gone: the curving wall of branches ran all the way round the room. She beat her hands in vain upon it and turned away, tears welling in her eyes.

'The Horse,' she murmured, 'I must get out and rescue him . . .'

But nothing seemed to matter greatly, neither the Red Horse trapped in the river, nor her own predicament. The bed-place vanished and a velvet-covered chair appeared. A tin box stood on the hearthstone beside a spouted pot and two cups. Gry sat down on the three-legged stool and opened the tin: it contained dry leaves which had a sharp and appetising smell and a spoon with a short handle in the shape of a briar topped by a rose.

The kettle boiled, its quiet song bubbling to a crescendo and Gry, surmising that the leaves were much like those of the water-mint she used at home, warmed the pot with a little boiling water and tipped it to one side of the hearth with an automatically-muttered charm.

'May the grass grow sweet.'

She put three spoonfuls of leaves into the pot and poured the water in.

'Do you take it with milk?' someone asked.

Gry swivelled wildly on the stool and almost upset the pot.

The doorway had come back! But it had grown big enough to accommodate the tall, stoop-shouldered figure of an old gypsy-woman. In her large and capable hands she held a brown jug which matched the teapot in Gry's hand. She wore a scarlet skirt and a black bodice and the shoes on her feet had high, scarlet heels; her jewellery was made of gold and bone, of amber and jet; she had a wart on her chin and blood-spots on her apple-cheeks; her eyes, bright as a wren's, were full of knowledge and cunning; worse, her grey hair fell straight down to her shoulders where it began to twist and curl in waves as tumultuous as water in a rocky rapids. In short, she had all the signs and hallmarks of a witch.

Gry was speechless.

'Go into the forest till you come to a fallen tree; then turn to your left, and follow your nose – and you will find *me*!' said the witch and cackled with laughter. 'And here you are – a little, thieving Ima woman.' The witch advanced and set down her milk jug on the hearth. 'A female horse-herder far from home. They don't let their women roam alone, those handsome, doughty horsemen; so this one must be a harlot or a murderess. An outcast, plainly.'

She bent over Gry and took the teapot from her unresisting fingers, poured milk and tea into the cups.

'Will you take a cup of tea with me, my dear?'

'I –' said Gry. 'I –' but she could find no other words.

'Drink your tea and then you will tell me all you know and every detail of your story,' said the witch; and Gry drank, feeling warmth and courage flood into her with every sip.

'Now!' The witch was sitting in her chair, leaning back against the purple velvet like a queen on her throne.

Gry recited her tale, without sentiment and without apology, right to the end,

'. . . and so I sat on the three-legged stool and put some leaves and boiling water in the pot –'

'Tea!' interrupted the witch. 'You made my tea! Witless girl: couldn't you see the house was waiting for me, making itself comfortable and laying out the things it knows *I* like. You've confused it, don't you see? – look at the wall, are *those* a gypsy's traps?'

Hanging from a peg were three Ima bird-traps and a horse-goad which shimmered and disappeared as the witch glowered at them.

'You are a gypsy?' said Gry hesitantly.

'Am I a gypsy! By all the stars and Lilith, I am Darklis Faa, the famous gypsy witch, the celebrated chov-hani.'

'The gypsies sometimes came into the Plains to buy horses of us,' said Gry, the picture from childhood strong in her head; though whether it was her own memory or a tale her father had told, she could not remember. 'The women carried willow baskets and their children on their hips and the men had bright neckerchiefs and big, gold earrings and sprigs of rosemary in their buttonholes and whips plaited from the hides of griffons. They prized our horses above all others.'

'Tosh! We use Ima horses to pull our vans, but never for riding: they are too coarse.'

'They are the chosen mounts of the Brothers of the Green Wolf.'

'Thieves and murderers all – perhaps your ingenuousness comes of true innocence after all. You seem extremely stupid for a woman with the Gift,' said Darklis crossly.

The hair stood up on Gry's neck.

'I am no diviner,' she said fervently.

'I, who can see a person's soul-light, say it is otherwise. The light above your head is clear as crystal – and if that does not

77

indicate a shaman who understands the speech of animals, I am not Darklis Faa! You were in luck, Ima woman. If I had not recognised a fellow-adept, you would have been a statue in my garden as quickly as Lord Koschei can say "Snipper-snap!" and turn his foes into woodlice.'

'I can understand the Red Horse, Madam Faa, and the wolf, Mouse-Catcher; but their speech is as thought to me. I hear nothing and they certainly make no noise – they are animals after all and have their own ways of talking with tail and ears.'

'I think you can also scry. Look at the tea leaves in your cup! What do *they* say?'

'I cannot read –' Gry began; but there were no signs or letters in her cup. The tea leaves had crowded together in a dark mass which bubbled and sighed like marsh-mud and, settling, became the bottom of a clear pool. In this mirror there appeared first the Red Horse and, as the picture widened, a second horse or pony with a coat of dapple-grey. Gry's hands trembled and the picture shimmered.

'Be still!' cried Darklis.

The Red Horse and his companion were grazing quietly in the glade, the Horse cropping near the mare and gallantly leaving her the most tender shoots.

'That is my Streggie,' the gypsy explained.

Gry smiled, and felt a small pang of jealousy.

'Your Horse is a finer specimen than the average Plains animal,' said Darklis carelessly. 'Fortunately for him, I discovered him before the nivasha got her teeth into his tender flesh. She's a good girl, Hyaline, but she loves to tease animals – and drown them.'

The picture spun in the cup and the horses vanished. When it was still Gry saw a stoat, which had run into the clearing and frightened Darklis's chickens into a huddle of ruffled feathers which the cockerel protected with neck and spurs outstretched.

'What a fine house I have!' gloated Darklis. 'Better at guarding my possessions than a whole army of the Archmage's soldiers.'

'How does it turn itself about?' Gry whispered. 'For that is what it did when I arrived – and I did not believe my eyes.'

'On its four feet – and by my enchantments, addlehead!' cackled the witch. 'How fortunate you are, little woman, to have found me and my canny home. What is your name? Will you give it me, for I have told you one of mine.'

'The Ima have no superstitions about names,' said Gry. 'Our souls are our own and free. My name is Gry and I am the daughter of that Nandje I told you of, the Rider of the Red Horse and Imandi of all the Ima.'

'Are you sure of your name, girl? "Gry" is the gypsy word for "horse".'

'It is the Ima word for "Princess of Horses", Darklis Faa.'

'Look into the bowl once more, Princess.'

Now, the hut itself was visible, squatting like a mother hen on its feet of twigs. The little flock had run beneath it and settled in the dust to bathe. Gry sighed, but did not know if she envied the chov-hani or was merely tired of her questions and her conversation. She yawned.

'Show me – something wonderful, something I can only dream of such as Pargur, the illustrious Crystal City, or else the handsome knight I see when I sleep. Please, Darklis,' she pleaded. 'Show me a glad sight, something to cheer a fugitive.'

'No,' said Darklis. 'The leaves are spent,' and she tipped them into the fire. 'Instead, let us smoke a pipe together.' She felt in the pocket of her skirt and drew out a knobbly, briar-root pipe and a small sack of tobacco closed at the mouth by a piece of red cord. She filled the pipe, tamping the tobacco down with a horny thumbnail, and gave it to Gry.

'Take a glowing twig from the fire – there is one! – and hold it to the weed; but suck on the pipe and draw your breath in as you light it, or there will be no smoke and no satisfaction.'

The pipe-end was worn and marked by the chov-hani's teeth. It tasted foul but, persisting out of fear and a wish to propitiate the witch, Gry persevered, sucking hard. Smoke shot into her throat and she choked.

'More gently. As if you tried to suck a spirit in, for that is what

79

you are doing, communing with the soul of the tobacco. Which brings contentment.'

And now the smoke flowed, cool and aromatic, by way of Gry's throat into her nose, her vision, her heart and soul, and she was filled with calm and good will.

'Aah!' she said and handed the pipe to Darklis. They smoked quietly together, turn and turn about, until the Swan, the Hoopoe and Bail's Sword itself were visible through the smoke-hole in the roof.

'Like you I journey,' said the gypsy, 'but my quest has an object where yours discovers its objective as you search.'

Darklis Faa's Story: The Silver Dwarf and the Golden Head

Once upon a time, not so long ago, I was camped at Lythabridge with my tribe. My sister, Lurania, had been taking the air and improving her fortune by cheating the men of their gold – which they have far too much of. She came to me in high spirits and with merry mien, accompanied by a dwarf of lofty ambition, resplendent courage and singular appearance.

I recognised him at once: he was Erchon, the Silver Dwarf. You may know (or you may not) that the miner-dwarves of the Altaish are marked by their trade and take on the colour of the material they win from the earth. Thus an Iron Dwarf has a rusty skin and a Copper Dwarf is the colour of a new penny, an Emerald Dwarf is green – and these are easily told from their common brothers, the Stone Dwarves, who are merely grimy. Silver Dwarves are more rare and Gold Dwarves only heard of.

Erchon is famed for his dense colour, like a duchess's teapot – all over I don't doubt! – and is a fine rapiersman always armed. Also he wears one of those flourishing hats of the fantastical kind, large and highly-coloured with a gigantic cock's feather, for dwarves as you may also know (or not) are celebrated for their voracious carnal appetites and like to demonstrate their potency in an obvious and manly way. It does no harm!

The dwarf my sister had met bore all these characteristics. So, to cut the thread close, there was I exchanging pleasantries with the eminent Erchon outside this very bender-tent, which was pitched by the roadside.

He is bold and he is brave, I thought. I will test his courage and see if it can bring me gain; I will try him for my own amusement. So I made him a proposition and would have offered to pay him whatever his heart desired – but that, he was already in pursuit of though he knew it could never be his. He loved the Lady Nemione, his mistress: she who could never be his Mistress for she was courted by both Koschei and by the Kristnik, the stranger-knight. He took up my challenge out of goodness of heart and his love of adventuring. I thought that he, of all brave hearts, could find what my heart desired and bring it to me.

I wanted him to bring me Roszi, that wonderful gold head which sees and speaks all; Roszi, who was once a beautiful nivasha in the Falls of Aquilo; Roszi whom Koschei, by joining her icy soul and head to the body of a fire-demon and enchanting them both, had made into a puppet, a mere bed-toy to play with in the dark.

Ah, how I long for the Golden Head, spoiled and wayward though it be. How it would improve my shining hours! I would give it a proper, fitting use.

My wits are – a very little – sharper than Erchon's; nevertheless I was surprised when he obeyed me and lay down on the banks of the river, the mighty Lytha. Before he could raise his sword or otherwise resist, I kicked him into the water and at the same time spoke a spell. I turned him into a drop of river water and off he went to Pargur, which at that time was under siege from the Kristnik, Lord Parados, and which the Archmage, Koschei the Deathless, held.

Erchon tricked me, somehow, somewhere. He never returned from Pargur; much less carrying the Golden Head with him. I do not believe him dead, for no one has seen him or Roszi – but she is no longer in Koschei's gluttonous grasp, for she vanished the same day from Castle Sehol.

Darklis blew out a fan of smoke and idly watched it float above her head.

'I fear that he is using her, though I did not know he could work magic. Certainly, he uses her for his convenience and pleasure. Neither dwarf nor man, if he love a nivasha, will ever rest easy or be content with a common, mortal woman.'

She put down the pipe and leaned forward.

'Have you seen them, little Princess? Did they stray into your Plains, pretty Gry?'

'They are surely creatures from a fable – no!' breathed Gry. 'I have never seen nor heard of anything, of any creature like this Roszi. No. But I knew Githon, the Copper Dwarf –'

'Who is Erchon's cousin twice-removed in the female line?'

'Yes. Githon is a fine, upstanding dwarf, a travelling philosopher and lover of the curious. He was my father's friend.'

'Where is he?'

'I do not know.'

The gypsy witch stared long at Gry, paying particular attention to the luminous, unwavering flame above her head, which was the light of her soul and which only she could see, and to the depths of her dark pupils. Gry, like all Ima women, could hear the soft interior pulse-beat and other tiny sounds a person's soul makes within him; now, feeling the eyes and attention of the gypsy on her, she listened for Darklis's soul and soon heard it yawn and begin to snore, calmed into slumber by the strong tobacco. Soon, Darklis herself yawned.

'I am quite sure you are telling the truth,' she said, a little grudgingly. 'How late it is – or how early! You had better take my bed. I will sleep here, in the chair. There is too much of soft living in that bedroom for me: it is an ambitious conceit and I am happier by my smoky fire.'

Gry lay between clean, white sheets beneath a quilt of softest eider down and a coverlet embroidered with rainbows and clouds. The tobacco made her drowsy and her attention wandered, following the long journey she had made from home, and straying on the borders of sleep where the knight dressed all in silver waited to welcome her to his castle.

A gentle, querulous neigh broke into her dreams,

'I trust you are lying in the lap of luxury, dear Gry?'

'I am, I am, Red Horse,' said Gry, laughing.

'Then sleep safe,' the Red Horse answered. 'Goodnight!'

'Goodnight, dearest Horse.'

She fell asleep in the warm, dark haven of the bed. In the fire-lit room beyond, Darklis's soul was still snoring, while the witch talked in her sleep,

'What happened to the Kristnik, I wonder? Where's Parados, twelfth son of Stanko, the stranger-knight? I'll give a pound for a penny to any of you, man, mouse or maiden, who'll tell me. Where has the fellow got to since he disappeared at the Siege of Pargur?'

She is neat and slender-hoofed, thought the Red Horse in the glade; she has a small and pretty head and the hairs of her mane and tail are almost as fine as linen thread; her eye is kind and she smells good, of hay, horse-grease, mare's-scent. But she is not a Plains horse, not my white Summer, wife and mother of my Red Colt; nor any of my mares; she is not a Plainswoman, not Gry – she is nothing but a dapple-grey pony. However, I shall not stop her from leaning her head so comfortably against my shoulder. In fact I shall return the compliment by resting my head on her neck. His eyes closed and he lifted one hoof up to a tip-tilted position so that, should he slip into the still waters of profound sleep, he would stagger and so wake himself.

'When your Intelligence has passed out of the dense forest of delusion, you will become indifferent to all that has been heard and all that is to be heard.' I have these words from the Sage who begs outside the Temple of the Highest Thought and, having noted and learned them, resolve to use them as text and precept during my sojourn in this hot land of Sind. I shall make them the bread and wine of truth – or rather, since the priests and people here are sparing and ascetic by nature, the dry biscuit and water, the very stuff and staff of life. It would be a great convenience, could I close the doors of my mind on all the perils

83

and trials through which I and my divine Helen have passed and – no small benefit – on the bustle of our gypsy encampment; for it is the driest season, dusty, fruitful, abounding in deep noontide shadow and patches of bare ground too hot for a naked foot to bear. Our people are restless and tired.

To pass from delusion: what does the sage mean, do I want to accept his gift of mental peace? I live by delusion, by sowing and spreading it in the minds of others. Necessarily, my own temple of thought, my inner self, is full of strange creatures and fantastic images. To clear all this away, to prune and then burn as the gardener does when he tends an overgrown tree? To be empty, to be calm? What hard questions.

This afternoon, when I was in my usual perch, the cleft in the mango tree upon which blows the little, warm breeze which seems by contrast cool, I looked lazily down on the heart of the encampment. Surely its noise was not unbearable? Fragments floated up to me, a confetti of conversations, both human and animal; a salmagundi of music and song. The oxen were lying dully awake like opium-eaters, and chewing the cud; Mana's children played with their pet mongoose while she, squatting in the shade, was shaping dough between her flattened hands which she clapped together with a sound like self-applause as the paste began to fall and was caught. Raga sat on the fallen log, tapping his small, round drum while the flies buzzed unheeded about his shaggy head. The boy, Chab, accompanying him on the nose-flute, was so lithe and golden I wished I had carnal inclinations toward the male of our species. On solitary nights, when Helen was abroad with the snakes who are her soul-sisters, I had played with an idea of transforming myself into a sodomite and my redblood masculinity into something fittingly lickerish so that I might seduce and enjoy him. (Temperance, Koschei! Are you not about to make a resolution to quit such excellent diversions, to absolve, to abjure; to try the ascetic's way?) Laxmi, combing out her night-black hair, reminded me for an instant of my beloved, yet not so exquisite, not so voluptuous despite her curves in their wrappings of shockingly pink cotton, and her bell-hung, chiming rings . . . (Soon I will be free of such distracting images!) Slender Ravana waved to me and, again, I was tempted and tormented; he had the outward appearance of a woman, bright clothing, kohl-rimmed eyes, red-painted lips and beneath this frippery, a great piece of meat, a male tail almost as long as mine and two mighty testicles. He had been an actor with a travelling theatre before he ran away with we greater vagabonds.

I found myself half-aroused at these sights and thoughts; allowed the thoughts to reorder themselves until the recollection of magnificent Helen overcame them. Then, was I truly aroused – to what purpose? For Helen has gone. I write it again:

Helen has gone. Helen has left me.

and again

Eluned va da. Eluned mi da vyda, the language of the dwarves being most suitable for incantations mal or bona. All the languages that are and ever were or will be cannot contain my perturbation, my utter disquiet.

'For our good. For mine, but yours principally, dear Koschei,' she assured me as we took our last drink (the sweet juices of the melon and the passion fruit mingled, and a pearl against poison dropped in) together from her Cup. She kissed me on the lips and wiped the sweat from my face with the end of her scarf. I caught the phantom perfume which remained upon it in my nostrils; she had used the last drop long ago but, like its name, Sortilège, Spell, it lingers in the memory and wreaks sensual mischief there.

Helen turned the cup in her hand and sighed. I did not look at her again, being mesmerised by the spinning colours of the Cup, the sky-blue ground, the gold of the graven flames, the crimson and green letters. Words grew from her sighing.

'Must go – far – you know the Cup is dangerous – you know we are pursued, Koschei – Koschei-i-i-i-i.'

I looked sharply up, in time to see the Cup accelerate, turning now upon a seven-ringed shaft of light, and Helen's beautiful face above it, rapt. Then it and she vanished like a paper lantern crumpled, like leaves in a storm, and I was left alone to speak my question into the void.

'Where are you going?'

I listened, while the gypsies' talk hummed outside the cart, while the mocking jays sang. No answer came.

That was before noon. Hence it was that I sat like a monkey in the tree, hair tousled, body aching for love; and like a man, for I can reason:

85

Helen, knowing my arcane and sensuous nature as well as she does her own and, well understanding how I might yearn, provided for me before she left. She will be away for no longer than one moon, she told me, before we drank our loving cup, or the time it takes for a crawling grub to become a winged and glorious butterfly; long enough, think I.

'I have left you a gift,' she had said. 'Something of myself, you may call it; something I know will please you.'

She has left me Nemione, expertly plucking her senseless body from the great Plane of Delusion where she deposited it near the end of our last adventure and dressing it prettily in the female fashions of Sind – some lengths of more or less transparent, silver-bordered cloth, which go by the names of saree, yashmaq, fascinator &c – and bidding it lie in her place in our bed: for Nemione's soul is Helen's and so may my beloved put the pale, matchless Beauty to any use she will.

Nemione, my Lady, fair where Helen's dark, slender where she has abundance, voiceless where the rich tones of my witch surpass the beauty of the dove's 'curroo', the night owl's throaty hiss. Oh terrible asceticism, hard master, cold mistress! Must I spurn her? Must I abjure her? I stood up in the fork of the tree, reached out a little way and plucked a rosy-red fruit – so fecund is this little paradise. I tested the mango with my nail, making a shallow fissure from which its yellow juice ran out, and this I sucked, thinking first of absent Helen and then of present Nemione. (Perhaps my mind seeks the ascetic's way because I have excess of pleasures? I cannot believe it.) Decided for the time being, I climbed down and ran to my waggon, eager to share the fruit with Nemione.

Inviolate Nemione! Entire creature, unravished maid!

The curtains were closed beneath the tilt and I lifted a corner of the nearest to expose Nemione to my gaze. She was asleep, her snow-white skin flushed with the heat or from desire, perhaps, and she was sweating gently so that the womanly smell mingled with her jasmine perfume. Scenting her, I became excited and I dropped the mango in the dirt. Then, it was a moment's work to mount into the cart and, straddling the sleeping virgin while I uncovered myself, mount her. She woke as I drove into her; Nemione woke and smiled, who in Malthassa was cold to me as snow and ice, as the everlasting Altaish mountains themselves. I paused a moment in my exertions to put some words into her mouth, that she might speak and, 'Lord Koschei,' she whispered, her voice rasping with emotion and desire. It brought me to the brink and I erupted within her, a volcano released.

The first time is the last, I thought.

I looked down on Nemione, enjoying her transports, feeling her intimate grip and release as she sank panting in her own waking dream; and wondered, as we subsided together in the bed and lay close-twined, whether she could keep my seed and conceive of it. She was a toy; but she was flesh and blood and her blood stained my Parts, evidence of her chastity when she was a she-mage in our own country and proud proof I was the first to take her.

'Could you carry and bear my child?' I asked her, forgetting; of course, she answered nothing, being not only voiceless but senseless as far as mental matters go, and I heard Helen laugh in my mind, a ribald echo. Such a fancy would please her keen, malicious mind. The sounds of the encampment broke over me, pushing away the passing moment, demanding to be heard. I kissed Nemione on her parted lips and tasted her patchouli-scented breath.

'Say "Whatever you will, dear lord. I am here to worship and serve you alone, potent Archmage, king of my heart," ' I whispered and pushed the words into her mouth with my tongue.

'Whatever you will, dear lord. I am here to worship and serve you alone, potent Archmage, king of my heart,' Nemione breathed, her lash-fringed gaze the colour of an indolent, afternoon sea.

'Sleep,' I bade her, 'until I have need of you.'

She slipped from beneath me then and, turning her back, fell deeply asleep. Solitary again, I adjusted my clothing (the loose cotton trousers they call shulwars, nothing more), lifted one of the starry curtains which made the walls of our travelling house, and picked up a mirror, a common one, for grooming and vanities, no magic there – unless it was in the face reflected. My face, browned by the sun and the wind, blue-eyed; thatched with thick, greying hair in which still glittered many strands of yellow, a corn-colour; clean shaven. His face, browned by the sun and the wind, blue-eyed; thatched with thick, greying hair in which still glittered many strands of yellow, a corn-colour; clean shaven.

The even-contoured face, confident of life, its beauty enhanced by wisdom and the years, looked at me, Koschei Corbillion. Once, it belonged to Guy Parados. He's good as dead, lost in my world of Malthassa while I, in his, can do whatever I will, can travel as now I do, can live and love where I choose, can journey to his native country and claim all that is his.

When I last saw Parados, he had taken over the body of a horse and was using it for his so-called noble ends –

'Tis pity there's no notation in this alphabet for laughter.

We wise men of Malthassa think little of changing one body for another. It is from this, I think, my new ideas spring; for the sage of Highest Thought also taught me that by following his Way, any can become what is ordained be it dog, ape, or prince; and this notion, I wish to explore. My hunger for knowledge exceeds my lust by many a degree. Besides, it is written in the Twofold Scripture that the priest and the mage are one and the same and I suspect that he of the Temple is a deep magician.

These thoughts, which I now record, were mine while I regarded the face in the mirror. I put it down to look at sleeping Nemione. Asmodeus, she was beautiful, a perfection of soft colour and form!

'Snare!' I said, 'Delusion!'

But I could not forbear kissing her – thrice – in farewell.

So I went out into the evening. The sun had set and the heat his fires wake in the earth had receded to a gentle warmth. Fireflies and night birds were abroad. I stepped over the dry moat which divides the encampment from my garden, a magic garden I had made to surround the little annexe to my Memory Palace left in far Malthassa and in which I stored my most tender and amazing memories. It had taken seven nights to erect to my satisfaction, to decorate: a pretty thing, carved and ornamented in the style of this country yet cool and elegant, white as milk. I approached it through the garden, ducking under the branches of the flowering siris trees and passing the lake where the black swans and gold-winged divers swam. I paused to inhale the perfume of the night.

It was dark when I stood before my little building, if dark it can be when the skies are encrusted with jewels, and I went gladly in at one of its arched entrances and sat with crossed legs on the floor. It is the posture the sage uses when he exercises his body and mind to meditate and I had practised it until I was perfect. Such suppleness is the reward of discipline and I had my body well-attuned. I would begin work on my mind.

First, to clear it, I repeated the mantra the sage had given me and which I can record here in the secrecy of mind and journal. 'Jaa' it is, meaningless to me but, I know, a noise like that of the thunder and with an echo in my mind or the mind of this body which I cannot locate.

Jaa! No room in my mind for thought. Jaa! No room for hunger. Jaa! No room for desire. Jaa! Here is the engine of the body, pulsing, breathing.

I heard nothing but these, the sounds of life, and the near world fell away from me. I opened my eyes: the building had gone, the trees which surround it, the stars, the night. I sat in an empty place where a redness glowed. Sense of distance, sense of time: they had gone, but somewhere, maybe before me or to one side, I saw a rise in the ground and something indistinct upon it. I thought I was on the Plane of Delusion and blinked to clear my vision. The place glowed, red as the fire of a volcano. My eyes closed, opened. I was back in the annexe and the stars were visible, sparkling gladly beyond the arches.

I was glad, to be back, to have travelled; but I wondered, where? I took my journal from its place on the shelf beside the statue of Cyllene and wrote in it. At the end of the passage I drew a neat line and a sigil of protection, breathed upon that and replaced the volume. My hand, as I withdrew it from the shelf, knocked against something, the corner of a picture which had not been there before. I stared at it: I had no knowledge of it, had not conjured it; yet there it hung, framed in dark red mulberry wood and glazed with fine, clear glass. It was a portrait in oils and I recognised the sitter, Gry of the Plains, Nandje's daughter, or to put it in the hyperbolic, Ima style: the picture was a likeness of the Princess of Horses, Gry, Daughter of He Who Bestrides the Red Horse, the Rider, the Imandi. The woman looked serenely at me, dark eyes limpid – beautiful eyes! – her two plaits of hair bound with silver wire at the ends and silver in abundance, worked and engraved rings of it, on her bare arms and one, which had a cunning bone clasp fashioned to look like the tail of a horse, about her left ankle where the hem of her blue dress hung down.

Parados has done this, I thought. He intruded into my Memory Palace and now he is hanging his memories in my annexe. Yet I could not see how he gained entrance.

The rolling green Plains made the background in this pretty intrusion, hills and hillocks under the grass, some of them the dwelling-places of the Ima who burrow in the ground as if they were marmots or moles. The sky above the woman's head was clear and light. That is all, a plain composition truly yet a skilful one for it showed Gry as she is, untouchable and incorruptible, a true daughter of the Horse.

Marvelling the while, I saw that the sun was fully up. The fires aroused by my writings of Nemione above were quite damped by my writings of what passed here in the night, or maybe by the purity of the new portrait. I lay down to sleep on the hard, marble floor and felt its smooth cold enter my body and freeze my lust altogether. But when I emerge into the day and the camp and am again confronted by the startling beauty of Nemione, I may be in different case.

The witch's house, as Gry came in the morning from her sunlit, magic bedroom, had a disordered look. The chair and chest were gone, the stool was upended on the hearth and the tinware packed away. The light at her back, which gilded her dark hair and outlined her slight figure, snapped out as, with a suck and a sigh, the bedroom and all its luxuries vanished; but she spared it not one thought. The experiences of the night had taught her this, that magic may work for ordinary folk, and she ducked outside, through the original, low doorway.

There was Darklis, holding a steaming cup and a white plate on which lay two slices of dark, rye bread and a boiled egg. The chickens scratched in the grass at her feet. Beyond them, the Red Horse and Streggie waited, the pony laden with two panniers packed with all manner of gear, and a high-backed and embossed saddle. The expression on the pony's long face was resentful. I'd bet gold – if I had any – that she kicks, thought Gry.

'Ha!' said Darklis, as Gry advanced and Red Horse neighed a welcome. 'A tousle-headed lay-abed. Come, chi, hurry yourself. Here's a break-fast.'

The food was welcome and Gry ate it quickly and made haste to greet the Horse.

'We must never be parted, you and I,' she whispered.

'Never again,' he agreed.

With many a curse and sigh, the gypsy was dismantling her hut and Gry went to help her, but the willow-sticks whined as they were untied and separated from each other. She dared not touch them.

At last, Darklis finished loading her long-suffering pony and heaved herself up into the painted saddle, settling with a grunt, her feet hanging low either side. Gry mounted the Red Horse by knee and mane.

'Where are we going?'

'Where we are taken, I suspect; but I think her journey is ours and will take us to Wathen Fields.'

'Come, pretty Chickens and you – my fine fellow!' the gypsy cried as she touched the pony's sides with her scarlet heels, and the five hens and the cockerel fluttered in a panic after her and shot, one by one, into the sunny, morning air and so to their perches on the panniers and the pony's neck.

'Streggie knows where she's going,' Darklis called, over her shoulder.

furious fiery flanks narrow
brave brutal thick breasted

··

Deneholt that merry morning was full of light. The breeze touched but did not hold the autumn leaves so that they rustled quietly; the wood-birds sang with voices as golden as the leaves. Gry too sang cheerily:

> 'Your head and your heart keep up,
> Your hands and your heels keep down,
> Your knees keep close to your horse's side,
> And your secrets close to your own.'

The chestnuts grew in rows so regular, they might have been deliberately planted by an architect such as Garzon, who began Castle Sehol; but it was nature's doing, wild and accidental.

'We must enter the deep forest if we are to reach Wathen Fields,' said the Red Horse.

'Tilly vally! How shall we dare?' Darklis scoffed. 'The place rings with the cries of fell spirits and the beasts which dwell there.'

Gry listened, awash with fearful prospects, and gripped the mane of the Horse. It was clear that Darklis also had the power to converse with animals and she felt betrayed.

'You heard him!' she accused.

'I? O – ay. My name is Darklis Faa and I am the most famous chov-hani in Malthassa,' said the gypsy-witch smugly. 'And the most skilled, since Demeta Pennifold died – Barrac, girl! Out of my way! I know what's what, and where to find it!'

Although it was clear that Darklis had no more idea of where they were going than herself, Gry let the gypsy and her mount push past. They left the graceful chestnut trees behind them and rode under tall beeches whose boles seemed to Gry as thick and strong as giants' legs. Soon, the wind gathered strength and the brightly-coloured trees, as if they could no longer compete with the gathering clouds, gave way to yews and cypresses, to black birches and alders which held shadows in their sombre branches and darkness trapped beneath. The ground grew soft, and oozed moisture and the wind blew cold from every quarter, now in their faces, now at their backs. Soon the horses were stumbling over fallen branches and rotting tree-stumps so that they were forced to stop in the driest place they could find, amongst the roots of an alder. There was no space to put up Darklis's bender and they made a rough encampment where they slept fitfully, shivering in the bitter wind and silent because they dare not sing to keep their courage up. Nor did they dare admit the truth: that they were lost.

The drum of the shaman, Aza, echoed down the wind as far as the village of Russet Cross and again, as far as the settlements in the Plains, to Rudring, Sama, Efstow and Garsting itself, where Garron and Kiang had gathered loyal men about them who neither knew what to do for the best, nor where to look for Gry. A faction from Sama were camped out on the Plains, their watch-fires bright in the windy dusk and their flags billowing like shadow-garments. A second faction which, after much debate, had decided to follow Aza had ridden off in the wrong direction. And Leal, who was nicknamed Straightarrow as much for his honesty as for his skilful shooting, lay at Myrah Pits, on Hollow Down above the forest, as lost and strayed as anyone, his good name and his prospects destroyed for love of Nandje's daughter.

Only Aza, who had conversed with the zracne vile, the spirits of the air, knew where he was in the world. He was not lost, unless within his thoughts which heaved and bubbled like a cauldron in him, brewing up spite and ambition. He let his nails slide across the drumskin, and silenced it with the flat of his hand. It was time to call the inner voices out of the men, and to call up Tarpan from his sleep.

First, the shaman went about among the men, giving them sulphur-water from his iron bottle until they were all possessed. Then, sitting in the centre of the crooked and unruly circle of Ima, he undid the wicker basket which was Tarpan's stable and laid out the blackened bones of his horse. He took seven interlocking neck-bones, twenty-four spiny back-bones and eighteen tiny tail-bones and arranged them on the ground; he set out three rib-bones to stand for the horse's thirty-six ribs, and a shin-bone, a thigh-bone and four hoof-parings to represent four legs. When he had put the H-bone of the pelvis and the shield-bone of the shoulder in place, Tarpan was complete: except for the head, for that had been burned at his slaughtering to make ashes for a plague-draught.

'Be still until I call you, little Tarpan,' said Aza, crossed his legs and listened to the words which were roaring from the throats of the Ima all around him:

'I see the death-ship, Hespyne: has the woman gone to the Palace of Shadows?'

'I see a great wolf running: has the Pack devoured her?'

'I see sheep scattering in confusion. The woman is a ewe and soon we shall catch her by the leg!'

'She is by the sea!'

'She bathes in Pimbilmere.'

'She is in the Forest!'

'She has been taken by the Gypsies!'

'The Red Horse protects her!'

Which, Aza thought, is the nub of the matter though I do not understand it. But it may be that she was born with a puvush inside her – for Lemani gave birth out on the Plains, amongst the horses of the Herd, and not in a house as is customary. Or it may be that the Red Horse himself has eaten some wayward and evil spirit with the spring grass.

He watched sleep embrace the Ima, pushing them gently to the ground, and slept eleven dreamtimes himself. Then it was morning with a gale blowing and the men shouting loudly to make themselves heard as they caught and mounted their horses. He spoke to Tarpan, to wake the bone horse from his sleep,

'Rise up and run. Carry me, Tarpan, wherever I want and wheresoever you take me and let us go faster than the wind and more swiftly than the storm-clouds until we overtake and take the woman who was Nandje's daughter. Arise!'

Tarpan stood up, forelegs first and then the hind, just like a living horse. Every bone of his skeleton was in place, from tail-tip to atlas; except for the head, which was ashes in Garsting. His neck-bones stood up all in line like a stalk which has lost the flower which completed it and made it a whole. With a hop and a spring, his necklaces rattling and his skins and feathers dancing, the shaman flew through the air and perched upon the wide blades of bone which were all the shoulders Tarpan had.

'Follow us, Ima,' Aza taunted. 'Follow us if you can and you dare!'

Tarpan whirled once about, and they galloped away in a white cloud of salt. Battak drove hard heels into his horse.

'Spare nobody, neither man, nor horse,' he cried. 'Ride!'

The forest exhaled, a dense and freezing breath which filled every glade and hollow and hid the trees, one from another. The puvushi burrowed deep and the nivashi, whose hearts are as ice, froze in their pools until their long white bodies looked like dead travellers embedded in a glacier. The birds were silent, clinging with cold feet to their perches. In a single night, all the leaves fell. But the leshi did not sleep. They sat high in the trees where witches' broomsticks and ivy-crowns grew, and they hid under the crystal-covered leaves on the forest floor; the leshi were wide awake, and the forest beasts also, of which the chief is the wisent.

Beneath the alder where the travellers sheltered was a mossy niche warmed by the breath of the four who slept there; but the leaves fell on them all the same, steadily as each leaf grew mortal cold and was severed from its twig. The Red Horse opened his wise eyes, shook and shivered his russet hair and his new coat of leaves. He looked knowingly about him. Some beast was near: he hoped it was not a bear. He waited, staring into the haze and, after a while, walked quietly away from the sleeping women and the pony. The fog drew its grey curtains behind him. It was as if he had never been.

Bonasus, as day breaks, likes to graze alone. He is taller than a house-door and as broad as three strong men, and his family of cows and curly-coated calves is numbered in hundreds. While his wives and children sleep in Deneholt he is abroad, eating the sweet raxen which grows in the forest pools and wading belly-deep to reach the best.

He scorned the weather and this new cold. His coat was thick, the colour of cream. His sharp-edged hooves broke through the ice and found the mud he loved to stand in, while his hot breath thawed the raxen at which he snuffed and snorted, well-pleased. The fog troubled him not at all, as he bent his great head to the grasses, for he kept one ear cocked warily backward and the other forward.

Yet the weather was ill and unnatural, and he knew it as he stamped in the mud and let his woolly coat soak up and soil it until his underbelly and his submerged legs were dyed brown. Also, there were strangers in the forest, come to disturb his peace and, very likely, to try to cut the trees down or set traps.

Gry shivered in her chequered gypsy blanket. It was the one Darklis used as a roof for the bender; the witch herself was well-wrapped in purple, a magnificent redingote which, together with her scarlet and her jewels, made her look like a queen. They stood together, staring at the tree-tops, and marvelling at the great, bare branches which, in one night, had thrown off their golden coats to greet the cold.

'Something's wrong,' said the gypsy. 'It comes from Koschei, perhaps. The last time he was crossed, his bitter anger brought a winter which lasted an age.'

'I remember it,' said Gry. 'It was not so long ago. Something else is wrong: the Red Horse has gone.'

'Pshaw – the horse! His animal nature has got the better of him. I daresay that, even now, he is galloping back to the Plains and lusting for his mares. Plains horses, as I told you, are coarse creatures.'

'Not my Horse!'

'Well then, soft-heart, perhaps a bear has got him.'

'No!' She could not abide such a thought, that her beautiful warm-bodied Horse should be dead and cold, his red coat torn by sharp claws and his solid flesh devoured by pointed, ivory teeth. She hid her face in the blanket. 'Bears don't eat flesh,' she said.

'What? Forest bears? Those brutes do – anything they can lay their claws on, beetles, honey, grubs, nuts, fish, sheep – I know bears. We gypsies bind them and teach them to dance.'

Gry was silent, miserable and defeated.

'You will feel better if you eat a little bread,' said Darklis. 'Here –'

'No. Not until the Horse comes back.'

'Well, you will starve,' and the gypsy bit into her hunch of bread and bit off a second piece for the pony, Streggie.

'Caution does not get you grass, Horse.'

Bonasus spoke with a good will, his terrible horns lifted and his remorseless guard lowered now that one of the strangers had appeared, walking out of the foggy shadows to beg him for mercy and aid. A horse – but this was the Horse of whom the wood-birds had sung, before the coming of the cold. This was the great stallion of the Herd, the chieftain of whom the leshi had whispered as they got news from the samovile. The Horse approached awkwardly, wading through the hock-deep, icy mud, but neither his slow pace nor the mud-stains on his brilliant, red hide (which was veiled and silvered over with beads of mist) detracted from his stateliness and potency.

One like myself, thought Bonasus, a master of females.

The great wisent and the Horse looked at each other, and their minds met.

'No nivashi there to tread on, thanks be!' the Horse said pleasantly. 'Though the morning might be a better – is it Koschei's doing once again?'

'I know not. There is talk, in the trees, beneath the earth, but no one has the truth of it. Have you newer rumours?'

'Hearsay only, the chatter of the fox in the night, the wild imaginings of the grey wolves. But I have come on another's pilgrimage and she travels because all is not well.'

'Then tell me your story.'

The Red Horse's Second Story: Gry, Nandje's Daughter
Three journey with me. One is of little account, a pretty, flirtatious pony mare I should hrmmm! – one is, like myself, equine, and the second is Darklis Faa, the gypsy witch, whom you know well for she steals the milk for her tea from the women of your herd. But the third! She is Gry, the daughter of Nandje of the Plains, of the Ima, who, if she is not a princess by birth, is one in thought and deed; though you would think her no more than a small dark-haired woman, much bedraggled with her travelling.

'Are you in love with her?' Bonasus interrupted.

'I am not human,' said the Red Horse dolefully, 'so there is no hope for me.'

'Yet you may comfort and help this Gry. Continue!'

Gry, Nandje's only daughter, Lemani's beautiful girl baby, was born about seventeen years ago (an approximation, since you, like all Malthassans, know how flexible is time in these unpredictable latitudes). Her mother dropped her in the spring grass just as a mare drops her foal and so, most likely, comes her kindred-feeling with we horses. She is one of three: there is Garron, her older brother, and Kiang, her younger. Both of these are honest, honourable men.

They made a happy family, Nandje and his wife, Lemani, the two boys and the girl – for there had been other girl babies, four of them, who had lived but an hour or a day. Lemani rejoiced in what she had and in what she did, working in her house and with the Herd and journeying, in the proper season, to the Forest-fringe for the nut harvest, with her husband to the Cloth Fair at Flaxberry in SanZu and with husband and children to the Horse Fair at Vonta – It was there that Gry, a child of nine (say), first saw a boy: that is, first noticed how bold and distinctive they are. She smiled at this creature, the boy, who was only a linen-weaver's son of Flaxberry visiting distant kin, but most handsome with yellow hair the like of nothing except perhaps fine silk thread . . . this boy of (say) ten years, with his white grin and his scarlet blush, woke her female heart.

Gry lost her mother to the winter-fever before she found another beside her father and brothers to love as dearly. She began to see, because of the grinning boy, that Leal, in her village, looked at her with the same bright, brave eye. He used to bring her polished pebbles from the River Nargil, or the striped feather of a migrant hoopoe he had found in the grass, and gently give her these pretty playthings; for he, being fourteen (or thereabouts) and as honourable as Gry's brothers, knew he could do no more until he was made a man and she had become at least almost a woman.

When Gry was eleven, let us say, and long-legged and gangly as the young of the Herd, Leal brought her his best filly-foal, a roan horse called Juma, and put the halter-rope in her hand.

'A gift is like a promise,' he said.

'Why?' Gry asked. 'And why do you give me a present when it is not a feast day?'

'It's Juma's feast day. She outran her mother today – And I promise to come back and see how well you teach her.'

The boy ran off without another word and leaped up on his own horse, Tref, which as he was trained to do, was passing at a gallop. Yet soon, being devoted to horses and their care and especially to the filly foal, he visited Gry again and many times – though not often enough to disturb her father or her brothers.

'This teaching of beasts and their mastering with bit and rein is a thing I do not understand,' Bonasus remarked. 'You and I need no straps and buckles to make us act. We do not have to put saddles on our backs to run.'

'It is to help the rider, not the animal he rides,' the Red Horse explained. 'I allow Gry to ride upon my back because she needs my speed and wisdom. When I was made to wear saddle and bridle I fought them. No one but that sagacious horse-master, Nandje, could get up on my back and no bridle but the enchanted binding made of the Om Ren's skin could hold me back. But let me finish my tale.'

So the matter between Gry and Leal stood and continued, in peace and friendship, and Juma was both grown and made, a fine and steady mare, when Koschei's Winter came down upon the land and the horizons of the Ima closed in and were bounded by white drifts and falling snow. They began to kill we horses out of season, for the pot, as the stored vegetables and grain ran out. The dreadful, magical winter seemed to last many years until the coming of the Kristnik, Parados, to Malthassa brought it to an end. He came alone, out of the blizzard, and springtime came with him, walking in his footsteps and before him like a herald. At that time Gry was perhaps sixteen and Leal probably one-and-twenty.

Leal, though he fought the feeling, was jealous of the Knight. Nandje had commanded his daughter to care for Parados, body and soul – she must bear all the duties, except that final, dark and secret devotion which binds man and woman, he-beast and she, of a wife; so, Gry cooked for Parados, gave him fresh clothing, bathed him and oiled his body; and she was pleasant to him and pleased him. I think she loved him a little and, certainly, she pitied him because he had come mutilated and a cripple into her country: an enemy had cut off his hands. He could not even feed himself, unless he chewed his food on the floor as you and I do; but Gry cheered him by saying often 'All will be well' and by her singing: she has a sweet voice.

Parados, who sought Koschei to challenge and overrule, soon left the Ima and Leal, for a while, followed him; but that is another story. In the Plains the time for the horse-harvest neared and, while the grass grew up and seeded the ground again, the Om Ren was seen at the edge of the forest.

'The Forest Ape is looking for his death,' said Nandje. 'We must hunt him and give him what he seeks.'

Nandje did not seek his own death then, but he got it, early and untimely. The Herd killed him as they kill anything that gets in their way, underfoot, with tread and horn, after the Om Ren knocked him from my back; but that, too, is another story.

Nandje's death is the beginning of this, my new story. It happened that I made a friend of his poor, sad daughter and made enemies too, amongst the men of the Ima and of their shaman, Aza. It happened that one of the men forced himself on Nandje's daughter and died. And so it came to pass that both I and she have fled from the Plains and that she seeks something but does not know what it is that she seeks. Perhaps it is her father or a lover; or her life or happiness. The only certainty is, that we have lost our road amongst the samovile-haunted thickets and the puvush-ridden earth of your forest.

Bonasus breathed out a great, hot gust of air. The fog about him dispersed and that which was wrapped, like a walking shroud, about the Red Horse began to dissolve and fall as water droplets into the mire.

'You want me to help you,' he said. 'You should never have got mixed up with that gypsy.'

'Darklis is kind enough.'

'She is like all her tribe, and mine, and yours: in the end loyal to her kind. Beware she does not desert you in the thick – but, very well. I am a soft-hearted fellow when it comes to the female of any species. I will lead you as far as the leshi go, which is beyond briar rose and bramble: their parish ends before the fields, which are the province of the poleviks. Once there, you will easily find the high road that leads to Wathen Fields.

'But, Brother, I will do this only if you give up the fair Gry to me and let me carry her while we walk in my forest. I should like to try how it feels to be a beast of burden.'

The Horse nodded his head from side to side and it may be that he was thinking deeply, or that the flies which were rising from the raxen now that the fog was fading away, had bitten him. Or else he did not want to entrust Gry to another.

'I must carry her,' Bonasus said.

'You will find her light as a leaf,' the Horse said, at last. 'Though her troubles are heavy.'

'Here I am!'

'There you are!'

Gry believed she had never been so happy, never so glad, and pulled the blanket from her head to smile so lovingly at the Red Horse that Darklis was filled with envy and thought, All I have is that miserable, changeling pony – and all she has is my old, crabbed self, and my sharp heels in her sides!

'By Lilith!' she cried. 'He has fetched the Wisent.'

Gry, looking up from the shelter of her blanket, seemed to Bonasus to be as tender as a new shoot, and as green – not much more than a child. Sometimes, on summer afternoons, he had glimpsed the children of swineherds at play in the forest fringe. He had seen women too, almost as large as men and heavy, like his cows, with fat and milk. This creature was liker a spirit, light, willing, adventurous. He admired her and bellowed, though he thought he spoke softly as to a calf.

Gry ran helter-skelter to the Red Horse and flung her arms round his neck. The gypsy stepped backward and fell over a root. Her pony was tied and could only rear and neigh, but her chickens whirred up into the trees.

'Be brave,' whispered the Horse in Gry's ear. 'Bonasus is chief of the wisent herd and comes to lead us to safety.'

'He is so big!'

'His strength is his virtue. Stand firm.'

The gigantic bull came slowly towards her and, so carefully, trod the miry ground until he stood beside her and she could feel the heat of his body and breath. She looked steadily at him; did not move, though she knew she should flee. His white head was curly at the top where his two shiny and murderous horns jutted out. His eyes, set deep in their masonry of bone, were like the worst and most untrustworthy stallion's, flushed in the brown with red. A tremor ran all the way down her spine; her legs shook by themselves. Bonasus bent his left foreleg and his right; his head sank low and his great body came to rest in the mud as he kneeled to her.

'And you are afraid of him!' the Red Horse whispered.

'He is still enormous, kneeling there!'

'He is a proud beast. He has humbled himself to pay you his compliments. He will carry you safe and sure to the other side of the forest. Ride on his back!'

'He might run off with me! And what about you, dear Horse – are you leaving me?'

'I shall never leave you, Gry. Only grant Bonasus the favour he begs for. Let him carry you.'

'Let him carry Darklis!' Gry looked behind her. The gypsy witch, her magic spells forgotten and her velvets streaked with mud, was cowering against the tree.

'He does not kneel to Darklis. Besides, she will ride her pony when it is calm again. We will all travel together, just as you and I with Mouse-Catcher to guide us, travelled from Wolf's Castle to Pimbilmere. Give Bonasus what he asks: ride on his back!'

Gry looked up, as if she wanted a sign. The sky was visible again above the treetops, grey as despair, and full of snow.

'We must travel onward, while we can,' she said and touched the dense fleece of the wisent. Like sheep's wool, it gave and sprang back to meet her hand again, like a soft sleeping-mat. She wound it about her hands, advanced a foot, stood on Bonasus's knee. He did not move, only softly breathed. So, she climbed his shoulder and straddled him behind the hump of fat and muscle which sat like a huge shield-boss at the base of his neck.

'Bravo!' The Red Horse stamped and mud flew high.

Then Bonasus stood, a mighty force rising from the sodden ground. He marched, his shaggy back surging up and down as each leg strode, and Gry felt as though she rode the flood for he was alike unstoppable; nor could he be turned aside once he had decided upon his course. She had no fear of falling but she thought she would be carried off and looked anxiously behind her. There was no need of alarm. The Horse was close behind, and trod in the wisent's hoofprints.

Darklis was left to follow if she could.

'Drat!' she said, and 'Cursed be he, that wretch Erchon, who set me off a-wandering out of the way – for no gain I can see.'

'Calm yourself,' she told her pony. 'Who would expect you to be afraid of a mere animal?' and Streggie, though she stopped plunging and rearing up, rolled her eyes until the whites showed. Darklis, after vainly trying to brush the mud from her wonderful clothing, climbed on her back and dug her high, hard heels into the pony's sides. The chickens fluttered down from the trees to their customary perches; and so, equipped with all her necessaries, the gypsy set off in pursuit.

It began to snow, flakes like goosedown falling from the grey above. Darklis pulled up the hood of her redingote and the chickens tucked their heads under their wings.

No branch dared touch Bonasus, nor Gry lying warm on his back, snug in his wool and the chequered blanket. She saw the nivashi, suspended and immobile under the ice of their pools, until the falling snow covered them and hid them from view. She saw the tiny leshi scurrying over the snow, in which their feet wrote wavy tracks like the footmarks of birds and, when she looked into the distant shadows, other leshi tall as saplings and they, too, were following Bonasus. The crowding trees drew back from the wisent's path. When he came upon one fallen to the ground, he thrust it aside with his horns; then, Gry felt the power in his body. Soon, the snow lay thick and deep but, underneath it, the forest floor had levelled out, smooth as the lawns in

Castle Sehol's gardens and the trees were oaks with heads like old stags.

Bonasus bellowed. Gry felt his voice echo in the vault of his ribs; she heard what he said.

'Behold the heart of the forest, the Weatheroak!'

It was greater than the rest, an old, old tree. The snow had clothed it in white so that it looked like a king in his ermine.

'You must get down from my back,' said Bonasus. 'I am too big to stand inside the Weatheroak but you, if you will, go beneath it and learn what weather we shall have.'

The Horse moved close to the wisent so that Gry, by sliding first on to his back, easily reached the ground. She gasped as her feet sank into the snow and the leshi, gathering about her, chattered and pointed. Their feet were covered in moss and lichen from which their toes stuck out like needles from a pincushion.

A patch of earth, brown and bare of snow, lay beneath the Weatheroak and Gry stepped to it and stamped her feet to warm them. The leshi surrounded her, squealing loudly.

'Give her air,' Bonasus roared. 'Give her space to be and think her thoughts.'

Gry lapped her blanket about her, covering her head and closing her eyes to shut out the light and to let the noise of the leshi and of the breathing of the Wisent and the Horse fade from her mind. She laid her hands upon the trunk of the ancient oak and the snow melted beneath them and slid to the ground. At once, she knew what she had to do and moved closer to the tree, embracing it and pressing herself against it as if it was her golden-haired dream-lover, the knight of the stricken castle, or brave Leal Straightarrow from her past and distant life.

The bark beneath her hands, against her face, was rougher than a beard. It smelt neither of oiled steel and leather, nor of sweat and horses, but of ancient odours, damp, fungi, pollen, honey; like a distillation of all the barks and resins that have ever been or of a rare incense from a holy place. She felt the oak sway with the movement of the earth and time itself and found her inner eye bright and clear of vision and looking on scenes of mayhem and

105

destruction. The earth split and crumbled, rivers ran reversed, forests, mountains and cities crumbled. She saw a great castle but it was falling as she watched, its stones dropping from the tower-tops and its walls and bastions cleft from top to bottom and there, on the highest tower, was her knight shouting into the storm and waving a silver banner. She saw Leal, alone on a steep hill surrounded by lightning-blasted trees. He was holding two bridles and looking about him with a horrified expression, but there were no horses in sight. And then, the worst thing in the world, she saw the Red Horse stretched out still and dead upon a grey and stony ground and she beat her fists against the Weatheroak which groaned and trembled in its roots and began to lean and fall upon her. Scattering the terrified leshi, she screamed and ran from under it like a madwoman across the clearing and amongst the lesser oaks.

The Red Horse ran swiftly after Gry and stopped her with his bulk and body before she had run too far and lost herself in the forest.

'What is it? What terrors live beneath the old oak tree?'

'It fell on me!'

'No, it stands there. Look. You went into the future, remember?'

'It is terrible,' Gry moaned and buried her face in his mane. 'All fallen down, the earth gaping, everybody dead.'

'Did you hear the voice of Koschei? Did you see him? Is that what has frightened you?'

'No Koschei. Only death.'

'Bonasus is waiting for us.'

'I want to go home.'

'Alas, little Gry, I am your only home. Courage.'

'The tree spoke to me, Red Horse. It said, "This is not Koschei's Winter. It is the end of the world." It showed me in pictures and you were lying dead.'

'Nonsense!' The Horse shook his head so vigorously that his mane whipped Gry.

'Don't doubt me, Horse. Don't leave me.'

'On then. Let us find a place to rest and afterwards travel on with quiet minds to Wathen Fields. That is surely a blessed settlement, sheltering in its clearing in the Forest. I have often heard you Ima talk of it – your tobacco is grown in the fields which surround the village.'

The Horse carried Gry back to Bonasus and she climbed the woolly mountain of his body and settled in her place behind his hump.

'You are cold,' the wisent said, 'and full of terror and foreboding.'

'The tree told much more than mere weather,' she answered. 'It showed me the end of the world.'

'Every living thing must die but that great death, that too, must come sometime,' he murmured and a cloud of warm air gushed from his nostrils to surround and comfort her.

'Look!' said the Red Horse softly.

The leshi were creeping from beneath the snow and out of the cracks and hollows of the oaks where they had hidden themselves, quiet as mice. When they reached Bonasus, the tall ones lifted up their arms to Gry and then bowed low, while the small ones climbed up to her through his wool and stroked her with their mossy hands until she was calm. One of them, as yellow and warty as lichen, crouched before her and offered her a pair of shoes.

Gry smiled at him and took the shoes which, miraculously, were just the right size, and made of silvery birch-bark lined with soft, cream wool. She put them on her feet and Bonasus turned his head to look.

'Ah, wonderful!' he said. 'They gathered that wool from the coats of my little ones. Now you are more comfortable – and full of courage, I hope.'

'I feel better,' said Gry cautiously and the leshi beat their hands together with a muffled, drumming sound and scurried down to the ground. It was not long before Darklis and her pony, hurrying in their tracks, caught up.

'My child, my rikkeni chi!' the gypsy cried. 'Pretty one, what has happened to make you look so hot and queenly?'

107

'I was frightened, but the Horse and Bonasus took care of me and the dear leshi were kind. Look at the shoes they made me.'

'Sweet Bartholomew! They might not take the golden guinea in Pargur but they are rum rigging and skilfully-wrought. We gypsies know a good thing when we see one – but what has happened to put you in such a taking?'

'It was the Weatheroak,' Bonasus said. 'This little lady is not used to seeing visions.'

'Stuff! The tree is but a fancy weathercock, and a faulty one at that. I have used it myself – why, I clearly remember leaning up against it only a month or a day ago. It showed me a sunny, balmy summer – and look at the weather today, all cloud-down and sky-feathers!'

'Something is wrong, indeed,' said the wisent and broke into a trot so that Darklis had to kick her pony on and had no time for conversation. Although the leshi, tripping along behind, seemed able to walk fast and talk faster.

Bonasus halted suddenly and bowed his head so that his neck before Gry became a steep hill and she must hold the hair of his hump to feel secure. Behind him, the Red Horse slithered in the icy mud and Streggie bumped into him, nose to tail, tipping Darklis forward on her neck. The five hens squawked and their cockerel, woken suddenly, stuck his head in the air and crowed,

'Look-where-you-go-o!'

Gry yelped too, 'Sky!', and 'Arsy-varsy, rorty horsey!' cried Darklis, working her way back into the saddle.

He does not mean to alarm me, Gry thought, looking ahead. I see why he stopped so suddenly!

A small monkey, or ape, was playing on a fallen tree, making merry there by scrambling along it, leaping from the end into a drift of snow and running to the trunk to begin all over again. His agile body had marked the snow with a deep imprint, as if an angel had fallen there and, as the travellers grew quiet and stared, the sun came out and the snow upon the branches overhead began

108

to thaw and fall in clear droplets on their heads and shoulders and into the melting snow upon the ground.

'It is the Om Ren,' the Red Horse said, his voice awed.

'The Forest's Father!' Bonasus echoed in the same, reverential tone.

He is so small, thought Gry; an animal at play. His father, the old Om Ren, helped kill my father; and then the Red Horse killed the Om Ren. And, once upon a time, no one but Nandje could ride the Horse and he only with the bridle of Om Ren skin. And I, Nandje's daughter, can ride the Red Horse without this awful magic, though I do not understand why any of these things has come to pass.

The young ape jumped from his tree and scampered off without a sign that he had seen her. For a moment, she was sad and wished he would return; but one sight of him had been enough to give her new courage and she sat tall on Bonasus's back.

'His mother must be somewhere about,' said Bonasus to the Horse.

'The Weshni Dy – I saw her once. She was kind to me. She is a shape-shifter and could take any form – she might be that puddle of meltwater and the primroses flowering beside it, or that crown of ivy atop the leaning oak.'

'I should like to behold her – just once before I die and my son Marha takes my place. But we must continue, Red Horse, and help Gry onward. This is the place where we make our turn toward the briar rose and the bramble. From there it is but a step to the high road and Wathen Fields.'

Darklis rode slowly after the two great animals, deep in thought. I have seen him, Him,' she said to herself. 'Himself, the new Ape, the Om Ren of the Forest; and it is He who has put the weather back on course and made the flowers grow and bloom in an instant. Look at the buds breaking on the trees, dear Streggie! The Weatheroak was right after all when it showed me a fair summer. Look at the sunshine dappling down through the leaves! Listen to the birds!'

'What have you found?' Bonasus asked Gry, who stood ankle-deep in new grass beside him. The red stems of the bramble arched upward on her left and, on her right, the green stems of the briar rose climbed high into the trees and were covered in sweet-scented white flowers.

'It was caught in your wool – it is a stem of the sweet raxen you graze in Deneholt.'

'Good. Eat it, Gry, and remember Bonasus. The grass will help you to endure the hardest rigours. I must leave you here and return to my herd: it cannot prosper long without me to guard it – the young bulls are much too wayward, and silly with fighting each other. Besides, one of them may rob me of a cow.

'Goodbye, little shaman. Fare thee well.'

'Goodbye, Bonasus. Thank you for showing us the way.'

'Remember, Red One,' the wisent cautioned the Horse. 'From here, it is but a step to the road; and it is, besides, a fine place to make camp till morning.'

His shoulders bunched and his head went down as he swung himself about and charged away. Gry watched the gouts of earth his heels flung up and thought of his gentleness and his strength. Soon, he was out of sight.

'He could be meek as a lamb,' she murmured and put the raxen in her mouth and chewed, expecting it to be both tough and sharp. The stem was as sappy as the spring grass in the Plains, sugary and easy to eat. She sighed as she swallowed the last of it and stretched her arms and her body. It was good to be alive.

I came through the forest, she thought. I crossed the Plains and the salt-lands; I was a guest in Wolf's Castle; I climbed Russet Cross – O, Darklis has made a fire and got the tea-things out while I've been dreaming. Bonasus was a king too, as great a ruler as the Om Ren. He called me a shaman.

The Horse was grazing quietly. Gry went to him and put her arms about his neck

'Are you well, Horse?'

'Extremely, little Gry. I am both replete and happy to be so. I should not eat more but I am greedy today, and this grass is tasty.'

110

'So was the raxen. Horse, did you hear what Bonasus said? He called me a shaman.'

'You look like one, filly-girl. It is the weird and wonderful mix of your clothing. Common people do not wear shoes made by the leshi!'

'Where have they gone? – I did not see them leave.'

'I think they are here still. You may see one if you watch carefully. Stay quiet and still.'

'Coo-ee!' Darklis cried. 'Time for tea!'

'You will not see one now – go to the gypsy and get your meal. She is kind, in her way.'

Darklis, sitting close by the fire on her three-legged stool, served boiled eggs and rye bread and cups of hot, sweet tea.

'What a blessing to be out in the open and no need to struggle with my bender's sharp claws; and what another blessing my chick-a-biddies are,' she said. 'Always ready and able to lay. But, look, sweeting, above the smoke and branches where the sky is clear. The first star shines. It is the newest wandering star, which is why my people call it the Cuckoo-light for it is a strange bird in the nest of the stars.'

'We call it the Guardian of the Herd,' murmured Gry. 'It shone first over my village – not long after Parados came among us. To see it is always a good omen.'

The Red Horse, who was nibbling some fresh, young hazel leaves, drew back his long and whiskery lips in a smile that was almost human.

Raxen would make her journey bearable, tobacco made it easy to rest. Gry drew on the gypsy's briar pipe and, while the smoke drifted through the halls and galleries of her body, took the pipe from her mouth to examine. It was something like Nandje's: the stem stained yellow, but the knobbly bowl shaped like an upturned hat with a rose like that on Darklis's tea-spoon carved on it.

In this state of bliss all the senses were lulled. The stars were bright and very far away. The burbling of the spring amongst the hazels was a noise on the edge of consciousness but Gry could

111

clearly hear the Horse singing to himself, and she blushed in the dark, knowing that Darklis also heard him:

> 'When I was a little colt,
> My mother kept me by her side,
> But now I am a great horse
> I'm fit to be a king;
> I can fight all-comers,
> I have ninety sons,
> And I know a pretty girl
> Who likes to smoke at night.'

She was glad when his voice died away and she heard the deep, even breathing which meant he was asleep.

The day came when it was due and proper time to dismantle our encampment and take the road once more, if road you can call the rutted jungle track which lay between us and our goal, the pleasant (so Raga told me, his face creased with smiles of delight) land of Utter Hara which I suppose lies near the ends of this earth. I went with heavy heart to pack away the Annexe, grieving as I made and worked my spells and thinking sorrowfully of its sister and parent, the Memory Palace inaccessible far away. When I had done, I was exhausted and yet full of a good, proud humour: the little, pillared building was flat and two-dimensional as a picture and the size of a pocket-grimoire. I placed it carefully inside an envelope of oiled silk and sealed it with black thread and the thirteenfold knot. There was nothing left of it in the clearing but a circle of worn earth.

Ravana met me by the pink siris tree, swaying with a light step over the intervening ground. His kohl-rimmed eyes were heavy with disquiet.

'We must turn northward and cross the Dusty Plain; and we must be on our way before it is dark,' he said, his voice low, his eyes wary. 'Have you noticed the grey monkey which comes every day from the jungle to me to be fed?'

'A lively fellow, fond of mangoes and rambutan?'

'Yes, master. I am sorry I fed it. Laxmi says my pretty playfellow is

no animal. It is a Spy and it heard me speak with Jasper, discussing our route.'

'A Spy! Of Asmodeus? Of Urthamma?'

'Of Lord Yama himself, whom you call Zernebock. It is a peri and those lissom, treacherous creatures are the pets and servants, the eyes and ears of the king –'

'The King of the Lightless Garden?'

'Indeed, master, and of the Palace of Shadows. He who has many names as there are races in this world and all others, as many as there are nations and wars in every sphere of existence. As many as there are stars in the skies or sunbeams on a clear day or different sorts of love.' He linked his arm with mine and led me over the adamantine, sun-cured ground to the steps of his cart.

'Are you lonely, master?' he whispered, 'Are you desolate without the Lady to supply your venal wants; melancholy because she has left you a mute toy in place of herself?' He pressed his body against mine and I broke roughly away, though I was excited by his touch.

'Pray!' I said. 'That is what I must do – pray for help and enlightenment.'

A long way away, in the heathlands of Malthassa, by Birkenfrith where Mouse-Catcher had left Gry and the Red Horse, Aza rode through the night. He had long ago left the rest of the Ima behind, for the bone horse, Tarpan, needed neither food, water or sleep, and the shaman was tireless, driven by the bitter and caustic energy of hatred. Tarpan seemed to float, though his fleshless legs moved energetically, galloping a little way above the ground, following the star-shadow he cast. Mouse-Catcher and his mother, Mogia, watched them carefully from the shelter of a rock and heard the scritch-owl and night-raven cry out in fear.

Aza, clinging to Tarpan's shoulder-blades, smiled grimly to hear their songs of alarm. He looked forward into the future and up, at the stars. The great star burned above and he spoke his thoughts aloud, 'She is in the Forest with a gypsy and the Red Horse: that I know. But why should the One Star watch over her? She is certainly a witch who has more powers than ever I could guess at. All the more need to be rid of her! If she does not die in her pride of the night-cramp or the cold – if she does not perish in water or heat, Stribog grant that I am the one who cuts her throat and sends her to her father in the Palace of Shadows.'

Bold in his speech, yet wise and full of tact,
There was no manly attribute he lacked
....

Colley Switman stepped out of his front door to look at the sky
and sniff the wind and the weather. He was as content as it is
possible for a hard-working innkeeper to be and smiled to see
the sun rise from its night of rest beyond the Altaish and flush
Wathen with its first light. The breeze was already thickly laden
with the scent of the tobacco flowers.

Colley walked into the silent, empty road which ran past his
front door and looked up at his pride, the Live and Let Live Inn.
In his eyes, it was perfect; and his customers and guests shared
his opinion. The golden thatch of the roof dipped low over the
pink-washed wooden walls and the inn-sign which showed on one
side, a happy man drinking his ale, and on the other, a smiling
dwarf before a sumptuous spread, was newly repainted. The door
was tall and broad, of thick oaken plank and the windows, some
of which were glazed with glass and some with butter-coloured
horn, were framed by grenadilla-flowers and creepers. By the
door stood a mounting block said to be hewn ten thousand
lives ago by the dwarves of Saxum; and Saxum was said to
lie in the foothills of the far-away Altaish. Far, indeed, and
nothing certain, Colley thought and turned his head to look in
the direction of the mountains while frail wings of fear fluttered
close to his heart and stilled again. If the mountains looked so
huge at this distance, what must be their true height? – and what
on earth could live up there, in the snowy wilderness? What lay
beyond them? Earth? Air? Water? Or was it true that – could

115

you scale the mighty Altaish – you would walk into the house of the sun?

Asmodeus! He saw a dog-turd lying in his precious bed of gillyvors and came from this fruitless contemplation to himself as he kicked it away into the roadside dust.

He glanced along the street. Still no one about, no one on the high road nor approaching it through the fields; not on the village green nor beyond it, in the crofts and gardens of the housen, nor yet by Fortuneswell where the Game would begin. He was ready: all was in order. He was ready for the day, whatever it brought. Tightening the strings of his dark green canvas apron, he turned indoors to wake his wife and, on a second thought, emerged again, picked a bunch of his sweet-scented gillyvors and strode off to the well. Keep its nivasha as sweet, he thought, and maybe fortune would favour his side in the Game. Then, all truly in order, he would climb the red-carpeted stairs to the bedroom, duck under the closed bed-curtains and kiss his fey darling – no, first, though they were in shining, supple order, he would attend to his leathern byrnie, his sallet and his gloves for was he not captain chosen of the Wathen Men? But – yet – it was not possible for such a loving fool as he to be testing stout buckles and stouter straps while his fragile beloved slept ungreeted and unkissed; so first, he would climb the stairs and rediscover her whom he had left a short hour ago.

Sib opened galena-grey eyes. Her husband's round face was beaming between the bed-curtains; fiery like the sun and suffused with love. She blinked at him. His smile, she thought, might crack his face in pieces. He took her hands in his and played with them, kissing them and comparing her long and delicate fingers to ash twigs, angel's limbs, the bones of mice.

'Sib,' he sighed. 'Sweet by nature – and Sweet by name, since you took mine. Shall we have children? Two or three sturdy sons, think you? And a daughter like a little elf, as winning and dulcet as her mother.'

Sib sighed in her turn.

'I would rather three elfin daughters and one strong son: my

116

body is made to deal with dust and cobwebs, fallen leaves and the beetle-wings flittermice drop in the attics.'

'But if you eat your cream –' he said, releasing her hands. 'I have brought your breakfast.' He drew the curtains aside and put a wicker tray on the bed. The room – o! it was a clean and pretty one, the best in the house – was full of light and the busy sounds of morning rising from the yard below. Sib pulled at her dusty floss of hair until it cast a deep shade over her eyes before she sat up and began hungrily to eat. The food seemed to strengthen her, even to tint her shadowy complexion with the golden colour of the day. Last of all she drank the cream in the blue basin, right down to the last drop which she licked from the basin's shiny depths.

'The cream is smooth today,' she said. 'The red-and-white cow's.'

'A good guess. It is hers,' said Colley, answering her statement as if it were a question. He watched his wife arrange the dirty dishes tidily on the tray and marvelled. It was not so long since he had found her, cowering beneath the slate shelves in the food-cellar. A thieving vagabond he had thought her, or a runaway, as he caught her by one arm and pulled her into the lantern-light. She would give no account of herself nor explain how she came there and he had locked her in the broom cupboard under the back-stairs until, bethinking himself after closing-time, he had remembered his strange captive and crept, when all the servants were gone to bed, to release her and put her out in the street. She had made no sound all afternoon, neither whimper nor shout, and he half-expected to find her gone, released by one of her kind for there had been both lame and able-bodied beggars in the village that day. The door was still locked and, when he opened it, expecting to find her crouched as he had left her on the untidy jumble of tools there, he had found a saucy creature and a neat array of the mops and brooms, arranged in order of height along the wall.

'Well!' he exclaimed. 'You have improved your dark hours.'

'What a mess, sir, what unhallowed disorder,' she returned, with a smile. 'Your servants are idle.'

Her smile, which tilted up the corners of her pale-as-curd mouth,

117

had undone him. From that moment, he believed, he had been in love with her; and had kept her in the tavern as a hireling-servant responsible for household order and neatness.

'I am good at that,' she'd said, when he first proposed it, and laughed like a silver chime hung in the evening breeze.

He paid her in kind with aprons and a print dress, with food-stuffs and the daily basin of cream she demanded. As she did not seem to need long sleep like her fellow-servants, but napped on a settle between moonrise and cock-crow, he took to sitting late with her in the snug of the closed and silent tap-room, tickling her unsophisticated palate with dry sack and the sweeter wines of Arcadia; soon he had embraced and kissed her; then, made bolder perhaps by the fumous wine, he had proposed marriage and been accepted with a soft 'amen' and the chiming laugh. She said she had no name, or would not give it, so he called her – who would soon be close kin – Sib. In this he also honoured the great-aunt who had willed him the inn and now lay in black SanZu silk in the boneyard, silent at last: Drusilla Sibilla Dowshier, virago and harridan.

At the wedding, his bride was described as Sib Abigail, domestic, and he by his proper style and title of Colley Aloys Switman, Esquire, proprietor and keeper of the Live and Let Live tavern at Wathen Fields. As the priest read from his book, Colley thought he had found true happiness. He had bought his bride a veil of embroidered gauze, fine as spider's thread; it had been delivered to her in a tiny red-paper parcel which contained a walnut shell and she had pulled the filmy veil from the nutshell until it clouded the polished floor. She looked up at him from wan mists when he lifted the veil to kiss her before the altar, the priest and the congregation; and blinked in the sudden light. Now, she was here, in his bed – almost as solid as he was as she reached for her daytime shift. He had her clothing specially made in greys and eventide blues, for the bright skirts and ribbons of the village women did not suit her at all. He detained her for a kiss which multiplied, as they must, and became prolonged dalliance on the bed until she said, 'Should you not be tapping at the bungs of

118

your ale-barrels, Man-that-I-married? The players will call for it by quarts and yards.'

'Not till after the Game.' He caressed the strange band of white fur which grew from the nip of her waist all down the globe of her belly as far as her womanhood, and whispered in her ear, 'I took the nivasha some flowers.'

'That is well; for who can tell, my Colley, what is, or will be? Only, I know that Wathen Fields will win the Game.'

Smoke filled Gry's dreams, spinning blue and grey fibres about her which were trailing threads of silk and the infinitely small needless of moss-stalks through which she ran, her broken wings dragging and holding her back. She heard the six feet of the stag-beetle drumming his pursuit and the snip-snap of his claws as they scythed the air. He had got her, caught by the hair! and she opened her eyes and put up a hand to scratch her head. Fleas, perhaps from the thick wool of the wisent or the gypsy's chequered blanket. Something was holding her hand and she rolled over and pulled it from her head.

The leshi landed in a clump of grass. She could see how frightened it was and did not know how to soothe it or say sorry. Her head felt very strange and she touched it again. Her hair was plaited – that was what the leshi had been at! There was another, and another, peeping at her. She smiled at them and stroked her hair until they had crept close again, even the one she had scared.

It was just light enough to see them, and the Horse, asleep on his feet in the green twilight before dawn.

'Thank you, leshi,' she said.

They made tiny, high noises like flittermice.

Her hair was scarcely long enough, but they had made five plaits, two each side and one at the back into which – she felt – they had worked the spiral shells of grass-snails.

They had slept under the stars to save Darklis the trouble of putting up the bender. Gry saw the gypsy stir in her blankets and lift an arm to the sky.

119

'Dishilo!' Darklis cried as the sky above the treetops flushed pink.

Daybreak, and the Forest passed. Wathen Fields was somewhere – there, perhaps. Gry look beyond the briar rose, where the trees thinned out, and saw a pair of doves fly up. She imagined the road, sweeping in curves across the cleared land. Perhaps there would be other travellers on it, good people like the Ima used to be; or horses and wagons carrying cloth and wood; or wandering musicians and storytellers.

When Gry had fetched water and Darklis had lit the fire, they settled to cooking breakfast. Another party of the smaller leshi brought them mushrooms and the white hen and the speckled cackled loudly and each laid an egg.

'What could be fresher?' said Darklis, breaking them into the pan. 'All we need is a bit of bacon, but we might as well wish for the moon.'

'I'll wash the dishes,' said Gry, 'and myself, for we will soon be among decent people who mind their manners and their purses.'

'Tish! girl. You are with a decent gypsy and never mind the king of horses and my good dapple-grey.' But she laughed as she loaded her pony. The Red Horse stood by keeping watch, his ears pricked.

'What do *you* hear?' the gypsy asked him.

'Nothing, Darklis Faa, but leaves rustling in the morning air – and Gry splashing in the spring.'

'That is a curious hairstyle she's given herself.'

'The leshi fashioned it while she slept. They are fey and clair-voyant and have taken to her.'

'She is no ordinary mortal, for sure.' Darklis fastened Streggie's saddle-bags and paused in her work, hands on velvet-clad hips. 'Horse, I have a question to ask you while the little lady is at the spring.'

'Then ask it.'

'It is this, Red Horse. Why does the light of two souls shine over your head?'

'A-hem!' said the Horse. He stamped his left forefoot and neighed up and down the scale three times. Gry called out.

'What is it, Horse?'

'Nothing, dear Gry. I am only clearing my throat.'

'You are trying to dodge my question, brother Sharp,' Darklis accused. 'Listen once more to me. With my native skills and all the canny learning I got from my dear mama and sweet grandam, it is no trouble to me to see the two soul-lights over you. Clear and certain as sunrise, they are, or as the Crane-stars in the sky.

'Now, as you know well, Ima women too can hear souls and see them – far better than their menfolk, who must listen with an ear laid to the belly. So, comes their odd way of greeting a stranger.

'But all that's flummery, for the question is: why Gry has noticed nothing awry? In short, *Sir Parados*, she thinks you are no Man and all Horse.'

'You are a canny woman, Darklis Faa, and I would take my hat off to you if I had one and were capable of it. The soul of the Horse is, indeed, in his belly and Gry often hears it. But my human soul, my poor bound soul, is sitting – comfortably enough, to be sure – just behind the Horse's right eye, *inside his brain* where the wild crackling of the currents there and the swishing of the bodily chemicals masks his little cries and movements; and the reason he is there is because I cannot subdue the Horse's iron will and fiery temper unless my soul rides in his head.'

'You speak of your soul as if it were a prisoner. Why do you not send it back to your own body and become yourself?'

'I do not choose to, at present.'

'Liar! Sneaking cove! Something prevents you – is it Koschei?'

'I've lost my dear, well-used body, which I left in a safe place far from here but perfectly accessible to one with my talents.'

'Lost? Stolen!'

'I trust not, chov-hani. That would be inconvenient – no, a disaster. I think it lies where it always did, but the erratic times and tides of Malthassa have obscured it.'

'Tosh! You forget to whom you talk! I am Darklis, Queen of the Faa Tribe and all the Canting Crew, and as you rightly say,

I am a gypsy witch – but no mere dukkerin chi or hedge-rigger. I am Empress of the chov-hanis.'

'Then I bow before you,' and the Horse bent his forelegs and dipped his head.

'You know as well as I, and in your heart of hearts, Kristnik, that the Fifth Circle of Limbo where you left your soul is outside time. That cannot move nor be obscured. No, someone has stolen your body and Koschei is the chief suspect, wherever he may be.'

'I have seen his corpse, Darklis, but I cannot believe he is dead.'

'He is not vainly called "the Deathless". Like yourself, he is a master of the shape-shift. Nonetheless, when you tire of being a horse, you will have to find a fresh body.'

'I enjoy my present state. I am in no hurry.'

'O, self-deceiver! You enjoy the love of the little Ima woman and bask in her devotion – pah! Seduction and docking with women! These and suchlike diversions are not the reason you came to Malthassa. You are here to defeat Koschei, not to continue your last life as a top-diver, tupping all and skirted sundry for love of the game – though I suppose that now it is all and tailed sundry . . . In Albion you were a Christian. In this world, you are the Kristnik, the man who won the love of a nivasha, of Nemione herself. Here, you are the twelfth son of a twelfth son, of great Stanko himself.

'You have lost your way, Parados. If you don't soon change direction and your skin you will lose Malthassa and everything in it.'

'Enough, gypsy. Enough scolding.' The Red Horse was tempted to complain, to ask Darklis how she dared take the place of his conscience. He contented himself with curving his neck proudly and arching his long tail. 'There is method in my madness and I must hide my true self and travel with Gry,' he said. 'While I am a horse, I cannot change the world but later, when Gry has found what it is she seeks, her father, her lover, whatever it may be; when all the obstacles which lie in her way have been surmounted, we may discover who is telling this story. If it is myself, why fear? If it is Koschei, or even some other, I shall fight him.

'So be content, or leave us and make your own way.'

'Then, Sir,' the gypsy bowed, in her turn. 'We won't tell Gry any of this – just yet.'

'No, we must keep mum, you and I; hold our cards close to our chests,' said Parados. 'I am the Red Horse. If I were to become Parados all suddenly, it would be too much for her, in spite of the raxen grass. She is almost a horse herself at times and, horselike, she could be scared into a fit and stampeded out of her senses. She is too precious to put in danger.'

'And you, Kristnik, are too fond of her.'

'She is mine. I invented her.'

'Did you so? There is more than a loss of body and travel incognito here. There is miching mallecho and the cursed and interfering hand of Koschei in the matter. How is it you can no longer turn the tide of events? Who has robbed you of your power to cleave mountains and change the course of rivers? Perhaps you should, after all, desert your cause and remain a horse forever, Parados. It is a simpler and more noble way of life.'

'Like your continual wandering, gypsy?'

'If you think my life and the ruling of the Faas is simple, Parados, I bid you return to the dame school and learn your alphabet again. We wander and we live on hope and what we can catch, on good fellowship and whatever we can snatch for ourselves. This is not just the boundary of Bonasus's kingdom: it is Solomon's Haven, well-known to every gypsy. How sweet is the water of the spring in which the little horse-herder disports herself, knowing we cannot see her! And the wild white rose – here it is, in effigy, on my pipe-bowl. Aye, we gypsies stray across every man and beast's acres, like the stems of the rose, though we have no lands of our own.'

'Call me Red Horse, Darklis, not Parados or Kristnik – do not let a slip of your tongue uncover me until I give you leave!'

'I swear I will mind my speech, Red Horse. By the Upright Man and by our mother Lilith! Now let me finish loading this stupid nag and you, do you walk amongst the hazels and fright Gry from her joyful ablutions.'

'How many miles to Wathen Fields?
Three score miles and ten.
Can I get there in daylight?
Yes, and back again.'

Gry was singing, as they trotted along the road beside the forest. The Red Horse listened and smiled to himself. He felt her light weight high upon his back and, looking round, surveyed her supple left leg where it projected from under her absurd and makeshift skirts and disappeared again into the deerhide wrappings and the neat birchbark shoe the leshi had made for her. When he turned his head the other way he caught a glimpse of her young face with its mix of the wisdom the wolves had given her and the endurance she had got from Bonasus's raxen-grass. She was horse, tree, water and woodland too, a free spirit, lovelier without those female distractions, the long plaits, blue raiment and silver jewellery with which she had been decked when first he saw her. He remembered how he had compared her with others of her sex, and especially with Helen Lacey, and concluded that she was without guile, entirely blameless.

'What is it, Horse? Do the flies trouble you?' said Gry.

He made no answer but put his two pictures of herself into her head.

'Me, Horse. What of it?' she exclaimed. 'Gry, Princess of Horses, and Gry, chief of beggars. I don't know which is the odder for, surely, what happened to me in the Plains is a sign that I am cursed.'

'Not cursed, princess. Do not be so harsh with yourself. Sing again, sing to me.'

Gry, with an effort, put the sad thoughts their conversations had woken away and began again:

'How many miles to the high Altaish?
A thousand miles or more.
Can I get there by milking-time?
Yes, there and home before.'

Wishwash, fudge, galimathias – Darklis has infected me with her
canting hyperbole, the jade! the Horse thought. What nonsense,
unless you ride in your imagination. He shook his head to clear it
and to clear away the flies which buzzed about it like the insistent
words he once was able to master. Without waiting for Gry's
voice or heels, he cantered along the grassy strip between the
wheel-ruts.

Soon, the forest curved away from the road, its crowded trees
retreating in a dense, dark line. The croaks and eldritch chirrups
of the leshi grew faint as they were left behind. Different vegetation
crept at first, then flourished, burgeoning in the intervening space:
small larches, weeping willows, prickly bushes of gorse in full and
yellow flower. Gry drank in their rich, coconut scent. The gorse
gave way to thick bushes of green broom which, in their turn,
made room for grass and meadow flowers. Here, they stopped,
Gry and Darklis to smoke a pipe and the Red Horse and Streggie to
graze. When they rode on it was between tall white-flowered plants
whose leaves were already beginning to droop in the morning sun.
Dust pothered up from the road, coating them all with fine, white
particles and they felt themselves invaded and coated also in the
perfume of the flowers.

'Tobacco,' said Darklis. 'There it is, is the powerful weed. We
are riding through Paradise Grounds where the best smokes are
born strong and reared on blood and the ground-up bones of the
finest cattle.'

Something chirped amongst the plants like a homecoming bird
and whiskered faces peeped out between the leaves. Gry watched
them as she might a flock of rare birds and they cheeped at her
with sweeter voices than the leshi and waved seven-fingered hands
as green and sappy as the tobacco stalks. She recognised them
for what they were, the spirits of the place, pithy but benign,

happy to lie all day in the tobacco-flowers and watch the bees forage.

In smaller fields with neat hedgerows grew crops of half-ripe melons and squashes. The pea-bines in the garden closes were hung with fat pods and the orchards crowded with pear and apple trees which sheltered hen coops overflowing with yellow chicks, while their brown mothers pecked in the grass and gaudy cockerels strutted. Darklis's fowls clucked in sympathetic unison and her cockerel crowed.

'Hold, my noisy cacklers and you, my chuckle-headed klaxon, swallow your pride!' Darklis cried. 'The whole village, from house-proud hussif to babe-in-arms, will hear us coming.'

This place had a different sort of fruitfulness, not the lawless abandon of the forest's trees and wild weeds, but tidy growth kept in check. Yet the neatness and order were no comfort to Gry, who felt only that she had come to another foreign place. For some long moments she yearned for the endless steppe and unbounded skies of her own Plains. She nodded her head in agreement when the Red Horse said, 'This is a land of people who conceal their fear by pruning and trimming everything that might threaten them.'

There was no time for more philosophising. The Horse shied violently and Streggie, with a great clash and clatter of saucepans and a squawking from the fluttering and unseated hens, baulked, hooves dug in.

'Come up!' Darklis kicked her in the ribs.

A remarkable figure rose from the ditch to confront them, a tall man whose brown face was streaked with dirt, whose jet-black hair curled and tumbled from under his hat. The rest was as green as the hedge behind him, shirt, breeches, boots and long coat of heavy broadcloth, a bowler hat into whose brim was tucked a single spot of brightness, a scarlet game-cock's feather. Old leaves and twigs and other ditch-bottom litter clung to the skirts of his coat.

Darklis spoke out in a ringing voice.

'Why do you leap so headlong and sudden upon us, hedge-creeper? Our horses are not used to such uncouth sights as you in the morning, my sturdy ruffman.'

126

The man looked at her with his dark and piercing eyes and a scowl stretched his well-formed mouth, about which a good deal of stubble showed; but soon, as he caught sight of Gry in her high place on the back of the Horse, a bold and merry twinkle grew in them. The feather in his hat glowed like a spot of heart's blood.

'See the herb of grace, the rosemary in my buttonhole, lady,' he said, and touched his hat brim and bowed to her. 'The gypsy does not care to recognise it though she knows it is the sign by which all we Rom know each other.'

Gry shifted in her seat, uneasy at his rude waylaying of them, alarmed by his careless beauty, while the Red Horse tossed his head and pawed the soft, yellow dust of the road. Darklis said, 'Oh, I spy the sea-rose, and I see what a rum duke you are, a handsome fellow indeed, quite the bedroom charmer. You must be a Starling or a Moongazey. You are not of my tribe.'

'Not a Faa, nor yet Starling or Moongazey. I am one of the Lovelaces, the original roving kind.'

'Never heard of them!'

'They come from Arcady, very far away on the other side of the forest.'

'Which side, man? Never mind! Do not let it be said that Darklis Faa knows everything! – so, what is your business with us?'

'To wish you good day, sweet ladies. To tell you what you may expect in Wathen Fields today. I heard your party – and your chickens – on the road and resolved with myself to greet such resourceful travellers personally. For is it not unusual, though a grand sight, to meet with a woman of the Ima in this part of the world? Especially one mounted upon such a fine and regal specimen. You are fortunate ladies, the Fair begins today in Wathen Fields.' He turned to Gry. 'The town will be full of young bloods, my pretty, a ruck of handsome men there for the Murtherball and for the drinking afterwards. You will surely find yourself a lover.'

Gry was fascinated, as much by his glittering eyes as by his whirling words and manly body.

'I already have a lover . . .' she said and faltered in her speech. Certainly, she would never see Leal again.

'Not so sure? Think then of the Fair and its delights, its extravagant shows, its music! Who knows what manner of handsome fellow may accost you there – poet, merchant, prince, soldier, gypsy lad?'

'Flummery!' Darklis interrupted. 'Is this the way to talk to a stranger? Leave the girl alone, sir! Go, find yourself a crack jade to dance the blanket hornpipe with and leave honest folk to follow their own affairs.' She tossed a silver coin into the dust and the gypsy man looked down at it and up again at her.

'Is that to bring me luck or make me rich, Darklis Faa?'

'To be rid of you!'

He bent, picked up the coin and tried it between eye teeth which seemed to Gry to be as strong and white as a wolf's.

'A good one! Thank you – when I spend it on ale, I shall toast you, Ima princess; or, if I spend it on a doxy, I shall think of you in your heyday, Queen of all the Faas and *Empress* of gypsy witches, and wish I had met you in those springtime days.'

Darklis snorted, loud as any horse. She spat on a finger and made a sign in the air.

'Farewell, Stranger, see how I give you my malediction! Hie on, Gry. We will leave the hedge-creeper to wait for his next prey.'

They trotted on, kicking the dust up over his dandy clothes, and were a yard or two beyond him when Darklis, her scowl turning suddenly to a smile, turned in her saddle and called.

'Romanichal! Will you give me your name, Sir Lovelace?'

'Avali! I will. Hyperion, that's it: Hyperion Lovelace, Lord of Little Egypt. Remember it tonight when I visit you in your dreams!'

The sun was high in the sky when Colley chanced to step out of the inn again. As usual, he looked up at the sky – and beamed, seeing it cloudless, blue. A perfect day. The village was filling up with fairgoers and players, many of whom were already inside the Live and Let Live tasting the new ale and, he hoped, praising it to the heavens. Stall holders were setting up, laying out their goods in a leisurely way. No hurry: they would be selling all night, once the fair got going. On the green, Wathen's brass band was practising the March of the Men in gusty and vigorous fashion. Colley stood by his door watching them, and the road.

Now here came true travellers. A woman of the Ima, if he wasn't mistaken, but dressed very strange. And a gypsy. Both of them well-horsed: the Plainswoman on a great, red animal – and riding it, by holly green! without the benefit of saddle or bridle! Not 'it', either but 'he' for sure, with that thick, muscular neck and a full purse of seed between his hind legs. The gypsy's mount was a neat dapple-grey, burdened with saddlebags and other traps – and fowls, too, by the four Alls! What a wonderful gift for Sib the pony would be. How its dappled coat would complement her cob and mousey greys; if the gypsy would sell.

The women were talking nineteen to the dozen, the gypsy in a whirligig of vagabonds' cant and the other in the buoyant accent of the Plains. He heard the Ima woman ask a question.

'What *is* Murtherball?'

'The reason so many are gathered here, princess.' He bowed respectfully. 'It is a game played by a hundred men who tussle with each other for possession of the ball – a cannonball it is, big as I can safely hold in my two hands and heavy as a twelvemonth's child, that's near two stonesweight . . . There are two sides, fifty each, and one or other of them must get possession of the ball and carry it, against all comers, from Fortuneswell (over there, beyond the Green) to this mounting block.' He patted its worn and dusty top. 'Can I help you dismount?'

The Ima woman laughed suddenly, and he was reminded of falling rain. It was a fresh sound, without guile. She dipped her head as if she was about to assent and, in one lithe movement, had slid from her high perch to his side. He looked down at the top of her head. The hair of the five plaits in which her hair was dressed radiated tidily from a central point. Yellow snail shells were tangled in them. He stared at her weird clothes, recovered his good manners and bowed to her once more.

'Welcome to Wathen Fields.'

'My father told me of this place: he came here, I think, in his youth. And our tobacco is grown here.'

Her smile was warm. She was small, weird like his darling wife; and human like himself.

'Your father –' he began. 'Was he –'

'He was the Imandi, The Rider Who Bestrode the Red Horse, Nandje Skybrow.'

'Ah, O,' Colley stammered, embarrassed: should he bow again? 'I am sorry if he is Gone; and of course, I know the name although I never set eyes on him. My old aunt would have known him, Drusilla Dowshier. But she has Passed On, too.'

'You are sad about this.'

'No, not overly, Princess – she was stricter than a school-master.'

'But you are sad. You think she did not love you.'

'She did leave me the inn.'

'You see? She thought well of you. That's love, isn't it? Now be still, Innkeeper. You bowed to me but I have not greeted you,' and the woman tilted her head to one side and stared intently at him.

'She listens for your soul,' the gypsy remarked.

Lords and Ladies! Colley's face burned firily.

'It is our way. And so greeting, sir Tavernmaster.' The little Princess stood up straight and looked him in the eye.

'Switman, Colley Aloys Switman.'

'A name to match your soul, Master Sweet Man. And I am Gry, Nandje's daughter.'

The gypsy had scrambled off her laden pony while he had been paying court – the proper name most surely for his solemn and respectful behaviour. But such a traveller did not happen on him every day. She must be a lady in her country; a princess certainly. The best rooms? And the end stall for her horse. He liked her serenity; she looked about her, to be sure, but carefully as if she wanted to remember every new thing she saw; she did not 'ooh' and 'aah' and gape with slack jaw and popping eyes like some travellers from distant parts. He considered: her companion would

130

also require accommodation – a room, the cushioned bench in the taproom? Her flock of chickens had flown to scratch and bathe in the dust at the roadside. That settled the matter. They – gypsy, horses, fowls – should be made comfortable in the stable. He knew who she was and stared keenly as she talked and gestured: Darklis Faa, queen of her tribe; and a witch too, it was said. But he was the master in his house.

'You have seasonable weather here – if this be summer,' she remarked. 'It snowed on us in the Forest.'

'Snowed? It never snowed here,' said Colley incredulously. 'The Forest – have you ridden through it?'

'We have indeed. We are seasoned travellers.'

He could hardly believe the successive wonders so, hoping to go on mining this rich vein of a day, he spread his hands and arms to indicate the inn behind him and said, 'Please step inside the Live and Let Live. You will do me great honour if you will consent to take a drink with me, ladies – and a bite to eat as well.'

I am mad, he thought; and what will Sib say? Usually, he was wary of the gypsy kind and kept a close watch on any who strayed within his walls.

'I do not think that the Red Horse will fit through the door – though Streggie might,' Darklis Faa declared.

Colley clapped noisily and an ostler came running from the back parts of the inn. He took the grey pony's rein and gaped and mopped and mowed at the Horse.

'Can't lead a norse wivout a bridle,' he said.

The woman in rags and tatters smiled and spoke to him.

'He will go with you,' she said. 'Walk on and he will follow. He is very hungry.'

Then lo! the great red stallion followed the ostler as gentle and sweet as a lamb and Colley led his ladies into the inn and through the crowded tap room, where men both broad and tall made way, into the parlour where a round, polished table stood by an open window. The innkeeper pulled cushioned chairs from beneath it and a young man came hurrying towards them with three tall

131

foamy-headed tankards gripped in one hand, and set their drinks before them.

'This is my summer ale,' said Colley proudly.

He watched the two women lift their tankards to their lips. The gypsy got a white moustache to go with her black one but, on the Princess's curving lip, the bubbles looked like those shining globes of air a nivasha breathes out as she swims down to the still stream-bed. He lifted his own, admired the golden liquid, spilt sun through the glass, and supped.

'It is a lively creature,' said Darklis Faa.

'I never tasted water like this before,' said Gry.

'Child,' the gypsy murmured. 'This is water made potent with hops and barley, fermented like your horsemen's kumiz.'

The innkeeper drained his tankard and jumped up.

'I will send you your dinner – as quickly as may be,' he said, bowing for the third time in his bustling way, chiefly to Gry. 'As soon as the best dishes are washed and filled for you. My duties –' and was gone into the crowded tap-room.

Gry smiled at Darklis as the ale began to work in her.

'Alcohol,' the gypsy said, 'which awakens the senses. Tobacco, which pacifies. Two of the four Alls; and here comes the third of these necessities, good food which appeases the pangs of an empty belly.'

They smelt the food before it was placed on the table and their senses combined to make their mouths water. The servant-girl, whose be-ribboned sleeves and embroidered apron and skirts were smirched with gravy not one whit, took off the dish covers. 'Forest game,' she said, 'In a sauce of Arcadian wine and juniper – and Dolly's cream. Peas from the kitchen garden. Butter from Polly, the red-and-white cow. I made the bread but the flour's from Wathen Mill, by the river Lytha.' She piled their plates high. The potboy brought more ale.

Then Gry and Darklis were silent until their stomachs were full and their lips buttery and stained with the purple sauce. Gry cleaned her lips and chin with the snow-white napkin the girl had spread on her lap. The company in the tap-room, which they

132

could see through the open door, seemed very far away and its noisy chatter no louder than a memory of the sea. Darklis wiped her mouth on her scarlet skirt and belched; she lit up her pipe.

'It was good – as my Aunt Jennet's best,' Gry said, and sighed sleepily.

'Ay, the cook is a hero and Switman the king of innkeepers,' said Darklis. 'Hist! – here comes something quaint, a bleached mort dressed in smoke. Can she be his wife? – they talk of her as far away as Tanter . . .'

The creature danced across the room towards them. Her light clothes and spiderweb hair floated as airily as eventide mist; her eyes glowed huge and grey as moonstones in her delicate face.

'They say there's a spirit for every place and occasion,' Darklis whispered.

'She is like one of the vile,' Gry agreed.

But her voice was deeper than they expected, husky as if with dust and ashes or from the pipe-smoke which hung in the air.

'I am Sib Switman,' she said, with a dip of her strange head and a slow widening of her mirror eyes. 'My man has fed you well, Strangers – I see your clean-licked plates. But you will get thick heads from drinking Colley's ale. Will you walk with me outdoors?'

'She will,' said Darklis at once and waved the stem of her pipe at Gry. 'But I shall remain in this comfortable parlour – which is a place I like more and more as the ale goes down – and try a half-dozen more tankards of the foaming tide. Never look a gift horse in the mouth, I say, and this one trots out well –

> 'Fill up the mug, then, fill it high,
> Fill all the glasses there – for why
> Should every creature drink but I?–

'When I am drunk as a Pargur countess and merry as a cricket (yet no danger to any man or pretty canting lad, for I am old and past the amusements of youth). When I am well-basted but only lightly oiled (for Darklis can hold her ale); then, I say, darkmans

133

will be on us and the sun well set and I will make my way outdoors to the fair and see who's there to sell themselves and what there is to buy. So bring me another tankard, potboy – if you're quick with it I shan't ask you to kiss me!

'And I give you a good teasing proverb in return for your greeting, Mistress Switman:

'Gypsy vans are gay and smoky,
Be they old, new-made or fine,
The house where dwells a kikimor
Will prosper, sparkle, shine –

'like yours, Mistress, and so, good day.'

Gry, left her place at the table and followed Sib Switman from the room. A frown of puzzlement creased her forehead for neither sigh or sound had emanated from the innkeeper's odd wife to show that she had a soul.

'Climb here,' said Sib to Gry in the stableyard. 'Can you see your horse? He is safe, is he not? Comfortable? Foddered? Colley's locked all the horses in because there are so many in town, rogues, vagabonds and murtherers who wouldn't shy from stealing a ride home. Colley says it is always best to lock the stable door before the horse has bolted . . . what does he mean?'

'I don't know. Our horses run free.' Gry looked down on Sib from the top of the water butt where she was perched, and back through the high window. The Horse was below her and a little way away in a low enclosure of dark red wood whose walls sloped up to meet the stable-wall. Small statues of rearing stallions were mounted on the posts of the enclosure: she liked those and liked, also, the look of the fresh yellow straw in which the Horse stood hock-deep; the bowl of oats fixed where he could easily reach it; the rack of hay. Someone had brushed him, for his coat shone like a burnished copper shield, and she wondered at that; at her silent bidding he had gone quietly with the stable-man so, suffering the man to brush him, he perhaps hoped to please . . . Several other horses were stabled near him and she could see Streggie directly below, clean and shining like the Red Horse, munching hay. The Horse snorted into his oats so that they flew up in the air, and settled to eating again.

'Horse!' she called, in her mind. 'Horse dear, do you hear me?'

No answer came, although she waited for it; but she heard him belch, not sure if the sound came through her mind or the window-glass and then his unhorsey voice, singing: 'Beloved –' There was a new note in it, a wildness and loss of constraint, like Darklis's after her ale.

> 'Beloved, I will give you the key of my heart,
> To lock it up for ever, that we may never part,
> If you will be my bride, my joy, and only dear,
> To walk and talk with me everywhere.'

He slurred the last word, 'ev'rywhurr,' and she thought of the Ima mad on kumiz in their Meeting House and shuddered. Was everyone here drunk, men, women, animals, all? She had liked Colley's ale well enough but the desires the alcohol brought her were not her own, being crude, animal and selfish. She pushed the hair back from her hot face and felt the snail shells in it tumble and click together. So, putting on a cheerful face, she jumped down and followed Sib into the shade cast by the stableyard wall. They passed a high-walled enclosure with an iron-bound and padlocked gate. Sib darted forward.

'Come away!' she called. 'The watchdogs live there!'

They ran into a cool and grassy orchard. Here was a flock of hens many times larger than Darklis's pecking in the grass beneath the apple trees. Sib ducked and darted under the branches which hung low and heavy with codling apples.

The chickens came clucking when they were seated on the grass. One hen boldly led her chicks up Sib's outstretched leg and left them there, ten balls of golden down perched in a row.

'The hens are in my charge,' Sib explained.

While the flock gathered about them the two, grey and fey, brown and brave, talked. Gry felt at home: there was grass a-plenty, as tender as that of the Plains, and she plucked a juicy stalk to chew on.

'Like you I am a stranger in this homely place,' Sib began. 'I was not always a creature of the house and garden-grounds and I see that these rich fields and neat houses are strange to you also. You do not dress as others here. Have you the glamorous touch? Do you speak with the creatures of the Otherworld?'

Ale for mankind, oats for horses: too much of both dulls the senses and opens the door to sleep. Inside the shadowy stable, the Horse, stuffed full with oats and contentment, stretched himself out on the thick straw of his stall, asleep before his eyes were fully closed. His legs twitched as if he were walking over loose and stony ground.

He who says the Tropicks are all verdant, lies. True enough in Sind but here, in the thrice-accursed Plain, which men liken to the worst Night Mare or to the tortures unshriven souls must endure in Purgatory, we stumbled over the stones and walked slippered and veiled in dust. Hence its inventive name. Dusty we were and so remained, for we could not wash. The wells were few and those we passed smelled rank and were surrounded by crowds of people and animals waiting their turn to draw water and drink. We carried all the water we needed for drinking, and for the animals too – which we could not ride, only drive slowly to conserve their strength, helping them often by blowing the dust from their eyes and nostrils, to save their choked breath, or by shoving the lumbering vehicles with shoulders, might and main.

Why did I not use my Power to avoid this trial? As I have observed and noted many times before, and doubtless shall again, Magic is not to be wasted, for its working costs a greater effort than a five days' walk; and so I, too, conserve my strength for greater efforts and let the body toil.

136

I sat aching and satisfied on the tail of my cart: it had been good to exercise the fine, fit body of Parados. It was eventide and we had halted for the night with such sigils and circles as gypsies can make about us. The sun's rays came striking in brilliant and ruddy-hued patterns out of the west and I wondered idly, Is this the same sun we see in Malthassa? Behind me, in the cart, Nemione was sleeping. I could see one of her graceful arms ringed with gold and silver bangles – nothing more, and I thought Shall I lie beside her and enter her in my dreams? I could not: it was my watch, for the grey monkey, or the eagle, or the camel which were Lord Yama's spies – or for any other beast or like enchantment which might be a peri in another's skin.

I thought – in my heart of hearts – it profitless to look for such in the crowded Plain. Were I one of the Dark Lord's eyes, I should seek my prey when it lay alone and unwatchful, at ease in a grove or by a plashing stream. And so, when I had gazed all round me at the horizon and seen the sun creep closer and colour the near acres gold, I felt in the pocket of my shulwars for my broken prism and turned it over and over in my hands with slow and regular movements like those we used for our prayer-beads when I was a novice religious in the Cloister of my youth. The prism grew warm in my hands. I stopped turning it and held it up for the sun to shine through, amusing myself with directing his broken and coloured rays in shimmering lines across the ground.

Then, looking at the prism as it took in and emitted the changed light, I saw it had kept to itself the fourth colour of the earthly rainbow's seven. (There are others only the beasts can see.) It shone like an emerald, a deep and wondrous green. Puzzled, yet delighted by this change, I held it to my eye – expecting to view the dust, tinted marvellously, shattered viridian, through it, a kind of poor man's Pargur, city of crystal illusions –

I saw a new scene, at which I drew a long and heartfelt breath. The prism worked again! I looked into Malthassa, distant, miniature, as a child looks wonderingly into the wrong end of a telescope.

In a green shade, I saw an intimate scene – not of the bedroom and its pleasures alas! but of two females sitting close and talking from the heart. One, I knew instantly: the Princess again, old Nandje's daughter, the Princess of the Ima whose portrait by appearing in the annexe of

137

my Memory Palace had given me pause . . . She was clad in rags and skins like a dirty, uncouth shaman, but delightful all the same to look on – smooth skin revealed by her torn garments, pretty face, curves and hollows glimpsed in repose. The other I had never seen before. Certes, she was no woman (though lovely) but a spirit or elf. Something scratched in my ear-porches and I shook my head to clear the sensation away; the sound grew louder. It was like a pair of wind chimes shaken in a summer breeze, like conversation in the next room. Asmodée! Urthamma! I was able to hear their talk as clear and intelligible as if I stood behind the tree which shaded them from their sun's intemperate heat.

'Perhaps you are a priest, or a travelling acrobat?' Sib demanded. 'Is your hair plaited in that curious way because you are married – or unmarried? Have you a lover? Are you in love?'

So many questions, thought Gry, and streaming from her fast as the winter wind.

'I love my Colley,' Sib swept on. 'My Man is very dear to me – but it was not always so. I am like the silkie seal who leaves her skin on the seashore while she goes a-visiting and finds that her lover has kept and hidden it so she must remain with the humankind and nevermore swim the green sea to her heart's content. I am like a black sheep in a flock of white or like the ugly duckling before he turned into a swan. I do not belong here; and nor do you.'

She pushed her cobweb hair from her eyes and stared at Gry, inviting her to speak.

'I will tell you who I am,' Gry began. 'My name is Gry and once I was the dear daughter and sister of a family; but I believe they are all killed now, nobly or by treachery. As for how I come here, that is a story I must often tell. My clothes are not the usual kind. Everyone knows a gypsy by her extravagant dress and her gold and brass rings. People recognise a lady, or a lord – silks and satins, a full purse and servants. But me! Look, this is all that is left of my old, blue dress which once was long and full; which I wore with my hair in two braids like plaited horsetails and my silver bangles and ankle-ring. When I was truly Nandje's daughter of the Ima, a horseherder and not a runaway. And these leggings I made from the skin of the deer the wolf-pack killed for me. My beautiful blouse I got from the shepherds of Russet Cross – and these stones to make fire whenever I need it. Darklis gave me the blanket and my shoes – look how well-made they are, and how warm, too warm today! – were made for me by the leshi in the Forest. They plaited my hair, which was as rough and tangled as a briar, for I have had a hard journey to this place. And, as you say true, it is fair and prosperous; but is not my home in the Plains where the grass grows green and fast in our moist mother, Earth, and the pale sky is lively with the seventeen winds as they carry the voices of the zracne vile and the salt smell of Russet Cross and Stribog's tears when he weeps.'

Sib sighed. 'You and I are wilder than a red demon when he dances in hellfire. Or snowflakes in a blizzard on the high Altaish.

'These days I wear women's finery, though it was not always so. Colley chooses my dresses. He does not like to see me in the village costume, but in gowns which remind him of the place where he found me, hiding in a blue shadow in one of his cellars and my hair, which is like spiders' spinnings anyway, covered in webs. I have told no one, not even my Darling, how I came there – he thinks me a runaway servant and, so, I am. It would frighten him to know where from, and he never frets or asks me, the dear.

'But I will tell you, Gry of the Ima, for loyalty and discretion are two of your virtues, I can see. Besides, one who is a friend of the leshi and whom the leshi honour is no ordinary woman.'

Sib lifted the chicks one by one from her leg and tucked them carefully beneath their mother. Then, contorting her thin body into a knot of limbs and knobbly joints and resting her pointed chin on her knees, she began to speak.

Sib Switman's Story: The Sharivila
The gypsy was wrong, for all that she is a queen and an empress, a wise woman and a witch. I am no kikimora or household goblin, no lob-by-the-fire or pisky of the dairy.

Far away beneath the earth is a land where the black water

seeping from the bedrock becomes the trickle that jets into the spring that fills the runnel that rushes into the brook that flows into the river that surges to the sea that is Ocean which surrounds us; there, in that damp, dusky place, was I born, the child of a white deva and one of the sharivile which live in the cellars of the Palace of Shadows. I was born at the heart and kernel of the earth, in Lord Yama's castle where the passageways are narrow and dark and his servants tremble when he walks them. Why, the Lord Yama keeps everyone in thrall, even Urthamma and his fires!

In the cellarage where I used to live are the vaults where my lord keeps his wine, and the pantries where the dark-lamps are prepared before they are carried upstairs to darken his diwan, his harim and his feasting hall, his courts and gardens, his stables, library, jousting-yard, archery walks, long galleries and bathing-pit; all his closes, enclosures and lands. And I was one of those who carried a lamp.

Understand that this place I tell you of is beyond the imaginings of mortals. And realise that, since it lies in the centre of the spherical earth, at the core of the great globe, that anything which is dropped will fall not down, but up through the fissures in the rock – which is no older and no younger than I.

I fell, balancing a lamp in my hand as I stepped over a chasm in the harim floor. It swallowed me, that chasm, as if I had been a gnat and it a gape-mouthed frog; and it ejected me, bruised and torn though not bleeding, for I am half sharivila and such only ooze a little water like the rocks. I shot out of it as fast as lava from the cauldron where the unformed mountains are brewed, falling downwards out of hell and upwards to the surface. This stuff, this plant you call grass, was very strange to me. I lay a long while in it, on my face, until I had the heart to get up and see what else in your world was unhellish.

The light was the worst thing I had to bear, hard as the Dark Lord's anger, and I could only be about after dark. Even then the moon shone bright. I travelled over mountains and through the Forest, crossed rivers and marshes till I came to this settlement. A house stood near the forest-fringe and this I entered, creeping fearfully in the shadows and making hardly any sound – though you Men and She-men have dull hearing. At night I cleaned the house for the old man who lived there and he, in his turn and finding that the rooms he had left dirty and all of a jumble were sparkling and in good order, left basins of cream for me and, each se'nnight, a glass of sack which was very good. So, I continued a long while, growing strong on my new diet, until one day the man brought home a dog pup which could smell me out wherever I hid myself. I took to the attics, but still the whelpting found me out. I could only live safely on the rooftop itself – besides, the pup grew into a dog with teeth big as pocket-knives. I left the house I had called home and sought refuge in the cellar of the inn – for I knew that Colley Switman kept his mastiffs locked up.

There Colley found me on a winter's night. I have been a long time in his village, though he does not know it. I used to see him out bird-hunting with his catapult and stick, his hair shining like the rays of the sun and his face scarlet from running in the heat – a vigorous man, I saw, for he never missed a shot; kind-hearted too for he killed no more than he needed and never the nesting birds or their young. He gave me work in the inn and began to love me. I love him. We married when the tobacco plants put up their green fingers from the earth. I am happy now and only yearn for the Palace of Shadows when evening comes and the shadows here grow long.

We all yearn for the shadowy Palace so I am no worse off and no better than you. It is Death, that place, and Life as well. Every thing and creature that is in Malthassa and has a soul comes from my birthplace and must return there when its time is come. Once we were all pikulik, the souls of the unborn which play in the Asphodel Meadows beside Lethe-waters until a child is conceived and wait their turn to fly to it; but the dead, those who have passed once through this world or any of the others, must remain in and about the Palace and serve Lord Yama for ever.

Sib's great, grey eyes shone with a eerie light.

'Do you long to be with your father?' she asked Gry.

'I wish each day and night that he lived; but he is dead and I have seen what time and corpse-moths have done to his body! If only I could be with him again.'

Sib smiled, showing a double row of tiny, polished teeth each one of which was needle-sharp, like the eye teeth of a polecat.

'If you want to find out how he does you must cross the Altaish mountains and walk to the ocean shore. That is the only way I know for a living person to see the souls of the dead.'

'Cross the Altaish! Fall from the edge of the world!'

Sib laughed softly.

'Do not believe everything your shaman told you. You still might travel to the end of the world with your good horse, and come to no harm if you have strength and courage enough. Listen, there is courage and high hearts! Hark to the battle-songs and shouts. The Murtherball players are gathering at the inn and it is almost time for the Game. I must help my Colley put on his battle-clothing – yet we have time enough.

'Time to wander and time to wonder,' continued Sib, unwinding her arms and straightening her legs. She wrapped her left arm tight about Gry's waist and led her from the orchard and into the garden-grounds of the inn. Artichokes grew here, raising their jagged limbs and tight-packed flowers to the sun, and purple-podded beans entwined with climbing brighteyes, scarlet tomatoes like round-hipped flasks, devil's garlic showing its black spears above the loamy ground, speckled chard, rue, wormwood, and the puce leaves of lightswort splashed with white patches like a diseased lung.

'I choose the crops and tell old Harry, the gardener, where to plant them – as if I were of humankind,' Sib proudly said.

One whole bed was filled with sunflowers, which turned their black and yellow faces up to the sky to follow the course of the sun. Another held blackheart peas and in this, to scare the blacktops and other thieving birds, a scarecrow was planted. It had a white face made of turnip scarred here and there with marks like tattoos and long, black hair made of a horse's tail, which made it female, for in the tail were still the plaits with which the horse had been

142

dressed. The princess of scarecrows, it wore an old silk blouse with hanging sleeves, and a crown and jewellery made of plaited sticks and white birds' bones.

'I save the crows' bones when I have sucked them dry,' said Sib. 'And hang them here. They warn the others not to steal.'

Gry touched the scarecrow as they passed by and heard the bones swing together and utter their dry alarm. She looked up into the creature's face and saw that it had white shells in place of eyes.

'She's blind,' Sib whispered, 'but beware you greedy birds, beware! She hears your every chirrup and hop and the silent beat of your wings.'

But Gry, hanging back for a moment, spoke to the scarecrow. 'You are a beauty, in your way, like the Lady Byely.'

The tiny bones of the scarecrow's necklace slid together and tapped out a dry tune.

At the very end of the vegetable garden, where a high wall divided it from the fields, stood a small, octagonal house covered all over and roofed with shells and finished, at the apex of its pointed roof, with a flourish of wrought-iron, a weather vane in the shape of a fork-tailed demon.

Gry felt Sib squeeze her waist until the hilt of her father's knife dug into her flesh.

'Shall we bathe, sister?' the sharivila said. 'Let us dip the water from the bath house well and fling it over each other until we are wet as the west wind and squeal and laugh until we are like men drunk on strong ale. But there is no time, for Colley waits – yet there is time to speak with Bannika.'

Gry saw the sprite before he moved, a muscular figure perched on the beam above the dipping-pails. His naked body, about the size of a full-term child's, glistened like the wet slate of the floor and was the same leaden colour. He swung down on finny arms and his webbed feet slapped the floor as he landed beside them.

'Io, Sib Switman, Man-Borrower,' he said, silver spittle running from his wide mouth as he talked. 'Io, Spirit-woman! Let me help you out of your dusty, sweat-stained clothing. If you will step into the tub, I will soon wash you clean of your grime and your cares.'

His touch on Gry's arm was seductive and cool and she began, herself, to untie the strings of her skirt.

'No time, Bannika,' Sib said. 'Let her stay human and dirty. Can't you feel the minutes hastening, can't you hear their racing pulse? My Colley's waiting.'

The bath house sprite drew back into the shadows by the bathtub. They heard him muttering, 'Time and tide are flowing fast, time is water, tide's a race,' as they went out again into the unrelenting sun and passed under an archway guarded by a matching pair of stone greyhounds.

'I can pat a dog of stone,' Sib said and did so, laughing.

The rose-garden drowsed, drunk on the heat and its own myriad scents. There were sweetheart roses, gallicas, thrupenny bits, Nymph's Thighs, the Rose of Peace and a hundred and one other kinds, which Sib named as they walked and came, by following a path mown in the knee-high grass, to the back door of the inn.

Colley stood waiting in the empty tap-room, his gear ready on a table and his yellow hair bound back and hidden under a black scarf.

'They are all ready, but me,' he said.

Sib ran to him.

'Here I am, Love. I can make haste.'

She held his leather byrnie open and helped him into it, fastening it tight about his broad chest; lifted and placed his shallow hat of iron on his head and tied the strings which kept it in place. Last of all, she put his mail gloves on his outstretched hands and kissed him on the lips.

Then Colley was no more the genial keeper of the Live and Let Live Inn but a man armoured for Murtherball. He unlatched a glass case which hung above the bar and took the iron ball from it. Cradling it in both hands, he held it out for Sib to kiss.

'And you, Gry, Nandje's-daughter. Seal the murtherball.'

It was a hard, cold thing to kiss in summer but Gry obeyed him.

'Be sure you watch and cheer us on, my wife,' he instructed Sib, smiled briefly in a challenging and predatory way and hurried from the house.

'It's perilous on the ground,' said Sib. 'See how the crowd surges like floodwater!'

They stood side by side on the mounting block before the door of the inn. High as the shoulders of a tall man, it was a good place from which to view the Game, and Gry could have mounted the Horse with ease from its flat top; ordinary horses were mounted from the fourth step of the narrow flight which wound about it.

The old stone was hallowed: Gry felt its magic creeping upwards from her feet. Dwarves had cut it, digging it out of the ground and carving it to shape, before they danced and beat their hammers against it in prayer.

Hard to see which men were players, which spectators; some seemed to be both, hurling themselves into the mass of shoulders and flailing arms on the other side of the wide village green at the end of the street, standing back to take breath or exchange a few words with a neighbour. And the murtherball, most of the time invisible in the scrum, occasionally shot high and fell heavily earthwards to be caught in brawny hands; or dropped like a murderous rock shoved from a cliff or castle battlement, scattering players and spectators both.

Like Gry and Sib themselves, the village women were elevated and apart, leaning from windows, or high up on chairs and ladders at their garden walls so that they could lean across the mossy tops, lace and ribbons dangling, and look down on the Game.

The All-comers had the ball. One of their men, dressed all in blue, was running hard with it. Then a white-clad boy of Wathen overtook and doubled back to attack him. Soon, Wathen had captured the ball and were heaving it from hand to hand overhead and Gry saw Colley for an instant as he caught and passed the heavy cannon-shot.

Sib pulled at her hair until it covered her face entirely.

'Let us go in,' she said. 'The sun has struck me hard. You can watch from a window, but I must rest.'

The inn was dark and empty. Sib and Gry mounted the broad flight of oaken stairs which led up from the hall and so, by another narrow stair, to an attic high in the thatch which the thick straw kept cool. Cobwebs hung from the underside of the thatch and filled the corners of the room, each one with a round, grey cob listening at its centre.

Sib knelt by them and chattered shrilly. She lay flat on the floor and spread out her arms and legs, her head like a giant tangle of webs and her thin body in its grey and blue draperies no more than the shadows. Her voice floated eerily to Gry.

'. . . the window. Open. Watch my Colley. Keep out the sun with your body . . .'

The yellow thatch stretched down in a steep slide. Gry, leaning out into the warm evening, saw that the Game had come halfway down the street, that its players were fewer in number because some stood by exhausted or bleeding; though there were yet as many men as make a raiding party of Ima. For a while the two sides heaved and shoved and no one gained an inch of ground. It was all over suddenly. Colley had got the ball and was running hard. Nobody could get near him as he pounded down the street, a bull, a charging warrior with a battle to win. Jumping high, he lofted the ball to the top of the mounting block. The spectators shouted once and fell silent as they watched Colley pant and dash the sweat from his face. Someone untied a knotted balloon and let the air out of it with a long squeal. Everyone squealed, a great and noisy herd and, rushing forward, carried Colley, ball and players into the inn.

It was all over and done with until next fair-day. The women had disappeared, gone in to put fresh ribbons in their hair and sleeves. Gry closed the window and latched it tight. Sib was invisible now, overlaid with evening shadows and the coming of night. Perhaps she could be felt. Gry knelt and crawled across the floor, reaching before her with one cautious hand – which soon encountered cloth, a long bundle of it, and the soft-head of a mop. These were the images in her head and what, in the gloom, she saw, until she tugged at the cloth and it billowed up. There was Sib, pushing back her clouds of hair and rubbing at her eyes with bony knuckles.

'Is it over?' she said, and yawned.

'Colley won – Wathen won. *He* put the ball on the mounting block.'

'I wish that I had seen it . . . my Darling will be happy. I told him he would win, and he gave the nivasha his best gillyvors.' She stood and shook out her dress. 'I must make sure the tankards are clean. Nathan washes them but they must be inspected! And the fires to see to and the lamps! Come, I will give you a seat by the ale barrels, where you can see and not be seen. Hasten! Fly!'

Animated now, a phantom come to frantic life, she caught Gry's hand with hard, clutching fingers and pulled her down the steep stairs.

Colley, in his innkeeper's clothes, his glistening red face the only sign of his part in the Game, was busy, serving tankard after tankard of ale. Once, he turned and gave Gry a broad and welcoming smile. A great heat flowed through her, flushing her face: here was the first man, since Leal and her brothers and before that dark time in the Meeting House and darker in the storehouse, to treat her with honour. (And such a man!) She smiled, although he had turned back to his task. There were no other women in the inn, the servant-girls all on holiday, and no sign of Darklis. Sib darted in and out of the crowd and the fires glowed warm and the lamps burned bright.

A fiddler struck up a tune – 'Haste to the Wedding' it was – and soon, a piper and a hurdy-gurdy man joined him. They played 'Strip the Willow' and 'Bonny Green Garters'. At this, Colley told Nathan to take his place and drew Sib from her lamps with an 'Enough now, the place is bright as day and the fires burn hotter than need-fire.' He sat on a high stool at the bar and swung her on to his lap. Nat offered a clear glass flute of the golden summer ale

147

which Colley, laughing, took and pressed to Sib's white lips until, with nose wrinkled, she sipped a little and sneezed. Colley drained the glass and laughed again while Nat charged it and brought a second glass, the twin of the first, which was filled with cream. Sib pressed her drink on Colley and the pantomime was repeated; then, each laughed at the other with such an air of love and good fellowship that the company pressed in the tap-room and in all the other public rooms shouted together:

'One huzzah! And two and three! Huzzah, huzzah, huzzah!'

'To the Four Alls, Drink, Tobacco, Food and Love!' cried Colley.

The musicians played 'Salute the Victors' and 'John Barleycorn'; then Nat, turning from his customers, brought Gry a tankard of ale and a thick sandwich filled with beef and spread with mustard, which she ate with relish, dusting the last crumbs from her lap, and spreading the chequered blanket about her shoulders, for a draught blew in from the back parts of the inn.

Someone was behind her. She turned her head. It was the gypsy, Hyperion Lovelace, decked in all his former finery and more for he had stuck a new feather in his hat beside the scarlet one, a long peacock's feather eyed with sapphire and purple and fletched with green and gold. He smiled white and bowed to her before passing into the crowd, which swallowed him up so that only the crown of his hat and the nodding end of the peacock's feather could be seen.

Gry was tired, her bones cold, her legs and shoulders aching. Colley smiled across the bar.

'Princess! Gry! The third door in the first corridor,' he said. 'Sleep well!'

Gry went yawning up the stair, the candle Nat had lit for her in her hand. Beyond the third door was a cool room where a white bed gleamed in the dark, inviting sleep, and pale curtains billowing at the window wafted in the soft, coherent perfume of sweetheart roses from the garden.

Gry woke, not knowing if she had slept long or a little. It was dark

148

yet and the curtains hung pallid and still. Everything smelled of roses. Someone was singing outside, and she leaned on her elbow to listen.

> 'The gypsy rover came over the hill
> And into the garden so shady,
> He sang so sweet and so complete
> He won the heart of the lady.

> 'She came tripping down the stairs,
> All her life before her;
> As soon as he saw her pretty, pretty face,
> He cast his glamoury o'er her.'

Gry stole out of bed and, hiding herself behind the curtains, peeped out. A man stood in the starlit garden below her window. He sang in a tender, yearning voice, many more verses of the lady in her castle and the gypsy who loved her.

> 'Will you go with me, my honey and my heart?
> Will you go with me, my dearie?
> And I will swear on the hilt of my sword
> That no other man shall come near thee.'

The singing stopped as a shaft of light fell suddenly into the garden. A shadow rose on the garden wall, the silhouette of the gypsy, tall and long-haired with his round hat and his peacock's feather.

'I never sing idly, lady,' Hyperion said. 'I would bring you the fourth and best of the Alls which is life's greatest pleasure, Love, and the delights of the body enchanted. Come with me to the fair and beyond, to the greenwood. Come roving with me and see all Malthassa, Tanter, Pargur, Myrah, Castle Sehol, Castle Lorne, the very Altaish and the Donjon of the enchantress Lilith, the fortress of the gypsies itself that, 'tis said, rears its golden walls and towers of lapis lazuli as far as heaven's gate. Come, I am waiting! Come to me!'

Gry trembled.

'Are you there, my sweet?' the gypsy cooed, 'I know you are, my beauty! – draw aside the curtain, just a little.'

But Gry remained where she was, though her heart beat fast and for a moment, as the gypsy spoke cunningly and wooed her, lifted a hand; and lowered it.

'If I had a ladder, lady, you would not be so shy,' said Hyperion stoutly. 'Well then, stay pure, stay virginal up in your bower. I shall not wait to beg so proud a lady on my knees. I'll go alone to the fair and find another doxy who is willing. Farewell, sweet dimber, forget me not! I'll wear a lover's rose for you.'

He raised a hand in mock-salute and sniffed the rose he held. Then, thrusting the prickly rose-stem into his mouth, he bit on it and bowed low, looked boldly up, the red rose jutting like desire between his lips. His serenade was done.

A sigh and soft footfalls followed; the gypsy was gone and the shaft of light too, which had come from a window below that now was shuttered again. Gry shivered, wide awake, reached out and, too late, drew back the curtains. Others were singing in the garden, children with high and merry voices,

> 'Boys and girls come out to play,
> The moon doth shine as bright as day.'

Though it did not; only the small stars pricked the cloth of heaven and the great Guardian sailed into view, filling the dark garden and fields beyond, even to the edge of the Forest, with silvery, spangled light. Gry heard the leshi calling and her body quickened, wanting to be with them amongst the trees, alone and free from humankind. She touched the tight plaits they had made, leaned out and watched the Forest's star-shadows reach into the fields.

Small lights were dancing through the garden, the children carrying candle-lanterns, shouting, boisterous, 'Drive the Shadows back! Scare the spirits! Boo!' Sib, she knew, was sitting in the dark, with her fingers in her ears and her shaggy head tucked in her lap.

Some of the children spied Gry and held up their lanterns to see who it was, watching them.

'Princess!' one called, 'Princess, give me a wish!'

'Horse Lady,' another said, 'a ride on your horse, Lady, for the love of Lilith!'

Gry laughed.

'My horse is the Red Horse of the Plains and he will not give rides. Besides, he is asleep. I cannot grant wishes, but I will tell you two things. For you, little brother, that once and not so long ago, I talked with Mogia, the great Wolf Mother, and she was kind to me and gave me food and clothing. And for you, littlest sister, that only two nights since, I rode upon the back of Bonasus, the mighty Wisent of the Forest and he, too, was kind and gave me shelter and his own food to eat.'

Then 'O', said the first child in wonderment, and waved his lantern about until the night was filled with red and yellow snakes of light. 'I have a little bull-calf in my father's barn,' said the second. 'Hurry, Pol, we'll be left behind.'

They ran off after their friends. Gry pulled on her clothes and thrust chilly feet into her warm shoes. She wrapped her blanket tight about her so that she looked more like a gypsy than like the daughter of the Imandi, and crept down the stairs. Though the house appeared deserted, the front door stood open and the street and Green beyond it was another world full of colour, noise, and the smell and light from tallow candles burning at the stalls and lighting up the wares on sale, buckets, pots and pans, hot chestnuts, ice-cream, beads and laces, dog-leads, cure-all embrocations and potions in purple bottles, masks, balloons and twists of toffee, yellow cakes and curious silver medallions made and sold by dwarves. Buskers were playing all along the street and conjurers and illusionists dazzling folk with their colourful tricks. A pair of clowns tossed a scarlet diabolo back and forth between them. A man in a golden domino and tights walked along, banging on a huge bass drum; gypsies danced their czardas and flamenco and, somewhere in the crowd, the hurdy-gurdy man was turning the handle of his instrument and calling forth a haunting tune she knew of old. In the Plains it was called 'Follow Your Lover'. Altogether, there was so much bustle and racket that she could not understand how it was that the garden had been so still and peaceful and, wrapping the blanket even closer to hide every element of her jumbled clothes, she stepped out in the wake of a half-naked wrestler and a tiny, fur-stoled dwarf-woman who carried a pied terrier almost the size of herself.

Through all the racket, posturing and pizzazz, the Red Horse in his stable behind the Live and Let Live Inn dreamed on.

Nemione slept, as always, as ever, inert, lovely, mindless. She had lifted up the thick-fringed curtains of her eyes, revealing the sapphires, as we passed from the Dusty Plain into lusher country. The province we now travelled in lay in the shadow of Suleiman's Mountains – at once I was made easy, at home here: was Suleiman not a mighty sage and magician called by Men and the Beasts 'Magnificent'? Why, he could command the Beasts with his Ring!

The air was fragrant, rich with the sandalwood and pacculi which grew by the roadside in dense bosks or thickets. A look of surprizement stood a moment in Nemione's eyes and she parted roseate lips – but it was only to yawn. She nestled in our bed of silk and tasselled Kashmir coverlets – those I had exchanged for good rupees with the same turbaned ruffian who sold me my howdah pistol, heavy, murderous thing that it is. And marvellous that my hands can load and fire it and also enjoy to touch Nemione.

Though I held her hands in one of mine and with the other, stroked her lily limbs, she slept.

Therefore I desisted and left the cart, springing light and gladly from its little red-painted flight of steps and pacing across the tree-shadowed glade where we had made our encampment. I saluted one or another, Laxmi, Jasper, Chab, but kept resolute on. It was in my mind to find a fresh and innocent site on which to raise the annexe of my Memory Palace. Also in my mind were several resolutions of which I'll write anon. And, item, a fine thought: I should name my annexe suitably as, Little Palace, Demi-Pavilion or, and this name as it formed itself pleased me, the Treasury. If memory holds no treasures, it is sad grey history.

I soon found myself in a new glade where a freshet of water flowed in a stone channel and birds-of-paradise hopped and displayed in the trees. I think the place had once been a temple or a garden for it had an odour of faded sanctity. I sat beside the water reflecting that I had a new treasure in my annexe or, now, Treasury, the portrait of Nandje's daughter which had inexplicably appeared there while the water, in its witless way, reflected my face broken up into a thousand features and transported hither and thither across the surface. Might I see Gry again, not a princess as she was in the painting, but dishevelled and wild like her companion, the kikimora, the house-spirit – as I had supposed from the waif-like creature's looks – who was now discovered to be a grey spirit from Lord Yama's palace? I unpocketed my prism and held it to my right eye and, as before, beheld a green-coloured light or radiance which seemed to enter my very eyes. I waited, turned the prism, waited long. Nothing passed and at length I took the prism from my eye. The greenness, I realised at once, was mere refraction and incandescence, the dancing light of the leaves on the trees. I put it away.

Now, for clearly I was trapped in Parados's world, was the time to erect my Treasury, the only place in which I could be private to inspect my thoughts and memories. I took it from its protective envelopes and, minded to make a pleasant addition, set the folded Treasury afloat in the centre of the freshet where a spring bubbled up and the water flowed to both left and right. Raising my hands on high and pacing to and fro as I felt an onrush of the nervous energy necessary to the working of magic, I spoke the words (never recorded except in Memory) and made the signs and signals (never drawn but in Memory) the manifestation required. The Treasury, from its first unfolding, a lotus on the water, rapidly built itself about, beneath and above me and a refreshing shade and coolness descended, the light and heat being obscured.

I looked about me. Nothing in the building had changed from before, I was relieved to see. I made a deep and courteous bow to the picture of Gry, sat on the floor beside the pretty fountain I had unconsciously raised to enclose the spring, and tried the prism. No green appeared, nor pallid colours of marble, the material illusion of which the Treasury was built, but a kaleidoscope of whirling colour. For a moment the vortex threatened to engulf me, body limp and aching, mind confused from my Workings.

Then I saw fair Gry at a Fair. She blushed and breathed before me, all tender and sprightly as she was, wrapped in a gypsy blanket no more colourful than the tent or booth she stood trembling in. She was consulting a fortune-teller (I peered close for mayhap he was kin of Helen's), a handsome, raw male of the wandering species who sat at a gimcrack table, the red-eared head of a gaze-hound resting against his knee, comfortable with himself, experienced in the delusive – and, I did not doubt, seductive – arts. His many-pocketed poacher's coat hung on a peg behind him and his scrying bowl, a poor thing of painted tin, stood on a rough pedestal made of a new-cut log. And clearly, though he concealed his purpose well, he itched and smarted with lust for the little Princess and was composing speeches and endearments for later use on her the while he told her fortune.

'You are not so coy now,' he began, 'and safe as a nun in her cloister here amongst the crowds. Look, sweetness, into my descrying bowl and espy what you can spy.'

The woman drew back a few steps from him but, cat-curious about her fate, forced herself to advance until her bent head was close to his. Wondrously, the prism's perspective altered so that I, too, could see into the bowl where small waves, the miniatures of ocean breakers, smashed themselves in glittering droplets against its rim.

'I see nothing,' she said as she stared at the broken water. 'Yet – o, it is me,' in a tremulous tone, 'and you, Gypsy – o-oh!' For there, under the clear water which capped the little drama as the sky does Malthassa, were he and she entwined in lovers' dalliance on the greensward of a walled garden where grew such fragrant flowers as Diana pinks, Snow-in-Summer, and Lavender Blue and a dark, old tree on which red berries hung. These, he reached up to pluck, thrusting them into her open mouth with lecherous tongue. Sometimes, he missed her mouth and then, the berry dropped upon her breasts and burst there like a drop of blood.

'No!' the Ima woman cried. 'Show me no more of this – it is all lies.'

The man laughed, light but cruel.

'Who knows?' he said. 'But, for nothing, I will tell you this: You will not find what you think you seek. And now, since you cannot be seduced either by songs or pictures, I'll use words. Meet me at dawn by Fortuneswell, or meet me at starshut in young Colley's garden (I'll be there at the gate alone). Or here and now, in my striped booth in the middle of Midsummer Fair.'

He sighed so bitter I half-believed him sincere.

'But you will not, so go your ways and I'll go mine and so Farewell and be –' he faltered, for the picture ceased to move and he was frozen there in mid-speech while she stared at him, dumb and motionless, and was overlaid by a flock of sheep in a rainstorm and a crowd of Ima men haranguing a poor shepherd. The tempest raged, I could not hear what they said. Gloom and mystery – ah, yes! – the shy grey hell-sprite cowering underneath a cold-cellar shelf, her head with its ball of cobweb hair tucked between her knees.

Magnificent! The young Ima archer they call Leal for his fidelity and Straightarrow for his skill at shooting was there, running at full stretch along a deserted road, leaping and hopping the ruts and potholes as if they were bushes and he a stag. I had time to observe a bridle of the ornate, Ima kind, waving and clanking in each of his hands before he ran away and I beheld another scene, a bout of dicing between a sturdy Copper Dwarf and a hireling tobacco-cutter. Him, I knew, by his brown-striped smock and dusty hair. The games were close, fast, exhilarating; but the dwarf was not Githon and, eventually, the pair faded away. My senses were jolted and my fancy woken by a different kind of bout, keenly-fought by a country wench in white stockings and stays and a lad with a fearsome weapon. Their fencing-ground was a hayloft and I was pleased to see out the play, comparing his technique (crude, energetic) with my polished style. Well, thought I, the greatest game cannot be escaped, it seems; and were that sage of Idra in my place, he would not surely turn away to meditate.

Like a hag in a fable, like a leather-pinioned bird of the Herodian Plateau, that old trickster, Aza, the Shaman of Garsting came winging. He was flying high, an eagle amongst birds, and I thought the prism showed me his entrancements, as a warning perhaps or as pure diversion; but I saw that he did fly and that his mount and vehicle was a horse without a head. Therefore, I shivered in my gilded sandals and my shining spirit quaked. Like Death he was, all dry and sinewy and spindle-shanked, but his white hair was thick and his eye keen. The horse was a cunning creation, all unjointed, fleshless bones and each of these as black as charcoal out of the fire. I supposed the horsehead was not needed since Aza's mind drove on the steed and I watched and wondered as he rode it through the air and high above the tall heads of the tallest forest-trees until he, too, was lost to sight in the immense distance.

A wolf howled, far away in the night. The Ima were riding, a host through the darkness; but they are always riding and hosting, death-hungry primitives that they are and soon they faded into their bloody past and future, and a pair I knew of old appeared who were sometimes in Pargur and once, in Castle Sehol at my bidding, to entertain a crowd of workmen with their tarot cards and crystal balls, their stomping dance and raucous song. Darklis and Lurania Faa were walking together along a country road by starlight, that is to say by the light of that great star called Custos which appeared when Parados was a man and abroad to my chagrin, tampering in Malthassa. Lurania tapped the road with her white stick. Darklis sucked on her pipe.

'– and did you hear them, sister dear? The twice-shining doubled souls I see?'

'Aye, daughter of our mother! I heard the sweet tenor of the man and the hayfed neigh of the horse.'

A tunnel mouth opened, sunlit in the afternoon. A saltier pranced there, come up out of the mines on some filthy errand or, more like, to find and ravish a dwarf maid or three. His erect phallus bobbed like a drumstick. Better not to wonder. The only good saltier is a dead one. The best, skinned and boiled down, make a potent musk. I use it. It attracts females as honey does ants. This one exhibited himself beside a fire – no, that was another picture's glow which penetrated the whole prism, a prospect of destruction as red as any in the Pit, the Plains afire, the Forest burning, and in shuttered darkness the Red Horse asleep below a roof of wooden boards and a night sky where Custos shone brighter than Valdine's prize diamond. High among the

156

stars, in the swaying basket of my Frostfeather, my white, soaring balloon, I spied Aurel Wayfarer embracing Friendship. Frostfeather! – I used to ride him high, above the storm – sailed on, sublime, majestic. The prism went dark.

He has his lusty Spring, when fancy clear
Takes in all beauty with an easy span.

....

'– be damned.' The bitter words of Hyperion Lovelace rang in Gry's ears as she fled from his tent and, willy-nilly, through the fair. The crowd shoved and jostled her. She tripped on a sharp cobblestone and stumbled against an old and stinking dwarf who shook his fist and tobacco-stained beard at her. The crowd roared, running with her, tumbling through the night and the echoing, twisted streets; between the glaring booths and flashing mountebanks' swords, the twirling batons of the jugglers and the masqueraders in their harlequin suits; over the dark, rutted ground.

She could run no more: her chest heaved under the yellow silk blouse, her throat was dry as the desert. At last, when she was able, she looked to the sky for solace, deep into the unending space which was all that remained for her of the soul of the Plains. The Guardian burned stilly above the open ground she knew to be the village green. A chill wind ruffled the grass and her hair. The star was bright as a dewdrop, as silver, as the eye of the storm; she struggled for comparisons. All at once, Gry saw another great star, a new red light like hellfire falling fast, like a comet ablaze, a fireball about to hit the earth in Wathen Fields, on the green just where she stood.

The crowd behind her screamed and the fire fell, wild, un-stoppable; not ten yards from Gry who cowered in the useless shelter of her bare arms and blanket.

'I am dead,' she thought. 'This is Lord Yama's palace.'

158

Now let me write what befell, while I have her picture fresh in my mind, her dirty deerskin garb, her young flesh, her coal-black plaits with the yellow shells tied in them, for all this world and Malthassa like a nixie or a drow-goblin. Let me write, for 'tis is the first time I have employed the mighty pen, sharper than the sword Durendal, that Gry, Nandje's daughter, lay half-dead upon the yellow, trampled grass of Wathen-in-the-Forest's playing ground, her hands in the muddy pits which had been trodden by the Murtherers, and dog-shite on her face; and – yea, also this: her gypsy blanket fallen from her and her skirts tumbled up so that her sex (as black-crowned as her head) was wantonly exposed to the brute gaze of the yokels.

'A sight to match any in Pargur,' said one.

'Ay,' another answered him. 'But if this is what happens when the stars drop fire, then let them all – and give us maids a-plenty.'

'Is she, think you?'

'A maid? Surely. The Ima keep their women intact until they marry them. Any that fall by the wayside, they kill.' He nudged his friend. 'Or would you be brave enough to verify her purity?'

'You're an addlepate, Vladi. Sensible men avoid the Ima – or would you be brave enough to risk a horseman's arrow?'

So they left the princess where she had fallen and turned away to gape at other wonders. She did not know what a Subject she made, her eyes and ears in Hell. In that other place, she knelt upon a rocky road, all mired as she was before but awake and seeing, greater than the forest's trees, tall pinnacles and hollow arches sculpted out of black shadow.

Her father was walking towards her out of the pitiless gloom, his hands raised in welcome and all his fingers' ends luminous with corruption. His face was ravaged still from the corpse-moths' burrowing and his teeth showed yellow and decaying in a wide grave grin. He bent over her and she saw that his eyes had become like those of a demon's, scarlet, malevolent, gree

dy

The cursed pen is bro

The fire hissed in the bottom of Fortuneswell, and the water bubbled. The limbs of its nivasha flailed and thrashed as she was thrown up and sank again, dead as a lobster dropped into a boiling pot.

'Ai-ee!' wailed the crowd, 'Bless her poor soul!'

Men ran forward, awkward in their fair-dress. Harlequin was the first to reach Gry, though the black bear was at his heels, and he stretched out a timid hand, afraid to uncover death; and slowly pulled the blanket back.

She lay on her back, wide eyes staring at the sky. Harlequin thought the fire, her last sight, burned in them yet, poor innocent, poor beauty. He had seen death no more than twice, when his twin cousins had died. It felt as though she was staring at him. He saw her eyelids move, her lashes trailed towards her cheeks. She blinked, distinctly.

'A miracle,' he whispered, tearing off his mask. 'Thanks be!' and the tears rolled from his eyes and wet his downy beard.

'I think she is not hurt, only stunned.'

The man at his back was speaking. It was not old Aiken in his bear suit, but a stranger, a fine gentleman somewhat ragged and distressed. One of his sleeves was torn right off.

'Let me see.' Harlequin gave way. Perhaps the man was a physician. 'I have seen mazed bodies like this before – often, in the field, when the cannon have fired. She –' The stranger felt the girl's head and her hands. He took a steel mirror from the pocket of his shirt and held it to her mouth. 'She breathes strongly: see the mist. Ima, isn't she? What does she here?'

'She rode out of the Forest – only yesterday. They say she has taken a quest, to look for her father –'

'She looks brave and sturdy, even in this plight,' said the stranger.

He looked about him and Harlequin admired the keenness and purpose of his gaze, and of his words when next he spoke.

'The heart of the Forest. I saw it as we came down, and the lights of the town. Wathen Fields, is it not? – too neat to be Lythabridge.'

160

'Wathen Fields, ay sir,' Harlequin agreed. 'And I am Vendigo, the smith's son.'

'Then run, Vendigo, to the inn – for there must be one – and bid them prepare a bed for this casualty.'

'Yes sir, but sir – you said "I saw it as we came down". From where, sir? The land's all flat about Wathen.'

'In the balloon, boy. 'Tis in that tree – but run now as I bid.'

Vendigo gaped once where the stranger pointed and nodded. Then he was gone, running hard, an arrow of motley through the crowd as it surged forward across the green. There, in the crooked beech the leshi planted when Wathen was forest, hung the remnant of a passenger balloon, is basket rocking like a huge cradle, its white fabric rent beyond repair. People were chattering loudly, the accident passed by, and some were cheering a second aeronaut who was dropping light and controlled from the branches, just like a circus acrobat, a happy comparison the more apt as she landed on the grass and saluted gaily, for she was clad in trousers and bolero of ruby silk, her glossy hair was tied with a glittering ribbon and her beautiful face was painted like that of an actress, especially the coral-coloured lips.

But the stranger, ignoring it all, lifted Gry and carried her towards the inn.

The young star-man, whom the crowd glimpsed and had by heart in an instant, noting every detail, walked like a lion, proudly, his mane of fair hair bound back with a fillet of gold, his long legs cased in tight breeks of nut-brown leather and tall boots, his upper body in a gleaming breastplate and a white and billowing shirt which had lace on it and a golden feather pinned to its collar; and, picturesquely, its right sleeve missing, only a tatter of lawn to cover the fighting-muscle of his arm. His sword hung at his side.

He smiled on Gry and she, looking dizzily up at him, like the crowd had him by heart; but completely, hopelessly, inexorably. His eyes were kind, his lashes fair as his head, the tilt of his mouth both fond and dangerous, his soul as clear and sound as the purest diamond. He, the star-sailor, born of the midnight, delivered of

161

fire, was the man she had dreamed about when she slept beside Pimbilmere and in Darklis's silken bed. She forgot faithful Leal, the brave Red Horse, Hyperion Lovelace with his honeyed words and stinging taunts and loved the stranger on sight.

'You look better already; you'll be fine,' he said. 'I'll make sure of it, or my name's not Aurel Wayfarer.'

His companion danced behind, nimble and free as air. She carried a tattered flag on a broken staff; silver it was and embroidered with a green wayfaring tree, and it fluttered bravely as they hurried along the street.

They made a fine commotion at the inn. Nathan was sent for pillows, the maids roused to boil kettles and make broth. Sib ran for the pipkin of bragget, a sweet ale renowned for its restorative powers, which Colley held to Gry's lips even as she rested in the arms of the brave (that was certain) knight (that was obvious), Aurel Wayfarer. Then Gry, when she had drunk her medicine, was laid on a pile of pillows before the fire with Sib to bathe her head with cologne and the two strangers placed in the best, stamped-leather chairs on either side of her. Vendigo Smithson, his harlequin's costume aglow in the firelight, lingered near to worship and adore the hurt Princess, so brave, so beautiful. Besides, the scene was splendid, zestful, and he had never seen a soldier close before. All the while the crowd, held back by Nathan and a line of hastily-set stools, roared in the far part of the room, in the doorway and in the street outside. Colley rounded on them with a cry of, 'Time, gentlemen! Have you no homes? No winsome, willing wives who stay even now at the cold hearth for your return?'

'Pipe down, Colley,' someone called. 'Keep your voice to yourself and let us hear the Balloonist. Who is he?'

'How do we know he is not the advance guard of Koschei's army?' another cried.

'Or the Archmage's spy?'

'Or the Dark Lord's envoy sent to destroy us?'

The blacksmith pushed the flimsy barrier of stools aside and shouldered Nathan out of the way.

'Who are you, sir?' he demanded. 'Fine and fair enough, I see, with your pretty clothing and your prettier lady, but whence come you and what is your name?'

The fire burned brightly up and Gry saw the wonderful man clearly. Sib dabbed at her brow with her scent-soaked kerchief, and she shook her head and pushed away the bony hand. The soldier's eyes were fierce with impatience but he took an unhurried sup of ale and handed his tankard to his lady. Then he stood up and bowed to the blacksmith.

'Aurel Wayfarer at your service, sir. I come from Pargur.'

'Then you are of Koschei's party.'

'Not I. I am the Kristnik's man.'

'So say you. All I see is a dishevelled soldier and a Pargur fancy-woman and all I know is that they were riding in Lord Koschei's balloon – for I helped drag the basket from the tree and saw a name I know and all the world knows upon it: Frostfeather. Honest folk do not travel in that wondrous conveyance.'

The stranger pressed his lips together as if he were secretly annoyed and bowed again.

'I can only tell you my story.'

Again, the crowd began to murmur like a great hive of bees and some called mockingly above the noise, 'Look at the lace on him!' and 'Who bought your finery, soldier?'; but Darklis Faa's voice was louder than all.

'These men are farmers, brother Blade, who hardly stray from home,' she cried. 'Give us your history!'

She stood, arms akimbo, amongst a band of gypsies by the window, another old woman, whose face was as pocked and lined as hers, leaning on a white stick at her elbow. Hyperion Lovelace twirled his round hat in his hands and smiled in a raw and disparaging way which made Gry uneasy.

'Let's hear the cavalier's tale. Then we can judge if he is to be feted or put in irons and sent to Parados,' Hyperion said, his voice clear and scornful.

The stranger ignored him, took another mouthful of ale and examined the room and the crowd with his fierce and intent stare.

163

The torn flag, which had been propped against the chimney breast, hung at his back and gave him a gallant and courageous air. He finished looking about the room, found Hyperion's eye and held it with a stern glare.

'Listen well, gypsy,' he said, 'and do not interrupt me or you will spoil the telling.'

Aurel Wayfarer's Tale: Ruined Pargur

We do not hail from the stars, people of Wathen, but from Pargur which is renowned throughout Malthassa, the crystal city of luxury and illusion to which all lovers of beauty and all men who search for glory must eventually come. But the life of ease and featherbedding has ceased, all the synchronicity and variety of the city come to an end, for the Kristnik, Lord Parados, has vanished and Pargur and Castle Sehol, where Koschei and Valdine before him held their courts, stand blasted and destroyed, opened to the four winds and to any bold rover.

The men of Wathen Fields who believed in lovely Pargur and its changeable, rainbow-hued stronghold as maids in unicorns or children in Holy Nicholas, bellowed and jeered.

'Pargur destroyed – never!'

'Never in a madman's daydream!'

'Not till doomsday or the day after!'

Aurel Wayfarer, whose head ached from a blow got from a branch of the beech tree and whose arms and legs were badly bruised, laid a hand on the hilt of his sword as if he would draw it and fight any and all who disbelieved him. His fair companion, who had been meek and silent until now, jumped lightly up and laid her hand on his.

'I will tell the tale,' she said. 'My lord is weary and out of sorts for he fought the fire in the balloon and shielded me with his body when we crashed into the tree; besides he will tell you military matters and political conniving and leave out all the scent and colour which make a tale come to life. He is a man of action. I learned storytelling at the feet of Polus when he came to Nether

Pargur and from Scheherazade's book. I know how to choose my thread and weave it into a fantastic tapestry – how to make your blood boil up and your hearts beat faster. I had a hard prenticeship, for it was I who told Koschei the tales which beguiled the long, cold nights in Sehol when his winter blotted out the sun and laid the land to waste.'

Now the crowd was a nest of snakes, hissing its venomous abuse.

The woman waited until the turmoil subsided, twirled once upon the very points of her long slim toes and bowed low.

'I am Friendship,' she said. 'And I beg you, sirs and ladies, to remember my name and so act with judgement reined and amity at liberty until my tale is done. Be still as lovers after their play and quiet as the catamountain when he sleeps in his den, while I tell you what has passed in Sehol and in Pargur to bring us so far from our home.'

'Shall we hear the Archmage's doxy?' Darklis called.

'Aye,' answered Hyperion, for all. 'She who can spin her yarn and enmesh Koschei's dark mind in it can beguile this country company for sure.'

'Then,' said the woman who had known Koschei, and smiled and made a curious and lively courtesy which caused her hair, her breasts, and the gauzy fabric of her red trousers to shimmer and shake. 'Then, my sweet gentlemen and lovely ladies all, I shall begin.'

Friendship's Tale: The Knight of the Golden Feather and the Magic That Remained
Aurel Wayfarer, Regent of Pargur the Mutable City, sat alone in the Babylon Chamber and tapped his fingers on an inlaid box. The two colours, ebony and ivory, twisted over the box in an elaborate pattern of severed arms and broken wings. He unfastened the fetters which bound the box and began to take the chessmen out of it and set them out on the chequerboard.

He had placed half a dozen when he grew weary of his game, sick at heart: the chessmen were shaped like horned demons and the king and queen were gargoyles which leered and dropped black diamonds from their fundaments when they were moved. They had a beauty which was wayward and dark for they had belonged to Koschei.

On the chessboard, the black king impatiently lifted his sword.

Aurel wanted no more killing. He would rather be what once he had been before he met with Parados and went adventuring, a simple flax-grower in SanZu. Honour and wealth came with preferment, sure, but troubles came also and enemies; and Responsibility which always had a capital R and its companion, Guilt. The city was a mire of treachery and death; the castle, which had been magical, embowered, mutant Sehol of a thousand tales, was likewise sullied, ruinous and drear, unknown acres of it in the hands of Baptist Olburn and his horrible crew. Olburn, whose career had been long and evil and who had once been Koschei's Chief Torturer and Executioner, delighted in the chaos and cruelty. The corpses he had made were spiked and gibbeted on Vanity Tower.

Aurel tapped his fingers on the box and suddenly flung it from him so that it split and broke open against the marble of the fireplace and the crowd of pieces scattered, the black overwhelming the white.

It was cold. The wind howled in the turret tops and beat against the long, glazed windows, looking for a crack. Aurel looked out over the castle gardens toward Pargur, but the city was overwhelmed by a glassy mist. He went to the fire to chafe his hands. Turning on the hearth, he warmed his leather-breeched buttocks and his fine and manly legs. Vaurien and Thidma kept the watch, with a detachment of loyal guards; he was supposed to be sleeping – which was out of the question. What might he do, to pass the six hours till he was called?

– Climb Probity Tower perhaps, to see if he could find the room with the arrays of model soldiers he had once spied there, Koschei's battle-plans no doubt; or search the undercroft of the Shield Hall for the missing archery targets. He could go to Toricello's Bower, which he was fairly sure of discovering by going downstairs and opening every door in the Long Gallery until it chanced to appear. There, lissom Friendship and dextrous Concordis would be at play, juggling or practising their acrobatic skills on the flower-bedecked swing; always, despite their long residence in the castle and service under (his mouth curled in disgust) Koschei, prodigious beauties, splendidly dressed.

He moved from foot to foot, full of longing and unease; musing. This impatience came from inaction! So – if he could find Hadrian he would fight a bout or three with him – if he could find the gymnasium.

The Copper Dwarf, Githon, licked the butter from his fingers and turned a page of his book. By Cypris and Cyllene – an interesting diagram! He studied it, holding the book out in the firelight the better to read the script which covered each section of the diagram like spider's footprints: Koschei's metamorphosis engine! 'To transform the Heart of the Subject, set the dial to o,' he read, 'and switch on the mercury pump.' He took another bite of buttered crumpet.

Wondrous, the knowledge Castle Sehol held within its fluctuating contours and myriad migrating rooms. He had been the first to enter Koschei's study, knowing in his stout dwarf's soul that books were only ink and paper and therefore could not harm him.

He had been wrong about that but, no matter. The study had accepted him, let him take down and read whatever he fancied; allowed him the comfort of this cushioned chair before the fire. He scratched his beard, which had grown long during their time in the castle and covered half his copper-coloured face; the lowest hairs of it hung well below the third button of his shirt. He had an idea of asking Friendship to plait it and of dressing only in black leather.

The book was heavy on his knees, but he read on. This engine, it seemed, could turn flesh to metal and metal to flesh, could unite the two in one body – better, (he turned the page) was able to create women. The creature in the drawing was both fragile and robust. Her head had the immobile, everlasting beauty of a statue, while her body seemed fleshly – indeed, an absolute exemplar of ripe womanhood who had, instead of a navel, a curious jewel like a green water-lily. What a man Koschei must be to have thought of this – of her! And where, if he had made her, was she? Perhaps, if he searched the castle . . . ? Why, he was part-metal himself, having breathed in copper-dust and felt it grind, like pigment in a mortar, into his skin when he worked in the mines.

Githon marked his place in the book with a spill from the grate and stood up. There was Koschei's desk, just as he had left it, furnished with a freshly-cut quill pen, the silver pomander which perfumed the room with this heavy, addictive scent, the sheaf of clean paper, the glass for his wine. He dared not sit at the desk – yet. The thought sent a shiver through him. His keen ear caught a stray sound, metal on metal: well, the castle sometimes resounded with its noisy memories of fights and sieges; but this sounded fresh and – he listened hard – full of endeavour: as if someone strove to cleanse himself by action. Ducking under one of the vines which invaded all parts of the castle at random, Githon left the library and hurried along the corridor flinging doors open to right and left.

Boxes and bins: a storeroom. Chairs, table: the Council Chamber. Dresses: women's stuff. A balustered gallery and the sound of men breathing hard after exertion: the gymnasium, and there were Aurel and Hadrian below, wiping the sweat from their faces with towels monogrammed $\mathcal{K}$, in gold.

'Bravo!' Githon shouted and ran down the steps to the arena.

'Another bout!' Aurel said to Hadrian.

'Are you sure, Regent? You fought well.'

'Not well enough. You beat me –'

'I am an old soldier trained.'

'And I hope to be! The old must instruct the young. Once more, Hadrian – take guard.'

Githon watched them critically as they strove, but from an equal elevation, for he had sprung up and caught the exercise rings which hung from the ceiling. There, he swung, flexing and relaxing his formidable arms. The rings were not dwarf-height and he was proud of his jump: what would it be, to have the graceful, easy stature of a man? Perhaps the metamorphosis-engine, if it existed somewhere other than in Koschei's experiment-book, could increase his height?

Aurel forced Hadrian back and followed him, pressing a slight advantage.

'There –' he panted, 'I – have you! –'

'Not!' returned the soldier, as Aurel's rapier clattered to the ground. 'There, you are wounded in the arm.' His rapier, with another thrust, would pierce Aurel's upper arm. Hadrian put his weapon up.

'Never be hasty,' he said. 'Rash acts have been the undoing of many a good man.'

They noticed Githon, swinging like a monkey in a tree.

'Can you turn a somersett?' Aurel idly asked, amazed when the dwarf, tucking under his round head and heavy beard, rotated between the two rings. 'Why, you are as good as Concordis!'

'Not I.' Githon dropped to the ground. 'No, I am a thick-set miner whose arms are made to wield shovels and picks, while the ladies were bred up to bend their supple bodies and entertain us males – let us visit them.'

So, for a time, the three followed the tedious tactic of walking along corridors and flinging open doors until they found what they sought, Toricello's Bower.

'Decimus Toricello was an engineer who delighted in the anomalies of time and space, in topographical puzzles and in massy structures – such as the Devil's Bastion where Old Roarer used to fire on our enemies,' Githon was saying as Aurel turned the gilded doorknob. 'He loved the greenwood too, especially those shy plants which grow in its glades and secret places – he built this room for a fernery –'

But Aurel and Hadrian scarcely heard him; they had neither visited Koschei's study nor read in its books and had no idea that Castle Sehol's many, varied moods and colours had been the thought-child of a mortal man – besides, just as Hadrian pushed open the door, they caught a glimpse of a naked, female back and a suggestion, beyond the floral swing and swags of depending ivy and vines, of an unclothed breast. Then Concordis, her bolero gaping, came tumbling from between two stone satyrs and Friendship after her, more slowly, pirouetting on her toes and closely wrapped in the transparent yardage of three of her seven veils.

'You have disturbed us at our rehearsals!' she said, her voice stern and her expression welcoming. Indeed, her smile was so inviting that the two men and the dwarf bowed. Githon, indeed, at once forgot the wisdom of his race and years in contemplation of the two Graces who leaned close to one another, and were all female charm and harmony.

'I will call for wine!' said Concordis and clapped her hands. Soon, one of the Bower's mechanical fauns attended her, setting with a tick-tock of his clockwork heart and a sweet groaning of his oil-hungry joints, crystal goblets out upon a glassy table. The creature pouring a sea-green wine which sparkled as much as did the fountain in the centre of the Bower; and Concordis, looking at the arrangements and at the two cushioned settles beside the table, was satisfied and bade the faun begone.

'You have forgot the vittles,' said Friendship. At once the automaton reappeared, its four hands burdened with ripe fruit and dishes of nuts.

'There is a dwarf!' said Concordis. A side of bacon so huge it seemed as though it would crack the great ashet it lay on was offered. A well-honed carving knife was slotted through its glistening skin. 'Come, Githon, be seated and you, sir – Hadrian – on my right.'

Friendship and Aurel were left to occupy the other seat.

The unease which had troubled Aurel in the Babylon Chamber returned: it was impossible to disregard the bare legs and scarcely-covered body so near. Yet he could not stare at Friendship as he used to ogle (from the safety of his mother's windows) the vagabond dancers who came to Flaxberry for the Linen Fair. She bent closer and handed him an over-brimming goblet at which he sipped. The bubbles in the wine burst in his mouth: the sensation was – not disagreeable. He took a good mouthful and remembered what he should do, for they all, the five of them, seemed close as conspirators around the laden table, Githon with his loyal heart, Concordis in her silk trousers and glistering bolero, stolid Hadrian, Friendship wrapped in her gauzes, himself – Aurel raised his glass.

'To Friendship and –' he began and they burst out laughing before raising their glasses to drink.

'But I –'

Friendship's slender hand touched his.

'You meant both,' she whispered and, louder, 'It behoves us to be good friends. Companions who have no secrets from one another. Countless myriad legions of ghosts and spirits which are the legacy of Koschei and his forerunners abound in Castle Sehol; Baptist Olburn and his men are resident also, somewhere in these hollow halls, but who, besides us and your Ima friend, Thidma, is true to Parados?'

'My friend and fellow, Vaurien,' said Hadrian at once.

'And Estragon Fairweather,' said Githon, 'who has changed sides once and may again.'

Concordis counted them.

'Eight,' she said, and held eight strong fingers tipped with silver in the air. 'Seven who are loyal and one whose character, as the dwarf says, is written in his name. Estragon was once a castle guard and has a liking for order and discipline. The castle, lordless as it is now, does not suit such changeable natures.'

'As changeable as the castle itself,' said Hadrian. 'Once, soon after we came to live in it, its variance and moods were a delight. These dark days, I see them as a curse. Who knows where Olburn walks when doors, windows and the jakes by Hades! must be searched out anew each day. But give me more of this heady wine – and a good slice of ham, if you please, Concordis. Let us forget care and spend our leisure time like dwarves in carousing.'

'Men see dwarves as jolly, companionable fellows. They do not know we must be harder than the metals we work,' said Githon mildly. 'I will also take a slice or two of ham – and more wine, lady.'

He held his goblet out and, just before the wine began to flow, watched with amaze as it broke of itself in pieces, which fell out of his hand. They looked at the jagged shards lying on the table and Aurel stared at Friendship's legs beneath its pellucid top. She reached suddenly down and uncovered more of their shapely length.

'I am not ashamed of my body. It is a good servant,' she said.

He, moving as swiftly as she had, grasped and lifted them into his lap.

'The table may shatter next,' he said. She laughed, delighted with his boldness.

'Or,' said Githon, smiling at the ceiling, 'that great crown might fall on us. It is obsidian, hardest of stones. I think we should withdraw, Hadrian, for a game of poker in my rooms. Concordis is a nonpareil at the game but Friendship, I know, is no hand at dealing and Aurel is too much of an innocent to play against me.'

'I –' Aurel began, but Friendship, still amused, laid two fingers on his lips and, in a moment, the dwarf, the soldier and the juggler were gone.

'How occasions conspire,' she said, laughing. 'I've watched you often, my lord, of an evening when you take a walk along the battlements –'

'I have not had the privilege of watching you.'

'I think you are a little afraid of Toricello's Bower, and not because the glass broke. It is true, we used to give our shows here, to Koschei and his guests – once indeed, I danced before Olburn; and I have shown my body to many men, such as that old money-grubber, Tate the Furrier and, more happily, to some of the younger lords who used to dwell in the castle. And I have displayed it, against the dancers' code and all custom, in the solemnity of the Shield Hall.'

'It is of no account to me,' the young Regent said.

'Nor me! I am not a whore, Aurel, though I have been bought. Not everyone born in Nether Pargur is a harlot.'

'I know little of Pargur. I was a country boy.'

172

'And I am a city-bred girl. Resounding, mutable Pargur once was all to me.'

'My birthplace is stable and quiet. I doubt I shall ever see it again.'

'Then will we two orphans be friends, and true to each other?'

'I never had a woman for a friend.'

'Or lover, I think. Let us wander about the castle together and see – whatever it will permit. Sit a moment longer, Aurel,' and she darted away into the tangle of vines. They are growing without check, he thought, and watched one: sure enough, a long tendril extended itself from the vine's end, reached out and found itself a crack to which to cling.

I shall be trapped! he thought. Grown over – suffocated. Where has Friendship gone?

Then he heard her feet pattering back across the floor. She was properly dressed, he saw, and breathed hard out in relief: a pair of gauzy trousers, to be sure, and a bolero like her companion's but with a shirt beneath it, and red leather slippers with curly toes. Those parts of her which should be hidden from the general gaze were covered. She had tied her hair back with a ribbon.

'No time to dress it,' she said, touching her tresses. 'Follow me – no, better take my hand. It is easy to get lost in Castle Sehol: the name means 'nowhere' did you know? In the old language of the dwarves.'

'Had dwarves a hand in building it?' he asked her, but she smiled and shook her head.

'Ask Githon,' she said. 'I know only what Koschei saw fit to tell me.'

He held out a hesitant hand, and she grasped it. 'Don't let go!'

Following Friendship, whose hand was warm and pliant about his, Aurel realised how little of his castle he, the Regent, knew.

After all, he thought, I am a plain fellow who had never left SanZu until Parados took me adventuring; and poor Mother no doubt is thinking of me and wondering how I fared – but how can I send messages home to Flaxberry when I don't know where it is? Nor how to find my way back there. We travelled league upon league in the balloons, flying like eagles over field and forest, mountain and moor. I kept our balloon up, for sure, but Parados knew the way.

And how long is it since we came to Castle Sehol; how long have we been trapped inside? Perhaps time itself has been overset and is in pieces – like that archway.

'Run!' said Friendship and pulled him beneath the tottering stonework and safely out on the far side.

'It is always like that,' she explained. 'Koschei made it to scare trespassers. Hurry.' She pulled him along a grey corridor which seemed to have no end, and into a niche in the wall. 'The statue is gone. But we can rest on its plinth.'

'How long have you lived here?' he asked.

'It's best not to count – impossible anyway! You would end up in Bedlam. "Take city and castle as they be / Or lie with the madmen in Sans Pitie" – don't you know the saying? Now, just here there should be – a catch!'

He pulled her roughly back from the stone she had been caressing as she spoke, for the wall had dissolved and become a door.

'Koschei loved such devices,' said Friendship. 'There is no need for alarm.' Nevertheless she did not immediately move out of his embrace but kissed him lightly on the mouth. 'Open the door, Aurel. There is nothing to fear beyond it, unless you dislike Koschei's taste in furnishing. These are guest-rooms which have another entrance in the Shield Hall, and I daresay you would have found your way here in the end.'

He looked with wonder on the damasked and brocaded rooms they passed through, all at first glance in the very highest of taste and, like the chessmen, of exquisite depravity when examined closely.

'He entertained ambassadors and potentates here,' said Friendship. 'With roast faun's leg and pickled songbirds, with devilled bones and messes of raw larks' tongues, with wine and cordials of poppy and mandragora. They slept well after the feasting and Koschei, dressed like a playactor in mask and black gloves, would

174

come into the bedchambers and stifle them in their dreams. I dare say they deserved it.'

'Weren't you afraid, for yourself?'

'Not I. He needed me to bolster his vanity and I loved him, in a way.'

'That is vile!'

'No. He was a monster, surely – but, do you know the story of Beauty and the Beast? Well, no matter. Here is a pretty thing which must have escaped Koschei's notice. Take it, you are Lord now.'

It was a cockade-pin, lying on a gilded chest of drawers, and it was pleasing. He laid it in the palm of his hand to examine, turned it over: silver and gilt, shaped like a love-knot framed in a wreath of flowers.

'You could wear in your slouch hat, to pin the feather.'

'Or I could give it you, a love-gift.' Too soon for that. He put it back on the chest, but the dancer snatched it up.

'Koschei stole it from Lord Lucas. You may safely keep it,' she said, drew out his lucky feather from the buttonhole he always wore it in and pinned it by the love-knot to his shirt collar.

'There!'

'We are too bold,' he said, while admiring the brooch, himself and her in the mirror above the chest. 'You, Friendship, Githon, myself and the rest of us. We took the castle, but it was by trickery and treacherousness – Estragon let us in, we killed some defenders and have assumed that all is well. Koschei might return.'

'All things are possible. If he does, you will fight him.'

'Fight Koschei? You would not dare!' someone said. Aurel turned, hand to sword.

Friendship was laughing and the voice repeated its threat.

'Fight Koschei? You would not dare!'

She is a veil-dancer, he thought. Her companion is a juggler and they both come from Nether Pargur, home of all kinds of tricksters, whoreson knaves and mountebanks.

'You are clever to throw your voice like that,' he said.

'Not I!' Her laughter made her most desirable. 'It's the mirror – see?'

He noticed then that its frame was a black-painted mouth of gross, irregular proportions and listened to it repeating its message over and over – until he stepped to the side. 'Enough,' he said. 'I see how the thing is set in motion.' Then he held her by the slender shoulders, bent and kissed her long.

At last, 'I think they chose you for Regent,' she said, 'because you kiss so well! Let us go, Aurel – let us climb. There is nothing in these rooms but old glamour.'

'And the ghosts of our new love,' he said and followed her down a narrow, turret stair and out into a courtyard enclosed by high walls of dressed stone.

'The inner bailey,' she said. 'You have seen this before.'

'Yes. I meant to move the quintain there to a better place. To use it.'

'I think it is too late for that, for games. Do you know the name of this tower?'

'The Virgin Tower,' he guessed, for it was white as skimmed milk. 'The White Tower?'

'Indeed. Pale as Nemione's skin: she was such a beauty – I do not know why I say "was", as we do when speaking of Koschei. Nemione is as clever a magician as he and might also return. She lived in this tower – the key is in the lock. Turn it, Aurel; and lock it behind us. There is a device on it which transforms the handle to a cockatrice if the door is left open.'

They each took a deep breath and began to climb the narrow, twisting stair so fast that even limber Friendship panted, until they reached a landing and a door.

'In here?' Aurel reached for the latch.

'No. Have a care! I do not know where in this world or the next it leads.'

They climbed again and he paused at the second landing and the second door to wait for her instructions.

'Not there! They say it leads straight into the Palace of Shadows.'

They passed three more doors, and she let him open one. It led into the room with the model soldiers, all their legions armed and ready, set out on a vast table ready for play, or for plotting. As he looked at them, admiring their neat, miniature weapons and shining helmets, he knew that, like Koschei's chess pieces, they could move themselves and he backed through the doorway.

'This room is in Probity Tower.'

'Sometimes – but we are at the top,' she said, and she stepped up past him through an open arch. Here was a huge, attic room whose floor of pale, bleached boards was scattered with feathers and bird-droppings and strewn with cast-off clothing and other finery. A dead butterfly lay on the floor beside an unglazed window, its colours brave in the gloom. Friendship walked about, picking a bead up here, a jewelled hairpin there.

'Once, Nemione's room was here,' she said. 'I suppose I had half a hope she might be in it. I wronged her once, in my boldness – I could have apologised, which would have made her laugh, most icily. She was quite as cruel as Koschei. This comb is hers – see the emasculated ape on the top of it. Poor thing, he is so slack-jawed. I suppose she wore it to tease Koschei. I might steal it but – you remember what happened to Snow White when the witch gave her a comb?'

'She slept the sleep of death until it was taken out of her hair.'

'Bravo, Aurel! Stars, look what has been thrown in the corner – by the window! It is Nemione's fur, the one she had made up from the skins of a hundred silver foxes. No, don't touch it.'

Friendship extended one scarlet slipper and kicked the fur robe, which only slid a little on the boards. She touched it gingerly, lifted it cautiously and dragged it about.

'It looks big enough for a giant. When she wore it, it trailed behind her along the paviours. Sometimes Halfman, liveried like a page in her colours of white and gold, rode on its train – he was *my* pet monkey. Koschei took him from me and gave him to Nemione. I suppose he is dead.'

'He was lively as a cricket when I saw him in Castle Lorne. You forget, Friendship, that I also knew the Lady Nemione; though she had become more of a soldier than a lady when I at last dared speak to her.'

'A soldier? Nemione! Don't tell me: I can imagine *her* armour, all feminine glitter, gold baubles, satin sword-hanger – and breast-plate cut low! Ah, Aurel, I should not mock nor should we have come up here. The place is a museum of Nemione's sorrows. And it is getting cold. That rain you hear drumming on the tiles has snow in it, you may be sure. I know by the muffled sound of it.'

'Put on Nemione's fur. It will become you, I am sure, as much as her. And warm you.'

'I dare not – it may indeed "become me", or I it! Never be half cautious when magic is abroad. But we might sit on it.'

The fur felt like the best silk floss at home. He touched her hair to make a comparison and could find no difference.

'My pride and joy,' said Friendship. 'Longer than Nemione's!' She stood up and unbound her hair, flung it forward so that it kissed the floor; bowed to him. Then she knelt on the fur and kissed him and he her. Soon, enclosed in warmth, he was part of her and they were dreaming ecstasies together. It seemed as though they floated, one twined with the other, close as mouth and tongue or heart and soul, spiralling softly downwards like leaves falling from a tall tree, or like thistledown drifting or the shining hairs of a silver fox brushed gently into the air.

Waking, he believed himself at home on the swing in the mulberry tree, but remembered he was in paradise and that paradise was nothing but an old fur coat and the dancer, Friendship, who lay naked and asleep beside him. He moved to kiss her and saw, beyond her, white fluffy clouds and a tilted horizon. Alarmed, he raised himself on the fur; half-sitting, was afflicted with the vertigo which had threatened to unman him when he first learned to fly a balloon, for the coat, and himself and Friendship on it, had lurched like a balloon which has lost its upcurrent. The sky was far above. He looked out, and down: there were rocks below. Also, it was growing dark.

Aurel reached for Friendship and clung to her. Eldritch voices screamed about them and snatches of ethereal song eddied and faded. Friendship, waking, whispered, 'Zracne vile. Where are we to be among the spirits of the air?'

'Falling.'

'This is the end of Sehol. Maybe we have died.'

'In bliss then. It may be so – we have no clothes.'

'We took them off, remember? This is high magic.'

The motion slowed. They floated gently downwards and came rolling to rest in a damp gutter. The fur robe vanished but their garments dropped about them and they crawled stiffly to retrieve and put them on. Aurel found his sword and, caught under a ledge, the belt still attached; his breastplate was standing up like half a man; he buckled them on. Friendship's hair blew like smoke in a fair wind; indeed there was a wind and they and the roof were lit by the rising moon. They were lying in a gully at the edge of a roof shaped like a wizard's hat. Familiar stars shone overhead, the Crane, the Swan, the Hoopoe, Bail's Sword and Custos, the Guardian, the great single star which had appeared when Aurel had journeyed with Parados and which Githon had named. He glowed more brightly than the rest.

'He stands guard over Sehol,' Friendship whispered, pointing at the star. 'Where is the castle? Where are we?'

'Perhaps it has moved. Or else the castle has moved. We seem to be on a tower top – there is a little turret. With a door in it!'

Aurel examined the steel-banded door and warily turned its handle, expecting it to be locked, or enchanted; but the door opened easily, swinging in without a creak as if it was kept well-oiled. They looked down a broken, twisting flight of stairs, and further down on gaping walls and a tumble of jagged rock and cut stone. The cone-shaped roof, which had appeared so solid moments before, they now saw was full of holes, its rafters shattered and its slates either fallen or hanging loose. One slipped and slithered as they watched; crashed somewhere far below.

Aurel peered into the void.

'I am certain we can climb down.'

'Where to?' demanded Friendship. 'I see nothing there but moonlit rock; and it looks as cold as charity.'

179

'Then take my hand as I took yours in Castle Sehol. There is nothing to fear. This is an old pele tower, a watch tower, ruined many years ago.'

'I wish we could go back,' said Friendship.

'Can you fly without Nemione's fur?' Aurel went down a step and reached behind him for her hand. 'Now follow me. Tread where I tread and all will and shall be well.'

Friendship stole after him. He felt her shudder, but soon she remembered her dancer's training and, shaking off her fear, tripped lightly down the shattered stair.

When they came at last to the base of the ruined tower and stood amongst the rocks and the great blocks of dressed ashlar which had once been an impregnable wall, Friendship sniffed the air and squeezed Aurel's hand.

'Brimstone, zedoary! – that sharp scent. And saltier's musk.'

'Plants perhaps, even in this wilderness; or perhaps the tower gives up its stored perfume to the night.'

Friendship was brisk and roughly shook his arm.

'There are no *flowers* here, Aurel, nor saltiers neither; they live in the silver mines. Those are the body-smells of Koschei – beware!'

In that hard, moonlit place where the rocks and their shadows could hardly be distinguished from each other; where the fallen tower loomed threatening in decay, there was no safe hiding place. Friendship, who had seen Koschei at work and at play, knew well he had no need of mortal eyes to see a fugitive and hunt him out, but might use lenses, mirrors, pocket cabinets, a scrying stone or, worst, his brilliant mind. She took a timid step forward and screamed.

She had trodden on a book which, being rain-soaked, gave like a living thing under her foot. They bent to examine it in the moonlight, Aurel prodding it with the point of his dagger. The white binding looked new, inviting touch, and was marked on the spine with sigils and deep-etched golden Φs, Πs, Ψs and Ωs. Aurel used his dagger to open it.

'Don't turn any more pages!'

'I am nobody's fool, Friendship; and I can read what is written there.'

'Then hold your hand to your face and read through the cracks between your fingers!'

'Stop fretting. These words will harm no one – it says: "The Book of Castle Truth which contains the names of all my subjects: Jerusalem, Urdiv, Kristnik, the Lady Lilith, Chastity, Poverty, Obedience, Courage and Meekness, or the Blessed City, the Lustrous Angel, the Man of Destiny, our Best Beloved, the First Ideal, the Cardinal Rule, the Golden Thought, the Right Hand and the Spirit of Peace. These are the nine common names and identities of God and my name" – oh, listen! – "is Parados Constans, son of Stanko. I am Prince of Pargur and Paladin of Malthassa." Look, it is written in a firm, manly hand. This is his book, Friendship. We are quite safe.'

'Fool! Koschei's scent is strong – don't you think, if Parados had been here, these pages would be charged with his body-odours?'

'Maybe – train-oil, cordite and castile soap, all clean, honest smells. I have it! This a message from Parados, written here by just and whitest magic.'

'Anything is possible in Malthassa – but it sounds like a description of the Virtues, or notes about a place and the people who live there. And we must find a better place and some friends! Let us try in this direction.'

Aurel followed her, muttering: 'A city – a castle. Called Jerusalem?'

They scrambled over a huge rock and up to the summit of another, but Friendship did not stop, only said, 'Ugh, the reek!' and went on, faster, jumping recklessly across the chasms between the great blocks of ashlar so that Aurel was forced to hurry after her. The moon made the ruin bright as day. Friendship stepped into a pool of light and stood still. Her hair flew up as she raised her arms and cried out.

'Devilry! Ai!' Her wail, shrill as a bat's, terrible as a banshee's, made Aurel's heart go cold in his chest. His own hair stood on end. 'Ai! Ai! Ai-ee!' She sobbed plaintively while her hands made grasping movements in the air as if she would tear out her hair.

'Are you hurt?' Aurel said stupidly and she rounded on him and spoke bitterly,

'Ay, in my heart. My lord lies there.'

Aurel, leaping to her side, looked down and saw the Archmage of Malthassa and onetime prince of Pargur, Koschei the Deathless, sprawled amongst the rocks.

'He is dead,' she wailed. 'Dead!'

'Then his vaunted title was so much braggadocio.'

Some shreds and tatters of his magnificent crimson robe clung to the magician's burly shoulders but, apart from these, he was naked. He lay on his back, the scars and weals on his abused and altered body there for anyone to see. In the full woman's breast which swelled on the left side of his chest, rising from the hair like a smooth, white hillock, there was an old and hideous sword-wound covered with thick scar tissue and in his ribbed and muscular stomach, ragged rents and piercings edged with burnt flesh.

'Poor thing,' said Friendship.

'To come to this? It is a fine sight, Love, for it means that we and Malthassa are free,' said Aurel. 'It means that you will stay with me, Friendship. See, he has been shot with a snaphance pistol. He is most certainly dead and we have nothing to fear from him.'

Yet Friendship continued to lament and Aurel, though he grew impatient, kept his arms about her while he used his eyes and nose. There was no question of touching the dead man; such foul corpses were better left and the quicker the better too in case, beside the sickening vapours, any unloosed magic hung about them. The smell of musk was very strong. Koschei, he supposed, had anointed himself with it – was it not said that saltier-grease made strong men invincible and weak men virile? His nails were as long as a catamount's claws; his eyes, thankfully, closed and his fine, nay, noble features, in repose; but the altered chest with the taut male belly below it was an abomination and – he felt his own mouth gape in horror – the man had a grievous wound. He had been unmanned, ay doubly too, with one cut from a Pargur blade. There was nothing of his vaunted masculinity but a short contrivance like a fowl's arse.

So she was never Koschei's, he thought, and spoke to Friendship in tones which were at once challenging and tender.

'You are my lady, Dearest, for better or worse.'

She did not answer but only looked at him with eyes that might have been vacant with horror or empty with longing, took a ribbon out of her pocket, captured and tied back her billowing hair. She took a deep breath of the cold, night air and pulled him away from Koschei's corpse.

The moon was full and great as their new love, balancing on the horizon like a white ball on a precipice edge.

'Is that the moon, so close?' said Friendship, and he saw that the sphere was moving slowly towards them, revealing, as it descended, the ivory circle of the moon in the sky.

''Tis Frostfeather,' Friendship breathed.

'We must capture it if we can, and fly from here in its basket.'

'There is no need. Koschei put a commandment on it to fly between Pargur and this place. I know now where we are stranded, for there was pillow-talk between us. This was Peklo Tower, where the Archmage worked his most puissant spells. From here he controlled Malthassa and all in it and of it, the land, the people, their thoughts and actions, the tallest mountains and the deepest mines; the seasons and the weather.'

Friendship laughed suddenly, a glorious sound in that gloomy place.

'You *are* a cautious fool, my man of gold, you, Aurel, who flew Parados's balloon for him. Look, there is the ladder rigged ready.'

The white balloon, child of the waxing moon, sank lower and offered Aurel and Friendship salvation. Its glowing canopy rose proudly above them and Aurel took hold of the long rope ladder and held it steady for Friendship to mount. She went up it like a soaring lark and he, following, felt his spirits lift.

Frostfeather rose as soon as they were both safely in its basket and Aurel went to tend the fire in the round-bellied furnace; but Friendship hung over the side, as a famous beauty leans from her balcony to see the scene below. The body of Koschei was hidden in shadow but clear, on the top of one of the ashlar blocks, a coloured globe, a map of Malthassa in the round lay in pieces; and Friendship marvelled to see it and thought sadly of the transience of beauty, of love and life itself.

Aurel came to her with a cup of hot wine.

'His hampers are well-provisioned,' he said. 'See, there are blankets and a down-quilted mantle.'

The mantle was embroidered, like the sky about them, with silver stars. He wrapped her in it and in his arms and kissed her and, when he had tasted all the sweetnesses of her eyes and mouth and stopped to draw breath, she murmured drowsily in his ear,

'You smell of summer, golden man, of hayfields and warm earth.'

'And you of May-blossom and clover honey.'

From Frostfeather's hampers he brought grapes and manchet-bread spread with butter and, while they ate, they looked down at the moon-enchanted sea and the last of the rocky promontory on which Peklo Tower had stood. Among the white-capped waves, Aurel saw a ship a-sailing, which he pointed out to Friendship; for he, like any man of Malthassa, knew that no mortal man had ever built such craft.

The ship battled through the waves, all its billowing black sails set and pennons flying. It gleamed in the wave-troughs and glittered on their crests and was a strange, brave sight; but it was so far below them it seemed more an illusion or the model of some vessel of destruction foredoomed.

'That is Hespyne, the Ship of the Dead,' Friendship said in a solemn voice and made the triskele sign in the air and on her breast. 'They talked of her in Nether Pargur, in the hour between wolf's dusk and cock-crow, when fell spirits were abroad and haunting.'

'And where does she sail?'

'Why where else, but to Hell? – to the Palace of Shadows where the Dark Lord is King. Kiss me, Aurel; though I'm wrapped in swansdown and silk, I am cold.'

They sat down on the pitching floor of the basket and he held her close until she was warm again and drowsed and slept; then he tended the magical furnace and took a lookout's vigil at the basket's-side. The waves were huge below and the sky growing lighter, though the clouds which sailed high and alongside them were ruddy, as if drenched in blood. He recognised the land they were approaching with a start: they were on the seaward side of Pargur, where mighty cliffs stooped sheer to the sea. No man, till now, had seen it from that viewpoint. Friendship stood beside him, rubbing her eyes.

'Oh pity!' she cried, 'That is Nether Pargur.'

The time-enchanted strata out of which the city's pleasure quarters were fashioned lay exposed like a gigantic doll's house or a theatre of the world. The streets and plazas were in a confusion of dazzlement and panic, figures running hither and thither, dolls disturbed. A roof crashed in ruins, the front of a lodging-house fell forward and bodies tumbled from it in the various attitudes of sleep and love, of commerce and thievery. A hurdy-gurdy man, winding away at his instrument, patrolled the wrecked streets, his one-eyed cur behind him; a soldier blew his flugelhorn and naked men and women fled, tumbling into the ground as it opened like a yawning mouth under their feet and swallowed them, hearts, limbs and souls. Then Frostfeather was close against a stone gallery where painted ladies and eunuchs ran, some crying loudly for help from the miraculously-arrived pair in the balloon-basket who rose like a vision of salvation before them and passed over the edge of the land. Frostfeather flew over Upper Pargur.

The rising sun lit up successive scenes of havoc and commotion in its bloody light. All the city's bells were ringing of themselves, without bell-ringers, as the buildings shook and quaked, and stone columns, statues, towers of glass and crystal, shell-encrusted fol-lies, civic monuments, bridges, plaster ceilings, frescoes, murals, tessellated pavements, tiles, fountains, roof-trees, gutters, sluices, bathing pools, inlaid furniture and grandiose avenues and pleasant prospects came crashing down and jumped in pieces over the heaving ground. The effulgent rainbows which used to arch about the city and make bridges tower to tower, golden finial to weathercock, had melded together and laid a patina of light across the ruins. Above them, dispersing like bubbles or wisps of morning mist in the heat of the sun, were the city's illusions, save for their dying shimmer no more than brief dreams.

Frostfeather rose again to reveal Castle Sehol, ruined and grey, its light gone out and, without veering from its course, carried them beside the devastated walls in which gashes were torn out as if they had been made in cloth not stone. Of Probity Tower and Vanity, there was no sign, for they had toppled and lay in heaps of tumbled stone athwart the smashed courtyards which once had surrounded them with acres of smooth paving-stones. The gardens below the castle were riven with chasms, trees, follies and statues upended in them, the flowering shrubs turned all to firewood and the clear waters in the ornamental cisterns and canals drained away into a sea of mud; of the pretty pavilion Koschei had called his Memory Palace there was no sign.

Tears stood in Friendship's eyes.

'My friends, my treasures,' she said.

Aurel held her cold hands and kissed her brow. The brisk wind pushed them along and made Frostfeather's taut wires thrum. Some thing or object was flying with them, whirling along in a mad flapping dance. It was a card table covered with a cloth of green baize and three people sat about it on wicker chairs and clung however they could to the table and to their hands of playing cards. There were none on the table: they had all blown away with the stakes of paper money, the IOUs, the glasses and the wine.

''Cordis!'' screamed Friendship, reaching vainly out from her mantle and the basket.

Aurel hung down on the other side, his feet jammed in Frostfeather's ropes. As the table hurtled past, so close it almost knocked him from his hold, he grabbed one of its legs; at once the table collapsed and the baize cloth twisted itself into a rope to which clung Concordis, her garments flattened to her body, Githon the Copper Dwarf, and the soldier, Hadrian, whose weight on the cloth threatened to drag them all from the sky. Concordis got a hand on Frostfeather's basket, then two, and swung there upside down: was she not an acrobat and strong as a horse? Githon swarmed up her body as if it were a tree, relishing, despite his perilous position, the differing textures of her body parts, bony chin, taut neck, firm breasts and firmer buttocks which he needs must use as handholds on his way to safety; tensed legs and he was up in the basket next to Aurel and hauling up the cloth and Hadrian, who fell over the rim with a thump which shook them all.

Concordis came up last, having stretched her body to remove all impressions of the dwarf, relieved herself into the wind, and hung inverted for a little longer to see the broken buildings hover above her head and the sky and balloon under her feet. She embraced Friendship.

'I thought I should never see you again, nor Malthassa either. I thought we would be blown straight to Hell,' she said and Friendship, who had waited very still and full of fear while Aurel worked, kissed her and took breath to tell her tale when, ''Ware below!' called Hadrian, and the company in Frostfeather's basket looked down together.

The Devil's Bastion stood unbreached and untouched above the ruins of the castle, its flat top still paved evenly and Old Roarer and the other cannon in their places. The bastion was alive with figures battling with each other and with the cords and tackle of three of the castle's best fighting balloons.

'There's Vaurien!'

'And Thidma!'

A standard waved near them, Aurel's canting arms, a green wayfaring tree upon a silver flag. It leaned precariously, for Estragon Fairweather was trying to pull it from its socket while Vaurien clung to his legs. Thidma had fallen on his back and was shielding himself from the blows rained on him by the tyrant executioner, Baptist Olburn. Aurel roared his battle cry.

'On your feet! Who fights for me?'

The cry, coming out of the very sky like a dragon riding the wind, woke Vaurien's rage. He pulled Estragon from the flag and began to belabour him with the flat of his sword. Thidma found courage and strength, stood up, parried the next blow and dealt one himself at which Olburn bellowed like a wounded bull, and cursed him for a whore's kitling and a dirty, Ima savage whose mother was a goblin and whose father lived by selling his sisters to the trolls.

Frostfeather began to sink toward the great bastion, coming home and, as they all sank into the fight and confusion on its broad top, Aurel snatched up his flag, breaking the staff as he wrenched it from its mounting. He stuck it in the basketwork. At once, there came a change which thrilled through every one of Frostfeather's crew: a change of heart in the enchanted balloon. It floated smooth and steadily and answered with a dip of its canopy and a creak of its basket-work when Aurel woke its fire. He steered it close to his loyal men so that Hadrian, by leaning down and grabbing the plume of Estragon Fairweather's helmet, removed him from the action.

Fairweather hung helpless in the soldier's hands, the steel ribbon which kept his helmet in place cutting deep into his chin and his neck stretched out like a turkey cock's upon a chopping board. Hadrian spoke to him in kindly tones.

'Fear not, turncoat, I shall not strangle you with your own chinstrap.'

'Mercy,' Fairweather squawked, casting away his sword.

'That's for noblemen and lords to grant. I'm a common soldier,' Hadrian said and dropped him. The traitor's body fell swiftly, now on its back and now its face, as the wind pummelled it, and burst apart upon the blocks of stone below.

The men on the bastion had rearranged themselves. Vaurien and Thidma had seized one of the balloons and Olburn, his lieutenants and his dowsabelle, the she-boggart he bought with counterfeit gold, held another, while the rabble of his soldiery swarmed into the third. They soared aloft as quick as corks blown from bad

188

wine bottles and Aurel manoeuvred Frostfeather into place. His plan was to wait for Thidma and Vaurien, fly swiftly aloft and lose the foe with altitude and daring.

Then was battle-royal and aerial. Saving Frostfeather, Olburn had the best craft which he flew up against the white balloon and essayed to capture it with grappling hooks. He wanted Koschei's magic craft for himself and feared to fire on it or on its passengers. His boggart-wife longed to tear the finery from Friendship's and Concordis's backs to bedeck herself; especially, she coveted the star-patterned mantle which hung like temptation over the basket's side. She licked her grinning lips and, while she waited for tender flesh to bite, combed out the lice from her pelt.

Thidma and Vaurien fought bravely, rest their souls, but they were no match for Olburn's soldiery which outnumbered them five to one. They plunged deathwards; but they took ten men and one balloon with them.

Olburn closed for the kill, his piebald craft soaring as fast as Frostfeather and wedded to it with three grappling irons embedded. Concordis and Hadrian hung from the ladder, trying to dislodge them, Githon waited with drawn sword, Friendship with a cutlass and Aurel fully armed. He had found pistols aboard. Like the foe, he hesitated to use such weapons in the air. Olburn's men began to haul Frostfeather in, pulling like bargees on the ropes. Soon, the fight would be hand-to-hand.

The end came quickly, as night falls in the tropics. Brave Concordis and bold Hadrian cut two hooks away, and fell; stout Githon, jumping for the foe, dropped into the chasm of air between the two balloons; Aurel fired into the canopy of Olburn's balloon as Friendship severed the last, binding rope.

Like gulls' cries on the wind, the terrible screams of the dying hung in the air, a chorus of despair. Friendship clung to Aurel.

'If the gods have any pity, they will be senseless before they hit the stones,' she said bitterly. 'Soar, Frostfeather, and go where you list. You have a lighter burden now.'

The wind-gods, which till now had toyed with them, drove hard against balloon and basket. Pargur was gone, fallen behind them,

189

a far-off memory. Malthassa's dark, eternal forest passed below them, tree on tree, thicket on thicket, brake on brake and still there were trees from evening to morning, from sunup to sunset, until all but one loaf and half a bottle of wine were left of the provisions and night fell for the seventh time. The great cuckoo-star Custos, the Guardian, shone above them. Friendship, staring up at it, crossed her fingers and made a secret wish. Aurel turned from kissing her to tend the fire and saw that it was running out of control. The furnace was glowing scarlet and the ropes and silk above it turning brown as they smouldered.

'The Fates forfend, Sweetness,' he said, 'but I fear 'tis our turn for farewells and perdition. Kiss me.'

Friendship did so, soft and full, and then pulled out a tiny casket, or compact box, from her trouser pocket and began to powder her lovely face and smooth coral-coloured paste upon her lips.

The storyteller made a pretty curtsey.

'The rest, my gentlemen and sentimental women, my lords and ladies of Little Egypt, you know, for you saw it: what passed when Frostfeather took fire and Aurel Wayfarer and I fell like the children of the stars to earth. I give you my blessings and thanks for your hearing and ask yours for my tale.'

Uproar leapt out on her ending, some yelling 'Encore!' and some 'Fantasy!' Hyperion Lovelace raised a hand for silence and spoke sardonically.

''Tis a fine tale in which the teller is the heroine and her lover the hero.'

Colley got up then and planted his bulky body firm on his hearth beside Friendship and Aurel; in front of Gry on her pillows and Sib with her kerchief and her bottle of cologne.

'Enough, gypsy,' he said, 'unless you wish me to show you the door,' and Hyperion, politic for once, bowed elegantly and doffed his hat from black curls that tumbled, put it on again and sat quietly amongst his people. Colley made a short speech in praise of Friendship, and of Aurel too for he, though pale and silent now, was shown to be a true hero and a follower after good.

'Perhaps, mistress,' he finished, 'you will hasten the morning by giving us one of your Pargur jigs or sarabands which, if they be as fine as your tale, must be the best.'

'Gladly.' Friendship smiled. 'Certainly I'll dance for you. I can easily turn my feet to a country measure, a courtly galliard or any dance that is danced in Pargur or the length and breadth of Malthassa, but I shall give you my best, the Dance of the Single Veil.'

She pushed back her chair and Colley cleared a space. Standing there, alert and graceful in the bumpkin crowd, she placed her feet in the correct position to begin, raised both arms in a sinuous line before her face; and, realising she had no veil, laughed aloud.

'I must make believe, and you also,' she cried, looked about her and saw Gry leaning forward with flushed cheeks, the chequered blanket across her lap.

'Lady –' said Friendship and dropped suddenly into a real curtsey. 'Ima lady, you are such a one as Thidma was, brown-faced and dressed in cloth coloured like a summer sky.'

Tears filled Gry's eyes.

'I knew Thidma,' she said. 'He was my uncle's eldest son.'

'Then, for his sake, will you lend me your wrap?'

'Why not? Thidma was a fine fellow and a great horseman and hunter of wolves.'

Then Friendship danced and made the company believe that Darklis Faa's old blanket was a SanZu veil of thinnest silken gauze and that she was naked behind it. The men cheered her wildly and the women with a sincere enthusiasm believing, each one, that did she try, she could dance in just the same schooled and abandoned manner to win both hearts and flowers. Ale and wine flowed and high language, extravagant boasts and barbed jests. Yet Gry, with Sib a shadow at her back, soon looked away from Friendship's gyrating figure and saw that Aurel Wayfarer was not watching his Love but herself, Gry, Nandje's daughter. He smiled and held her gaze; then, like a wounded swan or a salmon on a hook, she was drowning, sinking in a rapid current of blue riverwater and the dark pupils at the centre were paradise

191

islands. She wanted to lie upon their shores and feed on honey and lotus blossoms. Aurel's eyes, as she looked at him, seemed to dissolve and she felt instead the greedy gaze of Heron and felt his hands clawing at her skirts. She rose quickly and hurried away to her room.

THE PALACE OF SHADOWS

pass with me
Through an eternal place and terrible

Excelsior!

....

*Since my pen is broken irrevocably and my penknife lies in my cart, I'll
put away the story, seat myself upon the floor and try the journey of
negation once more. Jaa!*

*Ah, God, all the gods – by which I mean my old master, the Absolute,
and the many deities of sorcery and cunning, those who attend and
are Zernebock (or Lord Yama), to wit Abrahel, Asmodeus, Babylon,
Bel, Cyllene, Lucifer, Moloch, Sinistrus and Urthamma; by the Dark
Lord and by the spirits which dwell in earth, air and water, let me
have enlightenment!*

*I sit, I practise the disciplines, lose myself and come again upon
the level place before the Rise. But this time the redness has abated
and I see green and flowering trees, birds and beasts like those about
us in Idra yet brighter, so dazzlingly limned upon my perspective I can
scarcely bear to look. The creatures, the plants themselves hold in and
at the same time spill out pure light, all the colours, every hue of the
spectrum and* beyond it.

*I hear sweet music, sensual, spiritual. Dancing girls approach me.
They carry flowers which they strew to make a path, and garlands which
they hang about me till I am almost overcome with the fragrance –*

'Follow us, Koschei,' they chorus, 'Follow! Follow!'

*So, at last, coming by viridian-shadowed dells and paved pleasaunces
where other maidens sit in the sun or sport with pet deer and tiger cubs,
they bring me to a lake the colour of marigolds. A boat lies against the
bank and, in the lake, an island. They put me in the boat and, with
much dainty pushing and laughter, send me off. Without sail or oars*

I am carried to the island.

Landing I find, in the scarlet grass, stepping stones which lead me to the centre of the island, but by a tortuous route. I pass many on the way, men three and four times my height, all of them dressed in the most splendid clothing of the same eye-confounding hues I saw on the dancers, and hung about with gold and all sorts of precious jewels. Each one greets me with an elaborate bow.

So, coming where the stones lead, I find steps and a throne atop them where sits another of the giant men, more richly dressed than his fellows and holding a lotus-flower of purest white in long fingers of bright blue. His face and feet are the same unearthly colour and his smile, which is welcoming, shows teeth of pearl. He, too, know my name and speaks it.

'Clever Koschei!'

I bow, and he holds the flower out to me so that I can look into its heart where, at the bottom of a deep shaft suffused with yellow light, his image – or rather, himself, dressed now like the lotus in white, stands. He speaks again; that is to say his giant and his lotus-enclosed selves speak to me:

'A pilgrimage, Koschei? Or intellectual curiosity? These are questions you must debate with yourself.'

I bow again and answer.

'I have already done so and journeyed here to find the solution.'

Then the god is angry and shakes his fists and roars.

'Go back to your world! Humble yourself with discipline and fasting! Fold your arrogant limbs into the semblance of this holy lotus, empty your mind and begin again. Only then will you be fit to kneel before the meanest, prentice sage and beg him to instruct you.'

He lays the lotus flower on a jewelled cushion and reaches for me. Once – only – I try to dodge him; once – no more – to call up a protection spell, before he has me, a prisoner on the palm of his hand which is now as big as a Turkey carpet. He purses his blue lips and blows me from him on a gust of breath.

I wake safe in my Treasury. The outlandish flowers with which the maids garlanded me are still about my neck, fresh as dew. By this, I know I have been in an Otherworld.

I shall not admit 'I am afraid,' although the blue god gave me good cause to tremble and shake at the knees. A heathen god, powerful. As great, possibly, as Urthamma.

But – by that fine fire-dwelling fellow! – this world of Parados's is a wonder and a gateway to others – so I may yet find a road to Malthassa and Helen; and when I reach her I will put this garland about her neck, kiss her and bring her back through the splendours of the garden of the gods to our chosen path, a-roaming with the gypsies until it is time to claim Parados's goods and inheritance.

Helen has been gone too long. I admit anxiety, nay, jealousy of the unknown wherever she is, of those she has met or spoken to, exchanged a smile with or, by the black hound Despair, invited to her bed and body. Let me open the journal; find, many pages back, this verse,

> For thou wert of the sunless day,
> The heavy fields of scentless asphodel,
> The loveless lips with which men kiss in Hell.

Parados must have learned, or written this. I did not. I believe it is a tribute to Helen and know I am afraid, not now of Urthamma nor the blue god and his crew, for I have mortal longings greater than my spiritual. I dread to lose Helen and, setting aside those resolutions and questions I should address of pilgrimage and curiosity, pose the terrible query once more:

What if Helen, loving me who am the same in body and looks as Parados was, should tire?

Think, Koschei. Reason it out! She loved me in my own body, passionately, ecstatically among the rocks and stars between our worlds, in the fallow sky-fields where we lay together. That body's gone, lost to me and ruined like my city and my castle. She loved me for my wit and abilities and these remain, residing in a better case, this fine, fit body Parados abandoned. Further? Then this: I could as easily get another body, one which she'd find novel, entertaining – that of a boy, Chab say; that of strange Ravana; of an ape, a toad, a dog, a demon.

I forget! She's mistress of all bedroom arts, of each descending step of debauchery. Has she left me to seek a younger lover?

So, snap the journal shut, return it to its place, perambulate, pace up and down. Here, beside Cyllene's statue, is the portrait of the Ima woman – changed by all that's ensorcelled and mutable! so she is neither the chaste princess of the Plains nor the dirty shaman I saw in the prism but a living, breathing woman who leans forward, still in rags to be sure, *but so infused with the light of love as to be positively desirable – who leans towards me and stares from Eros-enchanted eyes. And I stretch forth my hands to take hers, so life-like is she – I want to touch her youthfulness. The paint is hard and ridged against my fingertips.*

After these sad discussions with myself and with the new portrait, I must leave the little building and its garden for the camp. Its noise is welcome: I come to better thoughts, eat well on biscuit and doves spiced with the condiments of this land, hot peppers, cumin seed and fenugreek, drink sour buffalo milk and so to my bed, restored in body and spirit both. Nemione, beside me, as the night grows deeper, is a most fit substitute for Helen. In the haunted hours I wake alert and enervated, exhausted yet afire, athirst for new knowledge and experience. There is my draught, in the carafe. I take a long drink of Ravana's preparation, tasting each spice and each drug as I come upon it in the suspension: nutmeg, mace and cinnamon, zerumbet, zedoary and cassumunar, red Arcadian wine.

Then come ye sprites of the abyss, pluck out my body-hair, pinch me, prick me with your red-hot irons; bring me at last to Her who with nails of ice and acid spittle will tear me and devour, beginning at my tongue. I feel her volcanic breath . . . I drown in the fathomless pit where, an intruder! I perceive a small figure dance towards me. Nixie, nivasha, demon? It is my bed-companion of old, Friendship, she of the ebony tresses and light feet. She prances, mocking, hiding herself behind an old chequered blanket and I reach for her, throwing aside the blanket, fastening my hands about her neck and pushing her face into the pillows as once I would in amorous play. For she is falling with me.

Gry rose late and guilty, thinking of the Red Horse abandoned in the locked stable, of Darklis talking with her own folk, of the noontime sunlight and a missed morning; then, forgetting all of these, of Him, of Aurel who had fallen from the sky and who was now, she must suppose, asleep in the embrace of his (there was no denying it) beautiful lady. She washed herself with care and tried to tidy up her rags. Her hair, that was impossible to change but, while she stared in the mirror over the washstand, seemed well enough in its weird, wild style.

The stairs were broad, uncarpeted, with carved banisters and a shiny rail. At the turning of the stair she leaned on it, looking down. No sound rose to meet her but the ticking of the grandfather clock as it marked the wayward Malthassan time, no sound from above but – a foot on the stair, descending. Aurel swung boylike round the newel-post and saw her. His sword was buckled to his belt and he carried the torn silver flag which was his badge of courage and her chequered blanket. He blushed as he handed it to her.

'Thank you,' said Gry, 'I think it is late.'

'I think it is after noon. I am hungry!'

'I hope you slept well – and Friendship?'

'I slept. Friendship, very likely, dances still among the ashes and the cold fire-coals. She is used to the night. I am a day-bird. No owl, me, but a lark or, better, a fighting-cock.'

He came down two steps to the turn and stood beside her.

'Why do you wear snails in your hair?'

'Because I am –' She laughed. 'The leshi put them there.'

'You are far from the Plains. I guess that many miles and great adventures brought you here?'

'Yes – and the Red Horse. I must let him out of the stable – goodbye!'

His presence made her nervous and she began to run down the stairs.

'Wait!' he called after her. 'Let me come with you –'

The stable was hot and full of the sweet sleep-inducing smells of hay and fresh dung, of ancient dust and neatsfoot oil. The Horse himself was sleepy but butted Gry gently with his nose while Aurel looked on and, astounded, could do nothing but admire the huge, red stallion and the easy way the slender Ima woman commanded him. He stretched his own hand tentatively toward the Horse, who snorted and rolled his eyes to the whites. Aurel drew back his hand.

Though there was no outward sign, the Horse was deep in conversation with Gry.

'I thought you had forgotten me,' he teased. 'I thought you had given me to Switman to cart his barrels to and fro. I've spent a quiet night but I heard you carousing until daybreak. And, before that, a honeyed tenor sang in the garden. Darklis came in at starset, she and – but you will discover . . . Who is he, the parfit gentil knight – the man beside you, sweetest Gry?'

'That's Aurel.'

'Aurel!' the Horse exclaimed, and she felt him tremble.

'Yes. Aurel Wayfarer. He was Parados's man once – he came to Wathen in the night – but I shall tell you as we journey, for we are leaving today, aren't we, dear Horse? My thumbs itch and I long to be on the road. I shall not find my father here.'

Aurel, watching still, interrupted. It seemed to him that the girl had fallen asleep with her head against that of her horse, so he spoke quietly.

'Where are you going with your great horse, Gry? Where have you been?'

'That's a story which takes many hours' telling and is not ended yet,' she said. 'Nor do I know which road to take except that I must cross the Altaish.'

'It's possible,' he said. 'I have done it, but in a balloon. It would take a brave horse to climb that high.'

'The Red Horse is the bravest of all.'

'I don't doubt it. But to go alone –'

'I have travelling companions – the Horse and Darklis Faa. She is formidable and a witch besides.'

'Who takes my name in vain?' The straw of the adjacent stall rustled and Darklis rose up out of it, picking the straws from her hair as she came. 'Well!' She clapped her hands in mock-applause. 'Is this your newest fancy-man, gorgio rawnie? I thought that scoundrel Lovelace would capture your heart; but he's all bravado and sugar stick. This one, I can see, has a true heart beneath his ruffles; but your breeches are devastating, sir, quite the killing mode.'

Aurel, whose face reflected his astonishment, bowed with a Pargur flourish and returned the gypsy's greeting in kind.

'How else would a navigator dress, madam? Did you expect wings and a halo?'

'O, I saw you fall to earth, sir, you and your pretty doxy; and heard her tell her tale. I'm Darklis Faa, Sir Balloon-master, and any man or beast who threatens Gry here must answer first to me. I am her travelling companion and lady protector. I can snap my fingers and – look you! – daggers fly. So mind me before you go a-courting.'

She ducked and so did Aurel as a small cloud of silvery rain, which might have been daggers or could have been an illusion, fell into the straw. Gry took hold of Darklis's arm and shook it.

'Don't confuse him, Darklis, please. He has come to view the Horse. He is a knight of Pargur.'

'I know what he is. He is famous – but you, little horse-herder, would not know it, benighted in your vasty Plains. What do you now, sir? What else, after your spectacular entrance, can you do to terrify us?'

Aurel's eyes ceased their dance of amazement and the fierce gaze succeeded it.

'My Lady Friendship and I are searching for the Castle of Truth.'

'Truth, hey? That's a scarce commodity. I think you search after a mirage or an old tale half forgot. How goes the old ditty? – I have it!

'"And let me set free, with the sword of my youth,
From the castle of darkness the power of the truth."

'I trust 'tis not a dark castle you will storm, Aurel Wayfarer, you and your little lady, but one built out of golden stone, a fair fortress whose towers are topped with blue – which, I dare wager on it, is a description of Lilith's Castle where you and I, dear sister, are bound.'

A second gypsy-woman rose up in the straw, old and grey like

Darklis, and as deep-bosomed as the figure of Justice. Her bodice was scarlet spotted white, low-necked and edged with black lace, more of which she wore in her hair, anchored there with a tall diamanté-encrusted comb. She had been sleeping with her pony, it seemed, which still lay there in the straw, the head out of sight and the dapple-grey barrel of the body twitching comfortably. The gypsy-woman leaned on her beringed hands and first there rose her spotted trunk and then a pony's shoulders, dappled grey and enfolded in a flounced skirt of canary yellow, its forelegs, body, legs and swishing tail.

'By the Dark Lord!' Aurel exclaimed, stepping back. The Red Horse neighed loudly and the sound was like laughter.

'By Darklis Faa!' the gypsy centaur corrected him. Darklis herself curtseyed and said, 'My royal sister, Duchess of the Wildwood and Countess of the Moors, Lurania Faa!'

'Drinking All Nations, that's what did it,' Lurania complained. 'The dregs of all the bottles Nathan threw into the yard, dark rum, fine cognac, Hollands, white Caucasus spirit, bog-fire, sulphur-water, applejack, Zubrowka; and Strega in particular. A cocktail to take the head off anyone, flesh, fowl or fiend. Never make magic, sister, when you are in your cups.'

'You're fair enough, Lurania, until I get my witching strength back. At least you have good legs.'

'And my old, blind eyes. Why could you not give me the pony's head and sight and my own shanks and trotters, if you must make such mischief. You'll have to lead me.'

'I had to lead you before, or you would have run off when we met Bonasus. Look on the bright side, Lurania. You have your tongue and a ferocious instrument it is. You'll scare any scum or bug-a-boos we meet, on our way to the castle – 'tis time and more to choose a new King, for it's many a long day since my Towla was put to bed with a shovel.'

'I did not know that you too, Darklis, were a treasure-seeker,' said Gry.

'It does not do to hear everything, all at once. Yes, your dear father is your precious jewel and Lilith's Castle, which some call the gypsy fortress, is mine. Though neither Lurania nor I know where it lies except that it is built on high –'

'Our soothsayers tell us an enchantress lives there, she who is our immortal queen,' Lurania said, 'but that may be just another story.'

'Hyperion spoke of the place,' Gry marvelled. 'He described it, just as you have done – gold and blue.'

'May this be also the Castle of Truth?' Aurel asked. 'Like you, I know of it but know nothing of it. I should like to find it for I might then understand what gods guard Malthassa and how evil may be rooted out and destroyed.'

'Easily!' Colley's voice burst in amongst them. 'Simply! By the expulsion of all tricksters, vagabonds and boasting caitiffs like yourselves from Wathen – O, I have been ruined and deceived! Murder in my own house that was so clean and cheery. See!'

He strode into the stable, and they all turned to him and saw his frowning brows and ruddy face inflamed with ire; and Nathan at his shoulder carrying the limp and lifeless body of Friendship whose long tresses hung to his feet and were flecked with snow. Aurel sprang forward to take her from the tapster and to mourn, to discover the cause of her death; but Nathan forbade him with an angry look and held the corpse closer.

'Such a pretty thing, so bright and lively,' he said. 'So dead and cold. You gentlemen have hearts of flint. I saw you eyeing your new love last night; drowning in each other's looks you were. Every man knows what that means – and here you are in the stable where there's hay and straw enough to bed a dozen harlots. You didn't need to kill her –'

'Now Nat,' said Colley. 'She's been stifled, Sir Lace-and-Leather, by a pillow held in powerful hands. I don't want to know the rights or wrongs of it but I want you out of my tavern and off my land. Far from the village too, before night falls. If you're not on the road in two shakes of a donkey's tail, I shall set the dogs on you, ay, and call out the men to raise a hue and cry. There's plenty still here who are champions at the Murtherball.'

'Let me speak,' Aurel demanded.

203

'No,' said Colley. 'There can be no excuses.'

'But let me bury her! She was my love.'

'You've another now. I'll bury the dancer, I, the sexton and the priest, in our boneyard. She shall have the proper rite and a headstone afterwards. "Friendship" it will say, "who died believing her friends were true." By Hokey! What is that?' He raised a trembling hand and pointed at Lurania. 'Witchcraft! I am proved right and was so wrong to trust you, Darklis Faa. You've been a-conjuring devils in my stables.'

''Tis my sister, fool.'

'Then she is the sister of Old Nick, a creature the Dark Lord himself would be proud to own. Away with her! Away with you all!'

He turned on his heel and out of the stable, Nathan following with his sad burden. It was the last Aurel or any of them saw of Friendship, and Aurel collapsed in the straw and wept.

There was nothing for Gry to do but climb on to the back of the Horse and wait while the gypsies fussed about their goods. The hens had all flown up into the rafters and could not be coaxed down so Darklis, cursing, was forced to leave them where they were and to leave her precious chattels, the stools, the teapot, the mugs, the frying pan and the wonderful bender. All she had time to gather up was a shawl-load of bread, apples, cheese and cold pork, to which she'd helped herself about the village, and her carving knife. Lurania snatched up some horse blankets and draped them across her back.

Aurel, recovering himself, stood up pale of face and perforce allied himself with this strange crowd of vagabonds. He held one end of Lurania's white stick and led her from the stable. Darklis followed him and Gry and the Horse came last. In their pound, the mastiffs were already snarling, encouraged by the kitchen boy and the fresh, red meat he had thrown them. The kitchen boy caught the falling snowflakes in his mouth and tasted them. He held out his hands and when they were full of snow, moulded it round a stone and hurled his snowball at the nearest dog.

* * *

Peace, after the storm of anguish and betrayal, grief and expulsion, filled the stable. Colley's horses munched their hay and twitched their silken skins whenever a fly landed. The mice skittered over the beams and down the walls, in search of fallen grains, and the white owl which roosted on the biggest tie-beam snored and twitched, and tucked her head more firmly under her wing. In the darkest corner, something moved, a rustle, a sigh. Sib crouched there, grey eyes wild, long hands nervously scratching. Her shadow-blue dress had slipped from her shoulders and hung down as if it were in truth a shadow and she hiding in it. Her shoulders were bony and her eye sockets deep as wells. She had not taken her cream that day and, without its fatty goodness, was fading from the bright and decent world of Wathen Fields into her true place, the underworld of the sharivile, where she was Lord Yama's dark-lantern bearer, the servant of a grim master. She hitched up her dress and padded out across the snowy yard, flitted suddenly into the rose-garden where the coloured petals fell as fast as the snow and, turning and twisting in the blast, held up her arms and was whirled into the storm.

The snow, which had begun before they crossed the yard, was falling in thick white flakes as they rounded the corner of the inn and took the road for Lythabridge. No one came out to see them go; indeed, the curtains in every house-window were drawn. The village mourned.

The road stretched long and wide before them but already the snow was changing it, making bars of black and white as it fell into the ruts. The bright yellow light had vanished and its place was taken by an eerie snow-light as faint as hope. The travellers hurried on, their prints soon obliterated by the dancing flakes. Soon, they too had vanished, and all the fields and gardens were white and soundless for the birds had stopped singing and the village dogs gone into their kennels away from the storm; the poleviks, surprised as they went about their business of tending the ripening crops, were no more to be seen, every one of them in winter quarters deep in the hollows of the trees. Only, from afar, as if he too had begun a wandering, winter journey in the bitter weather, came the thin, disjointed sound of the hurdy-gurdy player churning out his melancholy notes.

A blue-grey haze blew across the travellers' path and stood up in their way. It was Sib, her dress rent and billowing so that her pale limbs were hardly visible against the snow. She held up her hands and the Red Horse halted. Gry leaned down.

'Sib! What do you here? Go home!'

'Home is behind me, in the past. I cannot return, for Colley will release the mastiffs soon, to be sure that you have flown.'

'But where will you go?'

'Never mind me. But heed my instructions and remember that you must cross the Altaish to find your father. Then walk to the ocean shore. That is the only way for a living person to see the souls of the dead. Go by Striving Pass!'

'Sib – come with us –' Gry reached down to help her up to the Horse's back, but Sib, despair and longing in her great grey eyes, only stood in the snow with her arms above her head. A gust of wind caught her and, with a flourish of her disintegrating dress, she was blown away.

Aurel, who had watched silently, shouldered his flagstaff and shook the snow from his shoulders. He looked up and his eyes met Gry's. Darklis pulled the blankets from Lurania's back and distributed them, one each, thick cloths of dull brown which smelled of horses and were heavy to wear. The hurdy-gurdy music had stopped. They heard Colley Switman's dogs baying.

'They are yet in their pound,' said Aurel. 'I do not think he will release them until dark, but let us make haste and cross the Lytha.'

Another waited to have words with them in Lythabridge where, past the church and past the chapel, across the Green and along High Street, a single arch of stone spans the River Lytha. It was here that Darklis had tricked Erchon the Silver Dwarf and tipped him into the river to go about her errands as a water-drop; in this village too that Lurania had enjoyed an afternoon of trickery and gaming with the men of her tribe, for Lythabridge was a favourite camping-ground of the Faas. The pickings were good and the folk gullible. So thought Hyperion Lovelace, as he waited at the bridge, the snow building up in layers on his hat until it resembled a giant mushroom and his red-eared gazehound waiting patiently by his side.

He saw them coming, blanketed and bowed, dark brown shadows looming amidst the falling flakes. His heart swelled, for he dearly desired the Ima woman, and he knocked his hat against the bridge to rid it of the snow, replaced it and licked his lips. When he saw who walked beside the great Horse, the fair-haired knight, he scowled but he composed his features and called out.

'Ho there! Will you toss me more of your largesse, Darklis Faa?'

Gry shivered though she was warm enough and, looking down on Aurel's head and the pricked ears of the Red Horse, was glad she had such protectors.

Hyperion Lovelace, before Darklis could reply to his taunt, had burst out laughing at the sight of Lurania half-transformed.

'Well done, very well done chov-hani! That is a fine punishment for sisterly jealousies – I saw Lurania cheat you of tuppence at the Fair.'

Darklis affected to ignore him and swept on, snatching the white stick from Aurel's grasp and leading her sister on to the bridge. Gry, learning fast, did likewise and rode on without looking at the gypsy man, who cried out, 'Farewell then, mistress High-and-Mighty, too high for me (though I love you) and mighty disdainful this cold evening.'

Aurel, who had met such cattle as this insolent gypsy many times in Pargur and who remembered him from the night before, halted with his sword-hand ready at the pommel and a frown on his face. The gypsy put up his fingers in mock-salute.

'Good day, Sir Soldier – or Sir Vagabond, as you are become, run so roughly out of town. You and I are brothers now, of the road and the empty heath.'

'Good day to you,' said Aurel and thought to himself, If this is all, he deserves nothing but our contempt; but he surely wants something of us, gold coin or some other gift. Maybe it's a good thing I carry only paper money in my wallet. And, sure enough, the gypsy was fumbling in one of his poacher's pockets – looking for a trinket to sell, no doubt.

Hyperion drew out a small, painted bowl, a cheap thing such as pedlars sell at cottage doors.

'Is that your begging bowl?' Aurel said scornfully.

'No, sir. This is a pretty thing for a pretty lady. I want you to take it and, when occasion presents, to give it to the lady there who rides her high horse so gaily. Say 'tis a gift without strings but, haply, it may remind her of the gypsy rover who tried so hard to win her. And say, sir, that were things otherwise I should be blithe to show her the greenwood and our wandering, gypsy ways. That, you may do after your fashion. You and she have been thrown together by the fates who order this cruel world.'

Aurel took the bowl from him and turned it over in his hands. It seemed an artless enough gift with its bright bands of colour, and what the gypsy said was fair enough.

'Very well,' he said. 'I will give it her by and by. But I shall give you nothing for, by your vaunting words, you are my rival.'

Hyperion grinned in a rapacious fashion and his eyes which, thought Aurel, were like nothing more or less than those of a snake which compels its victim to be still and be bitten, grew large and luminous.

'Yes,' the gypsy said. 'We are rivals.'

He gave his insolent salute again and stood aside for Aurel to cross the bridge. Gry and the gypsies were almost invisible, halfway across. He hurried to catch them and, as he ran, tucked the bowl into the neck of his shirt. Beyond the bridge the land mounted up and it was, as far as he could tell, exactly what the gypsy had described, a gaunt waste of heathland in which the ling bushes were blackening with cold and the thorn trees already sere and bent. They started across it, looking to left and right for a hollow or dell in which to pass the night.

In Wathen Fields the snow lay deep and even, choking the green plants to death beneath its smothering blanket, causing the apple trees to miscarry their fruit. Colley, in the last drop of daylight, went to loose his dogs. Their howls echoed across the village and its townlands for a long time, scarcely more desolate and forlorn than Colley's voice, as he went from room to room in the inn, then from barn to hovel and through the garden and the snowy closes, calling 'Sib! Sib! Wife, where are you?'

Night fell apace and still Colley wandered, calling for his love. His breeches were wet to the thigh where the snow had clung and been melted in his body-heat, his boots were caked with frozen clods of ice. In Last Close where the Forest loomed darkly over the hedge, he stared at the massed trees and felt hot tears form in his eyes and, while he wondered if Sib had run away with the leshi, gush down his cheeks. The stillness was that sort which happens when the snow ceases to fall and the world is turned upside down by a perilous beauty. Colley looked up at the stars. The gigantic Cuckoo Star, which the poor little dancer had called Custos, rode high, over Lythaside where the Altaish loomed. He turned about, lost in the world of the stars, his tears drying. There, by the constellation of the Crane, was something moving, flying hard – geese perhaps, startled from their nesting grounds by the change in the weather; a second balloon carrying, for all the tall tales of the flamboyant pair, the deadly envoys of Koschei? It came lower and Colley, horror-struck, descried a long and frightful shape, a headless horse of bone which galloped over thin air. A wild figure sat astride it and clutched its jagged neck bones. The horse began to descend in a spiral and Colley, stumbling forward in the snow, saw that it would land in the yard of the inn. His heart pounded with fear and he lumbered into a wading run wishing, all the while, that he carried a sword.

He was in time to see the flying horse land by his door. It was neither brazen automaton nor winged Pegasus but kin to that the Fourth Horseman rides, he who brings Death. As soon as its hoofs hit the snow, it broke apart into a scatter of separate bones and its rider leapt clear and began to gather the bones into a lidded basket. He whispered spells and cackled to himself as he worked, bent double, and the drum he wore at his back slid up his neck like the shell of an ancient tortoise. Colley stood awe-struck and did not know what to say.

The wizard spoke, but never looked at him.

'It's Colley Switman standing there, little Tarpan. I shall take food and drink from him this bitter night, and go to the graveyard too. I smell death here, sweet annihilation, delicious violation. Do not tremble, Master Innkeeper, but bring me into your warm house and give me some of the strong drink my poor old body craves. I am not the Archmage Koschei, silly fellow, I am Aza from the Plains.'

Colley croaked and eventually spoke, though all he could say was, 'Indeed, sir. Be my guest!'

'Pah!' The shaman spat, a yellow spume of phlegm which lay like desecration on the pure, snow-white ground. 'Yours is an incorruptible soul. You make mistakes, Sir Ale-seller, but you are honest. Tell me now, have you seen aught of a woman of my people, a comely little body, Gry by name? She rides upon a sorrel-coloured horse, no ordinary horse you understand, but a great red stallion.'

As the shaman spoke the church bell began to toll for Friendship's funeral and he stood straighter, listening to its single 'boooom!', sniffed a hanging thread of rheum back into his nose and said.

'Let us go first to the rites. I know Death well. He is my friend and protector and it is my calling and task to speak with the dead and the spirits which dwell between this world and the Dark Lord's dominions. I will have words with the corpse before you pile the cold earth over her.'

The broken part of my pen being cut away and a new nib fashioned, I can write this only, 'the story continues,' before I must see to my own, collapse the Treasury, pack up my traps and load my wagon; move on. We are bound for Suleiman's Mountains and the pass of Balkiss, where the wind can cleanse lepers of their sores and the pox-demented of their pustulences. Thence, by Khash and Lash, avoiding Goktepp, its

210

cemeteries where djinns dance by night, and its towers of ill-omen, we shall come at last to the Sea of the Magi – which is a jewel in a barren country like our Septrential Ocean in the YenZu Waste. There, we may rest in safety for we are to take ship for the North and so lose ourselves from spying, scrying eyes amongst the valleys of Little Horde.

This Geography I have from Ravana and so I may depend upon it.

The Dom gypsies love best to travel by the byways which pass through pleasant country where food may be begged or stolen; yet, to avoid baleful magic or a hue and cry at need (as when we crossed the desert) will climb into wild country – and such are Suleiman's Mountains and the Nimbeluk which hang lowering above the gravelly shores of that emerald, inland sea where we are to find peace; but, Ravana says, even these mighty mountains have trackways and passes and our oxen are strong; and, Ravana instructs, the wheels are to be removed from our ox-carts, the carts dismantled into their separate parts and all piled upon the patient oxen. Only thus, can we ascend into the highest places.

To be a bird, to fly like the swallow, to soar as the eagle, o'ertopping these tiresome mountains! To exercise my talents magickal, alchymical – patience, Koschei, for fame and its bays and palms shall come, even here! Therefore, onward Body, climbing higher; upward aspiring Spirit!

My wagon, the last time

'Sweetest Honeysuckle! Nemione, Queen of Pleasure, Fount of Desire – wake now and walk, for you can no longer slumber in this wheeled bed. Rise up, Most Fair, stand firm and show your beauty to my wondering companions.'

Thus did I exhort her who once was nimble as a Forest deer and could dance like a wave of the Ocean and fence as nimbly as a sunbeam over silk. Nemione opened her eyes, the sapphires shone, and lo! she stood swaying like one recovered from a long illness, leaned on my arm. I led her outside and let the gypsies see her. One by one they came close to touch this wondrous woman of mine and, 'By Lilith our great Rawnie!' said Laxmi, 'Let her come and sit at my fire and she shall have rose lokum of Byzantium to eat and female talk.'

'She is tired,' I replied, stroking Nemione's pale cheek, mindful of her lack of original conversation. A tear as black as a drop of ink fell from the corner of her left eye which, coursing down her cheek,

211

left dirty marks like the blots with which I sullied the page when my pen broke.

'You have wearied her with your lust, Koschei,' said Laxmi, put up her veil and turned away. Jasper and some of the other Rom came hurrying to dismember my wagon.

Under the Stars

I sat beyond the high peaks' shadow and listened to the night and the whistling wind, so strong of voice I could hear neither wolf or malevolent ghoul out hunting; then, more perilously, looked into my mind where I found turmoil, frantic heartbeats and laboured breathing which, as the world faded, grew still. Here, at its centre, is a black pool. Is this myself, a reservoir of darkness?

Purged with figs and heavy oils, rested, fed – on plain pancakes and fermented ox-milk – I turned to Nemione who opened her ever-heavy eyes and blinked as slowly as if she had been practising the Disciplines of India and had achieved inner harmony. I touched her: the skin felt like paper and I turned away. Her hair has lost its lustre, her lips their roseate tint, her smile its readiness. I lay and slept where I had meditated, under the countless eyes of Night.

A Rock in the Wilderness

Goktepp safely passed, midday. The gypsies sleep, I watch and wake. No sign of any being, animal or supernatural, which might be a peri in borrowed clothing. Before he slept Ravana warned me to look nearby and afar. Since his slumber is heavy (I see his hennaed feet; the rest is hidden by this rock) I conclude there is no need of special care and, tilting back my head, stare up at the silent, spiralling kites which wait in the heavens for us to take our next refreshment when they will descend to snatch whatever bone or crust they can. They feed on corpses otherwise. Protect me, oh birds of death!

A Rock by the Wayside. Many days later

When I went to our bed, now spread upon the ground under a rude awning, I thought to find Nemione and comfort myself. Nemione, thin and hollow-eyed, her breath gone sour and her eyes lustreless, but still a woman. I found NOTHING OF HER, not a shed hair, a forgotten earring, a dropped scarf, a sigh left on the air. Only except this, which I copy here, the two words writ in kohl on a sheet torn from a book: KEEP FAITH.

Nemione, gone of her own volition (but where?) or torn from me by Helen's sorcery, has left me a message from our youth. Once, on a time, we were brother-and-sister in belief, co-religionists, until I went my way and she hers. The chief law of our cloister was that instruction, Keep Faith. She and I both deserted that rule; what means she now? That she will return to me, remembers me, cherishes the memory?

Lackwit! It is a message from Helen herself. Nemione was her avatar, no more. My Lady says I must desert neither her nor my memory of her. So onward, upward, with renewed energy. In time, she and I will love again. Be damned then to these foreign gods with their blue skins and impossible dicta. I, Koschei, am sufficient in myself.

I turned the paper over. There was printer's work on it, some lines of verse, which I read:

> She was a Goddess of the infant world;
> By her in stature the tall Amazon
> Had stood a pigmy's height: she would have ta'en
> Achilles by the hair and bent his neck . . .

I recognised them, and the page. It had come from an old, green-covered book which lies, amongst many, in my Memory Palace. How came it here, so far, such legions of thought away? I threw it down, I know not where, and ran from the cursed pillows and their hollow luxury.

Then I raved like a young buck who has lost his lady-love and his last game of dice and does not know which is the greater disappointment. I ran among the rocks and made them ring louder than all the bells in Pargur with my pistol-shots. Ravana and the women came running; Jasper cursed me. I shall fetch the bandits, say they, the dreaded thuggees. Or else the soldiers.

I should welcome diversion, some valid action to remind me that I am a man.

They were soldiers who came, not instantly, for they were but mortal men without skills arcane or chymical, but within a day. Heralded by drums and trumpets, they came marching – a brave company – down the track up which we toiled. The gypsies yelled greetings in their own

213

language, greetings which in truth were curses; but Ravana spoke out in the language of Parados, if his simpering can be called speech.

'Ai, fine gentlemen!' he said, and clapped his hands. 'Slay me, bold Rifles! O, for a fine boy such as you, sir, or you my darling!' as the regiment went by in a long, trailing column, officers on horseback herding the men. Every one of them was sweating, dusty, ruddy-faced; armed with rifle and bayonet, heralded by a red and white flag and a fine standard of red, white and blue. Manly, glorious, victorious – those are all the things they were. An officer reined in his horse to stare at me and, when I saluted him and gave him good-day in the gypsy tongue, bared even teeth under a crisp moustache and rode on. A drummer came last, all alone, so hot and red he looked ready to combust, or expire. Yet he beat on his drum which, like a porter's load in a market, seemed to bear him down with such force he must use all his strength to keep it in its rightful place upon his chest. As he came closer I saw that the drum was fixed there with leather straps and that it was so fine and precious an instrument that it had its own carpet, or bed, the silver-grey fur of some predatory animal – which, doubtless, this brave drummer had killed. When he was level with me, the even steps of this drummer faltered, he swayed upon his booted feet, and fell to the ground. His drumsticks went to left and right as the gypsy men ran up and dragged him behind a rock. The moustachioed officer at the tail of the column gave neither sign nor signal of anything amiss and continued on his way, his scarlet-coated back and the round rump of his horse diminishing in the distance.

I called the boy, Chab, to me.

'What men are those?' I asked him.

'Those who rule this country, Master Koschei. The English.'

'How can that be?'

'The English have conquered many lands and this is one of them. Their own country is many months distant.'

'Do you mean Albion?'

'Ay, some call it that, poets and such. It is usually dubbed England or Great Britain.'

'And what year is it? – for I suppose these English number their years which roll one after another as regularly as waves of the sea.'

'Eighteen-sixty-eight, Master. That is, the thirty-first year of their Queen, Victoria, who is Empress here.'

'A woman rules those men!'

'They say she is harder than any man, if she exists. Jasper says she must be a man in woman's dress, like Ravana, for soldiers, he says, would not obey a woman.'

'I know a woman who – but thank you, Chab.' and I dismissed him.

Eighteen-sixty-eight! I had thought myself in a newer world, peopled by men like Guy Parados, full of marvellous flying engines, invincible weaponry and fast, red cars in which a body may drive where'er he list, from the icy North as far as the snow-girt South. I had thought to take ship and sail to Parados's country but . . . adrift by some hundred and forty years! How we had wandered, my Helen and I, not only through the arid regions and the mountainous, the populated and the empty, but backward through a century and a half. I called Chab again, who came with impatient air. I had interrupted his dinner.

'But do the English live here always?' I asked.

'Many do, or else how would they keep the people in order?' he answered.

'Very good, child. I suppose those soldiers on the road were hastening because of some rebellion?'

'They are always marching, Master Koschei. To and fro, up and down. A little like us, except that they journey with coercion and death of opposition in mind.'

'That is a fine exposition for a boy of nine!'

'Ten, Master.' I gave him a whole anna, the kind with a hole right through it. He would not spend it, I knew, but give it to his mother to hang on her breast.

Guy Parados is English, I thought. Here are his grandfather's fathers adventuring far from their native greenwood for, in truth, Helen had told me that the fair country of Albion was afforested, but with beech trees and oaks which stand at apart from another in groves and make, instead of dense, impassable forest, pleasant parklands where ladies and gentlemen may stroll. Then, bethinking myself of the here and not of the far-off, I went behind the rock to see how my brave gypsy lads did.

The drummer they had stripped naked; he was at his last gasp, dying of the midday heat and his exhaustion. The men were dicing for his clothing, his drum, and his money. Jasper beckoned me.

'Well, we have got one of them,' he said. 'That,' he gestured at the dying man, and snapped his own fingers together, 'is all his countrymen care. So eager are they to get to their next engagement, they have not noticed their loss.'

'You have gained by it,' I said.

'Ay. Look, Master. We have set this aside for you, or for the Lady when she returns.' The old man reached out and pulled the skin upon which the drum had been cushioned to him. 'Tis fur of the best quality, wolfskin, I reckon; though Raga says it is fox.'

The fur was soft and I ran my hands across it, distracted by its silken texture. Then, seeing some papers rolling about in the breeze which, in the mountains, always sprang up after noon to refresh those wearied by the morning's heat, I retrieved them. The gypsies had all but destroyed them with their greasy fingers and carelessness. The first sheet, which I dropped immediately, one had used to wipe his fundament and, of the printing on the rest, all I could decipher was '21st Empress of India's Foot' – and, further on, 'Sgt. G. K. Young' – the drummer's name, perhaps. I went back to the fur and sat down on it, to try if it would answer as a saddle, if ever I found a horse, or as a cushion to spread on the rocks when I meditated (but such luxury is forbidden in that hard discipline). I fell to thinking of Parados again; which was not strange for, while I thought, I scratched my arm with his fingers and wiped the sweat from my face with the back of his hand.

Mayhap I shall spread this fine fur on your broad back, Red Horse, I said to myself, and pictured the scene.

My animadversions were rudely interrupted: I had indeed attracted bandits, or else the soldiers had or the gypsies themselves. Already, the gypsies were repelling them with shouts and with their primitive weaponry, mostly old and blunted swords and, their true speciality, long daggers fashioned from discarded bayonets. I fired my great howdah pistol in the air and felt my body shake with the recoil; the very ground rocked. The next moment, as I broke the pistol to reload it and Ravana, saree tucked up, came running toward me, the grey fur I was sitting

216

on rose with me into the air, fast, high, higher – and I was flying, O ye Gods of Malthassa and the Underworld! Magic at last, my familiar, my saviour.

The Red Horse plodded steadily up the track. He was tired, had been since they crossed Lythabridge, and he thought longingly of the stable at Wathen Fields and of the oats he had enjoyed there. Many other thoughts crowded in his mind but he pushed them aside to concentrate on the climb. Gry was not heavy, nor would he disturb her, but he needed to pause more often in the ascent than once he would have done.

Aurel walked more swiftly than the Horse, outpacing him so frequently he played lookout and scout. Sometimes he found himself so far ahead he was able to lie down upon a dry patch by the wayside and enjoy the sunshine, while his eyes were busily at watch and his mind ranged far and wide.

The snow, under the sun's fierce onslaught, was melting fast and water rushed in the runnel beside the road. All the streams they'd crossed had been high, lapping the parapets of the bridges. It felt like a day at home in SanZu, himself a laughing boy with his old white dog at heel; or, better, like a late winter's day, the kind when you sense spring flowers about to emerge from the earth, when greyness has fled the sky and the birds are strutting and singing for the first time.

He knew this was not so and did not want to dwell on it; nor did he want to think too deeply about the road, a substantial earthen track leading upward all the while – but where to? Instead, he thought about the gypsy's offering, the bowl, which, wanting a fairer place to show it than those they had been camped in since leaving Lythabridge, he had not yet given Gry. It was a poor thing, battered and dented by being, he supposed, used as cup, soup-bowl, saucepan and shaving-mug; but pretty enough. He felt to make sure it was still inside his shirt – yes, warm from contact with his body. But why was Gry to have it? A disappointed lover is not usually generous. And what of his own love, scarce born before being brutally killed? He frowned as he tried to picture Friendship

217

and found he could not. He could rebuild her image, certainly: red slippers, garments lightly moving as she walked, the glitter-shot ribbon about her hair and the hair itself, dead black like Gry's but so long – how long? Gry's was shoulder-length, all loose so far down and ending in those curious snail-bedecked plaits. He should like to untie them and see her brush – but that was Friendship's hair in his mind. He could not reconstruct her face.

The Ima woman's face was broad across the cheekbones, narrow at the chin. She smiled often (like Friendship), but there was wisdom and endurance in her smile besides another quality which he feared might be devotion. Here she was now, approaching on the Horse. She waved to him and he watched her smile blossom as she came nearer. The gypsies toiled behind. Darklis had taken Lurania's staff to lean on and led her sister by the hand, the human hand, while her four hooves clattered behind and the voices of them both, arguing as usual, shrilled through the air.

Yes, it felt like a day long ago, thought Aurel, a special day – not Fair Day in his hometown of Flaxberry but somewhere else. He had it! In Vonta, where horses were bought and sold, where the Ima brought their surplus horses for sale and he, sucking a strawberry lollipop, had been skipping along the street. An Ima family was coming the other way, father, mother, daughter, the females outlandish in their fantastic sky-blue clothing and silver jewellery and the man brave and fierce, almost terrifying, with his tail of greased hair, hard bare chest, belt of silver discs and the two long pieces of striped cloth, fore and aft, which were all his clothing except for a pair of tall, red boots. An enormous sword was slung across his back. Aurel's mouth, remembering him, dropped open. The parents were about his height and the girl much shorter but – pretty? beautiful? She sucked on a green lollipop but took it from her mouth as she passed by to smile at him. Then he had felt the hot and rousing sensation he knew in dreams, and had turned away to look in the window of a shop while he laughed with embarrassment.

Gry's lips were bent in the smile. He felt the same, the old

218

sensation; but now he knew what that was and blushed, because it belonged to Friendship.

Aurel stood up and approached the Horse. The beast was used to him by now and did not roll his eyes or shy. He patted the sorrel-coloured neck, surprised at the dust and dead hair which marked his hand; looked up to return at least a part of Gry's long-lasting smile.

'Were you ever in Vonta?' he asked.

'Yes, once – at the Fair,' she said. 'Why?' and then he lost his chance to question her further for Darklis shrieked so loud he feared she had seen a catamount at least, or a party of brigands, and fingered the lucky golden cockerel's feather pinned to his collar.

'Do you mean to climb to the skies?' shouted the gypsy. 'Wait there till we catch you up. My sister tires though she has four legs.'

'My sister is as weary as a she-cat that's been courting all night,' Lurania yelled.

'They will not agree,' Gry murmured. 'We had better wait. It's as warm as a midsummer day in the Plains – the grass would be yellow and the mulberries ripe enough to eat.'

'In SanZu too. Look, wood berries!' He knelt to pick them for her.

By evening they had reached high, summer pasture, and the sun went down as they crossed it, leaving a warm afterglow and a promise of heat to come. The ground was as wet underfoot as marshland but they paid little heed. A house stood beside a grove of thorn trees, a small house made of boulders from the mountainside. It had heavy shutters, a fretwork balcony and a stack of wood beside the door. Aurel holloaed but no one replied and no dogs came barking out; the chimney when he touched it was cold.

'No one at home,' he said.

'Then break in,' Darklis told him. 'We need shelter far more than you need your knightly sentiments.'

'No need. The door is open. It is the same at home on the farmsteads; no one locks their door.'

When Aurel had pushed wide the broad-planked door and the travellers had ducked under a low lintel, they saw, in a dim interior, a hearth, a meal-chest and, hanging from the ceiling, some strings of dried peppers. There were no beds but several large cushions were stacked neatly in a corner and, behind a low partition which separated the house-place from the empty cattle-stalls, a tin box which Gry opened. Finding both ground meal and whole corn at the bottom of it, she scooped some of the yellow grain into her skirt and took it out to Horse who, because of his great size and the lowness of the eaves, must stay in the open with Lurania.

'What kind of cattle are stalled here?' Aurel wondered.

'Giant fleas, my boy, monstrous lice! What else but dwarf cattle, eighteen inches high. Look at the mess on the floor – that's grit and grime fallen from them that rightly live here, Stone Dwarves.'

'But where are they?'

'At their quarrying I don't doubt. This is their summer house and pasture where they bring their kine to graze.'

'It's summer now.'

'Sometimes it is and sometimes it isn't – and you from mutable Pargur! It's my belief it isn't summer, no more than that was winter we had below.'

When the fire was lit, Gry made some flat cakes of bread out of the meal in the chest; they drank water from the spring at the back of the house.

'Tomorrow, I will hunt for game,' said Aurel.

'And I for mushrooms and berries,' said Gry. Darklis was already asleep on one of the cushions and so could make no caustic comment. Aurel put more wood upon the fire and stretched his legs to the blaze. He leaned towards Gry.

'It was you, so long ago in Vonta,' he said. She did not deny it and he closed his eyes to picture the scene once more. Hyperion Lovelace's bowl dug into his collarbone.

'I've something for you, Gry,' he said. 'Gry? You are not asleep?'

220

'Too tired to sleep,' Gry said; but she yawned. 'What can you have for me, Aurel Wayfarer, beside the helping hand you have already given me and your companionship on the way?' while, in her head, she made a franker speech, '... *beside yourself, heart, soul and body?*'

'It's this.' He offered her a tin cup on the palm of his hand; or bowl, she saw, as she took it to examine.

'The gypsy gave it me for you.'

'Why not give it me herself?'

'Not Darklis. That bold gypsy captain, Lovelace; he of the peacock's feather.'

'I don't want it, then. Take it, Aurel. You can use it as a drinking-cup.'

'He was most particular,' persisted Aurel, glad to see her refuse the gift. 'You were to have it as a keepsake without favour.'

'I fear it may be enchanted. The man was a fortune-teller. You surely know how many of the gypsy-kind have hexing knowledge and are in league with demons. Why, Darklis there is queen of them all. To enchant her own sister!'

'I will take care of the bowl for you,' and Aurel took it back and peered at its patterned surfaces. 'I never looked close before: there are flames all around the sides –'

'It is bewitched!'

'No, they are painted flames – and letters too which say, by my Pargur blade! what he and I agreed, that we are rivals –'

'For what, Aurel?'

'For – for that which all men quarrel over. Listen! It says "All's fair in love and war" and – something else – "Keep faith". What can that mean?'

'Keep the bowl, Aurel; put it out of my sight for what I say is true, there is evil in it. Perhaps we should fling it down the mountainside.'

They made their beds then, on opposite sides of the fire. Gry lay near Darklis but wondered, as she fell asleep, if she would not be safer with Aurel. Whatever was fated, tomorrow she would take care to rid herself and him of the bowl. Aurel, making sure his sword was to hand, stared into the embers of the fire and watched their scarlet fade away. As my love for Friendship has faded, he thought. It is as if some being greater than I has taken it from me. My heart no longer aches for her but . . . He slept and woke again when grey dawnlight came stealing through the smoke-hole in the roof. Gry had woken also. She smiled at him across the cold ashes of the hearth.

'I dreamed of the star,' she said. 'Of the Guardian of the Herds.'

'And I of Custos,' Aurel replied.

'It is the same, whether it guards me in the Plains or you in Pargur. And now it guards us both.' She rose and stepped over the hearth. 'I will sit by you until Darklis wakes.'

'I am glad of that.'

He laid his warm, left hand on hers, and she let it remain there.

We were whirled backward, myself and the fur, which on the earth had been of a size to cover the chest of a well-built man and which, in the air, spread itself until it was the size of a good, weatherproof cloak, but still retained its straps and the scarlet and white edging of the 21st Empress of India's Foot. I turned about and lay down, so that I could see where I was going; and beheld the mountains of Shalimar and the dry and fertile places of Kushan and Seistan unfold below, a map of the long journey Helen and I had made across Middle Asia. Hearing the cries of a bird and mindful of the shapeshifting peri which sought me, I looked about, above and below, and so saw Ravana dangling from one of the straps of my conveyance. He looked in no wise discomfited nor uncomfortable, but hung there, the strap wound about his wrist, his female garments parted by the wind and displaying his true sex. His hair was similarly disturbed and, looking down on it and about to open my mouth and hail him, I saw that where the black tresses were parted in two places, right and left, grew the short and conical horns of a demon. Stealthily therefore, I finished loading the pistol which I still gripped and fired at Ravana's hand, to shatter it and make him loose his hold. The hand opened on the impact of the shot, waved its fingers

222

about, and plummeted, finger by finger and bone by bone, while the strap it had been holding blew free in the wind. Ravana did not fall, but continued to travel forward. He looked up at me.

'Well done, Sir Mage,' he cried. 'but not well enough, by Yama!'

His hair billowed once and settled into a different shape, of tight-packed black feathers. The rest of him as I watched, not knowing whether to fire again, or try my rusty mind at Magick to be rid of him, folded in upon itself, lineaments dissolving, and became a raven.

'Kaark!' he cried, turned in the air and flew away east into the pursuing night.

Ahead, below, I now saw the rich purple glint of an evening-haunted sea; and the pelt began to descend, passing over the feeble lights of small villages and great swathes of darkness, until I saw a new set of lights arranged in a ring on the ground. Now, the fur lost height as quickly as a falling stone and, arresting itself suddenly, slowed and came gently down on solid earth. I stood up beside it, easing my cramped limbs and stowing my pistol in my belt. It was cold here and I, in my thin shulwars and slippers, bent for the fur, meaning to use it as a cloak to keep out the night. I knew it as I reached out my hand: Nemione's great fur, which she was used to wear at Sehol in the cold, trailing its grey length from her peerless, white shoulders as she walked. It felt as warm and soft as she. My hand closed on nothing. The fur was gone, vanished as if it had never existed.

'Now I am in an interesting case,' said I and went cautiously forward toward the lights which, I soon saw, were flares stuck in the ground. A single man tended them and his back was to me as he lit a fresh flare from a lantern. I ran silently to him (the ground was loose earth or sand), gripped his throat in my two hands and squeezed the life from him. It was soon done.

When I had cast the body aside, I looked about with more care. Some pavilions, or tents, stood at a distance and were lit within, softly glowing like those lamps we used at Castle Sehol to illuminate the gardens. Shadows falling on the fabric of them showed their inhabitants, tall men like myself; some had beards, one wore a wide-brimmed hat, one smoked a long cigar. For a while I watched their shadow-play and, as it unfolded, saw the conclusion: in their various tents, the men lay down to rest on low beds. One read in a book; the rest doused their lights.

By the light of the flares, I looked at the man I had killed. He wore clothing similar to mine, excepting the turban about his head. This I unwound and put on my own head. I took his lantern and moved forward.

The wide arena of darkness inside the ring of lights was some sort of pit and I speculated on its use: for fighting, man to man or beast to beast; for the acting of plays; for the discovery of precious stones? Then I saw that it was being digged from level ground and that the dark shapes in it were walls and buildings, broken turrets and empty streets which had at some time been buried by the earth and now were being uncovered. I jumped down into one of the streets and began to roam the buried town for, thought I, if the men awake in their tents and call out, I can impersonate their watchman until I can escape; or I can shoot if they become unreasonable.

These ruins once had been a place of importance; the city of a great lord or king, that was clear from the blue- and gold-glazed tiles, porphyry columns, alabaster cisterns and arched and fretted windows, all in ruins, all glimpsed darkling by the lantern light. I stepped over a headless statue, a man it was, in banded armour and in by a gateway to a smaller arena which the archaeologists' labour had made. At once, I knew I was in a garden. There were no plants, and nothing living in the dry, stratified earth which now surrounded it, but at its centre was another of the alabaster cisterns which had, still intact, a water-channel or course leading into it and finished with the open-mouthed head of a lion. Roses were carved in the alabaster, edging the basin with their twisted stems and, as I beheld them in the lantern's beam, they seemed to open and put forth their heavy scent and I heard the plash of water from the lion's mouth.

Yet this was fancy. When I looked again, all was quiet, dry and immobile. I walked in the garden. A seat which had stood, perhaps, in an arbour, invited me to sit and rest; a lizard poised itself and extended its crest on a rock but that, too, was carven; a step, half-uncovered, welcomed my tread. And I saw that the step led up into a building, also partly-excavated from its centuries-long burial. It had arches of white marble and, within, was another dry fountain. It was like a cave in there, the arches leading nowhere and backed with the walls of earth, but I recognised the annexe to my Memory Palace, my Treasury, all sullied and dusty as it was.

I felt in my pocket. There, indeed, was the envelope of waterproof silk in which I had packed it away, long ago now and far away, under the distant view of Suleiman's Mountains. I did not dare negate the sigil and untie the thirteenfold knot to see if the Treasury was inside for, as any magician, however humble, or any student of philosophy knows, Memory is infinite and infinitely repeatable. If I chose, I might build a row of Treasuries, all alike yet all differing slightly in the degree by which memory is inexact. Those uncoverers of ancient artefacts, the men who slept in the tents, have uncovered something of mine by chance, I decided, and, since this is not Malthassa, proves that I have been in Parados's world before.

For some time I stood still, as quiet as the stones, while I tried to revive the memories of those times. I could not and, at length, stirring and looking about me, I saw an inscription in the paving of the floor, which I read. It was in the language of the Magi so I understood it well.

> **I, JEMSHYD, King** of Kushan, Seistan, Greater and Lesser Persia and all the Sea and Mountains which surround them whereon sail my treasure ships and by whose icebound passes my silks are carried away and my spices are brought, **Inventor** of the Arts of Medicine, Navigation, Weaponry, Horsemastery, Writing and Composing, Painting, Musicmaking, Goldsmithing, Silversmithing and the Working of Gems, of Perfumery, Distillation, Weaving and Stitching, of Love and Hate, of Life and Death, **Lord** of the Djinni, the Div and the Peri, caused this Pavilion to be raised in my Garden at Persepolis in the five hundredth year of my reign.
>
> Marvel, Admirer, and bow your head before my
> **MAGNIFICENCE.**

I, Koschei the Deathless, Traveller Extraordinary, Onetime Archmage and Prince of Malthassa, Magister Arcanum, trembled in my shoes, for

Jemshyd is but one of the names of Yama, Lord of the Dead and of the Palace of Shadows.

Nevertheless, for I was also in my Treasury, I walked on, across the inscription and toward the rear of the building where should stand the statue of Cyllene and the portrait of Gry of the Ima. That I could not see at all, but a vision of the woman filled my mind, a colourful picture of the shaman she was becoming in her pretty rags and tatters and her charming birchbark shoes; carrying a round drum like the face of the full moon, and a little tin cup and the long and cruel knife which belongs to her father. To clear my head, I rubbed the sacred spot – where all the mind's nerves conjoin – between my eyes. I examined the statue. It was clean and bright as the day I invented and placed it there, the face of it smiling its enigmatic and archaic smile, the gold of its crescent moon headdress gleaming in the soft light of the lamp. They must have brushed her well when they uncovered her, I thought erroneously, for this was more than mortal intervention. I lifted my journal from the shelf by the statue, glad to have it again. (It is there I have written this account.)

This was more than the work of men: the fourth archway was infilled, not with earth but with a flight of porphyry steps of which the third was broken, and a pair of brazen doors. The doors of my Memory Palace!

Overwhelmed by my discovery and by the fatigue of my journey from India and the shifts I had been obliged to make to preserve myself, I sat down on the broken step to rest, felt my head droop and nod; and was soon asleep.

Come, my duck, come: I have now got a wife:
thou art fair, art thou not?

···

Roszi, once the sun was up, loved to sit outside the cavern and trail
her fiery feet in the chill waters of the torrent. Then, she felt for a
little while like her old self, the nivasha, and would long to dive in
and play with the sparkling waters. Always, she recoiled, drew out
her feet with their scarlet, fire-filled veins, and wept a molten tear.
If she plunged, the water would boil and kill the fish she longed
to sport among, besides cooking all the salmon Erchon loved to
angle for: Koschei had given her the body of a fire-demon, uniting
it cunningly with the golden head his predecessor, the Archmage
Valdine, had made of her nymph's face and weedgreen hair.

She hated them both, the old archmage and the new; and loved
them also for making her what she had become, a unique and
magical beauty, the paramour of Erchon, the Silver Dwarf, whose
ardour made sparks fly from her body and her hard lips part to free
the long, frog's tongue Koschei had planted in her shining throat.
Now, she opened that mouth in sympathy with the thought, shot
out the sticky tongue and trapped a passing fly. She did not need
to eat, but swallowed all the same and felt a flame arise inside
her as the fly was consumed.

Roszi looked up at the sun and felt a happy rivalry with him,
all ablaze there and alone. She had companionship, love, uxorious
unity; soon, Erchon, who had been at work since black night,
would emerge from the mine and set about the cooking of his
breakfast while she, as a good wife must, would lay a cloth of
tabby silk on the rock, set out the silver plate, the porringer and

227

Erchon's two-pint stein; settle herself to watch him eat. She leaned back, draping her translucent body across the hot rock and fingering first the argent necklet of toads and water marigold flowers which Koschei had caused to grow about her neck to hide the place where her golden head was joined to her body, and then the silver chains Erchon had fashioned and fastened in a true-lover's net from shoulders to wrists and from waist to slender ankles.

Way downstream, where a disused adit opened on the banks of the torrent, a creature of a different stamp had emerged, a saltier who chewed on a stalk of wild celery while he played skittles with a pile of pebbles and a skimming stone. This early, his staff, which he had laid on the bank, was stiffer than his phallus and the thick hair on his legs and back had dry bracken and dead leaves from his bed caught in it. Tiring of his game, he jumped into the shallows. The water was full of mirror carp, of light and rainbow flashes; suddenly he grabbed at one of these mirages and drew forth a brightly-painted bowl from the water. He tossed the empty bowl in the air and caught it, put it like a helmet on his head, struck it with his staff to hear the metal chink and finally, studied it with a frown across his whiskery brow. It meant nothing to him, but it was pretty and glittered well in the sunlight. He clasped it to him and scented the breeze which was filling with the sulphurous stench of hot metal. He knew well what that portended: the she-thing with the golden head was abroad and lying where her metal parts were overheating and where her female parts were on display.

Every hair on the saltier's body stood erect and his phallus with them. He exuded the musky smell for which he was famous and hurried off upstream, leaping the rushes where they were low enough and dodging around the taller ones, intent on the hunt.

The she-thing lay on her back, half-covered by her dripping sea-green veils; the saltier crept nearer, so near he could feel the fire, like the heat of the sun, burning in her foot. He spat on his fingers. There was a flower upon her belly, a green goblet of five curving petals with a scarlet centre and scarlet were the veins which ran beneath her skin. Her white body was adorned with the shining chains with which the dwarf bound her to him. The saltier raised a hand to touch Roszi; never before had he hesitated before ravishing a female. The pain which stung his hand and his head was not the searing heat of her limbs but a rain of blows from the hard hands of the dwarf. Erchon, as he came up out of the mine, had seen the saltier and assaulted him while he was in his reverie of lust; nor did the dwarf pause for breath or words but continued to lambast the despoiler, knocking his staff into the water and sending his new bowl spinning away.

'Filthy quadruped!' Erchon roared. 'Cesspond vermin, spawn of a sewer rat!' as the saltier bounded away. He wiped his ore-stained hands upon his leather apron and his mouth upon his shirt-sleeve. These actions made no difference to his overall hue which was silver, as was his clothing, the scob and swarf ingrained over the years. His hair, which was plaited into a long pigtail, gleamed in the sun.

She was still asleep. Marvellous! The dwarf knelt to kiss the flower which grew where her navel should be and, as he kissed, so Roszi stirred and yawned and stretched her lovely body. Erchon was eternally amazed that she could feel with all the varied surfaces of her body: gold, silver, glass as well as skin. Her fiery nature, which would never abate, excited him beyond the boundaries of all previous pleasures; that part of her which was eternally nivasha, her soul, in delicious contrast cooled her fires from time to time and kept him unscathed and sane.

'You should not sunbathe, my golden swan,' he said. 'A saltier was here – about to touch you.'

'It is the one from Wolfram's old mine,' Roszi yawned. 'I do not fear him, dearest love – one touch and I would fry him!'

'They are dirty beasts – his smell is here still, all about you.'

'Let us burn it away, Erchon – in the morning sun!'

And he and she did what the saltier had desired to do, ardently, while crimson sparks showered on the rocks and hissed in the water. Then the dwarf uncoiled Roszi's tongue from about his chest and set about the cooking of an al fresco breakfast, cracking a duck's egg into Roszi's cupped hands where it poached perfectly and toasting bread on her hot buttocks. Finally, he fetched himself a noggin of brandy from the barrel in the cave.

'That's all I'll take today, for I must sleep,' he said. 'A plain breakfast. We'll feast anon, but come to bed now, my shining lover, and let us both renew our energies.'

Their bed was an extravaganza of silver wire twisted into the shape and semblance of swans, of waterfalls (these parts encrusted with small diamonds) and many sorts of fish; they lay on pillows filled with a wet moss which was so soft and light they fell asleep at once and drifted dreaming along that shadowy river which is so akin to death. The bed stood in one of the many alcoves and niches in the cavern; others held the necessaries of joyous living, an ivory table, a tall embroidery frame on which Roszi's watery work was stretched, racks of fine wines and barrels of ale and spirits, a game larder, a billiard table, Erchon's wardrobe of breastplates and feathered hats, his armoury of rapiers, inlaid daggers and ballock knives, his angling rods, a tank of veil-tail goldfish and Roszi's collection of veils, myrtle-broidered kirtles and caps of water-lilies, rushes and yellow flags. A stout iron-bound chest held her pretty chains of many, intricate styles of link, the coral clasps with which she fastened her veils and the amber studs with which she decorated her long, frog's tongue, for Valdine, when he turned her head from flesh to gold, had neglected to make pierced earlobes. One alcove, whose walls were studded with garnets still in the rock, was Erchon's study or engineer's laboratory where he drew up plans for the cunning engines he devised for himself and other silver dwarves. One such engine had an egress near the head of the bed, an open funnel or tube by which Erchon could hear the approach of any creature from the valley below or from the summer grasslands where the Stone Dwarf, Bluejohn, brought his family to quarry the geodes from the outcropping rocks and his cattle herd to graze. Bluejohn did not know of Erchon's existence, much less of marvellous Roszi's, but Erchon knew a deal about him.

Erchon lay on his side, in a deep and now dreamless sleep, while Roszi curled against him and kept him so warm the silver in his skin and hair glowed white. The bed steamed gently. He was used to this; his head and limbs were heavy with a delicious vapour-filled darkness into which there broke, and half woke him, a familiar ring or chink, the sound of a sword being returned to the scabbard. It was coming from the listening-tube. The dwarf propped his head on his hand and listened:

'It is beautiful. I did not know a weapon could look so fine.'

'It is true Pargur steel.'

Erchon sat up.

'Show it me again.'

'Let it rest now. We are wearied to distraction and may get our strength back if we sleep till the sun is high.'

Erchon smiled and listened to the silence which followed; there were limits to his listening device, which could not relay lesser sounds such as whispers and kisses, the flight of a butterfly or the footsteps of an ant. Nonetheless, it was clear that two strangers, one of each sex, had come to Bluejohn's mountain house. He lay down again, rolled on his back and set up a snoring which made the crystals in the chandelier ring.

The dwarf and his lady rose in the late afternoon and took a glass of wine together. Erchon told Roszi what he had heard and she laughed.

'A pair of lovers like us, my silver strength. Their talk was amorous play.'

'What if he carried a real Pargur sword? Who, by my best rapier! might he be?'

'Some knight errant as I told you, dearest, erring from virtue's path with his lady.'

Erchon went to the larder and cut a mound of slices from the sirloin.

'I believe it is a knight, surely. Who else?'

He sat on the bed-edge and listened at his tube, but no sound was forthcoming and later, when he descended to the mine, he had dismissed the danger from his mind, preferring Roszi's explanation that a pair of sweethearts had borrowed the Stone Dwarf's house for a love-nest. Roszi talked to her goldfish; walked about the

231

cavern; washed herself with streams of water poured from a golden jug until the steam rose, and dressed in a new set of chains. She took up her needle of gold and began to couch a damp length of arrow weed with a strand of grasswrack. As she sewed, she mused and dreamed, hearing murmurs, hearing voices, hearing the eightfold tramp of a pair of horses, the fourfold footsteps of two people. The sounds were coming from the listening tube. She ran to the mine-shaft and pulled the rope which rang the bell below.

Aurel walked the whole time beside the Red Horse and Gry astride him, and the Horse let him. The gypsies tramped behind in an untidy rout as they went up from the high pastures and wound, over dry, rock-scattered ground, between the last of the trees. They were green birches, sparse and elegantly-shaped as garden trees. The light, which passed between their leafy branches and made of the steep ground a place where shadows caught the foot, gilded Aurel's head and breastplate and turned the Red Horse copper. As well as suffering Aurel near him, the Horse had allowed him to hang a brace of ptarmigan across his shoulders; their red tails and bronze wing-coverts shone. Aurel had crept close to the birds and shot them with his pistol, surprising the women with his skill.

'There's no end to your man's cunning,' Darklis said to Gry. 'Who would have expected a knight to carry a gun in his armour?' She gazed long at Aurel. 'Your soul has swelled so much, my boy, it's fit to burst.'

Gry, while Aurel tied the bird's feet together and draped them in front of her on the Horse, only pondered. She did not believe Aurel was her sweetheart; but she was not certain. The Red Horse said nothing to her, only twitched his ears. Gry hardly saw the birch vile as she rode, so intent was she on Darklis's words and on Aurel's fair hair and strong shoulders so close, just a little way from her left foot. The vile sang like summer breezes, 'Here she comes. See her, see her riding by, the One who spoke with our Sisters and Brothers in Birkenfrith.'

The travellers left the last of the trees behind them and found

232

themselves following a track. One used to being trodden by heavy feet, it seemed, a twisting, narrow line amongst knobbly boulders. Darklis sniffed like a bloodhound.

'What do you scent, dear sister?' Lurania asked.

'More dwarf kind, sweetest sibling. A stench of ale and honest sweat. And just a tang of musk – can the little folk have taken to drenching themselves in scent like the high gentry?'

The Horse neighed as if he disagreed with her.

Far above them, where the snowfields lay and water was eternally frozen and moulded into great glaciers, Aurel noticed thin threads of silver running down the rocks. Some dazzlement, or trick of the eye, he supposed, and turned his thoughts to the way forward, for soon they would be walking in those exalted places, on the crown of the world.

The Red Horse, listening to his rapid breathing and to the pounding engine of his heart, was alarmed. Yet he would not admit it. He paused and hung his head till Gry's heels lightly touched his sides. Then he walked on.

He could not speak to her. He needed his strength for the climb, not to form the kind of sentences she understood and dream them into her still-forming mind. There was solace in thought and the Horse considered his uppermost, human soul. He had stayed too long; but his navigator and lieutenant, Aurel Wayfarer, was close. Meanwhile . . . the question of Hyperion Lovelace; the question of the bowl. He had watched patiently when Gry had dropped the bowl into a mountain torrent and clapped her hands delightedly as the current took it and flung it from foam-covered ledge to rocky bank and so, away.

It had been Erchon's plan to live in secret with the Golden Head but, given strength by the mountains themselves, the mighty Altaish, he had made contact with others of his kind, and with his kith and kin amongst the Silver Dwarves. He had not forgotten the ambition and the cunning of the gypsy witch, nor how she had made use of him by pushing him into the Lytha and turning him

233

to water to go about her business. He was to bring her the Head; instead, he had run to the Forest and thence, to the mountains, with Roszi, she who was all love and life to him and who sat now beside him in the eyrie, which he had reinforced with iron plates as a defence and last refuge. His left arm lay lightly on Roszi's back, as it might along a fire-warmed fender, or the top of a tiled stove.

'Here, we are safe,' he murmured, 'and, most likely, will not be noticed at all.'

He saw Darklis coming into clear view and marvelled when he saw her companions: Lurania Faa by some ill enchantment half-turned horse, the tall knight of the Pargur blade walking beside a creature of fable, the illustrious Red Horse of the Plains and, on his back, a woman of the Ima. He stroked Roszi's hot neck and spoke in her ear.

'Let them feast on our dainties and sleep in our bed, if they will. They won't find the way up here, and they won't stay more than a night or two – see, all four have that mad light in their eyes which comes only to pilgrims who wander looking for they know not what –'

His lips stung and a smell of scorching came from his beard. He rubbed at it. Roszi's ear had glowed red-hot. Her body was taut with alarm. He looked out through the peepholes in the palisade and his composure left him. The knight was staring directly at him, as if neither hot-forged metal nor camouflaging sticks intervened. A long-barrelled pistol gleamed in his right hand.

'On your feet! Who lies in ambush and does not dare fight openly?'

Erchon did not move. He pressed Roszi down. The voice of the knight echoed from the rocky heights above them.

'You cannot hide – ide – ide.'

Erchon remained motionless behind his metal rampart. The knight fired his pistol and the puff of smoke it discharged with the shot hung in a little cloud before his broad chest. Erchon marvelled at it while he heard the shot ring home, ricocheting from his barricade: it was as if the world had slowed and nothing

234

existed in it but himself in hiding and his enemy below. But this was cowardly work. He stood up and showed himself, even as Roszi tried to hold him down. Her grip burned his wrist and he shouted with both pain and rage, 'You there, Sir Fanciful Flag! Hold your fire while I come down to meet you face to face like the silver-blooded dwarf I am.'

The knight put away his pistol, tossed his handsome flaxen head and stood to attention.

Parados knew them of old.

It is coming together, he thought, like a play at the dress rehearsal.

He watched the Silver Dwarf lower a wire ladder from his high retreat, steady it, and assist his beloved to climb down. Erchon was ever the gallant, splendid even now in his work clothes and in jeopardy; enraged too, by his situation and the dwarven pride which would not allow him to remain in hiding. And Roszi! What a transformation Koschei had wrought; what a body he had made her. Almost, Parados desired her for himself, such a fantastical, rare thing she was. The Red Horse pranced a little, despite his tiredness, as the man's emotion passed into his body; and Gry leaned forward to stroke his crest, where the mane began to flow and the forelock sprung from his brow.

'You are not so weary now,' she whispered, yet she slid from his back and put her hands against his neck to direct him into the shelter of the dwarf's cavern-mouth.

The gypsies were silent, Lurania listening intently to the noises of the descent and Darklis shocked into unaccustomed quiet by the sight of Roszi. She had not expected to see beauty fashioned by Koschei's hand. The Golden Head she had expected, stiff and singular as a statue in an alchemist's laboratory, and that crudely united with the scarlet body of some vile, grasp-limbed creature out of Lord Yama's firepit, the deathly shaft where his lieutenant, Urthamma, ruled over the eternal flames, the grid-irons and torturing apparatus, his demons and the damned, those wretches whose lamentations rang out of the heart of the tempest.

235

But this – this crystalline woman with living fire in her very veins, this silver-hung grace whose navel was a flower, whose clothing was a length of silk the colour of the finest aquamarines, of the Ocean on a fair day in spring, of mild jealousy: which was all Darklis felt, watching the dwarf hand his paramour from the last rung of the ladder and kiss her lips before turning to face his challenger.

By Silk and by Linen, by the Living Goddess herself! Aurel found comfort in the old SanZu oaths. He dropped the horse-blanket he had been wearing like a cloak, stood tall and brave, though he felt neither, and waited for his challenge to be taken up. The magic feather which preserved him from ambush trembled on his collar, from the breeze, naturally, for a knight of Pargur does not shake in his shoes. The dwarf turned from his lady who, swaying a little as befitted such a rare and, doubtless, anxious beauty, walked into the shelter of the cavern mouth and stood there as if the Horse and Gry did not exist. Erchon strode boldly across the intervening ground until a mere yard separated him from Aurel. He bowed with a flourish of the hand that usually doffed his hat, and his long pigtail flipped forward and fell back into place when the bow was complete.

So this was the Silver Dwarf! Tall for one of his kind, his eyes on a level with Aurel's belt, a sheen on him like a polished shield, as heavily muscled as a drayman, as arrogant as a gamecock, warlike, dangerous.

'We require seconds,' Erchon said. 'I propose Darklis and Lurania.'

'She is blind!' Aurel objected.

'Her hearing is keener than most men's sight. And I will take her.'

'Very well. It will be sword against rapier: do you agree to that?'

'It is impossible, but such niceties never hindered me ere now.'

'A *outrance*?'

'Ay, to the death!' exclaimed Erchon. 'What will be, will be.'

'Then let us call on our seconds to pace out the battle-ground.'

Darklis stepped forward, her brown brow dark and frowning, her velvets sweeping the ground. She took Aurel's banner from him and used its ragged staff to measure the distance between the man and the dwarf.

'Too close, too close! You are not wrestlers – step back, Sir Cockrobin, to this line I am drawing – and you, my Handsome, stand there. Now!' and she took her place in Aurel's half of the ground and planted his flag there. The breeze extended it, showing Aurel's device, the green wayfaring tree. Lurania trotted to her station, where she could listen for a false stroke or a cheating blow of the foot; and Gry and the Horse, and Roszi, watched in silence.

Gry turned suddenly to Roszi.

'This is an ill hap, lady,' she said. 'You may lose your lover or I my brave esquire.'

Roszi's white body glowed with her emotion. The weeds and grasses about her feet scorched and blackened.

'I am dismayed beyond all thought, madam,' she said. 'What can we do? They are dwarf and man and soldiers both, accustomed to settling quarrels in this perilous way.'

The Red Horse lifted his weary head and nudged Gry. He spoke to her, in the usual way, his words and phrases dropping unasked into her mind, but his voice was sharp with urgency and had grown in authority so that she knew herself to be in the presence of an exalted creature, one as courteous and knightly as Aurel Wayfarer.

'It is Parados the Kristnik who speaks,' the Horse said. 'I, Parados Constans, Prince of Pargur and Paladin of Malthassa. Ask not how I came here, inside my fleshly prison, the body of the Horse, but run now to Aurel and throw yourself upon his neck and upon the mercy of the dwarf before they raise their weapons.'

Gry, in whom, in that instant, the rehearsal had become the performance, darted forward. Her arms, reaching over Aurel's breastplate, strained upward; she caught hold of him and held him as close as he would have wished, in a happier hour, in a gentler place, and his sword remained sheathed, safe in the scabbard. Yet

237

what was more magical was that Roszi, perhaps possessed of Gry's new sense of wonder and completeness, or else merely imitating her, had run to Erchon and was embracing him and covering his face with tears and kisses, so that his rapier stayed at his side and was never raised *en garde*. And what was most amazing was the stance the Red Horse took, a bulk of horseflesh between the two opponents.

'The ladies will not have fighting – they are for loving!' cried Lurania, and began to laugh.

'The Horse will die before you two come together,' said Darklis. 'As for me, I am for peace too. If the dwarf wants to quarrel let him pick on me, for 'twas I who sent him on the fool's errand which has ended here. Erchon, you were supposed to bring Roszi to me!'

The Silver Dwarf unlaced himself from Roszi's arms and they stepped forward, avoiding the Horse who looked after them with a capricious light in his eyes. Aurel meanwhile, had done the same by Gry, but kept her still beside him and lightly rested an arm across her shoulders.

'Give the Golden Head to me, dwarf, as we bargained,' said Darklis. 'I need her for prophesies and scrying work; besides, she is justly mine. Here is gold in fair exchange,' and Darklis pulled a heavy bag from her bosom, tugged on its string and poured coins tumbling and bouncing over the ground. Erchon gazed at them without emotion.

'I have gold enough here,' he said, reached up and put his arm about Roszi's waist. 'Besides, we had no such bargain. We agreed only that I would be content with whatever was to be. I am, most content.' He turned to Aurel. 'A truce, Sir Aurel. You and I are for the same lord, are we not: for Parados?'

'Dead or alive!'

'To the ends of the earth!'

'Your male loyalties are not in doubt, fighter cleaving to fighter whether in anger or in amity, and both to the greatest soldier who, like yourselves, thinks only of expending sweat and blood in battle, or his seed in a woman,' said Darklis nastily. 'Yet I will have justice. Give me Roszi!'

*   *   *

The air inside the dwarf's cavern was warm and steamy, the dimness agreeable. A single light burned in an iron bracket. Gry moved away from the Red Horse's side and found the well. She dipped up water in a silver bowl and gave it him.

'I am glad we left the debate, for you are tired, dear Horse,' she said. 'Lie down on this carpet. And you, Parados – once I cared for you, cooking for you, washing your body and dressing it in clean clothes. And I sang to you and did every thing a wife does except lie with you.

'Where is your body?'

'I have lost it. I am lost and must remain where I am, fast inside this great, red-coated body which is so tired from climbing and striving further and higher, ever higher into the Altaish. All the same –' The Red Horse lay down on the silken carpet and Gry lifted the brace of ptarmigan from his neck and dropped them carelessly.

'What can I get you – him?' Gry walked about the interconnecting caverns finding bread and apples, a handful of milled oats, some nuts; and put them in the basin. Only when the Horse was eating did she think of herself. There had been meat – and she ran back to the dresser where she had seen it, cut a fat slice and ate. She had no time or stomach for the wonders about her, the silver diamond-encrusted bed, the wall of garnets, the jewelled chandelier, but only listened to the rise and fall of the voices outside as the argument ebbed and flowed. That did not concern her either; or Aurel, and she wished he would come in. She looked fondly at the Horse. He was fast asleep and she smiled to see him, her one true friend, her dear companion who *was also Parados;* and went to cut another slice of meat.

Aurel walked into the cavern. The glitter and dazzle stopped him in his tracks. Only one light burned, but its flame was reflected in a host of gems. He saw the ptarmigan he had hunted and shot, the sleeping Horse; bent, and patted him while he slept; straightened up: where was Gry? A number of small caverns, it seemed, led out of this. He took the first, which opened into a kitchen-cave where stood a well-head and a dresser heaped with crockery and food, a loaf and a huge sirloin with a carving-knife ready at its side. He cut a slice and devoured it before he could stop himself. The sickly odour Darklis had descried in the wood hung about the dresser. It was a perfume like – he knew it! Like the dandies used to wear upon the streets of Pargur. Aurel followed the scent.

One of the lesser caverns was a workshop and engine-house and, here, the musky odour was strong. To one side, was the wrought wheel and winding gear which marked the head of Erchon's mine. Without waiting to consult the dwarf, or for a companion-in-arms, Aurel stepped on to the platform of the hoist, threw off the brake-lever and, as the gear smoothly spun, disappeared down the shaft.

Roszi entered her home in triumph, cool enough now and mounted on the broad back of the gypsy-pony, Erchon to her right and holding her hand and the draggled Queen, Darklis Faa, on her left.

'We shall feast now our differences are settled,' Erchon was saying. 'Eat mightily and drink in gallons. And afterwards, we will try you, my Love, and see what you can divine of future secrets.'

Lurania avoided the sleeping Horse and halted with her old nose held high. She took a lace-edged handkerchief from her sleeve, blew her nose on it and sniffed again.

''Tis that scent, sister, which drifted past us in the woods.'

'That's no attar from a crystal flask,' cried the dwarf. 'That is the spoor-scent of a saltier. Be wary now until I catch him,' and he darted away through an arch, Roszi at his heels. The gypsy sisters patted one another, Darklis the dapple-grey neck and Lurania the velvet-clad shoulder.

'Hie now for a warm welcome, if there are saltiers about!' said Lurania. 'I wish for quiet and a pipe of your tobacco, Sister.'

'And I for my dues, as we agreed without. To sit with Roszi and question her about the gypsies' fortress and the way thither, for

I must not waste my fortune and 'tis a long time till next Agnes' Eve, when I may (Lilith willing) consult the Head again.'

'You think the creature has the Sixth Gift for sure?' Lurania asked.

'O, certainly. Koschei made a pretty plaything there. He did not reckon his account with her aright, for who would expect such a beauty to flit with the Dwarf! I can do business with the dwarf-kind who love precious metals as much as I; but to Koschei I say "Boo!" and "A gypsy's curse on you for a whoreson trickster! Darklis does not fear you." '

Night had fallen outside the cave, and the guardian star, Custos, risen alone in the clear and cloudless sky. The small animals, mice, lemmings, urchins, stirred and listened with pricked ears to the night. One by one, and group by group, they began to move down the mountain, far and away as fast as they were able. The greater beasts, goats, ibex, snow apes, ounces, were already gone, running in a vast, mixed herd from the heights; and Custos, cold and brilliant as a royal diamond, watched over a wasteland.

My body was cold when I woke and my mind as an empty room across whose windows thick tapestries are drawn. I had been dreaming of night, of its blackness, of a world without stars to cheer the benighted traveller. Thus I was already in receptive, penitent mood when, having opened the brazen doors and passed into my Memory Palace, I seated myself on the floor of the vestibule and bent my legs into that curious position the holy men name for the white lotus, or nenuphar, which blooms in their tropick waters. Jaa! The stale breath left my body. As speedily, I emptied my mind. I had the trick of it off pat and instantly shed the world about me and the delusions and distractions it harboured. I came to the red place and waited there, expecting the dancers, unafraid, for I meant to ask the blue god the way to Malthassa.

After a little while, the light increases, but it does not fill and swell with lurid colours, only grows more red and intense.

Flames roar close by. I see and hear them and gather my forces about me, ready to fight or flee.

Opening like curtains or, more exactly, like a dense, red fog cut through

241

with a knife, the flames part. I see imps and devils, a cohort of them; but they pay me no attention for they are bowing their heads and saluting with their spiked rods and toasting irons. The fiend, naked and terrible, walks up to me, straddles his feet and bends to take my hand, which he shakes as urbanely as if we had met in the gardens of Castle Sehol.

'Koschei! How do you?' he says.

'Well,' I answer, 'and better,' but my puzzlement must dwell clearly in my voice for Asmodeus claps me on the back in such a hearty fashion that I fall forward like one of those dolls with a weight in the base; only I can not rise again but lie stranded while I disentangle my feet.

'You are lost,' Asmodeus says, at which I stare for, though I love all things occult and hellish, I hope to keep away from the Lord Yama's domain for many a year – I am called 'the deathless' by reason of my hidden soul and cannot be killed while it is out of my body.

'But I mean, you have missed your way,' the demon says. 'Come, let me raise you to your feet – why, what a sorry sight you are, Koschei, half-naked and the tenant of another's body! Not an ill body, though.' He sniffs. 'I smell death. You have killed recently. Look! There is the landward gate to the Palace of Shadows. Let me offer you the ease and hospitality of my humble mansion in return for all you have done for me!'

I hesitate in fear.

'My soul –' I say, but he interrupts me.

'I do not know where you have hidden your soul, Archmage; but I know I cannot detain you without it, so be comfortable and welcome.'

'Very well,' say I, my composure regained. I walk with him between the bowing ranks of his underlings.

Soon we come to the gate, which stands open. All is dark within. The red glow falls behind us, sliding from our backs like a discarded garment as we pass through the gateway. My nose begins to itch and fill with a moist humour; I sneeze suddenly and am instantly back in my Palace, seated on the floor with my limbs cramped into a poor imitation of the folded petals of a lotus-flower. I rub at the irritation with the back of my hand and open my eyes. Something stands before me, blocking my view of the windows and of my memory of the garden of Castle Sehol beyond it and, as my eyes focus and my visions fade, I see a pair of shiny

242

shoes and elegantly-trousered legs; the portion of sock visible between the hem of the trousers and the polished footwear is black, like the rest of the items and, exactly upon the ankle-bone which is higher and more prominent than a man's, is an embroidered monogram, or initial letter:

A

The shoes themselves, I notice, are built up in a curious fashion with blocks of leather and high and solid heels.

I look up and touch my head in a gesture I hope is at once submissive and careless. Asmodeus laughs.

'It is my turn to visit you,' he says.

His face and body are transformed. He is as suave as a waiter, as graceful as a faun; his short, black hair curls abundantly on his forehead where it is artfully arranged to display a pair of gilded horns, his black suit is well-pressed, his white shirt neat and its pleated front stiff with starch, his silk bow-tie scarlet as his lips. He smiles and bows.

'Come, let me raise you to your feet,' he says again, and again I disentangle my feet and thighs and stand, while he pulls on my hands. 'My servants shall find you a decent suit.' He tries, ineffectively, to dust me down and his polished nails graze my chest. The hair on the back of his hands is as exuberant and curly as that of his head. 'There is no need for all this mind control and spiritual union with strange gods. If you want to visit me, why do you not enter my kingdom through your own communicating door?'

I looked where he points. In the wall between the two windows is a narrow, bronze door, in design not unlike that of the outer doors. It is open, but the view through it is obscured for Abrahel, the Angel of Lustful Dreams, stands there, his wings cloaked about his shoulders and displaying a wonderful rainbow of colour on the tip of each feather. Apart from these, he is naked and his flesh shines dully like unpolished pewter. His right elbow rests on the outstretched palm of my statue of Urthamma.

I cannot be certain, in these tense moments, whether it is still a statue or has assumed a living form.

'I made no door!' I protest.

'But you did,' Asmodeus insists. 'I remember the process clearly: a hard portion of your mind and your desire to fathom every well of knowledge cut it – a few nights ago.'

'Then it was while my conscience slept!'

'Your conscience? Is that an organ you have lately grown? Do not deny the truth! The statue of Urthamma is a mnemonic, remember? H for Head, Heart and Hands; A for the Amulet of flame which hangs about his neck; D for Demon, the whole of him; E for his glowing Eyes and his keen Ears; S for his Sex and for Sin, your first love. HADES: Hell, or the Palace of Shadows. Some call it Dis, some Jemshyd's Garden; but 'tis all the same. You know this, Koschei, so do not dissemble matters with me. Besides, I am waiting to bring you to my mansion to entertain you, as I promised.'

As he speaks, Asmodeus points to each feature of the statue while his smile grows wider until I can see the needle-pointed teeth on the inside of his gums, which he uses to tear up the damned. Then, extending an arm to take mine, he whistles a command to Abrahel who at once unfurls his radiant wings and flies off across my garden.

'Helen sleeps. She called for the Incubus,' says Asmodeus, and digs me mischievously and roughly in the ribs.

'Where?'

'Oh, Koschei! Green-spirited, jealous!'

'In this world?'

'What world is that, Archmage? Are we not standing in your mind?' His arm, linked with mine, feels stronger than thrice-forged steel, and he propels me forward and through the narrow door. At once, all colour vanishes: the world beyond the door is black and white. Where shadows gather is spread many a shade of grey but all is monotone and monotonous, like the prospect of a starless night.

I look back, comforted to see the bright colours of my Memory Palace and by the sight of the open door. A stretch of gravel, which chatters spitefully beneath our feet, is all that divides the new door from the huge, black door of Asmodeus's mansion. He turns the handle, which is shaped like a phallus, and flings the door wide. I gasp. A chequered floor stretches before me which, since it is without true perspective, turns my brain giddy. I can not tell where to walk but Asmodeus, still forcefully guiding me, does not pause and I stumble on beside him. Soon we stand at the foot of a great stair and this I see, as I crane my head back and look up, rises in multiple curves until it meets black darkness.

'Now you may call upon me with an "Asmodée!"' the demon says. 'This absence of colour has its own beauty, does it not?'

I readily agree. If I do not, he will make me; besides, a rout of demons are descending the stair, some naked, some feathered, some clad in skins and carrying skulls, some with the shapes of beautiful women. These carry pitchers of water and clothing and immense white towels. When they have saluted Asmodeus, they surround me, strip, wash, shave and clothe me there and then, not releasing me until they have thoroughly brushed my hair and tweaked the cuffs of my shirt and set my bow-tie at the correct angle.

The demon claps his hands.

'Darkness! Cacophony! Capers!' he cries, bends, and unlaces his shoes, which he throws off so that he can the better prance from white square to black upon his cloven hooves. I, staggering after him, soon become more adept and my giddiness leaves me, replaced by immense elation and an insatiable desire for the pleasures of physical congress, which the women-demons and their rough towelling of me have aroused. A thunderous music, which is entirely without melody or harmony, fills the hall.

'In my house all is Pleasure and Desire and none are satisfied!' Asmodeus cries.

He runs up the stair and I follow him. The music surrounds us and bears us upward and the wonderful, deep, and constant darkness of the stair hides our bodies and our minds. Time is of no account. I cannot therefore say when Asmodeus ceases to kiss and play with me but only this, that it is not I, but icy hands reaching through the darkness, which fasten my clothes.

'Do you think your sins will not stain you, without your soul?' laughs Asmodeus. 'When you release that poor, imprisoned creature, it will be quite decayed.'

'It may be dirtied, but it will be alive,' I answer.

The demon and I caper on through the darkness in search of more sins; which, in this marvellous place, are pleasures.

In white light which bursts continually like waterspouts around me, I work at sin. The hellish music has ceased and all I hear are the sounds my body makes, chewing, snorting, belching, farting, vomiting. I cannot abuse it enough to satisfy me and the jest, that it is pure Parados's body which I mar, is old and sad. I eat, vomit, eat and vomit again; and again; I sleep and wake weary, countless times; I sit and wish for nothing, sigh and am tormented by negation; women (though they are the demons) come and perform whatever lewd and filthy act I decree, with me, with each other, all of us together, and still I lust; my pride is aroused, more than my body. I am Koschei and I can conquer Hell. I am the Archmage who seduced Asmodeus; I am the Prince of Pargur, and shall soon encounter Lord Yama who will bid me sit at his right hand, and feed me delicacies from his golden platter.

Yet, does not Asmodeus relish his Pleasures more than I? Has he not a greater appetite, a house which, to mine, is as a mountain beside a hillock? Why should I not have all that he enjoys? I shall challenge him to a contest of wit, of magic-making; or to a passage of arms. My rage knows no bounds; with these soiled Paladin's hands, I might throttle him – As I stare at my hands, expecting to see upon them some indication of their supposed might, they stretch, inflate, grow huge upon my wrists so that I have great trouble to raise and part them, and bring them together in a volcanic clap. The white light vanishes: I extinguished it; I am invincible.

Asmodeus is waiting for me in the dark. He forces me to run with him, over perilous, rotten pavements which are bursting asunder, heaving and clashing as if they lived. My arms are bent behind my back; my hands small, weak and human. The demon hisses in my ear:

'This, my mansion, is but an anteroom without Lord Yama's grounds; yet you thought yourself in Hell. What fools you mortals are, even you, Koschei, with your empty vaunting and your minute, worthless, hidden soul.' He shakes me, holding me at arms' length as he runs. Lifting me above his head, he spins about until I can see and hear nothing. 'Open your eyes, Magician. See where I have brought you.'

My vision clears. His world has not changed: it is grey and white; the *shadows are dense and black. We stand at the head of a flight of steps and, when I look behind me, I see a door standing open; but there is no sign of the Memory Palace beyond it, for it leads into his mansion.*

'You are too timid to stay with me, Impotence. Go to Hell and try Lord Yama's impatience!' Asmodeus roars and throws me down the steps.

'Darklis does not fear you – Zernebock!'

As the gypsy finished speaking, the floor of the cavern convulsed like a living thing.

'Chov-hani Doro!' exclaimed her sister. 'See where your curses have got us, Great Witch!'

'Maybe I have raised some dark force, maybe not. But I can see where I am going, Sightless, and –'

'She-snake!'

'May the Old One choke you, Zingara. Lucifer! Be still, Sister; never move!'

Darklis stared at the ground, in which a fissure was opening, a narrow crack which scored the billowing rock as easily as if it had been putty. As the fissure widened she bent forward, fascinated by its serpentine motion.

'Yag,' she said. 'Fire – I see demons dancing there.'

Lurania, who could smell the flames and the powerful stench of sulphur which they carried into the air, tossed her head and stamped her four feet; but Roszi, wholly possessed by the sight of the flames, slid from her back, her body growing hot and glowing as she moved. She darted to the edge of the chasm and looked down.

'Sweet Urthamma!' she cried, spread her arms, turned once about and dived into the flames.

Then Erchon, the Silver Dwarf, roared in agony.

'Stay for me. We are one. We are electrum together!' and with one last shout of 'Roszi!' threw himself after her. The infernal fire burned blue and threw up a shower of mingled gold and silver drops.

'One for ever and ay, indeed,' said Darklis, and angrily wiped away the tears which started down her face.

'What's afoot? What passes?' Lurania demanded. 'I smell hot metal and burning flesh.'

'Roszi has jumped into the fire and the dwarf has sacrificed himself for love.'

'Then our journey has been in vain –'

'– and if we do not flee, so will our lives. Come, Lurania, I will jump upon your back and you shall gallop your fastest. Do not falter, for I shall guide you.' Darklis kilted her skirts and, with a deep breath, a hop and heave, was mounted. 'Fly now, straight ahead, straight on, right –'

With a clatter and a cry, 'Save us, Lilith!' the gypsies fled the cavern. The flames rose higher and began to consume the fabric and furnishings, first Roszi's embroidery and veils steamed and sizzled, took fire and were gone in a puff of smoke, then Erchon's hats and finery, his engineering drawings and his books. As soon and as quickly as these things had turned to ash, the fire abated, and the chasm narrowed and closed over.

The Red Horse, to whom fire, which often ran wild in the Plains in hot weather, was no stranger, awoke then, and found himself deserted. The cavern was full of smoke; the carpet he lay on was singed and his nostrils full of the choking, twin smells of brimstone and sulphur. He snorted and coughed but was otherwise untouched; not a hair or a whisker harmed.

'So Koschei cannot harm me,' he said aloud, the distorted voice of Parados booming from his long, horse's mouth, and echoing about the cavern. 'Cannot lay his bane upon me, whatever the fate of my friends and companions – dear Gry, brave Aurel, and the rest: those tiresome gypsy women, shining Erchon, wondrous Roszi . . . I must leave this place, for I cannot journey underneath the Altaish. I am too wide and tall. Even if I am the last alive of our expedition, I must continue.'

So saying, he rose to his feet and stretched. Then, walking slowly but with great purpose, he left the cavern of the Silver Dwarf and his paramour, and began the long climb toward Striving Pass.

A blanket of darkness lay on the Altaish, smothering the light of the last, melting snows. Aza had used these pale snowfields as markers to navigate by when the stars went out and the Guardian of the Herds was extinguished suddenly, as if a giant had reached out and snuffed it between his hands. Now, in the confusion of night and the sound of water falling from the mountainsides, he was forced to land and bid Tarpan stay intact, that he might mount and fly swiftly away at need. He did not see the mouth of Erchon's cavern, but only walked cautiously about and finding a wide, flat-topped rock and, near it, a stream in spate, dipped his hands and drank. As he wiped them on some grassy tufts, his hands touched something cold, which rang against his nails. He felt it carefully and picked it up. It was a small metal bowl which, his fingers told him, must be either painted or chased with small, flame-like shapes and letters. Then, while he touched the surface of the bowl, the flames began to glow. Soon, he had light enough to see by. His thoughts turned directly to Gry:

'She has come this far: she is not idly fleeing me, nor travelling hither and thither without purpose. I am certain she means to follow and find Nandje, even if she must go beyond the ends of the earth,' he said to himself. 'I am not angry with her, not now. I cannot wish her death as I did when the hosting fury possessed me. Indeed, perhaps I am pursuing her to praise her. Clouded and mysterious are the ways of the Spirits, and the greatest of these is Svarog. Hail to thee, O Sky, though you turn a starless face to me. And it may be, Mightiest One, that you have darkened yourself to rebuke me. I lingered too long at Wathen Fields, watching the people bury Friendship and setting a wrought mortsafe over her grave to contain their fears.'

The flames on the bowl burned, seeming to radiate heat. Aza saw that the bowl was decorated with seven bright bands of colour. He read the two inscriptions: 'All's fair in love and war' ('Very true,' he murmured) and 'Keep Faith'.

'Perhaps my faith is not strong enough,' said Aza and beheld, at that moment, small flames licking through the wet grass and across the ground. He dropped the bowl at once, and saw it bounce into the stream.

249

'That's that, and an end of its magic,' he said; but the flames only grew larger, licking the foot of a broken flagstaff someone had stuck in the ground. Aza examined the flag, nodding his head when he saw the device upon it.

'A green wayfaring tree!' he said. 'This is the standard of Gry's knight, Aurel Wayfarer, he who is unjustly accused of murder in Wathen Fields. It is clear that he is innocent, and clearer still that Koschei has a hand in the dancer's death and in these upheavals. I must travel on!'

Speedily, the shaman mounted his headless horse and commanded it to fly upwards in the direction of the mountain-tops.

The nursery rhyme beat a laboured tattoo in time with the hoofbeats of the Red Horse,

> Up the hill hurry me not
> Down the hill flurry me not
> When I'm hot, water me not,
> In the stable forget me not,

the first line recurring again and again as he struggled up the pass. It was Parados who had named it Striving Pass, long ago when the first Malthassa book was in its birth throes; and the name had remained, a marginal note, until the time had come for Sib to speak it. So now the place existed and the Horse, by the witchery of the imagined and the printed word, climbed there, one hoof before the next before the next – and so on, while his lungs could scarcely expand, so thin was the air. But Parados had ordained it: it was so; and the Altaish was the highest mountain range in the actual and the fantastic universe.

Parados's thoughts, as the Horse struggled for breath, were regretful: he could no longer move mountains or cause rivers to spring out wherever he chose. Koschei had usurped those mighty powers, those conjurations by the written word which, rightfully, were his. It was Koschei who had the power to melt eternal ice, flood his world and rend its rock by fissure. Especially, he regretted the words he had put in the Wolf Mother's mouth, 'Take care. The road to true wisdom is long and hard', for he was the sole character in a similar story.

He? Who was he? One who had carelessly given away his crown. One who had existed because he could divine the dreams of a multitude: he saw his readers crouched upon his pages, eager creatures following the spoor of the story from vicissitude to love scene, from death to glory.

Then, as a beggar stares in wonder at a king, he saw a solution: the story might even now be his. Was it not he, Guy Parados, who was its author? Koschei, being merely a character, should be suffered to do what he would for, *finally*, the last page would be reached and those words with which Guy Parados always concluded: THE END and, after them, his last words, his hand upon the creation: Guy Kester Parados, The Old Rectory, Maidford Halse; and the date. What year was it at home in Albion? What month? What day? How long had he been absent in this Otherworld? What of his children?

Parados suppressed the flood of memories. All he needed to do, whether horse or man, was wait and endure, minding those wise words of Mogia's, 'Take care. The road to true wisdom is long and hard', and order his universe accordingly, step by step to the end until the Archmage was outpaced.

Who am I? he asked himself, as the memories, not to be long set aside, came creeping back. Once, in the beginning, my name was Christopher Young, the married man, the poet, the romantic, the sole author of a set of six beautiful children. What are their names? I scarcely remember. There's Ben for sure, the little boy, and Gregory's the oldest, adult now. My daughters ... But 'Christopher' became 'Guy' and 'Young' 'Parados' so that in my second incarnation I was the author of these races, this world which belongs between the shining covers of twenty paperbacks. And so the Kristnik, Parados Constans, was born, and his dark counter, Koschei Corbillion; were born so many more, Nemione, Erchon, Aurel, Nandje, Gry, any of whom I can become (if I am not all of them already) by a mere rearrangement of the letters

251

of the alphabet. I am the Red Horse in whom I am trapped by my greed for experience and the loss of myself. By Harry! this is all extended metaphor and, in reality, if I close my huge horse's eyes and open them again I shall see the screen of my PC and the words pacing even and black-lettered across the silver field. So – the Horse opened his eyes and saw the grey, wind-shorn boulders of the highest Altaish and the summit of Striving Pass like a saddle at the top. As he looked, a ghostly figure flew toward it, the rags-and-tatters silhouette of the Shaman of Garsting and his bone horse, little Tarpan.

A shudder passed through him.

There is Aza, he thought, riding to interfere with the story. I have lost the plot. I have lost so many characters and am likely to lose more. If I am Parados, let the Gods and Goddesses of Malthassa grant my prayers – O, give me soon a man's body with which to make my mark upon this chimerical world. And let Gry come out of the darkness; let Aurel Wayfarer be saved; let me live!

'Amen!' said Parados aloud, and staggered on.

At first, the passages through which the saltiers had dragged Gry had been high and well-lit, the main highways of the Silver Dwarf's mine made long ago to accommodate the passage of large engines and of the ponies which powered them. Silver ores glinted in the walls and the place was so pretty and spacious that Gry, even as she was pulled and pushed by the legions of little, goat-legged men, was hopeful of rescue.

They will miss me soon, she thought, Aurel and Erchon and, since this is Erchon's mine, he will easily find me.

But, all too soon, the saltiers turned into a darker tunnel, lit only by the flaring torches they carried, and the roof became lower and still lower until it was dwarf-height and then too low even for their kind, and Gry, who had bent her head, was forced to her knees and made to crawl. The saltiers grew excited at this and called to each other in their high voices. Gry could not tell what they said for they spoke as the beasts, bleating one to another. She caught glimpses of them in the torchlight, of their hairy bodies, their beards and tails, of their sexual parts which swelled and grew the further they travelled from the Dwarf's territory. It was the same; it was ever the same with the male sort whether man, horse, or fiend – for these creatures were surely of Lord Yama's spawning, so small, so potent, so strong, filled with lust; demons of a subterranean kind, not kindly like the spirits of the grazing-grounds and the forest leshi, nor yet indifferent to her as were the zracne vile and the puvush-kind. Their small hands gripped her arms and legs and, sometimes, they prodded her with their staves.

She did not cry out, or weep. I am my father's daughter, she thought, I am Gry of the Ima. I will never again be overcome.

Nevertheless, when she was driven into a narrow place in the tunnel, where there was no room for any but the foremost saltiers to walk beside her, her heart sank within her and she felt her soul quail and cover its face. The saltiers were calling angrily. All at once the near ones pushed her to the ground and began to snatch at her clothes.

'I am Nandje's daughter,' said Gry and put her back against the tunnel-wall. The leading saltier, which had first captured her, and which was bigger than the rest, crouched down and crawled over her thighs. She drew her father's knife, crying out as she drove it into the saltier's belly. The two that held her legs uttered their high, goat-like cries. She flourished the knife, so that the blood flew from it and spattered their chests. The tunnel filled with choking fumes of musk and the torches flared up. She glimpsed the excited throng of saltiers who waited, jostling each other and bleating loudly, farther down the tunnel.

Another moved to take the place of the one which lay dead across her legs. He gripped her by the ankle. She lunged with the knife but he came on until he was within a handsbreadth of the knife-point. She lunged again and the good knife scarred his belly, cutting a welt in the hair. He guarded his huge phallus with one hand and reached for her with the other.

'Come closer. If you dare,' she said. 'Come and be spitted on my knife.'

Evidently, he understood, for he drew back a little way, scratched his beard and bared teeth which were yellow as old ivory.

'Enter the sacred gate of my body. If you dare,' said Gry. 'I shall drain the life from you and there will be nothing left but a corpse, like this one!'

The saltier grimaced again and stroked her ankle. His fingers touched her birch-bark shoes and turned grey; when they touched the wisent-fleece which lined the shoes, they withered. The saltier whimpered and sucked them, but they had become as lifeless as a tree which has been struck by lightning; and it seemed to Gry that she heard the deep voice of Bonasus saying, 'Now you have the advantage.'

The leshi whispered in the Forest, and she heard them: 'Strike out!'

Gry, first drawing up her feet, kicked out. The birch-bark shoes struck once, and twice, and two saltiers fell. At once, their hair turned grey and their bodies began to wither.

'Again!'

Two more fell, and a third.

'Prudence is the best portion of valour,' Mogia called from Wolf's Castle, and 'Flee, swift like running deer at your shins!' called Mouse-Catcher.

It was hard to move faster than a snail, in that low passageway, and in the dark. The silence was profound; it was as if the saltiers had never been, nor could Gry smell them. Chesol deer ran as fast as the Herd: the skin of the deer which the Wolf Pack had killed and which she had made into leggings and a cape and skirt felt smooth and warm to her touch. Gry understood that a person blessed by the animals has certain gifts; and that it is not always necessary for such a one to move her limbs as fast as her will in order to travel forward.

She crawled on, her hands testing the ground before her. There was nothing but stone: the tunnel floor, rough and gritty. It was not the floor of the storehouse in Garsting, beaten earth, nor Heron who had thrown her to the ground, nor Heron she had killed. She vomited, twice, three times, crawled forward twenty paces and sat

254

still to rest. Then, taking from their bag the sparkstones and some of the kindling-moss in which they were wrapped, she made and lit a glim and looked about her.

There was no tunnel now, but a high-roofed chamber. The walls were hung with tapestries of coloured rock and gems; whether this was dwarven work or Mother Earth's, it was hard to say. Iron Glance, Wolfram, Velvet Ore, Lead Glance, Black Jack, Silver, Morion, Mispickel, Blue John, Rose, Amethyst and Smoky Quartz, Heliotrope, Jasper, Sapphire, Golden Beryl, Topaz, Opal, Almandite, Pyrope and Cacholong had been set in wonderful, magical confusion in a ground of whitest chalk. Though some of these were the names of puvush-women and some of dwarves, and men and women, here was no living thing but Herself, Gry, alone with the secrets lying beneath the Altaish Mountains.

'My moist mother, the Earth herself, made these stones,' said Gry. 'If dwarves then made them into this mosaic, or picture without a subject, then they were surely doing her bidding. After all, the dwarves, we mortals, the animals and the stones are one, all made out of the same clay and moulded into different shapes by Her.

'If I had not been captured and brought underground, I should never have seen this. I have used the wisdom of the wolves and the strength of Bonasus. I have more gifts than I knew, from the leshi and the chesol deer which died for me. It is true that animals often have more kindness in their hearts than men. As for those terrible goat-footed creatures, I believe they are a kind of demon. What else could be so vile?

'I will put them out of my mind! This great cavern is worth thinking about, not they.'

The last glimmer of light from her makeshift torch showed something as luminous lying at the foot of the wall. The faint light remained when hers had gone out. She went to it and, bending, saw several kinds of toadstool or mushroom growing in a hollow where some moisture had gathered. One of these was shaped like a tiny tree, another like the shells she had seen lying on the Ocean shore, yet another was brown as dried horseflesh; the last, which had a green, metallic sheen, was soft to the touch as the Red Horse's muzzle, and inward-curving and leaflike as his mobile ears. She broke a off morsel and put it in her mouth. At once, she knew that the brown fungus was good to eat and picked several heads, which she stored in her carrying bag. The first two were poisonous, one more deadly than the other; this, which she had by now swallowed, was neither food nor poison but medicine and stimulant, the food of illusion and dreams.

Though she had lit no light and the fungus's light was faint as a candle flame in mist, the cavern walls were visible again, each stone and gem shining bright as the sun. Gry, with one last, admiring glance, turned away from them and stepped out. There was the tunnel-mouth. In an instant she was under it and travelling fast, not walking but floating, knee height above the ground. If she reached up, she could touch the roof of the tunnel. She felt embedded gemstones, moss-growths, the grasping fingers of puvushi, snails, slugs. The Lady Byely led the way, drifting forward on the wings of her indigo dress, her silver bangles chiming together and the tattoos crawling and twining on her skin. Byely looked behind her and smiled at Gry. Her black hair floated up and trailed along the roof.

'I was fair, in my day,' she said. 'As you in yours.'

Then Aurel was there, gliding along beside her, Aurel and the Red Horse miraculously made to fit below the tunnel-roof and still keep his great, vigorous mass; Aurel, smiling also, the Red Horse wisely nodding his head as he went forward with her, and her father Nandje, her mother Lemani, her brothers, her dead baby sisters grown to women, Leal turning his head to look at her and smiling as kindly as Aurel; all these and Sib too, her filmy dress gone with the storm, naked as the daybreak, skin snow-white, hair a thick and dusty web. Benevolent tongues of flame, hearth friends, licked the tunnel walls as Gry came down to earth and her companions vanished, each and every one a fancy, every one but Sib who dropped behind and crept from shadow to shadow, good as invisible.

'She is elf-struck,' Sib whispered, 'but the madness is waning. She will soon be herself.'

The firelight came from a small tin bowl which was standing on the edge of a pool or spring, since water welled up in the centre of it, making bubbles rise and burst. The bowl was upright, almost as if it had been placed there. The painted flames on the bowl's sides were burning and illuminating a great area of tunnel and the wide shore of the pool. Gry touched the bowl: it was not hot. She picked it up, causing the beams of light to flicker and dance over the rock.

'It is the gypsy man's bowl!' she exclaimed. 'Hyperion's gift to me that I refused. Aurel was carrying it and I flung it into the stream near the Stone Dwarf's house on the alp – so it must have been carried here by the water. Wonderful.'

She dipped the bowl into the water and took a long, cool drink. The water was as sweet as Colley's beer and that, the flickering flames and the rumour of far-away explosions that sounded to her like the Herd galloping for joy on a moonlit night, made her feel at ease and at home. She sat for a while at the edge of the pool, looking into it. White fish swam there and a long-fingered nivasha floated face-up, her necklaces of lovers' bones adrift with her and her eyes half-shut and dreamy. Gry's reflection floated beside her and another's, the brown face of the gypsy, Hyperion Lovelace, appeared. He smiled his tigerish smile and Gry, at peace, smiled back.

'You are friendly now, Princess Haughty,' he said.

'I have come a long way and have learned a great deal,' said Gry.

'May I kiss you now?'

'Yes.' His drowned eyes drew her gaze, right into them. She leaned forward over the water, ready for his kiss; more, ready to kiss him. And felt the water slide with its sweet taste over her mouth; with its power to kill. She drew swiftly away and saw the nivasha laughing at her. Hyperion was not there and she was herself again, the last of the mushroom's magic spent: Gry alone beneath the Altaish. She held the bowl out before her and, using it to light her way, continued her journey through halls hung with crystal icicles, along muddy passageways and through damp crawls, across measureless caverns whose floors were paved with fool's gold; by caves where towers, thrones and tables grew out of the ground, and met suspended waterfalls and intricate, fringed arras, all of these red and yellow, weeping stone.

'If this buried land was kin at first to hell, it seems now like paradise,' she said, as she threaded her way between these natural monuments or paused, with the bowl uplifted, to view them.

'They are the same, Paradise and Hell, the Overworld and the Under, Life and the Palace of Shadows,' Sib muttered, covering her mouth so that she would not be heard. 'They are one, as you will learn.'

Disturbed, dismayed, ay; the knees of my elegant evening trousers smirched with grey dust, I get to my feet. First – a defiant gesture – I pull out a handkerchief and clean away the dust, smooth my ruffled hair, bestow the white square in my pocket once again; and now (it comes upon me, heavy, alarming, as a hailstorm on a fine spring day), with that gesture, realise that I have lost my prism. I had it on the mountain track, upon the flying fur, in buried Persepolis. Therefore, along with my shulwars and turban, my sandals and howdah pistol, it was taken from me in the house of Asmodeus. When the demons washed me and gave me these clothes.

Ah, Perdition, Ruin! But I may find it again if I but retrace my steps, not to try and wrest it from Asmodeus in his house, but to return to my Memory Palace, where I shall be certain to find it, carefully set down as a trophy and a mnemonic. Prism: Parados, Peer, Pry.

I turn about, ready to march up the steps. The door at the top is closed, crisscrossed with many bars of iron and hung with yards of thick, padlocked chain. I cannot go that way. The only way out is – so, facing forward – through Lord Yama's abode, the Palace of Shadows itself; and perhaps that is the fearsome place yonder, that jagged line far away. This place has neither sky nor ground. Shifting planes of shade and inky mist are all the landscape here. There are no homely dwellings or shelters. I must keep that line of darkness in my mind and strive to reach it before night: there is no night, nor day, no sun, no moon, no stars, no wind to cool my heated blood and blow away my terrors.

Walking on the moonlight

....

Gry, for it was she and not an Altaish blind-worm nor a skarn murmont, pushed and pulled herself out of the ground. The tunnel was narrow and perhaps had once been the burrow of a murmont which, breaking through into the rocky halls below his comfortable, earthy home, had taken fright and left it what it had become, a passageway between the inner and the outer world. The round exit held her about the hips. She wriggled, and was free. She stood, on shaking legs, and wiped the soil from her eyes, bent to clean her hands on the sparse grasses at the tunnel mouth.

She had come through the mountains and stood in a new land on the farther side. It stretched below her and was grey as ashes. The moon, alone in the sky, lit it, the steep slopes of gravel and fields of shale and, afar, an expanse of wind-shot water stretching beyond the horizon: the Ocean. Even here, high on the mountain-side, she could feel its unrelenting pulse, a charm of variance, a spell of reverberation. There were no stars.

Clear of the mountains' enchantments, Gry lost heart. She was thin, starved in being and bearing, stooped from crawling in the arteries of the Altaish. Her fraying clothes were truly rags and her hair had grown so long, under the mountains, that the leshi's plaits bound only the ends of a tide of darkness which flowed over her shoulders and down her back. Her face, in its shadow, looked white. She breathed in the salty essence of the Ocean and remembered how her journey had begun and where, in every detail, she had been; whom she had met and spoken with or greeted eagerly and liked; those she had loved. Looking up at the cold silver world in the heavens, she prayed.

> 'Full moon, round moon, here am I
> Standing in your light,
> Make it so that only I
> May occupy his heart.
>> Aurel,
>>> Aurel,
>>>> Aurel.'

The last syllable of his name faded to nothing. Her prayer was half-hearted and her eyes full of tears. She talked to herself,

'If he is dead, he must be with my father in the Palace of Shadows, and to see him I must also be a Shadow. I have Nandje's knife.' She drew it from the waist of her skirt and ran her finger across the blade. 'It is sharp enough to skin game and it is sharp enough to take my life.

She was certain that every one of her companions had perished. She had been so long away.

'If I had not found the pool of water and the toadstools, I should have died of thirst, or starved – and whichever is the easier death of those, it cannot be as easy as death by keen steel.'

She looked up at the harsh lands behind her. The mountain peaks were dry as deserts, impassable as a string of fortresses guarded by evil men. She spoke her worst thoughts:

'The Horse is dead, I know it. I should not have let him bring me so far and into such dangerous country when his proper place is with the Herd. As for Parados – well, I have been elf-struck in the mountain and maybe have been always . . .'

Again, she fingered the knife-blade, and drew it across the back of her hand. The blood welled and ran in a thin line. Hastily, she untied the strings of her deerskin cape and let it fall. The wind cut into her, as sharp as any knife, and she welcomed its cold breath, tossed back her shell-encrusted hair and held the blade to her throat. Now, her thoughts were silent and terrible:

The moon is the last thing I see and this as simple as the first rent in the heath-jack's belly, no more difficult than cutting through a tough old horsehide; easy as moving, as breathing and this breath is one of the last three breaths I take as I draw my father's knife from here, under my left ear to . . .

The knife jumped out of her hand and flew, clattering, across the rocks. Her wrist was locked in a grip of iron, in fingers stronger than the talons of a hawk, which tighten as its prey struggles. Someone spoke.

'That is not the way, my daughter. I know you are neither craven nor cowardly.'

Gry, delivered, relaxed in his hold and the fingers slackened, just a little. She could turn her head enough to see him and, expecting Nandje with rejoicing heart, beheld the wizened old shaman, Aza of Garsting. Behind him, in the pied moon-shadow, stood Tarpan, his headless horse of bone.

'You!' she said. 'You, my accuser, my betrayer.' She spat in his face.

A dry laugh burst from the shaman's parchment lips. He wiped her spittle from his cheek and squeezed her wrist until she felt her bones grind together.

'Kindness is the wrong way, with you,' he said.

'You have tried imprisonment and rape already!'

'Not I, but the Ima. Not I, but Heron. But nothing deflects you from your purpose, Nandje's Daughter. Look into my eyes – look! I have much to teach you before I depart.'

Against her will, Gry looked, her own nut-brown eyes with their black and honest pupils drawn by the authority of magic and high enchantment to stare into the shaman's. His eyes were perfect circles of deepest yellow, the colour of egg yolks, and their centres great glass windows on his soul where danced its twin image, fiery, frenzied. She saw herself reflected, tiny, powerless, and grey and white as he, for Aza's lineaments had changed. He showed himself in his true form, that of a hawk eagle, crowned with a crest of feathers, booted in striated feathers and spurred with eight cruel talons. He spread his tail, shook out his wide

262

wings and and spread them on the wind, where they quivered in delicious anticipation of flight. Yet the shaman retained the shadow of his human-form. His beak was also his nose and its leathery gape his mouth, his wings arms, his fingers long, dark primary feathers and his drum a circle of purest white upon his downy breast. He parted his beak and whispered,

'Be still, daughter, be calm. My talons close upon your wrists and I lift you, so . . . but you are neither my prize nor my prey. I carry you up, so far, so lightly, into the night and, so gently, drop you down upon the silver dazzle which is the light of the moon. Walk now and see the difference between truth and reality.'

The ascent was slow and stately, as if it happened in a dream. Gry felt her feet touch down – on air which, when she looked, had the appearance of a field of short grasses that, though they could be seen quavering in the skyborn wind, were also transparent. Far below and through them, she could see the declivities and steeps of the Altaish, its hidden valleys and unmastered summits and, when she whirled about, the endless ocean steppe.

'Sacred Sky!' she cried, 'Blessed Air!'

'It is your element,' the eagle said.

'I thought myself a creature of the grass and plains.'

'So, in a sense, you are – but of these sky-plains which are like your nature, pure and receptive. Quietly now, my child. Stand on your four feet and tell me what you know.'

She did not know how it happened nor felt herself transformed but, when she did as the eagle told her, saw that she had horse's hooves and slender forelegs rising out of them. She tossed her mane and flicked her tail up and down.

'I am the sky-mare. I am Nandje's daughter,' she said.

'Good! The first is truth and the second reality.'

Gry, feeling her own mouth and voice within the ghostly horse-form, was ready to speak. The words were perfectly shaped.

'I have outrun my companions and reached the end of the world. I seek my father. From him I will obtain a blessing and the courage to live life alone.'

'Alone?' the eagle interrupted her. 'What of the golden youth?'

'Aurel? Isn't he lost – or dead?'

'Look below.'

Somewhere in the ultimate fastness of the Altaish is a meadow, an alp far higher than those rich fields where the stone dwarf Bluejohn brings his herds to graze; higher, and unlike the everyday world below, littered with wonderful boulders of agate, cobalt and opal whose sides glimmer by moonlight. One flower only flourishes at such an altitude, the wan moly which no one but the gods dares pick. Aurel Wayfarer, struggling free of the mountainous undercountry by a disused mineshaft, had come upon this fantastical field and lay asleep there, his blameless features upturned to the moon.

Gry expressed herself as horses do, by kicking up her heels and cantering in circles; afterwards casting herself down to roll in the moongrass: I love him, I love him. The eagle answered as though she had spoken aloud.

'You must decide what is to be done about the human predicament; but I will tell you this for nothing: he believes that the woman called Friendship was his first and truest love when she was no more than his mentor. In time, whatever passes, he will know that distinction belongs to you, Gry of the Herd. He will never forget you.

'Now let us be done with bodily matters and with emotions which only deflect the spirit and turn it from its goal. Come a little way with me – we will walk together in the Pastures of Heaven.'

'The Lady Byely spoke of this place, when I saw her at Russet Cross. Shall we meet her?'

'No; no, not now, not here.'

'But show me the Horse!'

'I cannot.'

'Is he well?'

'I cannot tell. Come.'

They walked together over the shining turf which, being made of light, was as soft and springy as a bed made all of thistledown. Gry paced forward in an elegant, stately way, her proud neck curved, and the eagle tramped sturdily on his strongly muscled legs. Soon, he grew tired of such slow, meditative progress and flew up to circle underneath the moon, where his shift-shapen body glowed outside and within, showing the bones of the eagle and of the man. He flew down and perched on Gry's back.

'You are a fine and courageous spirit,' said he. 'As for your soul, that is as clean and unblemished as the day it was born. Do you see the boon-tree? We will rest beneath it.' He bounded up and flew to perch in its white branches.

Gry approached the tree which, like the elder trees in Malthassa below, was bushy and many-trunked. It grew out of a starry hummock in the heavenly pasture and something, which she took to be a doll of the kind women leave as offerings and charms, rested against it. When she bent her neck to sniff and touch the mommet with her nose, it sprang upright and unfolded gracile limbs. It looked at her from fearless, beady eyes and scratched an unmarked skin as pale as the tree behind it.

'I am yours,' it said.

Gry shied and tossed her head and mane fearfully.

'There's no need of fear,' said the eagle, 'This is your child.'

'I never had a child!'

'Yet you should have done, had the Horse not called upon his storyteller's veto and prevented it. This creature is the soul which started forth from the Shadow World when you and Heron coupled.'

'He did not complete his violent work.'

'Indeed, he did; but you have hidden it in your mind and from your waking memory. Greet the pikulik kindly. There is no disgrace in being desired by Heron, who was a vigorous man and a great historian and lore-master. The only shame is in the way he chose to take you; but that is past now, for the Pastures of Heaven have made you whole again and healed all your wounds.'

Gry looked at the little creature sideways. She snorted and blew air in the little creature's face. It seemed as helpless and innocent as a real babe and boldly returned her gaze, its eyes shining like beads of black glass.

'I am yours to command,' it said. 'Aza, who walks between the worlds, sent for me. You may call me Umbra, which signifies my home, the Palace of Shadows, and also my failure to be born as a child. I shall never have a birthplace to leave on a sunny morning or go back to as the sun sets.'

It put up a hand and smoothed its tangled, black hair. A knowing expression appeared on its smooth face.

'You see that I took something from each of you, before I was called back,' it said and smiled warmly, just like Gry. 'It is time to come down to earth, little Mother, pretty Mare. Be still while I jump on your back. Now gallop as hard as you can before the Pasture dissolves and becomes what makes it, separate moonbeams as insubstantial as myself.'

Gry, alarmed and suddenly full of the fear of falling, reared up and plunged forward as if all the men of the Ima were after her. The spirit-eagle soared once more into the eye of the moon, his two wings stiff blades. And the pace of the world and of the heavens, of the universe both real and magical, slowed, so that first Gry, with her small rider, and then the eagle, drifted through the moonbeams and alighted on the bald mountainside.

Gry thought she must have fallen asleep and dreamed a while, so listless was she; but Aza was there beside her, with his bone horse which lay turned to separate, fire-blackened bones, on the rocks.

'I fear he has spent himself; his power is gone,' said Aza. He raised his left hand and made a sign in the air. 'Rest, little Tarpan. I shall not waken you again.'

The shaman wrinkled his beaky nose.

'I smell death,' he said. 'It is mine. Listen well, Gry of the Herd. Your child, Umbra, may be commanded as a mother does her child, firmly and with love – do not let it play out of your sight! To you, it will show itself as it did in the Pastures of Heaven. But it loves to lead the common sort of men a dance for, being unborn, it has no loyaly to the humankind, except you, its mother-elect. See where it comes with flickering footsteps among the rocks!'

The blue light, taller than a candle-flame but shorter than

the flame of love which burns in every true lover's heart, lit up the rocks with its eerie presence, turned and twisted, settled between her feet. It burned stilly though the wind blew strong.

'Is it you?' said Gry.

'It is I, Umbra, wearing my dancing shoes.' The voice rose upward from the flame at her feet. 'Let me sit in your hand.'

'Will you not burn me?'

'I would not harm my mother!' Umbra rose, floating through the air, and stood on Gry's outstretched hand.

'You cannot ride here – I need my hands in case I slip on the mountainside.'

'Then I will ride upon your shoulder.'

The wind howled suddenly and Gry, the flame burning now beside her right ear, turned, it was so like the cry of a wolf. Aza was kneeling stiffly on the hard ground.

'It is my fetch,' he said. 'I am called and I must go. Bless me, Gry. I wronged you and have redeemed you. Give me your blessing before I die.'

'Then give me your hands. Put them in mine.'

The shaman did so, reaching up to her.

'"My blessings in your footprints which will mark me no more, Aza", says our Mother, the Moist Earth. "My blessings in the hollow porches of your ears, which will fall in upon themselves and decay as do the houses of men and the beasts", says Stribog, the Wind. "And mine in the sockets of your eyes and in those orbs of gristle which soon will be no more than dust rolling beneath me", says Svarog, the Sky . . .'

Gry shook her head to clear it of the voices of the gods who had used her.

'Take my blessings with you, Aza, for you have shown me the truth – and – and –' The shaman's hands were slipping out of hers as death came upon and weakened him. She gripped them for a moment and held him back. 'Take my greeting with you, to the Lady Byely –' Aza was gone, fallen on the ground. His body twitched once in the cold hands of death and, rising like a great

267

grey gull from a wrecked ship, up flew the eagle, mounting high until he was lost in the moonshine.

Gry, bending over his body, heard the shaman's voice blow in the wind.

'My drum is yours. My drum is for you, little Gry. Take it . . .'

She did not know if she should mourn his death or celebrate it. He had been unafraid, had seemed to welcome the end of his long stay in the world. Without needing to puzzle it out, she knew where he had gone: to take his place at the table on Russet Cross and there converse with his kind, the shamans who had gone before; to listen to the messages carried in the wind, by birds, by water, by light itself. She took possession of the drum, carefully freeing Aza's arms of its carrying-straps. As she touched them, his arms grew translucent and disappeared, his head and neck faded; his legs, his whole body vanished. She spoke to Umbra.

'He has called his body to him,' she said. 'He cannot always be an eagle.'

She stroked the drum as Aza himself used to do, first letting her nails slide over its taut surface and then tapping with the pads of her fingers to make it speak in its most gentle voice. She struck the drum hard. It cried loudly, its shout echoing after it. The sound excited her for it reached deep into her soul and called on the restive spirit of her other self, the sky-mare. She struck the drum again and again, her head close up against it, her body crouched. The sound, as it filled her ears and then her head and all the bony spaces of her body, made her rise to her feet and begin to spin where she stood until she was the sound of drumming herself, a flash of indigo and flying skins in the moonlight. It seemed as though she had caught fire for the pikulik, Umbra, danced as fast as she, circling about her so rapidly it seemed to multiply with every revolution.

As the sun came up, a scarlet coin from the sea, Gry sat panting on the ground. Where hooves and their music, the Plains and the Herd galloping, had occupied her mind and come to vivid life there,

268

was now a cavern of darkness and peace. As her body quieted, she looked out over the slopes below and chose, glad and steadfast, her route across the screes. There was a path, perhaps, a zigzag scoring the slope; whether it led up, or down, she could not tell.

Gry opened her carrying bag and ate some of the toadstools she had stored there. She collected water in her tin bowl, squeezing it from the moss which grew among the rocks.

'It is good to eat and drink, I think?' said Umbra querulously. 'That is something else you and my father denied me, the ordinary comforts of a baby.'

'Well, I cannot nurse a flame!'

Umbra jumped from her shoulders and wandered amongst the rocks. Mindful of Aza's warning, Gry kept watch over it.

Soon, her pikulik grew tired of sulking and returned to her. Its flame faded and, in its child form, it clambered into her lap.

'You may mother me now,' it said.

She was surprised to find Umbra warm and soft. Sib's touch had been cold and dry; but they were different kinds of Hell-folk, the sprite never intended by her maker to live beyond the gates of the Palace of Shadows but this, her unfleshed child, made solely to be sent above to claim the gift of life. And so, holding her pikulik against her breast, she fell to thinking of her dead father and all the Ima, men and women, who had gone before him, until the sun was fully up. Aza's drum lay beside her, the manikin which was its holdfast innocent in the daylight. The surface of the drum was covered in marks and pictograms which meant nothing to her.

'I suppose I shall know them one day,' she said.

Then, gathering up her belongings, knife, cup, and carrying bag she stowed them in their usual places and put her arms through the straps of Aza's drum, so that it sat on her back like a great, round shell. Umbra flew from her, its white body dissolving into blue flame, and rode upon the rim of the drum.

Gry turned about. There, where he had lain down, was the bone horse which Aza called Tarpan stretched for ever dead. She did not dare touch the bones but bowed her head to them and said, 'Rest quietly, Steed of Bone and Magic.'

Lastly, Gry took up her blanket, shook it out, and cast it like a cloak around her.

'Now, we are ready for the road!' said Gry. 'If there is one.'

Gry, casting about the slopes and screes, came at last to the path she had observed from the heights. It led both up and down, its meandering course determined by the presence of outcrops and boulders. This land, spread pale in the morning sun, was unpeopled and lonely. None dwelt here, it seemed and there was no abandoned house or mineworking to explain the path, no fields or grazing grounds. Sometimes, the path passed between rocks so high they made a ravine and in these places, shadows were gathered, dark shadows not formed by the light of the sun.

'Have no fear,' said Umbra. 'They are cousins of mine, up on holiday – when they are born they will become wolves and bears.'

'I never met a bear,' Gry said, 'but I have friends among the Wolves. I will pretend these reaching shadows are Mouse-Catcher's brothers and sisters.'

It was in one of these gloomy passes, that a familiar sound came to her, the happy – but so long unheard! – music of horse-gear with its complex melodies of creaks and jangles, and an undersong of groaning axles. Yet who would bring a cart up a track that led nowhere? She pressed herself bravely into the shadows which yielded before her and fled away into cracks and clefts. Umbra perched on a ledge.

Soon, she heard the steady beat of horses' hooves on the track and saw an old and rickety cart approaching. It was drawn by two horses harnessed one before the other and, as it came near, Gry saw the driver, a heavy red-faced man who was sleeping as he drove. An old garland of willow-boughs and dead flowers swayed above his nodding head.

The pair of horses stopped abruptly when they reached Gry, who pressed herself against the rocks and tried to be herself a shadow. When he felt the cart lurch and stop, the driver belched and woke.

'By the great Koschei!' he exclaimed. 'This is no place to halt, my beauties. It might be an ambush!'

He caught sight of Umbra flickering on the ledge, and slowly blinked his eyes; put up one strong and slabby hand to wipe away his dreams.

'Still there,' he said. 'Well, little corpse-candle, I hope you are not here to foretell my death. I've far too much business to go just yet – and I wonder what you do here, yourself, for your kind is usually met with in marshes and such low, moist places. Up here there must be wind enough, in season, to blow you to eternity!'

Umbra danced eerily, twirling on the ledge; but the man took no notice.

'I've been a traveller far too long to be scared by that,' he said and gathered the reins in his hands, ready to move on.

'What's that I spy?' he cried suddenly. 'A boy in hiding – no, 'tis a girl. Come forth, you silly creature. I'm no robber-captain or ravisher of unsquired dames.'

Gry stepped forward, her hand on her knife, in case.

'I did not suppose you were, sir,' she said. 'But it is best to be prudent when travelling far from home.'

'That's true – and you are a long way off. An Ima woman, I see. Are you a witch who climbs to gather simples in the Altaish; or a strolling musician perhaps, who can drum till dancers fall in a frenzy?'

'No, I am Gry, Nandje's daughter.'

'Nandje's daughter, well, well! He was a famous man, a great tamer of wild horses and a good toper to boot. Many's the time I've drained tankards side by side with him, at the Horse Fair, each of us striving to be the last to fall amongst the table legs and the turnspit dogs.'

'Then who are you?'

'Me? Oh, I am old Georg Deaner, the horse butcher. They call me Peacock 'cos I'm so resplendent! I hale from Espmoss, where our satanic majesty – I mean Lord Koschei, my dear – spent his youth.'

'I know little of the Archmage, no more than anyone. But Espmoss I have heard of – you too are a long way from home.'

'My business takes me to all parts of Malthassa. I have only to hear of an imminent death, and I'm off.'

'Beyond the Altaish, Mr Deaner? That is where we are – in a country the Ima say does not exist. We believe – all, that is, except me – that the world ends beyond the Altaish.'

The horse-slaughterer laughed.

'The land hereabouts scarcely belongs to this world, it is so very bleak. But so is death and that is what my business is all about. There's a dead horse nearby – did you chance to see it?'

'Yes, I saw it; but you will find it a strange horse, sir. It died a long time ago and was brought to life again by the shaman, Aza. It is a skeleton only, and has lost its head.'

'Well, well. Then it will be easy for me to carry to the cart; and I can sell it to the glue-maker.'

'You had better bury it and lay a heavy stone on the grave; and afterwards call in a priest to make sure it cannot rise a second time and haunt you.'

'That will cost me money, not make it for me!'

Gry regarded him with a smile waking on her lips.

'Go with the Gods, Mr Deaner. You have more power over the galloping kind than my father in his heyday. I feel your butchering knife and the bite of your cleaver as if they cut into my own soul.'

'Devil be burned in his own fires! You are the first woman I've met who frightens me. Even witch-women and gypsies do not stand by and ignore a corpse-light.'

'That is my child, Georg Deaner. Come, Umbra!'

The blue flame sank through the air and alighted on Gry's shoulder.

'I shall leave you now, with a prayer in my heart and my lucky Parados button in my pocket,' said the horse-butcher fervently. 'Gid – HUP, my lovelies!'

'What is your Parados button?' Gry called after him.

'What he give me once, in return for a ride in this cart.'

272

'Lord Parados?'

'Ay!' Georg Deaner yelled and was gone, about a turn in the path. Gry, striding out, felt Umbra flicker on her shoulder. It was laughing. The voice of the butcher, singing in a loud, cracked voice, came to her.

'I'll be coming round the mountain when I come . . .'

'It is an affliction of the human kind,' said Umbra, 'to bellow in the face of danger. But the butcher will do his work and bring poor Tarpan to the glue-works.'

'And me, where will you bring me, Umbra?'

'Where you wish to go, dear Mother; nowhere else.'

A Soul, when it dies, yearns to leave familiar places and journey where it belongs, with the other dead. The body is cast aside, remaining only as a memory or Shadow – which some call a Ghost – and this shadow-self, which keeps its mortal outline, is grey and usually transparent to fit it for an eternity in the obscure Palace of Shadows. A host of these beings was walking in the drear lands beyond the Altaish, forming a loose column which ceaselessly altered shape and to which newcomers, drifting down the mountains' sides or floating silently to earth after strange, limitless journeys from the furthest corners of Malthassa, joined themselves. Their feet trod lightly, without footfall, upon granite setts laid edge to edge for many leagues along the shore. This was the road to Hell, an ancient road where the crowding souls pressed close together, an unnumberable legion in the country Gry believed unpeopled.

As they solemnly processed, the Shadows sang in unison:

'Through the night of doubt and sorrow

Onward goes our pilgrim band –'

Gry heard them from afar as she hurried downhill with Umbra, who sometimes flitted about her in a burst of flame, sometimes sat still on one shoulder or the other; or hovered above her and marked her as an original. She questioned the pikulik, and Umbra endeavoured to satisfy her thirst for knowledge.

'They walk together because they must all arrive at the same

273

destination, Dolorous Wharf; and they sing for the same reason as the horse-butcher: to keep their courage up.'

Aurel, bounding with the energy his sleep in the enchanted alp had brought him, leaping tussock and boulder and sliding down small avalanches of scree, heard the voices of the shadow pilgrims; saw their translucent masses moving inexorably to the shore.

'This is a place with as many wonders as Pargur,' he said, 'and truly is it a perilous land; but I have my sword, my pistol and my lucky feather and shall avoid harm.'

Parados, moving the Red Horse down the slopes with care, picking the smoothest way, was soon aware of the deathly hosting when the Horse laid back his ears and whinnied his disquiet.

'They are gathering,' he said. 'Soon they will be weighed and ready to embark.'

So intent were the four on the procession below them that they did not see each other nor realise what a level piece of ground and meeting of their ways they were approaching, but arrived one after the other on the pebbled margin of a small spring. Then Aurel saw Gry, who was sitting on a boulder with a flickering marsh-light in her hands, and Parados watched them greet each other with the embrace of true friends and many delighted cries, while the blue flame spun from Gry's hands and whirled in the air. They embrace, he thought vaguely, They kiss, his efforts and attention directed inward to the Horse. Feeling every exertion of that weary body and every ache and spasm in the exhausted muscles, Parados imagined the Plains for him, the fresh grass, the wind and the wide and open sky. The Horse arched his neck in the proud curve of old, drew in some breaths of the sea-salted air and broke into a gallop, such a clash and thunder that the stones beneath his hooves rang and the ground shook; and Gry and Aurel looked up and saw the Red Horse coming fast as the storm wind.

'Horse, my Dear!' Gry ran to meet him, Aurel close behind. Reaching up, she caught hold of the Horse's neck before he came to a halt and hung there, heels and skirts flying, laughing with joy. The Horse stopped suddenly, panted and shuddered; and Gry, back on the ground, kept an arm about his neck and stood by him as she used so long ago in the Plains, when first they began to know each other.

'Rest, Horse,' she said. 'Lie down and I will bring you food and water.'

She spoke bravely, all the while looking about her as if she hoped to see good grazing or a brimming haystack on the barren hillside.

'There is nothing here,' said Parados. 'The Shadows need no food. Nor do I. I am dying, Gry – he is dying and so must I, without a new body to live in.'

'Take mine!'

'You and I have different destinations. Poor Horse, he has served me too well and for too long.'

'I cannot tell which of you is my dear Horse and which is Parados.'

'I –' The voice in her head faltered. 'By all the gods, by Svarog, I must leave you, dearest Gry . . .'

The Horse, as if poleaxed, slid to his knees and toppled over at full length. His legs kicked once and then he was dead, his great brown eyes fixed and lifeless, mirroring the sky. Gry, who had stumbled as he fell, threw herself upon his neck and clasped it. She sobbed into his mane and cried encouragement, though she well knew he was dead. She did not see the tiny azure manikin which slipped out of his mouth and which was the soul of Parados. It ran across the rocks like a hunted thing, a fugitive looking for shelter, a miniature man; jumped up to the toe of Aurel's left boot and began to climb his leg. Aurel did not see it – who notices an ant? – until he felt a movement on his neck. He put up a hand and slapped at the irritation, scratched his lip and felt a creature scrabbling in his mouth. Then, his mouth twisted with disgust, he coughed and spat.

He was too late. Already, Parados's soul had shinnied up the cavernous passages of his nose and was sitting comfortably, at rest, behind the shield of his forehead bone, quiet as a dumb man at prayer.

Aurel bent to comfort Gry.

'My Horse, the best friend I ever had; Parados, the truest knight that ever was! It is a double doom. It is cruel,' she keened. Mogia, using the power of the Wolf Pack and the airy channels which pass by Russet Cross, spoke to her, 'Death comes to us all, little She-cub. Do not protest. It is the Way,' but Aurel, being a soldier and death's familiar, could only pat her back and say, 'Please don't cry,' for he did not understand how anyone could so distress herself over a horse. Parados kept silent.

After a while Gry stood up and wiped her eyes on her skirt.

'She is right,' she said. 'It is useless to weep for I can alter nothing and it my own grief I selfishly weep at.'

'Who is right?' said Aurel.

'The Wolf-Mother: I heard her voice.'

Aurel stared at Gry and noticed then how weird she looked, how fey, with her tangled hair and her rags of untanned skin and indigo cloth, her silk princess's blouse; her collection of strange artefacts, the old knife, the drum; the little blue flame which followed her about.

'What happened to you, under the mountains?'

'A hard schooling, Aurel, such as young fillies get to turn them into wise and steady mares. Look, golden man, the Shadow of the Horse!'

The grey shape of the ghostly Horse was rising from his bed in the great stallion's body, coming with a shake of his mane and a swish of his tail to stand, head up, tasting the wind.

'Look!' said Gry again, for the Grey Horse was watching her. He came softly to her, rubbed his immaterial head against her shoulder and uttered the ghost of that kindly whicker with which a horse greets a friend. Gry gently stroked the shifting planes of his neck. Then the Horse, well satisfied with her greeting, turned seaward and waited quietly.

By the shore, the wind blew as saltily as he did in the Plains and at Russet Cross, where the dead shamans sat banqueting: but the wind that came from the Altaish brought news of snowmelt and avalanche, of an untoward heat and a loosening of veins of gold and silver from the tight hold of the rock. It also carried the sound of Georg Deaner singing energetically as he rode in his cart toward the sea and the dead Horse.

'The man you hear is a horse-butcher collecting corpses like a ghoul,' said Gry. 'But he shall not have this horse. Help me, Aurel. We must gather stones to pile upon his body, or Deaner will carry him off and sully his dignity with his axe and cleaver.'

They worked hard, Aurel bringing the bigger boulders and Gry heaping up the smaller over the Red Horse. Umbra floated a little way up the path to keep watch. Gry took out her sparkstones and her tinder and burned a little of her hair and a few stems of sparse sea-grass as an offering to Svarog. Then, satisfied she had done her best for the peace and protection of the Horse and for Parados, she offered Aurel the toadstools she had brought from under the Altaish and they both ate a little and drank spring water from the painted bowl.

This necessary succour of spirit and of body being complete, Gry and Aurel walked down the last slope and came to the road. The Grey Horse followed them, a pale and hollow memory of his mortal self, the Red Horse, but beautiful nonetheless.

Gry took Aurel's hands in hers.

'We must part, brave Esquire,' she said. 'You to your destiny, which I am sure is a glorious and gallant one, and I to mine – for I am fated to follow in Nandje, my father's, steps and bring this, his own particular knife, to him.'

'I will come with you!' Aurel declared. When she had spoken so strangely before, claiming to hear a wolf talking to her, he had only noticed her oddness and her untidy clothing. Now, he saw the beauty he had admired before and being lonely and a young man and, anyway, half in love with his memory of her weak and ill in Wathen Fields and courageous and strong, journeying to the Altaish, felt a flush of joy and a surge of desire. He remembered how they had held hands in the Stone Dwarf's house and the half-serious, half-jesting conversation they had enjoyed when he had shown her his sword and told her its history.

'No, Aurel,' she said now. 'Once, not so long ago, just over the mountain-ridge, it seemed as though you and I should be together for ever or, at least, until death. But I have learned that this is not to be; though I begin to love you.'

'But I will come with you all the same.'

'You cannot, Aurel. You must find your own story.'

'I want your story to be mine and mine, yours,' he protested. 'Besides, this road leads to the Ocean. I will at least come that far and see what there is to see, for I do not believe that all these shadow people will walk into the sea. They must be going somewhere.'

'They are and it is called Dolorous Wharf. You will not like it there – the very name tells how dreary it must be.'

'I can weather that!'

'Then swear to leave me when you are sure of my safety, for you will need all your strength to get back across the Altaish, and I cannot turn away from my destiny.'

'I swear it, Gry – on my sword, Joyeuse.' And so saying, he unsheathed it, lifted it in a salute and kissed it where blade met hilt and there was a golden ornament in the shape of a cockerel and the motto in+battle+i+bring+joy. 'I swear it though I am not content: I could love you well.'

'And I you.' She smiled at him and they walked hand in hand. Parados also smiled and continued to keep his watchful silence.

The Shadows flowed about them, passing on either side as water does an island or the heavenly wind a star. On that starry island, Gry and Aurel paused to look at one another. They did not speak, for parting and sorrow lay in words. Aurel took Gry in his arms and kissed her. Sib crept close then from her hiding place among the thronging Shadows, grey like with like, peered at them and shook her head.

'Love is bondage,' she said to Gry. 'Free yourself, my friend.'

Gry neither saw nor heard her.

The Grey Horse waited at the side of the road and, though he was but the shadow of a horse, was not surprised when he saw a gaunt, shaven-headed man approach, a man whose character was in his appearance and who wore a suit the colour of a rainy day and carried a sack over one shoulder and a leather satchel over the other. The Horse's mother, the fleet mare, Hurricane, had told him many tales in the old days back in the Plains.

'He is a man whose work is arduous and trying,' she had said, 'though he is no horseman.'

The newcomer, noticing that the Shadows went out of their way, moved amongst them and came to the timeless place where the lovers stood. He tapped Aurel on the shoulder.

'Have you any sins for me, Sir Knight – you and the lady?'

Aurel and Gry stood apart and the thin man looked them up and down.

'I have sinned,' Aurel answered. 'And I,' said Gry, but the man shook his head.

'I can see that you are blameless,' he said to Gry. 'And that your knight, like all men, has committed certain peccadilloes which come of youth and eagerness. So I ask you again, sir, are you shriven, or did you die in sin?'

'I am not dead!' said Aurel. 'Neither is she.'

'Then what do you here, Sir Knight?' the man said. 'I can see now that you and the lady are to be numbered amongst the living, for (though I don't understand how she has happened on a pikulik) you both have the bright and shiny speech and bodily hues of life, and are not reduced to mere shadows like these pilgrim souls.' He gestured behind him at the endless procession.

'What do you, sir?' Aurel said. 'You, too, have the appearance of a living man with your long face and your burdens, which are like those carried by many a farmer and peasant.'

'O, I am exempt from both life and death. I have work here, amongst the shadow-folk. I am Gabriel Chrism, the Sin Eater, and before they depart I must devour as many of their sins as I can.'

'Had my father any sins, I wonder?' said Gry to herself, but the Sin Eater heard her.

'Who was your father?' he asked.

'Nandje of the Ima.'

279

'I remember him! A small man, very strong in life and bow-legged from perpetual horse-riding. His own horses trod him.'

'That is how it happened,' said Gry. 'Though I still cannot believe it of the Herd, which Nandje worked as easily as I can milk a mare – that is the leader of the Herd waiting there, Master Chrism: Nandje's own mount.'

'The Herd trampled him by accident after he was swept from the saddle by the Om Ren – it was really the Forest Ape who killed Nandje.' Aurel spoke abruptly and the voice that came from his mouth was as different from his own as the sound of a bassoon from that of an oboe, or as chalk from cheese indeed.

'How do you know that?' said Gry, astonished.

'I must have heard it somewhere – in an inn or perhaps some Pargur merchant's shop,' said Aurel in his own musical voice and frowned because he could remember nothing about it.

The Sin Eater rubbed his hands together as if he were trying to warm them.

'I must be about my business,' he said. Gry caught at his sleeve.

'You did not tell me anything about my father I don't already know.'

'It is not a daughter's business to ask after her father's conscience. Such matters are between him and his soul.'

'But you have seen him! Tell me please, Master Gabriel, if he passed this way?'

'To be sure he did!' exclaimed the Sin Eater. 'He had died and what other way is there to travel to the Palace of Shadows? He looked well for one about to enter life eternal,' and he nodded sadly to Gry and went on. Aurel and Gry, hand in hand again, also walked on and the Grey Horse fell in behind them. They watched the Sin Eater going from one Shadow to another and, if there were sins to be got rid of, sprinkling salt from his satchel on a hunk of bread from his sack and eating it and the sins.

'He is like Byely,' Gry whispered. 'Melancholy.'

'Who? O, one of your spirit friends that I can know nothing of,' said Aurel a little jealously.

'She was once an Ima princess like myself. The Horse – or Parados – told me her story. She played melodies upon a turtle shell and, when people asked her why her music was so sad, she said: "My songs are sorrowful because they have water in them. Salt water, of the sea. My turtle swam in it, breathed it –" The eye-bright closes tight because she wept over it, Aurel. She died for love.'

'That is tragic, but not unusual,' said he.

'How can he bear to eat all that salt?' wondered Gry. 'A whole satchelful.'

'It has given him a sour expression.'

The sun hung low over the water and transformed its grey waves into ridges of pure rose red before it vanished below the horizon and gave way to a thick darkness which hid the mountains and the shore. Without the stars, it was dismal and impossible to see. Aurel put his arm round Gry and held her as close as was comfortable while they walked through the night's uncertainties. The pilgrim Shadows had begun to sing again:

> 'Clear before us through the darkness
> Gleams and burns the guiding light;
> Sister clasps the hand of brother,
> Stepping fearless through the night.'

Georg Deaner heaved away the last of the boulders which had covered his quarry and rightful prize, the body of the Red Horse. Now, as he looked at it and smelled the corruption so soon at work on it, he saw that what he had exposed was nothing more than a Plains stallion, stocky and sturdy, with a thick coat of russet-coloured hair. He stood back to mop his brow and scratch a louse from his head, but did not scratch in wonderment or perplexity for the proper disposal, burial, last rites and prayers spoken over a carcass meant nothing to him. He was concerned only to prevent waste. The dead horse represented money; was rawhide, glue, cutlery handles and dogs' meat to others. He turned away and began to set up the block and tackle he would use to haul it on to his cart.

....

The Grey Horse, who had watched all night, looked about him.
Day was near. Close by, Aurel Wayfarer, though he sat with
the thronging dead, slept deeply; but the sleep of Gry, Nandje's
daughter, was buoyant as a falling leaf. She woke while the world
was still in darkness and remained where she found herself, leaning
against Aurel, while she watched the shimmering Shadows. They
were as quiet as she but their silence was that of vast ages contem-
plating eternity and hearing the slow music which is continuo to
the song of life. Aurel, who moved and softly breathed, clenched
and unclenched his sword hand about the horse-blanket in which
he had wrapped himself and murmured 'Who fights?' – all in his
dreams – was that.

The sky beyond the Ocean flushed red: the sun was about to
rise and Gry felt elation, a lifting of the night's solemn mood –
even here in this unhappy place, well-named Dolorous, for it was
as dark and grim as sorrow. An immense jetty of blackest basalt
projected into the water. The Shadows were crowded upon it and
on the road leading to it. Somewhere amongst them was the Sin
Eater and, she supposed, perhaps some men or women whose
lives had touched her own; whom she had known. The ruddy,
ascending light woke no reflection in the land: in the Plains at
sunrise every blade of grass became a fiery mirror. Behind her,
the Altaish remained unwoken and dull. Nor were the Shadows
touched. Yet she felt herself aglow with light and the prospect of
a new and unknown world. Umbra, jumping from her shoulder,

performed its own morning dance to the sun and then, shifting shape with a purple flicker, became the white-skinned unformed child and beckoned to her.

Gry moved slowly so that she would not wake Aurel, and followed the pikulik. She glanced behind her: in the new light, Aurel had truly become a golden man, his hair hot coals, his sleeping body the colour of a metal in a furnace. She crossed a little, watermarked strand. Below the towering wall of Dolorous Wharf was a stretch of shingle and there, Umbra came to a halt. It beckoned again, but not to her. Sib was there beside the pikulik, suddenly and miraculously unfolding herself from the darkness at the foot of the wall. She ran to greet Gry.

'So far, so good!' the grey spirit cried. 'O Gry, I have watched over you so long. I am worn to a spider's thread – such a hard journey you made by the heights and depths, through every kind of danger and wayside hazard.'

'I saw you, under the Altaish,' said Gry. 'You walked with me for a good while.'

'That was not I but your troubled mind building me from memory. I was there, but behind you, watching out for ghouls and saltiers and other underground folk. But I must not chatter so! Quickly now, before the sun comes up. I must make you ready for the last stage of your journey. I will untangle your hair (how it has grown!) and Umbra will show you how to cleanse yourself.'

'I must be very dirty from my travels.'

'Possibly. We mean a spiritual cleansing.'

While she spoke, Sib worked frantically to unloose the five plaits the leshi had made and to pull out the yellow snail shells, which she laid in a row below high-water mark. Lastly, she drew her long nails through and through Gry's hair until it was as smooth and thick as the tail of the Red Horse and hung down below her shoulders to lap the pale circle of her magic drum as the sun's shadow touches the moon at eclipse.

'Now I must hide my face while the sun looks at you,' said Sib, covered her eyes with her hands and crept into the shadow of the wharf.

Umbra led Gry forward until she stood within a footsbreadth of the Ocean.

'Salute the sun!' it cried.

Gry raised her arms to the sky and tipped back her head, as she had seen Aza do so many times at home. The sun's warmth flooded over her, and his intense, yellow light washed fear from her mind and weariness from her soul. Her dismal thoughts and uncertainties vanished, her hearing was cleared of the echoes of the night and the underground Altaish; her sight became keen and empty of the fearsome phantoms of the past. When, at Umbra's bidding, she turned away from the shore and walked slowly back to Aurel it was with a springing step. She looked at him with fresh eyes and saw him for what he was, a handsome, over-eager young man who had his own, separate life to live and much to learn there and many obstacles to overcome and adventures to enjoy; and she saw the light of his soul burn ardently and with much more vigour than is usual; and this, for she could not see everything, was because the soul of Parados had hidden itself in Aurel's and, therefore, doubled its strength.

Aurel opened his eyes and looked at her.

'By Linen Warp and Silken Weft!' he exclaimed. 'You are as great a beauty as that mysterious Lilith the gypsies speak of – your hair ebony, your skin amber, your eyes . . . your clear eyes shine bright as lamps at eventide . . . the very sun has got into you, to the very pith and bone . . . beside these dull Shadows you are the light of day – of my day, Gry!'

Gry smiled.

'It is time to part,' she said gently. 'You have sunlight for your journey but, soon, I shall have only the dark. I will find my father and I am sure you will find what you seek, even if it is not the whole truth.'

'I do not want to us to part,' Aurel said truculently and reached up to embrace her.

'Hush! Look – out at sea. It is Hespyne!' Gry moved aside.

Frozen in their attitudes of love and rejection, they saw the translucent, triple-masted ship lift herself up and over each long, foam-topped wave as it rolled toward the land. The new sunlight, which struck her as she rose and fell, gave her the yellow hues of deadly jaundice or the morbid plague. Her black sails were set to run against the wind.

'The Ship of the Dead! I saw her pass below me when I rode in Frostfeather,' said Aurel, so softly he seemed to breathe the words.

'As Friendship told us truly,' said Gry. 'Yet there were many who doubted her. I, too, have seen the ship – passing by Russet Cross when I rode the Red Horse there.'

Hespyne, tacking her wayward course, sailed up and down the coast and sometimes appeared small as a child's toy between the hills and troughs and sometimes hove huge against the skyline; but always kept her sickly, shining yellow light and drew nearer all the while, her sails straining on each even tack and billowing as she went about. Aurel saw that her figurehead was a skeletal Hell-Hound and Gry that the devices painted on her flying pennons were reaping-hooks and shrouds.

The Shadows were moving. All along the wharf and in the road, they wavered and parted rank to make two separate columns. The Sin Eater walked to and fro, waving his skinny arms at them and crying 'Thieves, Hypocrites, Miscreants, Murderers! True Religious, Charitable Ladies, Poets, Saints!' Gry, Aurel and the Grey Horse, perforce, moved forward, pressed by insubstantial backs and shoulders, thrust aside or held back by arms they could pass their bodies through, as if they swam in clouded water. So, they came to the wharfside and the ship, which lay there tossing beside the stone but never grazed her sides upon it. The two columns of Shadows filed slowly forward, one on the left and the other on the right.

A man stood at the head of a gangway made of linked and chain-girt bones. He, it was certain, was the captain of the ship, that curse-ridden wanderer, Jan Pelerin, whom Parados had described to Gry: a burly man, his hair cut close to his head but dense and upright like a sea-beast's fur, his hands calloused and his broad face burnt brown. Clearly, he was hardy and used to the wind's muscle and the sea's wet tongue, for he wore nothing beside a kilt of grey tweed and a heavy belt of salt-dulled leather patterned with hair and, on his wrists, bracers of the same, whiskery hide. As it came aboard, he marked each soul with the print of his thumb on the forehead, sinister or dexter, evil or good.

The last of the company of friends who had journeyed from Wathen Fields came to the gangway: Gry, calm as Aza facing death, with Umbra burning steadily on her shoulder; Aurel, his right hand straying warily about the hilt of his sword; and the Grey Horse steadily pacing. Gry set her right foot on the bones. At once, Jan Pelerin frowned and called out:

'Hold! No closer! None but the dead may walk here. The quick have no business with me and are not permitted to sail in Hespyne nor set foot in the Palace of Shadows.'

Gry bent low in an Ima woman's curtsey.

'I am Gry, Nandje's daughter,' she said. 'I must deliver his knife to my father, whatever the cost to myself, death or destruction – and see! Here is his horse behind me, which he would like to have for eternity, to ride about and gallop on as he used in life.'

The captain laughed loud as a gale.

'How pleasant death would be if every daughter could bring her father his favourite playthings,' he said. He bent his sleek head and looked sharply at her; she returned his gaze as keenly.

'Hoh,' said Jan Pelerin. 'Hoh, hum. You are carrying some rare cargo yourself – a descrying cup and a talking drum; you are wearing birch-bark shoes. I see that you are a cunning woman.'

'I? No, I am only Gry. Once I was a princess but, these strange days, I am just myself and usually alone.'

'But you *are* a wise woman. Your aura is as the wind on the moon and your unborn child sits on your shoulder. Therefore – since shamans walk freely between the worlds – you may come aboard.'

Gry did not dare turn to Aurel, nor say goodbye, lest her courage and determination should waver. She walked quickly up the gangway, which was slippery and wet, and the Grey Horse (though he was but a shadow of his former self) shoved Aurel

287

aside and followed her on to the deck of the ship where Sib, stepping from the crowd of Shadows, took her by the hand to greet her. Aurel, his good nature lost in the new worry-lines which creased his face, set foot on the gangway. Immediately, Jan Pelerin hastened forward and barred his way with arms outstretched.

'Do not anger me,' said Aurel in a grating, surly voice. 'I must go with Gry and make sure she does not come to harm.'

'She does not need you, hasty knight.'

'I must go,' Aurel said again and closed his hand on his swordhilt.

'I say you are forbidden.'

Swiftly, Aurel drew Joyeuse from the scabbard and threatened him with the keen blade upraised.

'I will go!'

'It is forbidden!'

'Defend yourself. I cannot slay an unarmed man.'

'Do your worst!'

Then Aurel brought Joyeuse hard down upon the captain's shoulder and such was the sharpness and temper of the sword that the brawny arm of Jan Pelerin should have been sheared off as easily as a woodman lops a dead branch from an oak. The blade passed through flesh and bone and a gout of blood spurted into the sea, but the captain's arm and shoulder remained united and intact. Aurel stepped back a pace. His fair face was flushed and he panted with the effort of his blow and with anger and desperation.

'You are a young hot-blood,' said the captain mildly. 'Know by the Lord Yama that you cannot harm or overcome me. The Dark Lord is my master – how could a mere mortal change anything he has decreed?'

Aurel looked up into the wide face and saw that the captain had a divided lip like a wildcat, or a seal, and that his chin sprouted long, grey whiskers.

'I am not beaten yet,' he said.

'Must I waste my energy to work magic on you?' Jan Pelerin sighed gustily. 'How would you like to leave this place on the back of a whirlwind, sir? Or in the jaws of Leviathan? Ah, witless boy, I was once an intemperate youth before my sins brought me here.'

Gry, looking down on both of them from the side of the ship, called, 'Gain grace, Aurel. Admit defeat. Look, I am safe aboard – say goodbye in friendship.'

'No need. I will come aboard – eventually,' said Aurel, reaching for the pistol in his belt; but his hand, before he could draw and prime the gun, faltered. He blushed, his heated face turning scarlet. He stepped back another pace or two and dropped to his knees.

'I have not forgot my oath – my solemn word sworn on Joyeuse here. I promised to leave you when I was sure of your safety,' he said, '– and you seem to be safe enough up there, for all that Hespyne bucks in the water.'

'I am perfectly safe,' said Gry. 'The Horse is beside me and here are Sib and Umbra who know the Palace of Shadows as well as I know the Plains.'

Aurel, jumping quickly up, gave her a brave, Pargur salute, turned about and made his slow way back along the wharf against the tide of Shadows. Parados, whose timely intervention had brought Aurel to his senses, lay still and neither subtracted from nor added anything more to the confusion that was Aurel's mind, though he wished most fervently that they might both go with Gry.

'Yet,' said he inwardly, startling Aurel, 'I shall not long be idle for I have many more pages to write.'

'Surely I am crazed with love and longing,' said Aurel, shaking his head to try and clear it, 'and shall be wholly mad soon for I am proved a white-livered coward.'

Thereafter, he climbed the hillside steadily, sometimes stopping to look at the dark wharf far below and wonder at the ghostly ship which waited there, with sails hoisted. The road to the wharf was empty and the glim and glamour of the pilgrim Shadows gone. He supposed they were all on board and climbed a little higher to a steep place where a rock jutted, proud as the bow of Hespyne. Here, he halted again. The pennon at the head of

Hespyne's mainmast dipped once as though someone pulled on a rope, and flew brave. On the wharf stood a tiny, stick-like figure which waved a white cloth: the Sin Eater, giving the dead a last salute. The ship of death set sail and pulled away from the land, bearing Aurel's love and hope with her. He flung himself down on the rock and hid his face. Tears sprang, which he allowed to flow until they wet his sleeve and which stained his face when he looked up, straining to see what passed over. Some creatures flew there, in the upper air, and their fluid voices reached him: geese, a trailing Y-shaped skein of them, so high they looked no bigger than flies. Even when they were gone, their cries remained to haunt this desolate place, all the home he had, with a yelping like that of hounds after a stag.

Then Aurel wiped his eyes and stared out to sea. Hespyne too had gone. Though he strained his eyes to peer at the stormy horizon, he could descry nothing of her, not a scrap of sail; not one curlicue of foaming, white wake.

'Perhaps I am asleep,' Aurel said to himself.

'Have courage!' Someone, whose voice was calm as a good schoolmaster's, spoke to him. He looked wildly about, but could not see anyone.

'I am surely mad now,' said Aurel.

'It is Parados who whispers to you, words of comfort, words of wisdom,' said the voice.

'Parados is lost – he vanished from our camp outside Pargur.'

'And is found again. You carry me with you: that is why you cannot see me.'

'How? Why? Are you invisble – shrunken perhaps and riding on my shoulder like Gry's little flame?'

'No. My soul holds hands with yours. I am with you and of you – no, do not clutch your chest, nor your stomach! There is no need for alarm, for you are my young self – Parados at twenty-two!'

Aurel, who had been twisting and turning with agitation; who wanted to flee, took a strong hold of his fear and kept still.

'How came you where you are – where you say you are, Lord

Parados?' he asked and at once looked behind him as if he feared someone would hear him talking to himself.

'Not "lord", Aurel. We are equal companions now,' the other answered. 'You have the strength, vigour and rash courage of youth and I a deep mind and much hard-won wisdom – not a little cunning either! We must work together. As for my story, it is long and entertaining, and I will tell it you by and by when you sleep. Thus, you will dream it and we shall not have to waste the daylight. It has its comic moments too, and I expect your dreams to be full of joy and laughter.'

'I cannot believe I am talking to you, Parados – that this weird, twin state is mine,' Aurel protested. 'It is like the tales the old men tell in Flaxberry's taverns, late at night. Prove that what you claim is true.'

Aurel heard no charm or word of command but, in spite of himself, sprang up and danced a sailor's hornpipe on the prow-shaped rock. He grew breathless yet could not stop dancing until, muscles weak and heart pounding, his legs jerked to a standstill and tipped him into a sitting position.

'I – am overlooked,' he panted.

'That was not witchcraft,' Parados told him. 'It was myself within you, making you move. Just as I made you retreat from your quarrel with Jan Pelerin.'

'Love's ecstasy compelled me,' said Aurel, unwilling to accept this proof.

'Speak then!'

'Breten is gar-secges iegland, paet waes geo geara Albion haten,' said Aurel, without stumbling once over the unfamiliar words.

'Britain is a sea-girt island, that was long ago named Albion. Good! You do not know that uncouth language. It is Old English to you.'

'This proves nothing,' Aurel objected, 'for lovers often speak nonsense.'

'Then . . .'

Three small stones which lay on the ground near Aurel flew up and, before he could blink, or say 'Living Goddess!' turned into a blue china jug, a footed wine glass and a white-gloved hand which lifted the jug and poured a sparkling, golden wine.

'Perhaps,' said Aurel doubtfully, 'I have gained an ability to cast spells: it could be that this has been granted to me by the same powers that made Gry a Wisewoman. She was not one when first I saw her, though she was always unlike any other woman I knew – my mother, my sisters, poor Friendship . . .'

'But taste the wine.'

Aurel was thirsty and the wine, bubbling in the glass, smelled of green grapes and summer. He drank.

'Have a care!' Parados warned. 'Perhaps Koschei tries to poison you.'

'Koschei is dead. I saw his body at Peklo.'

'Then all is well and you are free to believe in my superior powers.' Parados spoke cheerfully and made no effort to correct Aurel. 'Single, double, treble – Metamorfismo!' Jug, glass and hand clattered to the ground, stones again. 'Now let us continue companionably on our way.'

'It's all very well for you, but I must make the effort!' said Aurel. 'And another glass would have been welcome.' This was spoken with as much cheerfulness as Aurel could muster. He rose from his seat on the ground, stretched and, having cast about to locate the route he had taken from the enchanted Alp, set off uphill again.

'Crossing the high tops would be a fool's act,' he told Parados. I must find that old adit and use the dwarves' way.'

Parados lay silent in his nest of nerve and bone. His thoughts strayed, but he kept them to himself, for they were busy about the unlikely refuge of which Darklis had spoken, Lilith's Castle, the Fortress of the Gypsies.

Aurel, when he stopped to rest in a barren gully between two dizzying precipices, complained of his hunger.

'I have had nothing to eat for days except some toadstools and water!'

'And a glass of champagne,' said Parados. 'I treat you badly, I know, but you are the hero so I am sure you will survive – Isn't that a snag tree with fruit on it?'

'You can't eat them – sloes! Their sharp juices make your mouth wince.'

'But try.'

Aurel, who knew the bush had not been there, and growing strongly out of bare rock, a moment ago, picked a handful of the purple fruit and bit into one of them. To his astonishment, it tasted like the best SanZu plum.

'I do my best,' Parados said, 'and I will try to find you a good meal later. Tell me now, as you rest, do you know Leal Straightarrow?'

'Of course! He was with us when your balloon fleet travelled to Castle Lorne.'

'Was he? Ah, yes – I can't be expected to remember everything without my notes. Those who are following our story will wonder what has become of Leal, who is as courageous as you and a full Ima warrior. He was often in Gry's thoughts but she did not realise he was searching for her, to rescue her. He lost his horses on the road between Myrah Pits and Espmoss and was left behind. So bend your thoughts, Aurel, to his situation and imagine what he might do?'

'Is he in love with Gry?'

'Quench green jealousy, Aurel! What might Leal do?'

'Catch the horses? He is Ima!'

'Very well. Can you see it happening?'

'Yes. Leal follows the horses' trail – their hoofprints and some strands of hair caught on an overhanging bush. And their fresh dung – he travels steadily, neither running nor dawdling and all night if necessary, sure of finding them at dawn – er – grazing in a clearing.'

'And then?'

'I suppose he rides them, turn and turn about so as not to tire them, until he comes to a place where there is news of Gry – of us.'

'Good! I think he meets Hyperion Lovelace there, in a wayside bothy let us say, where a pretty wife sells meat and bread to wayfarers – and beer of her own brewing. Hyperion is surprised to find another fine young man riding after Gry and is taken aback, though not for long. He buys beer for Leal and lets him make friends with his red-eared hound. He questions him and, when he has extracted all the information he needs, advises Leal to try SanZu; Leal, being a native of that province, is glad to follow this false trail and so, rides off.'

'We have not been near SanZu!'

'No, but Leal's role in this story is to be honest, straightforward and, above all, loyal; whatever befalls him. Besides, there are heathlands near SanZu where anything may happen. Be content, Aurel: Each page is a promise that all shall be well.'

' "All shall be well", Parados? You can say that even as we sit gossiping on this naked mountainside? When we have abandoned Gry and seen her sail off with the ghostly dead and when we are ourselves without a destination? – let alone proper food or a roof for the night. When I am alone and raving, talking to you – or is it myself? – like a madman!'

'No more doubting, Aurel! You are young, strong and reasonably intelligent. As I told you before, you will survive. But understand this finally: it is not "you" or "I" or madmen's ranting. We are one, closer than lovers, bound with more ties than blood-brothers. We have the same desires and the same aspirations. As for a destination: what could be better than that to which you and Friendship were bound?'

'Is that your Castle Truth?'

'I believe it must be, though I have not thought so far. It cannot be a sin to search for the truth and it is likely to be found in a safe stronghold. I believe that fortress is also the customary refuge of the Gypsies, the Donjon of the enchantress Lilith.'

Already, the shadows were lengthening and the sun declining in the sky. Aurel watched its rosy tresses colour the Ocean.

'The sun came out of the sea – how can it set in the same place?' he exclaimed.

'Don't worry about it – surely it is far better to have the sun set in such a picturesque way, dropping like a hot cannonball into the dark water, than let it disappear behind the Altaish. Why, in such a case it would be dark already!'

'I still won't get to the magic meadow tonight.'

'Better follow this gulley, then. I am sure it leads somewhere.'

Aurel was only a little surprised to find, some way into the defile, a small cave beside a pool of clear water in which trout swam slowly, inviting themselves to be caught. Amongst the dry litter and gravel on the floor of the cave, he found two flints and, just outside it, a completely dead bush. Thus, he was able to make himself a fire over which he cooked three of the trout which had swum into his hand when he lay, his arm up to the shoulder in the water, to tickle them.

'You are still a country boy,' Parados remarked. 'It's good to see you use the skills you were born to.'

Aurel's fire drove the darkness back a little way. He sat contentedly by it for a while before lying down to sleep, wrapped close in horse-blanket from Colley's stable. The fire went out, but he did not wake. Soon Parados, aware only of the night, also slept.

Gry stood upon the lustrous deck, alone with the spirits and the dead. Those the captain had marked with his right thumb had gone below, to sleep on the coffin decks, but those uncharitable souls which in life had cheated, stolen from and killed their fellow men and women were crowded on the foredecks, whispering and gibbering to each other, pinching, nipping and kicking; restless as the ship sped on. Among them Gry recognised Heron, the Historian of the Ima, he who had pretended sympathy before he betrayed and raped her. She watched him disinterestedly: she had conquered the saltiers and her fears. In truth, so much had her wisdom matured and her detachment grown, that she was sorry to see Heron marked as damned, like herself travelling between the worlds but to a dreadful destination, Urthamma's fiery pit.

She saw no sailors and believed the ship, enchanted as she was, could sail herself, or that Jan Pelerin could raise the sails by wise man's cunning and call the winds to push and pull them. She rested her hands on the rail beside her. This, like the gangway, was fashioned from bones but Hespyne's gleaming sides, her decks and all, were made of small, overlapping plates of horn.

'Nails,' said Sib. 'She is built of the nails of the dead. My sister-spirits collect them still from tomb and grave-mound, sepulchre and catacomb. And the sails – see how wonderfully they swell with wind, pregnant by Svarog! – are the cauls of mermen plucked from their slippery bodies at birth. They are born adult, fully-formed and their straining mothers split and die as they give birth.'

'Hist!' said Umbra and leapt, fitfully flickering, to rest on the crown of Gry's head. ' 'Ware! Here comes Pelerin.'

Gry felt the Grey Horse push his nose against her arm and, remembering how it used to be, velvet, suede, smooth silk, watched her hand pass through him as she stroked that image. The captain was shouting at her.

'Too bright! Such irreverent dazzle!' A grey yardage lay across his hands. She feared it was a caul and ducked when Pelerin came close and threw it over her. Umbra jumped from her head, taking its childlike shape, and she pushed back the cloth, which had covered her.

'Far better for a mourner like yourself, Wisewoman,' said Pelerin. 'It is my seacloak. I give it to douse your brilliance, for grey garments and moods befit the Palace of Shadows.'

Gry, examining the garment, found two strings and tied the cloak in place so that it hid her dun and blue clothing, the white circle of her drum, and the chequered blanket she was wearing like a stole. Pelerin reached out and touched the blanket. He grasped it and pulled it suddenly from under the cloak, sniffed at it and laid it against his cheek.

'Exchange is no robbery,' he said. 'I will lie on this when I am below.'

'Thank you, sir,' said Gry.

Pelerin bowed from the waist.

'You may drink from my watercask and stand upon my poop deck in the stern – if you will,' he said, stepped past her and went to a stairway and below.

Leaving the Horse, a patient phantom of his old, untiring self, beside the mainmast, Gry climbed the stairs to the after deck, fearful for an instant lest, like the gaunt stairs at Russet Cross, they should lead to another banquet of the dead. Sib and Umbra, gliding behind her, seemed as alarming then as the wind-pickled shamans, needing neither food nor drink, not ever human. There was only the great wheel, with its narwhal spokes and rim of petrified oak, to fear, and a barrel of sweet water into which Gry dipped the painted cup. The watchful wheel turned of itself as the ship steered her own course, but the water in the barrel was still and sweet, soft in the mouth with a taste of ice and moss. A few drops of it remained in the cup when Gry had drunk: they magnified the blue paint until it was as vivid as the Plains sky, a boundless mirror. Gry saw herself there, her image undistorted, and stared at the small, cloaked figure which stood alone on the death ship's deck, hair streaming in the wind, head bent over a small, round cup, while all about her the rough water heaved and neither a crumb of earth nor a blade of grass could be seen. Truly, she was at sea.

And I, Koschei Corbillion, called Deathless, Traveller, Prince and Master of the Arcane? Wearily, I make my way across the piebald landscape which seems to me to symbolise every woe and hardship to which mankind is heir: war, sickness, love's illusions, learning, commerce, gain and loss; the struggle between Parados and myself, white against black, a veritable game of chess, a desperate bout of chequers played over eternity. And the greys, I tell myself, all the subtle gradations that are the printer's familiars, all the traps and disappointments of life. Here I must contemplate extinction for Parados and weary life everlasting for myself: there can be no greys between us, no compromise.

Such thoughts in such a place snuff out all light, all desire and hope. With an emotion like sentiment awash in my heart, I wonder how they do in Malthassa without me to light their miserable, mortal lives. Yet, O my soul, I miss your quiet presence within me! How do you, shut in your flat, green-covered prison, the pocket-sized book of poems on the library shelf? Do you slumber or wake and, waking, can you read the letters on which you must lie, 'dear child of sorrow – son of misery' 'when to thy haunts two kindred spirits flee'?

So, my thoughts in the Memory Palace, I pause under a black poplar from whose bitter branches depends a sorry confraternity: some winged seeds, a coiling serpent, two crested lizards hanging by their tails, and a hanged man who chokes in his halter – for ever, ay! The light of Hell is dull. Each bank and hollow is a pen stroke on the paper of anticreation; darkest and most heavily scored the jagged line upon the horizon which is the Palace of Shadows. So far. So near. My eyes fill with the waters of sleep. I fall to my knees on the stony ground – not to pray, but to rest, for a brief respite from the hideous monotony about me. I close my eyes.

Hespyne stood upon her bow to dive between the crashing waves, recovered herself with a roll of her stern and bucked again and Gry, not heeding her, watched the pictures in the cup. This seven-ringed, flame-encrusted little vessel was the same, the very one Hyperion Lovelace had used, in his booth at Wathen Fair! Fool that she was, not to see it before: had she used it correctly, she could have seen and foreseen what was to befall her, and the Horse, and Aurel, the gypsies, the dwarf, his lady – anyone. The two messages Aurel had read out, 'Keep Faith' and 'All's fair in love and war' were meant for her.

A red-specked darkness shrouded the blue in the bottom of the cup, the sparkling demi-night a weary person sees when, with eyelids closed, he rests his mind and stares oblivion in the face. That was the benighted face of Malthassa lying troubled and without moon or stars under a lightless sky. In Albion too, the sun had set and darkness fallen, but with the false dark of a summer's night. That sky was the colour of Friendship's mantle, the cloth-of-heaven Aurel had found aboard Frostfeather and which had perished when the balloon fell to earth. Stars in plenty shone.

As Gry watched, she understood, knowing the names and histories of the places and people she saw.

The Plough, the Pleiades, Orion the Hunter, a myriad more, lit the eloquent quarrel-shapen land of rural England, the well-tilled fields and unnaturally neat villages; gave light to the poacher and the thief, to lovers, insomniacs and witches, to badgers and foxes abroad by night. In Guy Parados's house, which stood in such a landscape, his deserted wife stirred and slept on, content, her children all grown and from home except her youngest son, Ben, abed in another room, her tabby cat out hunting, her dogs snoring in their basket by the kitchen stove, her sculptures frozen in the pallid light which fell through the lancet windows of her studio. She seldom visited her husband in dreams. He had been gone seven years and, latterly, another had taken his place. Living or dead, Guy had lost her – Guy Parados, the writer of Fantasy, Parados Constans the Kristnik, seventh son of Stanko of Castle Belgard. The dark had returned. There was a new world in the cup, one in which the light was murk, the grass and the earth the colour of gall. A tall black tree overhung a stony bank and on this Gry saw Parados kneeling, as if in prayer, his hands clasped before him and his eyes closed. She gasped and tears clouded her vision. Through them, she saw that though he was dressed in clothes as neat and black as a raven's wing, his grey hair was awry and his face ravaged with weariness.

Her mind struggled to make sense of what she saw. This, she did not understand.

Darkness, strange visions: underground in the airless halls Sib had described to Gry, those caverns which are the birthplace of rivers, one wakeful entity continued her solitary journey. The Lamia, the triple-banded snake, burrowed in the soft strata between the rocks or slid through chilly, infant rivers and delighted in her long, lissome body ringed in scarlet, orange, and black, the jewels which studded her head and formed a diadem above her eyes, those deep and fascinating wells which, now, she closed, for the ways were close and dirty. Thus, with blind golden eyelids, she writhed on.

It was expedient to keep this, her favourite shape, a little while longer: the most suitable for such earthy travel. When she arrived – that would be the time to change her shape, and the right time for other changes also. Briefly, while her tongue flickered out to taste the way before her, she thought of Lord Yama and sighed inwardly. Her thoughts turned elsewhere, to hot, dry hollows where the sun bore down, bestowing caresses on his creatures, the snakes; to the narrow holes by which her kind entered tombs to visit the corpses within; to magic and conjuration and their many disciplines: hieromancy, ieromancy, pyromancy, onomancy, nomancy, pen dukkerin, hokkani, scrying, shifting shape . . .

As one who sees another's image in an old, time-spotted glass, Gry struggled to make sense . . .

The Lamia came to a vent in the floor. She paused above it, weaving her head from side to side above her coils, breathing the uprising vapours which were chill and odourless. Her thoughts turned inward as she slid into the vent. She played the Game of Incarnations:

What am I? she asked herself and answered her question immediately: I am the moon and the stars, I am the tree and the leaf, I am the wind on the sand, I am water and ice, I am life and death.

Who am I? I am the Lamia, beautiful, terrible, bride of the Loathly Worm; I am she whose elected diet is the blood of spotless virgins, the terrible Grand Duchess; I am Lèni le Soie; I – but who watches? Koschei? I do not fear him! Yama? She raised her head and opened her gold-lidded eyes. The loose skin of her neck towered up in a hood and, though she lay in darkness, the thousand jewels of her diadem burned bright as beacons, dazzling Gry, whose hand shook. The water spilled from the cup. Gry closed her eyes and saw the red-specked darkness; when she opened them again upon the occult light of Hespyne's deck of nails and on the ashen waves, the picture in the cup was gone.

A ghostly arm embraced her, sliding about her waist and holding her close.

'Lady – Ima Lady.' The voice was gentle and persuasive but had about it the regretful tones of someone whose life has been blighted, scarcely used, come to death too soon. 'It is Friendship.'

Gry looked into a sorrowful face and lightless eyes.

'Do you see as I do, that all is desolation on this ship of doom,

300

this sea of hopelessness?' Friendship asked. 'We must be friends – sisters – for both of us have died young. How came you to your death?'

'I – I,' Gry hesitated because Friendship gazed at her so soulfully and with such tender sympathy.

'You cannot bear to tell, to recall the dreadful moment and the pitiless method,' said Friendship. 'And there are worse deaths than mine, which was to be throttled by Koschei's hands as I slept exhausted after my dance. It matters no longer, dear sister. All that lies ahead for you and me is an eternity of service under Lord Yama.'

Her weak hold loosened and she slipped away, as dreams do at the coming of daylight. Jan Pelerin stood close by, though Gry had neither seen nor heard him approach.

'You have friends among the dead,' he said. 'Well, that is true of most mortals. When I was Archmage of Malthassa, I knew many who had passed beyond the grave: Garzon, who began the building of Sehol and Toricello, who continued it; old Polus, the greatest of Malthassa's storytellers; Fabella, my rosy-bosomed Queen; the Grand Duchess, Helena – I had my time, and an immeasureable time it was: before Koschei Corbillion and Manderel Valdine that Koschei killed, before Zachary Monthelita and Caius Stadlin.

'Beware of Greed that breeds insatiable children and Power that corrupts, Mortal. I spelled myself into a seabeast, a silkie I was, the greatest, most mighty – a sealy creature who swam with the shark, the orca and the she-seals, with mermen and maids and King Leviathan too, far below and far away from the light of sun or moon, without human speech, without air – for I had learned, at my studies, of the Palace of Shadows that lies on the far side of the Ocean, and I wished to go there and contest Lord Yama for my beloved dead, for Fabella and the Duchess.

'Asmodeus was chosen to punish me. He tied me to the keel of this ship and dragged me through cold seas and hot. He beat me with many-tailed, wet ropes; he prisoned me in the Leucos, that white tongue of ice which flows out of the Altaish, and set me in the volcano's throat to thaw me. I wished for death – but that,

301

he would not grant, and quartered me on this very deck to be Hespyne's captain, a solitary ferryman for ever, always travelling between the worlds but at home in neither. And Asmodeus issued a decree: that no living being in or of Malthassa, knowing or unknowing, and no ship should sail upon the Ocean, only myself, Janus Pelerin, and Hespyne. You thwart his rule; but you are a shaman and may do what you please on my ship.'

Gry looked up at him. She could think of nothing to say. Here, she found herself to be and by her own desire; she must play whatever part was given her, as now that of listener. It was growing dark, truly dark, the waves dissolving into the overall gloom. Jan Pelerin had left her side and was leaning on the rail at the stern of the ship, looking down into her spumy wake. She went to stand beside him, holding on to the slippery bone lest she should fall. Something rose from the foaming water, a long, glistening figure, naked and phosphorescent, fronded, finned. Others, visible as ghostly, luminous shapes, thronged below him, but none, save him, rose to the surface.

'It is a merman,' said Jan Pelerin. 'See how strongly he swims. He fears nothing for he cannot die: being generated from the seed of dead men, he is already immortal.'

'Hail, Dagon!' he cried.

The merman looked up. His eyes were pearls and his mouth a coral flower.

'Throw us the dark-haired woman,' he called, his voice as forlorn and wailing as the cries of seals, seabirds and the westerly wind. 'Cast her down: we would sport with her.'

'Not now, not this one,' Pelerin replied. 'Her fate is elsewhere.'

The merman sank from view and shoals of gold and silver fish, coiling sea-serpents and water dragons followed Hespyne, swimming through the immeasurable night. Even so, it passed and Gry, looking toward the horizon she had left, saw a small globe of light rise above it, a red-glowing orb no bigger than a lantern.

'Daylight!' she said.

'That is not the sun, rising over Malthassa,' Jan Pelerin said. 'It is the light of Hope, which is absent here. Look forward, where we are bound. That is the coast of Hell.'

They turned to face Hespyne's bow and watched, as if spellbound, the long, black cliff growing larger as the ship approached; they heard the waters' song of desolation.

> As the sea absorbs rivers from all over the earth,
> so does that place receive every soul.

....

My eyes are open. I walk not certain if, while they were closed, I was haunted by apparitions, or if I slept and opened my mind to whatever dire influences and visions abound here. The Palace of Shadows lies like a wakeful tiger on the horizon and again I study its black steeps and pallid summits. I am closer, surely? The place is no longer a single dash of the pen but has visible features, flights of steps perhaps, towers certainly and a tall chimney from whose immense top there rises a dark column of smoke, a trailing cloud of the kind which clerks burning old paper create, or butchers when they send murrain-ridden cattle to the fire or indeed, the mageless, primitive tribes of Far Malthassa who burn their dead on pyres; but since I cannot smell the smoke, it may all be illusion yet.

To my right are the empty, colourless fields which lie between my wayfaring self and that house of torment where Asmodeus dwells, pursuing his pains and his pleasures with equal ardour – and there, by my Manhood! – on the left hand side I see the limitless Ocean of which I have read so much, in Valdine's books, and in the journals of Pelerin the Sagacious, all of which are to be found lined up, cover to cover, face to back, in the library of the Memory Palace; that Sea which, in ambitious youth, I used to watch dash itself in pieces against the great cliff at Nether Pargur. Almost, I think, the 'Blessed Ocean' so glad I am to see it. It is without colour also, a tossing graduation of greys, and a ship rides on it, a tall ship of three masts and gleaming ghostly aspect, which sails swiftly toward this dreadful land as if it means to put a cargo ashore: coals for Urthamma? whips for Asmodeus? fresh *concubines for Lord Yama? I amuse myself with these baubles of thought. I know the ship well. 'Tis Hespyne, in which the dead are brought to Hell; which Pelerin the Once-Sagacious, condemned to sail the Ocean for all eternity, commands. I will go nearer and see what dead she brings.*

The cliff is higher than that prismatic precipice which drops sheer to the Ocean at Pargur; the height on which I stood when first I went to the Mutable City and began my campaign to oust Manderel Valdine from his august seat, the gilded throne of the Archmage. Hespyne, below, is a toy. How shall they do, how land? By cranes and tackle, mayhap; or by a hidden jetty at sea level whence leads a tunnel – Asmodeé! The ship sails upward. She rises like a bird, her score of sails black wings which beat upon the air – and passes over me, I know not where.

Though I scan the leaden skies, Hespyne is gone. I must continue, forward, onward. Here, at the junction of several trodden paths, are some stones set up, waymarks which I read:

THE ROAD TO EVERLASTING SORROW
THE ROAD OF THE LOST
THE ROAD TO THE PALACE OF SHADOWS

Hespyne dropped steadily, buoyant as a fishing gull. To one side rose a lofty range of mountains and, below, stretched wide river-meadows. The river running through them would have been a fair sight with its ox-bows and meanders, its rushy islets and its tree-fringed banks had it not been dark as pitch and the land beside it shaded in every tone of grey and black; the shadows under the trees stark white. The ship came down in the river and drew close to the bank. The gangway silently placed itself to bridge the gap; and the Shadows of men and women began to emerge, walking from the hold and from the after-decks with sober mien, sinister and dexter-printed, evil and good.

'This is Lethe Water, which surrounds the Palace,' said Umbra to Gry. 'Be wary. If one drop of that water passes your lips, you will forget all you know and knew.'

'Stay with us,' Sib urged. 'We will see that you come to no harm.'

Yet the Shadows, Gry saw, were not yet passing across the gangway but standing motionless in the waist of the ship, a crowd of effigies. Jan Pelerin, passing among them, dipped water from the river and gave each one a sip, even the Grey Horse.

'Come!' he called. 'All must drink before they leave Hespyne.'

'We are exempt,' Sib answered and made a gesture to include Gry and Umbra, the pikulik.

'How so?'

'I am the child of a sharivila returning to serve Lord Yama.'

'Pass then and do not drink.'

'And I,' said Umbra, 'was summoned to the Pastures of Heaven by the shaman Aza, there to serve his will: which was that this woman, Gry, Nandje's daughter, should have me for a guide and comforter until we came to the Asphodel Meadows. I am her unborn child.'

'Pass. Do not drink.'

Gry stood before Jan Pelerin and felt herself condemned to Hell, to continual residence with the demons and the dead in the Palace of Shadows: for, if she drank and forgot, she would have no reason to be here and none at all to leave.

'She is not dead!' cried Sib and Umbra from the gangway's head.

'She must drink.' Pelerin dipped his hand in the pail. The water dripped from his fingertips, viscid and black. Shadowy faces peered from it, were elongated and dropped. He pressed his forefinger and the last, murky drop of water on it against Gry's lips and forced them open. The drop lay on her tongue and, though she tried to cough it away, slid down her throat. She swallowed.

'Now, Wisewoman, you may do as you will, for I have fulfilled my part,' Jan Pelerin said.

Terrible sadness and longing filled Gry's heart and she thought of her father, Nandje, as she had last seen him, lying dead in his tomb, and then as he had been alive, riding the Red Horse across

306

green grass and yellow, according to the season, singing to her, sharpening his knife. She touched the knife-hilt. Its bone was smooth and worn; familiar as her own hand. She remembered the Red Horse as he had been in life, when he journeyed with her, a wild force, though he harboured the soul of Parados as well as his own; a gentle animal, for all his great strength, one she trusted with her life. He, grey now as the rest of this nightmarish place, had already walked down the gangway and into the meadows. She saw him toss his head and heels and gallop away like a colt.

I cannot take him to my father now, she thought.

Aurel's picture moved into her heart. She was sorry she had sent him away. She wished she had gone with him and not come here, where she was lost, a living soul amongst the dead. And my brothers, Garron and Kiang, she thought; Leal, what of him? Is he at home, in the Plains, the leader of the men? The Plains in summer rain, in spring frost, changeable, wind-inspired, heart, soul, home!

'All is empty, colourless. Oblivion,' said Pelerin in a toneless voice.

'I see the birds hopping in the bushes, Stribog breathes over the Plains. My hearth, my round grass-covered home, every stick, speck of dust, and firelit ember are clear to me as your face.'

'That cannot be.' He looked keenly at her and a frown creased his broad brow. 'Unless – what do you carry that protects you from Lethe's spell? Can it be the drum, the cup, that narrow-bladed knife? None of these have sufficient power. The birchbark shoes, then? My seacloak?'

'I carry my most precious possessions in my heart,' said Gry. 'The pictures of my father and my brothers, of all those who love me.'

''Tis they that shield you; more strongly than armour or any conjuration. Go in peace, for I am powerless against you.'

Sib and Umbra were waiting for her beneath a black poplar tree. They took her by the hand, one each side.

'The Horse has run away,' said Gry. 'I must get him back if I am to give him to my father,' and, by this, the two spirits knew

307

that neither Lethe's potent water nor Jan Pelerin with all his learning and his magic had been able to overcome Gry's wise and courageous self.

'You are Ima,' Sib remarked, as she bent to pick one of the lily-like flowers which grew in abundance at their feet. She tucked it in Gry's hair.

'Every mortal man and woman will know where you have journeyed,' said Umbra. 'The asphodel grows nowhere but in these meadows – see, there are my companions! I must greet them!' It withdrew its hand from Gry's and skipped away, a white, half-formed shape darting between the grey stems of the asphodels and Sib and Gry saw others like it hastening forward. They danced, crowding together, and it was immediately impossible to tell which of the pikulik was Umbra.

'Umbra did not say goodbye!' said Gry.

'It was not even half a babe,' said Sib. 'Listen to me. "You are Ima," I said, and if anyone knows how to catch a wayward horse, it is you.'

'I have no bridle. The Horse can only be tamed with his bridle of Om Ren skin.'

'Even his Shadow, here, in the Asphodel Meadows?'

'I do not know, but the Horse will tire soon and seek grazing. I suppose we might find him then.'

'No creature eats in Hell but Lord Yama and the Lady.'

'Then he will lie down to sleep.'

'He needs no sleep: he is dead and his sleep is eternal waking here, in the Meadows.'

They wandered among the clumps of asphodels, Gry looking to right and left and all about her to learn what kind of country was this that she had travelled so far to find.

'There are mountains,' she said, 'Great peaks like the Altaish.'

Sib smiled; laughed, a glad sound in the gloom.

'That is the Palace of Shadows!'

'How can crags and sheer rock faces be a palace?'

'Look again. You will discern more of the Palace as we approach it.'

308

The building, if such it was – but how might such a mighty structure have been raised? – the Palace loomed ahead and soon, its outermost wings lay to right and left behind them and they and the thronging Shadows, in their two predestined columns, were enclosed in a shifting circle of masonry: towers, pinnacles, archways and battlements formed themselves from the all-pervading shade as they came near; they saw long flights of steps, narrow lancet windows, flying buttresses, deserted balconies, crocketed pediments, ogee arches, water-spouts, gargoyles; and the palace doors, too wide and too high for a single glance or a solitary thought to encompass. Pewter-coloured they were, with a dull sheen and many bands and studs of the same dull-faced metal. Almost invisible before them, Grey before grey, stood the Horse. He faced them with head lifted and ears pricked, listening and, when he perceived them, neighed, his forceful voice as little at home here as Sib's laugh.

Gry ran to him and, as once he had so long away, so far ago, the Horse moved close and rested his head against her chest. She felt its weight and soft skin in memory; here it was weightless and without texture and her enclosing arms passed through it. She kissed the Horse upon the place where his broad, flat cheek would have been.

'So you know me,' she whispered. 'Was the water too weak for you as well?'

He could no longer speak in measured and learned sentences, nor sing with the voice of Parados but, in his own horse-tongued language, said first 'My Mistress?' and then 'Mount' and bent his knee to help her.

'Attend first to me,' said Sib. 'See there, the paving stones beside the great door? That is the servants' path and I must away along it and into the back door, before I am missed. Goodbye, dear Gry. Remember me.'

'I shall never forget you.' Gry kissed Sib's brow and felt, for the last time, the whisper of her cobweb hair. The hell-sprite spun about and, whirling like a phantom head of thistledown, floated away; soon she was invisible beyond the shadows which were gathering thickly at the door. A memory of the Horse's muscular knee recalled Gry. She stepped up on it and was mounted, seated on nothing, astride the Grey Horse. The gigantic doors rose up before, behind, on every side; and the Horse walked on.

Air-drawn, reverie-built, the doors were not, but had dissolved or never had been there, so almighty and adamantine, so impassably blocking the way. They were travelling through an immeasurable, dusky arch, a cavern like none Gry had imagined in dream or nightmare and so thick and numerous were the shadows that she could not distinguish those which were cast by the archway or were echoes of it, black and white, from the host of Shadows, the dead which surrounded and marched with her; save occasionally, when one or two crossed the Horse's path and she saw the terrible wound which had killed him or the plague-marks which had ended her life. The host streamed on, but the Horse halted. A naked horror barred the way. He wielded a pike on which the blackened body of a girl-child was impaled.

'There is no place for this horse in the Palace,' he said. 'You must ride in the gardens.'

Gry cringed away as she rode the bodiless Horse under the blade of his weapon and the poor thing writhing on it, past the guard in his hideous vigour; and found herself upon a causeway (where Memory made a clatter of hoofs) and then, in a winding avenue whose verges were close-planted with white willows and black poplars in pied succession. The trees hung over the road and Gry, feeling their cold branches touch her back, dismounted; and the Horse followed her meekly, chastened as a motherless lamb following a shepherd. The garden gate hung between twin piers shaped with wit and cunning into Male and Female; and in the gloom these images looked as beautiful and as remote as angels. His name was carved upon his ridged and muscular belly: 'Sin'; hers on her breast, above the heart: 'Agony'. Gry, who could not read, glanced at the statues but they were neither strange nor sinister of shape. She opened the gate with a calm mind and steady hand.

The garden within was full of plants whose hueless flowers spilled from funerary urns and over ironwork wrought in the shapes of trees, jostled with trembling leaves in beds bordered with narrow stones; the path curved and lost itself in overgrown shrubbery and found a direction again and so, they came at last to a central, sunken court, the heart of the garden. Water dark as Lethe's plashed here, running from a narrow channel into the open-mouthed head of a lion and so, into a white stone basin carved with roses. Gry touched a rose – it was no carving but grew, perfect of form, upon a thorny stem; it was without scent. Close by, a long bench was set in an arbour of the same flowers, and, upon its seat, an empty water jug. Steps rose, a boulder marking the first of them. On this crouched a splendid pied lizard, its jaws agape for the black-winged butterflies which darted about the flowers. As Gry and the Horse approached, the lizard sprang away and hid itself amongst the briar roots.

The steps led up to a small building or pavilion made of four white marble arches. The sound of splashing water came from it and Gry, from where she stood on tiptoe, expecting to see a skeletal envoy or a grinning demon, but not this elegant harmony of the solid and the fluid, could see a fountain cascading within. She sat down on the lowest step and the Horse, half-closing his translucent eyelids, tipped one hoof and rested beside the rose-encrusted basin. With his grey skin and proudly curving tail, he seemed to be carved from stone, a new statue in the enchanted garden.

Gry sat long. If time in Malthassa was chaotic and obeyed its own random laws, here, it was without meaning. She was not hungry or thirsty; she was rested and resting here, hearing insects hum about the flowers, the chirrup of a bird from somewhere inside a bush, seeing the flash of wings as another flew; and – the tail of her eye caught it – a movement which, when she searched her memory, might have been a banded snake slithering past her, gone between the marble arches, out of sight.

The footfall was soft. A sandalled foot rested on the step beside her. Its fellow was poised on the step above. The rest of the presence bent gracefully towards Gry and quizzed her with a keen look in her deep, dark eyes: a woman whose body rose up proudly from those humble feet, a comely vision of a woman whose black hair fell thick and precipitately from the crown of her head to her bare shoulders, where it curled magnificently upon the frilled edging of a low-necked blouse, a garment pulled so low that not only her shoulders but the cleft between her full, deep breasts was exposed. Her skirts were decorated with more frills and her jewellery, beads of black stuff like jet, earrings of the same, and heavy, clanking bracelets of silver, was of a familiar sort. Gry recognised the ghost of a gypsy and, remembering Darklis and her sister, said, 'Greetings, Rawnie dook.'

'Avali,' answered the woman. 'Yes, I am a lady; but I am no ghost. I am one of the few not dead who are allowed to venture here. Walk with me in the garden – your horse will not stir, see! He reposes.'

The eyes of the Grey Horse were so completely closed that Gry feared he had become a statue with blank and sightless gaze. The gypsy rawnie led Gry past him and on, by a different path. Soon, they came to a circular pool whose dark mirror was studded with white water lilies. Fish with trailing fins and tails swam round and round below them and the lady, dipping a hand in the water, beckoned to them. Soon, they were circling her hand. She pursed her lips and hooted, clear as an owl at night; one by one the fish raised barbed heads from the water and sang to her with the hollow voices of frogs. The lady smiled.

'They are my toys, but their song is natural to them and not taught; nor is it magically composed,' she said. 'Sit by me. This aspect of the garden is the most pleasant; when night falls it is neither so exquisite nor so safe.'

The carved stone which edged the pool was wide, like a tabletop or a seat. Tasselled cushions were scattered on it; Gry took the one she was offered and the lady another.

'You are Gry,' she said pleasantly, 'and you seek your father's

Shadow, that last insubstantial remnant which was once Nandje, the Rider Who Bestrode the Red Horse.'

'I do – can you help me find him?'

The lady did not answer but said, 'You are fortunate to have a father. I have none, and never did have unless my memory is false.'

'Everyone has a father!'

'Well, I may have – somewhere; but I do not remember him, nor my mother. Your mother was Lemani. Should you like to meet her once again?'

'She is dead!'

'She is here Dinelo, Silly: a Shadow but still a beauty, a favourite of the Lord's as you, I must own, are a favourite of mine for all your honesty and virtue, which do no harm I suppose, in their proper place and at the correct season.'

The gypsy, if such she was, moved closer to Gry and laid a slender arm across her caped shoulders.

'Won't you shed your thick wrap – 'tis warm this afternoon.' Subtly, as she spoke, the shadows increased and Gry felt so lax and warm she untied the strings of her cloak and let it fall. Her unblemished colours, the tawny deerskins, the yellow blouse, the indigo relics which had been her dress, her rich, brown skin, blazed forth in the lightless garden.

'What beauty! What audacity!' the lady said and stroked Gry's hair. 'I fear I must steal one, tiny kiss.' Her soft lips rested for an instant on Gry's cheek, and her embrace grew tight, her kisses wild and passionate; her skirts became breeches, her legs grew long and booted, her blouse turned into a heavy coat; her beads and jewellery vanished and, on her dense and curling hair (which remained the same) appeared a round hat in which were stuck a pair of feathers, one small and black as sin, the other eyed with silver, tall, trembling. Hyperion Lovelace, colourless and in negative but very much himself, gazed into Gry's honest eyes, his snake's eyes bottomless and fascinating.

'I have you!' he cried exultantly, between kisses. 'At last!'

'Then I am truly in Hell,' said Gry.

'Unfair! I have pursued you with – if not true love – lust and admiration in my heart. But, so be it. I am beaten and shall desist.' Hyperion's masculinity fell swiftly away: the gypsy lady smiled. 'You were a challenge,' she said. 'To resist me – what daring! To refuse Hyperion's love! – well, let us retrace our steps and enter the Palace. This garden is, when all's said, an unsuitable place for dalliance.'

A chill which made Gry put on the seacloak and jump to her feet settled over the pool. Silent, dazed by what had passed, she followed the gypsy along the path.

'Do not forget your horse!'

The Grey Horse, as they came to him, opened his eyes and followed them. His unshod, insubstantial hooves made no sound on the steps of the arched pavilion. The cascading fountain was loud in the quiet there and silver in the dusk. A statue with a horned headdress pointed inward, at a second flight of steps. An extravagantly-framed painting hung beside it. As Gry turned her head to see what was pictured there, the lady exclaimed, 'By my Lord, 'tis a portrait of you! How came it there? By sorcery and foul magic, I don't doubt. Let me compare – you must unfasten the cloak again. Ay, it is you, the Princess Gry; as you are this instant in your pretty rags and tatters and your charming birchbark shoes; carrying a round drum like the face of the full moon, and a little tin cup and the long and cruel knife which belongs to your father. A good likeness, is it not?'

Gry could only whisper, 'Yes.'

'So Lord Yama has made a portrait of you to go with every other thing that is his,' the lady continued. 'Read the inscription there.'

'I cannot read.'

'Fie, can you not? You would be at such disadvantage in Pargur, where the ladies do nothing but read tales of venery and fine clothes! It says,

'"I, YAMA, King of Hell and Lord of the Underworld caused this Pavilion to be raised in my Garden at the Palace of Shadows. Tremble, Soul, and bow your head before ME."'

The lady's voice, so sweet and low, here took on such a sharp and cutting tone that it seemed as if the inscription was incised in her very brain.

'Hurry Gry, or you will be too late!'

At the top of the steps, a pair of graven doors stood open.

'Mount – and mind the third step,' the lady called. 'Some careless fool has knocked a great chip out of it and made the way uneven!' She stood in the doorway, an enigmatic smile playing on her lips; and was no longer there. The pied, the grey, the shadowy murk were also gone. Firelight shone out of the doorway. Gry, alone once more, walked on and the Grey Horse followed her.

'Shield us, Svarog; Stribog, blow away our fears; let us again walk upon you, Moist Mother, in the future time.' Gry spoke her prayer of protection. 'The place cannot be so frightful if there is a fire on the hearth,' she said, and entered.

The room was immense. She could not see the further side of it but only that part nearest her: the tessellated floor of interlocking masks and moons; the dark, booklined walls, and the back of a huge throne, all of which were tinted with the ruddy light and which, as she and the Horse walked forward, increased in size. The throne, empty, thank Svarog, stood at a carved table as tall as the Horse. The table was overhung by a skull encircled with black candles whose purple flames cast gloom about them. Somewhere way beyond it, at the farthest side of the room perhaps, was the source of the fire but it could not be made out in the constant battle between light and dark.

Gry stopped suddenly, her heart banging in her chest. She heard someone draw breath, an inspiration loud as a gust of wind, and the smack of spittle-gummed lips parting to speak.

'Who brings a horse into my library?'

The voice rolled like thunder over the Altaish. The shadows at the end of the table parted and he who sat there, in a throne exactly like the empty one, leaned forward. He wore a crown of black iron and bones and many diamonds set in his brow; his eyes were pitchdark abysses which overflowed with anger.

'Who dares disturb my thought?'

'I am Gry.'

'And who is Gry?'

'A woman, Lord Yama, who asks to speak with her father, Nandje of the Ima, and who brings him his knife and his Horse.'

The King of Hell leaned down, over the table-edge, until the two jutting forks of his beard touched the floor. His breath was sour and hot, like the gases of an erupting volcano. Its force swept up Gry and the Horse and moved them across the floor from moon to mask and mask to moon until they were dizzy. The air was furnace hot. Lord Yama knelt beside them, his great ringed hands spread on the floor and his robes trailing behind him. He laughed. The book he had been reading was blown skidding from the table and across the floor.

'Those who trouble me, I send to the Pit,' he said. He picked up Gry and the Horse, one in each hand, and set them down beside a grating in the floor. The fire lay couched beneath it. Lord Yama laughed again and the flames leapt high and licked the bars which covered it.

'Where is the miscreant?' he roared.

Then Gry and the Grey Horse cowered, wracked with fear; but Lord Yama reached past them and pulled a grey and quaking Shadow from the outer dark. Illuminated by the flames from the Pit, it soon took on the form and outline of the Historian of the Ima, Heron.

'You and he have old scores to settle, I think?' said Lord Yama.

'Our differences are resolved,' and 'Pity me!' said Gry and Heron simultaneously.

'In your hearts, but not in mine.' Lord Yama nodded to Gry and, lifting the grating in one hand and Heron, by the left leg, in the other, tossed him into the Pit.

'Urthamma!'

Two arms, all aflame, stretched up; taloned fingers opened wide. Heron, falling towards them and screaming, terror-struck, was caught and raked from neck to belly; and the flames, the

316

hands and he subsided. Lord Yama blew the grating into place, tossed a great boulder to lie on it, and bowed to Gry. Though he had made himself smaller, he was still twice the height of an Ima man.

'You are a good woman, if innocent,' he said. 'Come, sit at my table.'

That, too, was smaller, and Gry had only to climb up by the carvings on the base of the first throne to sit down. Lord Yama resumed his own seat and the Horse, remaining at liberty in the hall, walked sometimes a little way in this direction or that and sometimes stood stock-still.

'Perhaps you would like to see my collection,' said Lord Yama, lifting a glass-walled cabinet out of the air. It was lined with a myriad of shelves on which in order of size, living corpse-moths, which struggled against the pins impaling them, were arranged.

Gry, who knew that this display, too, was a test of her courage, said, 'These, on the lower shelves, are just the kind which fed upon my father in his tomb.'

'They are called Sphinx moths, for she loves their death's-head faces; but you Ima call them Death Heralds. I have made careful study of their habits and find that they prefer a meat-fed corpse (such as Nandje's) to that of – let me say – a fisherman or salad-eater. But perhaps you do not like insects. Should you care to see my hounds?'

'Certainly, though I never owned a dog: the Ima do not use them. Yet instruct me further, Lord.'

Then the Lord of the Underworld whistled sweetly and six hounds ran in, which milled and bounded about the thrones and the table-legs and wagged long white tails and pricked up ears which, in the light from the Pit, were red.

'Three couple of three hundred thousand,' he said.

'I have seen one of these before,' said Gry.

'In the Upper World? You were fortunate it did not chase you here.'

'It was gentle and did not even try to lick me. It belonged to a gypsy.'

'That is most curious, unless –' Lord Yama smiled in his beard. 'But these are handsome are they not, bred solely to run fast?'

'They look as if they might keep pace with the Horse.'

'You are loyal to your totem!'

'Our Law forbids us to be otherwise.'

Lord Yama yawned behind his hand.

'Such goodness,' he murmured, sent away the hounds with a snap of his fingers and removed the specimen cabinet with a discreet cough. 'Will you not unpack your bag?' he asked. 'I would summon a servant, but some guests prefer to manage the task themselves. And unburden yourself also. The cloak –'

Gry, without a word, untied the seacloak's strings, took it off and laid it on the table. Next, she laid down her drum and her knife and, placing her carrying bag beside them, turned it inside out to show that, beside a few dry fragments of heath-jack meat and toadstools, it contained only the painted cup of tin. She saw Lord Yama hide impatience in a smile.

'So like your portrait in the anteroom,' he said. 'The colours so bright, so solid; and the silk blouse becomes you well. Take back your shaman's drum and your father's knife; the bag. Those do not concern me. Give me the cup!'

Gry, with a nod and a submissive declination of her head, passed it to him.

'Precious Cup,' he said and sighed so long and gustily that Gry's hair fanned out in a broad tail.

'This cup is mine,' Lord Yama said, passing his hands over it. 'It made a useful traveller's contrivance, I am certain; but it belongs to me. It is the King's Cup which shows me all that passes in this world and the other. I have been lost without it. I have been lonely without my tragedies and farces to brood upon, without my alter-eyes. The peris who brought me news do not see the worlds as I do.' As he touched the cup, it grew a gracefully curving pedestal and the body of it elongated. The crude, painted colours deepened and grew glassy until it had the shape and appearance it should rightfully wear, of a sky-blue vessel ringed with letters and flames and footed with seven bands of colour, with blue, and

318

gold, with crimson, green, orange, indigo and violet. Lord Yama spun the cup and the coloured rings flowed one into another.

'My joy! My toy!' he said, and, 'Those are the colours of the rainbow that arches over Garsting after summer showers,' said Gry.

'My darling at last,' said Lord Yama, leaning forward in his throne. 'How came my Cup into your hands, little Mortal, which, being soiled with human cares, are no place for it?' His speech was measured and his voice pleasant, yet the frown which creased the skin of his diamond-encrusted brow was deep.

'It was a gift,' said Gry, cutting a long story short. 'From a gypsy.'

'That gypsy again!'

'I saw him a little while ago – outside in your garden. I do not understand either.'

'Oh I *understand*,' Lord Yama said. 'Everything.' All the while, as he spoke, he had been playing with the Cup, turning it in his hands until the colours blurred and the engraved flames flowed together and became a halo like the sun's corona which spun above the cup. He caught it on a fingertip and let it slide down his arm, wore it as a burning bracelet, flipped it in the air and watched it spin until it hovered over Gry.

'A crown becomes you!' he said, as the flaming circle settled on her hair. 'Ah, charming! You will not burn if you sit still.'

Gry, so tense she could not tremble, watched helpless as the flames became a necklace and then a burning belt and, finally, swallowing themselves, hopped on to the table where they took the form of a salamander which ran about and puffed out smoke.

'Idle tricks,' Lord Yama said, snapping his fingers. The salamander vanished; coloured rings and flames, the Cup itself, were still. A wine-jug materialised and poured a draught into the Cup, which Lord Yama raised.

'Your health!' he said, and drank.

'And yours, my Lord!' The voice was low, mellifluous. It came from the outer darkness beyond the firelight's reach. 'I trust you are well rested, my King!' The voice floated eerily about the hall. 'I hope you are rested and ready for a night of sport!'

Silk rustled, the unmistakable susurrus of a long skirt dragging on a step; at the door.

The doorway framed her, a conundrum of black and white, a fluid chaomantic whose curling hair moved as subtly and as dangerously as a nest of vipers. Her face was hidden behind an airy fan of feathers which she cast aside as she stepped forward, one sandalled foot tossing up the hem of her skirt; and displayed herself, the archetypal fantasy, the beautiful gypsy dressed in flounced scarlet, orange and black, brass jewellery chiming and clashing.

'Get out of my chair!'

Gry sprang aside and ran to shelter in the safest place, beside the Grey Horse.

Helen seated herself on her throne. She was magnificent and comely. Her dress, which, by a trick of the firelight or of the darkness spilling from the purple candles; or by some whimsical maggot of diablerie, had looked like the tawdry raiment of a gypsy, was queenly, black as fate, cut low and bordered with ermine and the pelts of winter hares, its stomacher embroidered with sombre mispickel, sulphur and turamali. The same crystals, set in a band of iron, bedimmed her pallid brow and the rings on her fragile, ivory fingers. Her hair, which in the doorway had flowed free, was braided and twisted into a high, coiled headdress in which the diadem nestled like a cockatrice on its nest.

Yama bowed his head.

'My Queen,' he said.

'My King!' said she. 'It has been a long afternoon.'

'I craved your company,' said Yama, raising his face and reaching across the table to take her two hands in his. 'Yet – it was peaceful resting here and reading old Lully by the firelight. Now tell me, Beloved Sister, where you strayed. Give me a full account of your travels.'

'Where shall I begin: in Troy, Galicia, Albion?'

'Begin with that knave, Koschei.'

'Well then – know first that he is not my truelove –'

'Nor only love, Sweet Mistress!' Yama laughed until the bones in his crown rattled and Gry and the Grey Horse shook with fear. 'Yami, Dearest, tell me everything about Koschei –'

'Very well. He is a – you drink from my Goblet, Brother!'

'My Cup!'

'My Goblet! Fie, Yama, you know well the vessel is called "the King's" because it once belonged to Suleiman. It is mine as much as yours –' Yami's voice shrilled as she spoke, but into laughter. She tried to snatch it and a game of hide-and-seek began, except it was the Cup – or Goblet – which was concealed by king and queen in turn, in ether and in earth, in water and in fire, until it appeared, brimming with blood, in Yami's hand. She drank and sighed when she had drunk.

'You let me win,' she complained. 'You let me dance across the Worlds and up and down the Years with the Goblet.'

'Why, when you left me after our pleasant feasting, did you not tell me you would take it with you?' Lord Yama frowned, and smiled.

'Time is slow in some worlds, Yama; and in Malthassa, unpredictable. I needed the Goblet to help me read the mortals and their habits. Besides, I never guessed you would miss it between the noon and supper boards. Much less that you would send an army seeking it. You caused poor Koschei much anxiety.'

'Tell me tales of that Mage.'

'Archmage and Prince! He never forgets his titles. No, I will tell you of Parados; indeed of Guy Young, as once he was and styled himself. Not a magician, unless with words, but one who –'

'Another of your lovers, Yami?'

'You know me to the heart and core!' Yami pursed her lips and blew a kiss into the darkness beneath the pendant skull. 'But these tales are better told in bed when they may act as sauces – My black soul, is she still there?'

'The shaman? Yes, she dare not move.'

'Get rid of her, sweet Brother. Cast her into the Pit.'

'I have already teased her with it; but I threw in a man of her tribe, a vile creature called Heron who was bold enough to rape her and so found himself among the damned.'

'Fortunately, Yama, you are above your own laws and may transgress them whenever you please.'

'Shall I grow guilty – as mortals do – and throw myself to my own Urthamma? Leave the Palace without a king?'

'Nonny! What will you now – play with your queen, or your new doll? Come, the afternoon is long past and 'tis time for action. Destroy the tiresome, virtuous thing!'

'You mistake her: she has a stout heart and a shining, courageous soul.'

'And she is pretty enough. If you will not hurt her, at least send her on her way. She can be set to work in the kitchens or, if you demand it, King of my Heart, can be placed in your harim.'

'Peace, Yami. I will send her away.'

Before they could protest or flee, Gry and the Horse found themselves standing beside the table. Lord Yama reached down and lifted Gry on to his knee. She felt his left hand beneath her, stronger than steel, and sat still and breathless as he stroked her hair and let his huge forefinger wander over her face and breast. He touched the wilting asphodel in her hair and smiled as it freshened and increased to a posy. Yami, watching, wore an amused smile.

'Wise, and forbearing,' she said.

'A beauty – of her kind,' said Yama. 'Give me the Cup.'

Yami passed it to him and he drank the last drops of blood that remained in it before setting it on the table and tilting it so that Gry could look into it.

'I will find you your father,' he said.

Smoke rose from the Cup as Lord Yama tapped it. Golden flames writhed and Gry, fearful lest her father had been sent to the Pit, drew in her breath with a sharp and anguished sound; but there, in the smoke, was Nandje, grizzled as an old wolf and so familiar with his double apron, gilded belt and soft leather boots, his brown skin and red-greased hair that all were grey

322

as ashes. Gry's arms, unbidden, reached to embrace him and, 'Father, dear Father!' she said.

'Nay.' Lord Yama touched her lips. 'It is the Imandi's image, not himself. See, there are willow trees and an inscribed stone behind him. Thus shall we find him: he walks in the Sally Grove and contemplates life without purpose and without end: do you wonder that we of the Palace delight in jesting and japery?'

'I believed that death was the beginning of better times than those hard days we endured in Malthassa,' said Gry.

'They were not all hard; and you see that death in the Palace is neither better nor worse than life, for it is like a vast plain that has no end and no beginning. Wander here for ever and discover nothing.'

'In the Plains of Malthassa there is much to discover, from a nest of fresh eggs or a newly-blown flower to the Herd itself,' said Gry.

'Those would be novel encounters for me! I should visit the other worlds as once I used. I should go a-wandering through Time as my sister does.' Lord Yama sighed and the smoke and the vapour-Nandje were dispersed, the shadowy outline of the Ima warrior curving and wavering before it broke up.

'You may go to your father,' the Lady Yami said as she leaned forward, her beautiful face animated with curiosity and envy.

'We permit you,' said Lord Yama. 'Wait, she needs a guide.'

'No, Yama, do not waste a peri on her: she has come this far on desire and hearsay. I am sure her horse will take her where she wants to go; or let her call for aid herself. Clap your hands, Gry. Summon one of your servants.'

'I have no servants; only my one dear companion, the Horse.'

'Clap your hands, I say.' Yami spoke as one unaccustomed to objection and Yama, covering Gry's hands with his own, struck one on the other.

Immediately, the small flame that was Umbra flickered there, between Gry's hands.

'What must I do?' it asked.

'The Lord and Lady say you will lead me to my father.'

'Indeed I will.'

'And they say that if I clap once, you will come to me.'

'That is true; and Sib will come if you snap finger and thumb together.'

Lord Yama lifted Gry like a child in his arms and set her on the back of the Horse, whose hazy silhouette he slapped without a sound. The Horse bounded forward, carrying Gry toward and through the darkness at the end of the hall. Umbra, whose light was scarcely a glimmer, flew ahead; and they were in a pale arcade where the muted light of Hell's short day broke the shadows into a flock of ravens on the wing. They passed a half-familiar figure, a stout old woman sweeping cobwebs from the roof. Something in her round face made Gry say, 'That must be Colley Switman's great-aunt!'

The paved floor sloped, the arches vanished and faint Umbra was the only light; and now rose a fickle dawnlight as they galloped across an endless courtyard or circus, for it appeared circular. Here, they overtook a dwarf and three soldiers marching steadily forward. One of these saluted sadly. 'Thidma – it is Gry!' she called, but they were past.

'My cousin and his companions, Githon, Vaurien and Hadrian, who fell from Frostfeather,' said Gry.

A man hewing stone which endlessly reshaped itself into an uncut block looked up at them.

'And that is certainly the turncoat, Estragon Fairweather.'

Then Umbra led the Horse by a transcendent gate into a cavernous room where sat a dwarf whose skin and clothing were all tarnished, as silver is when exposed to time. The poor fellow was weeping and Gry clapped her hands and brought Umbra to her; the Horse stood still.

'How did you die – you who were so brave and defiant with Aurel? What has happened to your shining skin?'

'Nothing,' said the dwarf. 'It is my outer covering, no better and no worse than it has always been.'

'Why weep? Everyone must die.'

'I have lost something; I know not what.'

'Your cavern home? Your life?'

'I do not know –'

'Hist!' Umbra for an instant was its child-shape and laid a warning hand on Gry's. 'He has drunk the Waters. He and those others have lost their memories – come, haste, we are near the Sally Grove, and your father.'

'It is all hypothetical and abstract for you, Brother,' Yami said and idly tapped her fingers on the table. 'You are a great scholar and a mighty thinker –'

'And an invincible warrior, huntsman and lover!' protested Yama. 'I was renowned for my practicality and inventions when I lived at Persepolis: did I not bring to the people the arts of Medicine, Navigation, Musicmaking, Goldsmithing –'

'Ay, and Silversmithing, Perfumery, Weaving, *etcetera*. That is another part of my complaint: those deluded people you speak of forget me. Inscriptions are found, which praise you; paintings and statues are discovered, of you.'

'While your stelae and your statues are buried still? The female arts were always covert, Yami – delusive too, intuitive, magical; and you, if you wish, may make memorials to yourself and your arcana.'

'Very well.'

'Not on the tabletop!'

'Who made the design and caused it to be realised?' Yami's tapping fingers began to trace letters on the dark surface.

'Letters of fire, do you think? They will bring some cheer to this gloomy library.'

Smiling, she rose from the her throne. The five letters she had written with her finger on the tabletop were blue and icy:

Ελένα

'Queen of Broken Hearts and Whole; and a worse vandal than Alaric who roars in the Pit,' said Yama, touching the letters which sundered and flew asunder in a storm of hail. Then Yama caught one of these flying icedrops and laid it on the table. The letters shone forth again and the King of the Palace of Shadows enclosed his queen and sister in a fierce and ardent embrace.

'Helen: is that who you are?'

'It is hard to say when she is the same being as Nemione and Ellen, as Silk Lèni and Yami.'

'And the Lamia. But I love Yami – although your gypsy ways seduce me, Helen. Become yourself!'

'Wait till nightfall. Then, I will decide who I am to become. I am tired: so many transformations sap my energies. Yet I have enough strength left to speak and, if you will come into the garden with me, I will tell you the story of Suleiman's Cup; where it has travelled and what it has seen: Old Lyon, for instance, whose narrow streets conceal many crimes and secrets; Arcadia, Pargur, Wathen Fields; Guy Parados, Aurel Wayfarer, Koschei the Deathless . . .'

When she saw her father, Gry clapped her hands with joy; and Umbra vanished. Nor did she notice – being happy and unlettered – the words which, celebrating the Queen of Darkness, were cut all round the pillar he stood beside and which, being plainly written, said: 'Yami, Sovereign of Hell and Queen in the Palace there Who has the Power of Life and Death.'

Gry slid from the Grey Horse's back and ran to embrace Nandje; she did not notice either that her arms passed through him, nor that a cold dew emanated from his shadowy form. To her he was solid and real and kept his warmth and scents of horse-grease, tobacco and the fresh grass of the Plains; the little house he stood beside was very like the shelters Ima built when herding far out in the Plains.

'Father,' she said, 'dear Father. Look, I have brought you your knife and your horse, your wonderful Red Horse.'

Nandje, though he gazed at her, gave no sign that he had heard; his face was without expression.

'Father! It is Gry. I am your only daughter, Gry.'

Nandje's lips parted slowly. He peered at her from those narrowed, half-closed eyes she remembered so well, staring out into the Plains to watch the Herd.

'I do not know you,' he said.

Something stirred in the willows and clattered up into the grey, tear-drenched air. It was a magpie, the pied harbinger of sorrow.

The land was white,
The seed was black

....

Nightfall in the Underworld, that fell, circumscribed and limitless land which surrounds the infinite Palace of Shadows, is rapid. The grey vapours darken, the half-light dims and vanishes as when a single candle flame is asphyxiated by the brass hood of the candle-snuffer. The silence widens for a moment before the cries of the damned break out again, but more loudly, most piteously. Those valorous or charitable Shadows which chanced to be outdoors have all gone in to shelter behind the strong walls and adamantine doors of the Palace. The land without gives itself to the night and to the beasts and morbid fancies of the night which, because it is common to all worlds, sects, religions, creeds and systems of belief, is mother to monsters as real as those which haunt our worst nightmares, and more.

And the reason this dire land has so many and is boundless in itself, is that all who die, save only shamans, must in one time or another come there.

The first to issue from the crannies and deep crevices, in which it hides by day, is Azidahaka, first cousin to the Lamia, who views the night through his six eyes and lashes any straying Shadow or pert demon with his six barbed tongues for, although there is no more death, there is always suffering. And soon creeps out the wingless Gorgon toward the hollow towers which lead, through magma, lava and rock, upward and downward to Malthassa and Earth; she, if seen by the men and women who live their lives out at the surface, will turn them to stone – and this is no common quarried stone but a dense, white adamantite which can be neither carved nor moved. Formless creatures follow her: no one should have to look on them. Their weapon is pure terror.

The Erinnyes, which some call Furies and which the Peerless Playwright dubbed 'the children of eternal night' next fly forth, leaving their cavern with ireful beats of their leathern wings, scourges flailing, viperous locks writhing. They grin, exposing their long fangs and give tongue as loudly as Yama's hounds, scenting crime and thirsting for vengeance; any who wish to speak of them must call them by the name they like best, which is the Kindly Ones. Chief among them are the three vengeful sisters, Destruction, Grudge and She Who May Not be Named.

Lesser terrors emerge from hidden dens and dark burrows: the winged djinn, Ako-Mano, whose body is that of a great lion; the grimacing Keres who fly off to oversee the battles men delight in and the wounded, who delight them more, and whose blood they suck and feast on until they are sated; the Duschma who, striding about Malthassa, brings pestilence, the cachexy and marasmus to all. She had heard of the new darkness which lay on that land when Koschei put the stars out and hurried to breathe her corruption over families sitting by their hearths and over the cattle and beasts in the lightless fields and byres.

As for the peris, those silken-tressed and shapely temptresses Yama sends to deceive men: they, transcending time and form, manifested themselves wherever they were desired, pausing on their odious, undulating, jewel-bedecked way, to touch a perfect rose or lily perhaps and wither it; to kill, by breathing poisonous vapours, a favourite bird or pet; to make a newborn babe sicken unto death.

Ask not: How do these fiends know where to seek their guilty prey?

Alecto, or the Unnameable She, flew high, ascending into Hell's heaven or vaulted sky, touching there the overarching rock and plummeting down to course Lethe's banks and groves. She saw the wide rings flattened by the pikulik as they danced in the asphodels;

329

the thick black water; the place where Hespyne, vanished now to fetch another cargo of Shadows, had moored. Something stank, something foul which had sinned, delighting to indulge in all the thoughts and acts men prohibit themselves from savouring. His black heart glowed blackly in the dark and so, she swooped on him.

He stood on the far bank, leaning against the trunk of a tree, surveying the night with the nonchalance of one who belongs in it. He listened to the agonies of the damned as their cries echoed from the Palace and from the distant poplars on whose sturdy branches they were hanged to suffocate, breathe once and suffocate again.

Alecto, though her hind feet and claws were already extended, stalled her flight; she turned a somersault and hovered: let him be truly terrified. Opening her long, hyena's jaws, she whispered, 'Hist, Koschei!'

The man looked up. He could not see her in the gloom.

'Who calls?' he said. 'Asmodeus, is it you repenting your cruelty and wishing us to renew our friendship?'

'A better friend than he!'

'Abrahel, bringing me a vision of milkbearing hills to lie on and a dark womb in which to pass the night?'

'No! You have many more friends in Hell.'

'Yama himself?'

Alecto howled contemptuously at his presumption and let her shrill voice ring until nothing was and no sound existed but her belling. The man's broad shoulders shook beneath their cloth veneer and tears ran down his face.

'I am female!' she hissed and Koschei, whose mind was immediately filled with memories of his fascinating, voluptuous lady, said, 'Helen?'

The time for laughter had passed. Alecto swooped again, skimming over him and touching him with the tips of her hind claws which passed like scythes through his hair and cut two swathes: he had no time to duck. She passed him again and lashed him with her scourge. At last when, clinging for support to the tree, he hoped she had tired and gone, she swung about and, flying fast and level, caught him with her hind legs about the hips and belly. She panted in his face and, licking his lips with her carrion-reeking tongue and pressing her voracious sex against his, bore him screaming aloft.

'You have hidden your soul, Koschei. You have no finer feelings. How like you this, how like you this?' she screeched.

They make you mad he said he said it in words which etched themselves into my belly and burned there without flames They come in troops Their breasts drip blood They feed on me! and passing me from claw to claw drop me falling toward the black water when I am caught again and played with like a kitten in hell without claws I am their ball their shuttlecock their relay baton they run races with me in the air as prize and victim spitting on me acid vomit gristle and the half digested hair of legless crawling things I come I come to

another place hell's kitchen where the fires burn without light and the grey spirits have doused the dark lamps and handed them forth to dim the place that the cooks may skin me gut me joint me fry or boil me alive and serve me garnished with a frill about my neck, a lump of coal in my mouth and a sprig of parsley in my fundament polluted I lie on a vast ashet dish with the gravy standing in its sailboat by but

here be dragons salamanders forked spears gridirons from which the heat is rising steam too from a great gob of phlegm discharged to test their readiness to grill me I am not to be kept alive the only other but she the horse princess in the palace of fearful night and flame

He lay panting soiled his mind stripped naked and flayed his brain turned to wool his smart suit of evening clothes stained with the Fury's slime and spittle and his own vomit his cheeks with tears and blood softly then a black tongue the size of a palliasse protruded from the darkness and licked his face clean.

Yama smiled grimly. Koschei saw his lips and megalith teeth only.

'The Lord of Death is mighty in holding mortals to account beneath the earth; and surveys all things with his recording mind,' said Yama.

He lived. He felt his heart beat strongly. He breathed deeply of the foetid air and felt fresh raw energy course through him.

'Behold!' said Yama, setting Koschei on his feet.

The page was vast and its margins pure as Altaish snow; upon the white page letters moved, ranking themselves into words, into sentences and paragraphs. Koschei began to read:

The pied bird flew before them, leading them out of the willow grove. A second bird flew up from the last willow tree and Gry, when she saw it, smiled at her father and said, 'We will follow them as we followed the single bird, whose name is Sorrow. Now we shall prosper, for two magpies mean joy.'

Gry unfastened the grey seaclock Jan Pelerin had given her and dropped it on the ground.

'I shall not need that again!'

The indigo of her old dress, the butter-yellow of her blouse, and her tawny deerskins shone clearly out, as when the sun emerging from cloud passes his citron hand across the landscape; the silvery birch bark of her magic shoes gleamed and she seemed to tread a path of pure light. The steps of Nandje and the Horse, following after, were glad and both tossed their manes, Nandje touching his greased hair as if he had only then realised its long, dense magnificence. Although the magpies went ahead, in dipping, wide-winged flight, it was certain that Gry, too, knew where she wanted to go. A small, grey figure walking in the distant Asphodel Meadows looked after the little procession; but Lemani, who had drunk the waters of the Lethe, recognised neither her daughter nor her husband. Gry, with a gasp and a pensive catch at her memory, shaded her eyes for a moment and watched her mother walk away; then she, understanding how life and death were separate and inseparable predicaments, resumed her own journey back to the Palace of Shadows.

They passed Erchon first, and the eternally labouring Estragon Fairweather who had betrayed all he ever owed fealty. The three soldiers were still crossing the courtyard, Thidma of the Ima first, sword in hand; Vaurien and Hadrian helmed and close behind and, last of all, the Copper Dwarf, Githon, who glanced fleetingly and blankly at them. In the arcade, Colley Switman's great-aunt, Drusilla Dowshier, swept the cobwebs, now and forever, away. The early-morning air was cool and stirred the curtain which concealed the last arch and whatever lay hidden beyond it; no dark damask this nor tenebrous cloth-of-secrets, but sinuous rows of fire opals which struck each other and rang with the enchanted sounds of starlight in lakes and moonlight charming the sea. Gry put up her hand to part it and pass through.

'Avaunt thee!' said Lord Yama and pushed Koschei out from his place of concealment behind the curtain.

The opals hung about him like drops of blood-saturated rain and there, within their all-enclosing canopy, shone some scraps of blue cloth, yellow silk, and tawny fur. Silver glittered low which, darting forward, came near his feet and she stood there before him, just like her picture in his Treasury: Gry, of the Ima, her dark hair stuck with fire and asphodels, her birch bark shoes a shimmering reservoir of light.

'Parados!' she cried.

He, glancing at his foul and spattered suit, involuntarily brushed it with a careless hand and inclined his head in a polite bow. Her scarce-ordered words tumbled out,

'How did you get here? You were dying in the Horse about to lose your immortal soul without a suitable body to house it. Did you die with the Horse? I saw you in Hyperion's cup, kneeling lonely. It was grim. O, how wonderful! I have not seen you in your proper shape – I've not been able to speak face to face with you since you were in Garsting – such an age since you left, so long ago. When I nursed and cared for you before you went to SanZu to recover your hands, before you journeyed to Castle Lorne and Pargur.'

His attentive mind made the connection he needed, the missing link: the soul of Parados, his eternal foe, must have leaped (quaking and terrified in all truth as any man would be) from the dying Red Horse into the body of the young knight, Aurel Wayfarer, and continued there. Such a brave and healthful body was a suitable house for Parados's restless questing spirit and a bold and obvious one, easy to detect and pursue: hardy, courageous, and too young for guile, a form which, with his superior experience or, most likely, his unsurpassable magic, he could easily destroy.

Or the authorship of Malthassa and all that went with it, even Albion perhaps or this shadowy Palace, would for ever be in question.

He smiled as he raised his head from the courteous bow and said, 'I am a great magician, Gry; a wizard with words; and it is very good to see you again. We must sit down together, if this vast palace has any place that resembles a comfortable bower or soft-furnished solar, and talk over the old times. As you see I have managed to locate my proper body, which has hands and no mark to show where they were severed and re-joined. Is that not true chiromancy!'

She examined his wrists while he, recalling what he had read in his Memory Palace of her old chaste and loving relationship with Parados, was quiet; though smiling still, with an expression as open and honest as the paladin he pretended to be. She looked into his face and gladness and relief shone in her brown eyes, which unshed tears made limpid and compliant. He thought: A curious matter! She has her proper colours whilst I am still all black and white. To prove this, he said, 'What colour are my eyes, Gry?'

'Sky-charmed,' she said. 'When I nursed you in Garsting, you likened them to English summer skies which are blue as speedwell flowers until a rain shadow crosses them and they turn grey and dour as winter.'

Was it possible that her blameless presence was colouring Hell with its charity and forbearance? Yet, despite all her untainted charms and eager artlessness, he must remember that she was of Parados's party and must hate Koschei. She smiled her amiable smile.

'My father Nandje is here,' she said, 'and would be glad to see you had he not left his memory on the far side of Lethe. Also, the Grey Horse who once was the Red.'

She reached among the pendent opals and man and animal approached. He noticed that, when she touched them, their true colours appeared and when she withdrew her hands they became lifeless and grey.

'I have a pledge with myself to honour,' she said. 'I must speak once again to the Lord and Lady of this place. Will you come with me, Parados, for I should welcome your wise presence?'

'I will.' As he spoke the words the certainty that her fate would mean his escape, a safe release from Hell, filled him with expectation. She was influencing him, waking hope. Now, she took his hand which instantly coloured, becoming sunbronzed as it had been in Sind and Idra, and her father's in the other. Nandje flushed more, his natural, warm brown hues spreading upward and beginning to colour his chest; his greased tail of hair flushing ochre-red. Even the Horse, who walked so close behind Gry that his head grazed her shoulder, was briefly tinted with his proper sorrel colour as if a skilled painter laid on pigment with a light touch.

The curtain of opals chimed as they passed through it, the last of its heavy tails dragging on their shoulders and falling behind. They stood in utter darkness.

'It is like the old adits under the Altaish,' whispered Gry, 'where anything may happen. You have your magic, Parados, and I have mine. We shall prevail. See! We are in Lord Yama's library.'

Koschei, looking about him as they crossed the vast patterned floor, compared this infinite library with his own in the Memory Palace, which he thought boundless and realised now was limited by the size of his imagination. This was hardly conceivable, the rows of bookshelves stretching away through the barred shade and having, in the furthest distance, the appearance of cliffs, or ledges of rock. Somewhere, perhaps about the centre of the piebald plain, they passed a carved black table whose shining top was greater than the polished dance floor in Sehol's Hall of Shields, where Friendship and her companion Concordis, the acrobat, used to cavort and display their graceful skills of veil dancing, handsprings, somersaults and the like to himself, their Archmage, and to his company of picked men. He stood still to marvel for there, somewhat to the left of the table's centre, someone had written a name in inlaid, frosty letters, most like ice. In the Old Greek it was, the true form of his own darling's name: Helen.

But Gry and Nandje hurried on, she urging Koschei forward. They descended a short flight of steps, the Horse trotting last. Koschei was sure he could hear hoofbeats, as if the Horse was alive and not a ghost; was certain that the steps resembled those of the Memory Palace – was that not the great chip that fool Segno had made with the eviscerator of the Metamorphosis Engine when he dropped it? Smiling quietly like a hungry tiger, Koschei wondered whether the fate to which he had delivered his servant, long residence in the dungeons and the nightly caressings of Baptist Olburn's steel-shod cat, was more comfortable than being sent to Hell.

They stood in a high-walled yard.

'O!' said Gry. 'I was sure those steps led to the garden. Never mind,' and she pushed open a sagging wooden door. Koschei was this time certain it had manifested itself at her touch.

'We are in the garden,' said Gry, 'but it is not the same one.'

Trees there were, the ubiquitous black poplars and white willows planted in severe patterns and formal groups of five and nine, grey urns and gravelled walks which whispered as they trod them. The sky was a pleated tester of clouded and rippling grisaille; or it was liker flowing water or wind-shadowed wheat by moonlight. Arches divided the garden into courts, great and blunt shapes covered in piebald tesserae; such vaults might grace the entrance to a pasha's saray, or a king's diwan. A chilly breeze touched them as they passed beneath the nearest and found within a colonnaded square where stood a mounting block and, waiting

336

beside it, a pale and dish-faced stallion whose bearing, caparison and jewelled tackle showed that someone had lately dismounted from his ornate saddle.

The Horse eyed him jealously and snorted.

Gry stalked the pretty stallion and did not alarm him with sudden movement or her own anxiety but, as soon as she reached out a hand to grasp his bridle, a pair of wings shot from beneath his caparison and he flew away. The sky grew dark and the ripples in it agitated. Living and dead looked up, stared confusedly about, for Gry seemed to have lost her purpose and direction.

'You seek the Lady.'

The familiar, melodic voice was in their ears and floating all around. Though the Horse and Nandje remained dull, Gry and Koschei spun about.

A tall black cypress grew out of the stone floor and pointed at the lowering sky. She who had called sat beneath it on a cushioned bench, her full and shapely lips enfolding a smile of welcome and her brow bent in a frown of displeasure.

'You trespass in my caravanserai,' she said. 'None are permitted here save Yama and myself, for this is the holy place where all my journeys end and begin and it is here in these arbours and loggias that I lodge my fancies and store my secrets.

'Yet you sought, and have found me. Brave Gry and her father, the dauntless Nandje who would be himself if only he had not drunk! The famous Horse who is almost as handsome as my Cham, that you have sent to his stable with your meddling touch. And Parados, is it not: the writer of fictions?'

Gry had bowed her head respectfully and Nandje copied her, but Koschei, throwing himself on his knees, clasped both hands together in the mute attitude of Christian prayer.

'You ask a boon for someone, Koschei – or is it a favour you want for yourself, my love to pour into your foul heart?'

'How, and why are you here, Helen, and in such elaborate guise? Why did you desert me in Sind?'

She made no answer but, instead, opened the bosom of her

mantle and displayed her breasts which were as round and prismatic as globes of ice. They dazzled Koschei, who half-covered his eyes. A huge scorpion lay between them and clung tightly to the flesh with his ten claws. His tail, a starry coil, lay close about her neck. Yami looked tenderly at the scorpion which raised its mailed head to her lips. She covered its body with soft kisses and Koschei hid his face.

'What shall I do with him?' she said.

A voice issued from the scorpion's grinning jaws.

'Charades and Forfeits are both good games. But I would let the girl depart before I played with him.'

'For death or life?'

'What said the cards last night, or the willow leaves you cast in my Cup; the Sphinx, the Entrails? Any one of these will give you your solution.'

'The Tower of Destruction told me there will be catastrophe and, for him, a ray of hope. The Leaves, in like manner, gave two outcomes, death and life, but the Sphinx, even after I brought her honeyed wine, said only, 'I cannot resolve your dilemma.' As for that dish of sweetbreads and pluck – I ate it. You are right, Sweetness: the sum of these oracles is clemency. Lead your old father and his horse away, girl, and do not forget how to snap your thumb and forefinger together!'

Gry curtsied.

'I remember, Lady. Very well. A snap brings Sib and a clap fetches Umbra,' she said. 'Yet nothing can help if my father has lost his mind so, by your leave, I will smoke a pipe with him before we set off on our perilous journey.'

Then Yami's frown faded. Her smile grew wide and she turned her new jocund expression on Koschei who, crouched in the shadow of his own fear, never saw it; and Yami was content to leave him thus, a fearful suppliant at her feet.

'Work your earth-magic,' she said.

Gry sat on the stone flags and patted them to call Nandje to sit beside her. When he was seated, his legs crossed under him and his pale hands easy on his transparent knees, she took one of the shadow-pipes from his belt and watched it become a substantial clay and tar-stained thing in her hand. She touched his tobacco pouch and the jackskin bag which held the chattels he had brought from Malthassa, the dishes, beakers, arrows, fish-hooks and snares her uncles and aunts had provided and remembered, as she surveyed these grave-goods in her mind, that there had been no strike-a-light. Aunt Jennet, Uncle Sweetgrass; they had all forgotten to provide Nandje with the means of lighting a fire. No matter. She glanced at her father who, with a fluid frown of concentration on his shimmering brow, was filling the solid pipe in her hand with grey threads of tobacco which looked like river weed and, tamped in the bowl, turned brown and unctuous. She could smell the honey in it. Nandje put the long-stemmed pipe between his lips. Now, for a light. Carefully, Gry drew her sparkstones from their bag, struck them together and watched – as tenderly as one watches a sleeping babe – the yellow spark grow red, glow and slowly begin to consume the tobacco. The magic, healing smoke arose and Nandje breathed it in; Gry saw its soothing coils drift like incense down his windpipe and nestle in his lungs, which flushed red. She saw his scarlet heart begin to beat and all the marvellous colours of Life return to him.

Behind Nandje, the patient Horse snorted as the plumes of smoke teased his nostrils. He breathed in. The Grey Horse sneezed and stamped his hind feet with the noisy vigour of being while, with the charged, enchanted breath, his hide and hair turned sorrel red and his long mane and tail resumed their proper colours. His kind eyes were full of sympathy.

'Take your knife now, Father,' said Gry. 'I have carried it long enough. The scabbard is not lost, for Voag keeps care of it; but I know where to find him and will fetch it for you when we are at home in the Plains.'

Nandje settled the knife in place in his belt of linked silver-gilt discs. His frown had deepened with the coming of life and colour. The smile which curved around his pipe stem and held it in a steady grip showed that the frown was one of concentration and not of anger. He took the pipe from his mouth; spoke.

'I never expected to see you among the Shadows, Gry. It was a noble act, this journeying of yours to seek and find me so far from home.'

Home, ah! She must tell him all that had passed, that the tribes were scattered and warring, that Aza was dead. In time, not now when he was so newly reborn and she felt like a child beside him.

'We must be on our way, Father,' she said. 'I cannot tell what kind of journey lies before us, from death into life; but we must be prepared for danger and hardship. I will summon a guide.'

Sib, quick as the click of Gry's finger and thumb, appeared dancing, her spiderweb hair whirling about her.

'Your asphodels have increased,' she said. 'May your happy days likewise. A posy is like a ring of words, each flower a spell. Keep faith with yourself and use every weapon you have to bring you safe through the trials of war, or love.

'What is your wish? Command me, Shaman.'

'I would like to go home to the Plains with my father and the Horse. But do not call me "shaman",' said Gry. 'I am your friend.'

'I cannot call you by any other name. I am your servant-spirit.'

'We talked and laughed together in Wathen Fields.'

'But this is not Wathen Fields. The Palace is ruled in another way, without Colley's sense of right and wrong, of fair play and justice. Come! I will show you a way.'

'And with all speed, Sharivila!' Yami spoke impatiently. 'The She-shaman defiles my scentless paradise with her foul tobacco, her stinking horse and her human sweat. Go!'

Sib grasped Gry's hand, Gry Nandje's, and he the mane of the Red Horse and all in line, a jumping and skipping riot of humanity and colour led by a cobweb, they ran away together through the arch; when Gry, turning suddenly, let Sib's hand go and started back. Yami rose tall.

'If you return you must bide here for ever.'

'I forgot Parados in my joy. Let him come with us, Lady.'

'I have words to exchange with him. Be gone.'

'I cannot leave my dear friend.'

'Go – or be for ever alive in death.'

Sib's frailty belied her strength. She pulled Gry away.

Koschei remained motionless, kneeling with face in hands before his goddess. The pressure of his fingers, hard against his eyes, gave him dazzling visions of scarlet, unvisited galaxies, of flying horses and stellar serpents.

'Look on me!'

Trembling, he opened his eyes; raised his head. Indeed, she might have taken any man by the hair and broken his neck, snapping the bones and the vital nerve apart as easily as a cook tears the head from a pigeon. She waxed gigantic, seated there. Her knee was as high above him as the roof of a house, her mantled body a cliff, her exposed breasts headlands, her head the summit of a hill from which her black hair hung in tresses thick as ropes. She stood up and Koschei peered into the undulating sky; her mantle, slipping from her, would have drowned him in its valleys and folds but he clambered over them until he stood beside a ridge of fabric on the stones. Yami began to unload from her naked body the creatures which clung to it, all but the scorpion which remained in its clefted haven. From her head, she lifted down a horned ram, from her neck a stamping bull, from her arms two grinning boys; from her heart she pulled a crab that clashed its pincers together and, from her stomach, a maned lion. She set them all on the ground where they surrounded Koschei, bellowed, bleated and yelled, prodded and pinched him. Yami's voice, unchanged in musicality and timbre, assailed Koschei from on high.

'Shall I also give you my Balance, Archmage, that I use to weigh the good against the bad? Shall my Archer pierce you to the quick, that you may know the pain others feel because of you? Shall my Water-carrier drench the breath from you? For you are like my chained Fish that pull in opposite directions, and like my Goat which, standing at the edge of time, invites lechery and death.

You would be the Scorpion who mates with the Virgin when you are no more than a failed priest, a scoffing soldier, a meddler in the arcane esoteric who is only fit to tup a whore.'

And she snatched him breathless upward and sat him like a doll astride her left breast which was indeed made of ice. The Scorpion eyed him from his haven in the rift and drummed his claws upon his lady's right breast, which was forged from steel. His eyes were the fathomless orbs of Lord Yama.

Yami trod the Plane of Delusion, dancing with her two suitors over rainbows; ducking under clouds, climbing unseen stairways in the ether. In Limbo she was, traversing its nine circles fast as light and slow as time, kicking aside the litter left by inquiring, spell-weary mages in search of Shangri-la, El Dorado, Utopia, Dystopia, memories, the philosopher's stone, the Future, the Past, Bigfoot, the Old Man of the Sea, the Yeti . . . discarded identities, broken vials and wands, gems of power, engines of regret, nightmares, dreams. Koschei saw there one of his own devices, a shuttered box which, when opened, revealed a simulacrum of the Sphinx that told tales and fortunes. Close by it lay a piece of Parados's writing, several paragraphs waiting to be summoned to their correct place in a story and beginning 'Koschei Corbillion one fine day walked out among the anthropophagi to seek –' and She had passed it by and he, digging nails and booted toes into the ice, was nearly unseated and dropped for ever in limbo. He began to slip and slide anew for the terrain below was airy and full of inconsistencies and lies. He could not stop himself. He began to spin. The seat of the chair had been buffed to the texture and sheen of glass and he, dumped on it, had nothing to cling to.

'A cushion!'

He sank into the feather bed which billowed about him as he crawled over and crushed its hillocks and subdued them beneath him. His head was on a level with the table-edge, with the rim of a glass, with Yami's face.

'Why, 'tis Koschei,' she said, and smiled Nemione's smile. 'Take a glass of Arcadian with me, Archmage, False Parados. 'Tis a noble vintage.'

He downed the ruddy liquid, glad of the strength and courage it brought him, for Yama sat on his great throne with his queen cradled, lissom and comely, in his regal, silk and velvet-shrouded lap. His iron crown was heavy on his brow and his look almighty.

'The sentence,' he said.

'O that, Beloved: obvious. Clear as your divinity. He must be deprived of his magical powers.'

'Then, so be it.' Yama raised his left hand. A thread hung from it and Koschei, staring at it mesmerised, a fly to a wolf spider, saw that its other end issued from his mouth. Yama tweaked the thread and magic spilled, falling soft as rain upon the tabletop, spreading there, congealing into sigils, the crooked letters of forgotten scripts, fragments of half-consumed pearls, a frog's tongue here, a birth-strangled babe's finger there, a splinter from Simon Magus's wand, a shaving of the bark of Prospero's staff, a promise wrung by threat and coercion from the Witch of Endor, a teardrop caught as it fell from Helen's eye when Menelaus died, a crystal of dissimulation, a stone of wonder, a luminous diamond of thought, a ruby of infallibility, a sapphire of enquiry. These and many more of Koschei's skills, every shred and atom of his mage's knowledge lay exposed on Yama's table. The god surveyed the countless objects.

'No small collection,' he said, blew on them and turned them all to moonbeams and dust which, rising for an instant into the air, formed themselves into the ghost of Koschei's true shape, tall, black-bearded, hook-nosed; and vanished. Koschei, locked without a key in the body of Parados, tried to speak.

'Nemen,' he stammered. 'Helione? Gorser?'

'What troubles your tongue, False Parados?' Yama said. 'It rambles like a crawling babe among the past syllables of your life.'

'Hyred, Gurados, Par?' said Koschei and Yami, kissing her brother's ear, whispered,

'Let him behold female beauty. The sight of a fair and nubile woman always revives him. Call Friendship!'

A clap of thunder, a clash of hellish cymbals and she came

leaping over the moons and masks of the floor, instantly called up from her ablutions in the sulphur baths. She clapped white hands together, spun upon her toes, unchanged, slender, nubile, desirable; save that her lovely hues and spark of life were gone and she was snow and shadow, flickering, undulating, unreal. Her veils were mist and her hair a splashing cataract. Dance had been her life, and also her soul. So, she had lost nothing when she died but her life and her memory. Koschei, whose eyelids flickered like an opium eater's, recognised her and remembered how he killed her by a dream.

'Friendship,' he murmured. 'How many times did you come to my bed and warm and comfort me when I had lost my manhood to the traitor's knife? You had better call me "Foe".'

He leaned his elbows on Yama's table and his chin comfortably on his hands, sure in the knowledge that Friendship could not know him. He watched her greedily as she moved and flung her inexhaustible, airy body through all the complex patterns of the dance. He savoured the sweet pain of unrequited arousal and, with the salt of memory and the pepper of fantasy, enjoyed Friendship in retrospect. Yama spoke a word of praise and Yami clapped polite hands. For an encore, Friendship gathered her cast vapours together and rolled them into a spinning ball of dew which she sprang atop and so, revolved about the floor, a circus of one. Her breasts were cirrus, her haunches cyclones and her thighs nimbus. Koschei sweated, running thwarted fingers along the cropped furrows in his hair. To lie with a ghost, to inseminate one of the dead: what child, what abortion? Then, remembering his body was not his own, he felt phantom kisses, the compelling lips of the many women Guy Parados had loved and lusted after, from his chaste wife to Helen, her divine self.

Friendship, woken to more frantic death by her own violence, caught up and tossed her spinning, shiny ball aside. At once, it sundered into mist and a flurry of snow fell. A suit of ice covered her rotating form and her waterfall of hair froze. Her feet became a carillon, pealing out as they trod the endless measure and she, her transmuted self, fragmented and became

344

one step in a maze of dancers, the host of the peri, who imitated Friendship to dazzle and outwit Koschei and please the Lord and Lady. Yami applauded, a mite more warmly. Yama spoke a desultory word, 'Brava!', and yawned, while Yami nuzzled in his neck. The occasion for change and for intimacy had come. Koschei sat unregarded on. They had forgotten him, a corrupt being of small account, a stray mortal who had blundered into the Palace.

'I feel the cold,' said Yami. 'This dance goes on too long. Are you not chilled, My Own? Would you welcome a little heat?'

'Of your making, Dearest, or the simplicity of a good blaze?'

'Cosiness is what I mean, the flowers and the fruits of love beside the domestic comforts of the hearth. I am chilled to the very ichor.'

'And I! I'll uncover the fire.'

Lord Yama rose, lustful and magnificent. He strode quickly to the Pit, where all was dark and silent, bent his huge body and, with a titanic wrench, lifted the boulder which confined Urthamma; bent again and threw back the grating beneath it. The fire demon's flames sprang high and Urthamma himself with them. The laughter of god and demon frightened the dancers, who fled, dissolving and mutating as they sped away, Friendship indistinguishable in their jostling throng. Yami spoke.

'Warm me, Urthamma, dispel my ennui,' she cried. 'The gloom of this bookish place drains me. Give me heat, bring unquenchable desire!'

The demon, reaching out with tangled limbs of fire, enfolded her and set her alight. He carried her to the lip of the Pit. She, in her turn, embraced Yama and they, all three, drifted flaming into the greater fire below, which roared but did not consume them. Yami, looking languidly back as warmth and colour poured into her unequalled body and ignited her beauty, said, 'He has some magic yet, a writer's skills, the ink and paper handiness of the wordsmith, the anvil of his experience.'

The last Koschei saw of Helen, of Nemione, of Yami, was her crimson blaze of hair which, as she descended into the Pit, cast a last, reflected glory over the library and showed him the universe of books and the excitement and sorcery of the writer's chosen task. A flame with five fingers snaked into the room and pulled shut the grating, put the boulder back in place. Wintry cold filled the room. The half-light hid many of the endless shelves of books from view and Koschei knew that with word-spinning magic comes the burden of creation. He spoke aloud ...

I am the author. That is what Yami meant, sealing my fate as surely as Urthamma has covered the fire. The first action I must take is to close my eyes, to visualise: Parados and Aurel, Guy Wayfarer and Aurel Parados, journey in the Altaish. What other place is left for them to travel, seeking refuge as they must? I envision the Way, a deep gully winding through the high peaks, made by ice perhaps or the action of water aeons ago. Aurel stumbles along: there is loose rock − shale − underfoot and it is greasy with its own exudations and with the rain which but now has just ceased to fall ... The whole gully is darkened by rain and the action of the mountain tempests and the sky, too, is dark though enough light remains to give glimpses of the towering precipices which rise about Aurel on every side; save where the narrow gully runs. I wish I had not extinguished the moon and stars. That makes my life difficult. Maybe it is day, yes, sometime after dawn and the sun hidden because the gully is so deep. Or shall I put out the sun and see how Aurel does in a darkness like the hellish gloom I stand in here, make him exist in twidark and perpetual gloaming?

Aurel pauses. Though bold, young and strong, he is already tired. He has been journeying for many days alone in body, if not in soul. He unwraps the remaining hunk of bread I cause him to be carrying and takes several hungry bites. All the while he looks forward and surveys the steep and twisted way he must follow if he is ever to reach Lilith's Donjon, the Fortress of the Gypsies and the Castle of Truth. He wraps the bread carefully in its cloth and tucks it away inside his shirt and hollow breastplate. Then, drawing his rondel dagger from the inlaid sheath upon his belt, he peers down at his chest and slowly and with great concentration, for he wants to make the message clear, scratches on his breastplate the single word PARADOS. He has solved a problem for me. Thus, with the reading of this name, anyone may see he is Parados's man; and yet he may keep his own mellifluous and symbolic name, Aurel the Golden, the Wayfarer who is a pilgrim in life and has about him the clean and vigorous air of a green and growing tree.

Now, Aurel sheaths his dagger and applies his young virility to the task again, striding forward (the way is smoother, the loose stones give place to hard and shelving rock), mounting upward.

'I must get on!' he says and shouts his battle-cries until the welkin (yes, I may use that archaic word in a Fantasy) rings.

'Who fights? Excelsior!'

His right hand moves across his body in a protective gesture and he grips the hilt of his long sword, Joyeuse.

The cold creeps on numb feet about the library.

Now, as the poet says, am I 'the master of my fate' and the 'captain of my soul' (which is safe in the green-backed volume of Keats's poems in the library of my Memory Palace). I will take charge of events both here in the Palace of Shadows and in Malthassa; also, I believe, in that England whence came Guy Parados. How speedily they faded, Urthamma the Fire Demon and Yama, Lord of the Palace, Yami, the Lady. Alas, my beloved Helen! She's proved as false a dissembler as Nemione, a divine trickster who delights in confusing us mortals and Life and Death themselves! I stand in this bitter cold twilight with Gry, her father and the Horse all patiently waiting in my fancy. Sib too. The book is in my hand. I read its title, *Lilith's Castle* and, opening it, turn to page 341. I read:

'Characters:

Gry, Princess of the Ima, a horse-herding people of the Malthassan Plains.

Nandje, her father, the Imandi, Chieftain of the Ima.

The Red Horse, stallion of the Plains Herd.

Sib, a grey Hellsprite, once Sib Switman, beloved of Colley, innkeeper at Wathen Fields.'

This will not do. These are words, not pictures. The characters are static. Gry takes the action from me, grasping Sib by the shoulder.

'You know the ways that lead from here,' Gry says to Sib. 'Those rifts you spoke of in Colley's orchard, those chasms which criss-cross the Palace floors and lead down – but up into Malthassa and the sunlight. Will you show us, dear Sib? Take us as far as you safely can for I must return home so that my father and the Horse can live out their interrupted lives and we may all breathe the clean Plains winds again and spend our remaining days under its wide sky.'

'Willingly!' said Sib.

By Yama! (and surely, I may salute him in his own place and palace) 'tis cold.

She was ready to be born. She felt the power of the muscles which seized and propelled her forth, along the channel, from darkness into light; and the blood which pounded, flooding through her heart, resonating in her ears, was it her own pulse and drumbeat, this song of Life? Was it hers or her mother's? Her mother the earth's?

The tunnel was steep, twisting about her. Its grip was tight; it spun her until she was giddy.

Death dropped her in the heather of SanZu, face-down. She smelt the damp earth, nuzzled it, tasted its dew on her lips; she rolled over and her eyes opened. The arch, the vault, the heaven high above her was bright blue. She blinked and let the space and colour fill her eyes, her body, her senses. She cried with happiness and laughed aloud.

Then Gry, the Shaman of Garsting, stood up shakily like a new foal, brushed the dew and heath-stems from her skirts and her silvery birchbark shoes, and watched her father and his Horse, the great red father and leader, husband and sire of the Herd tumble out between the stone lips of the vent. She unloosed her drum and beat it joyously.

I add one word: 'Leal'.

The warrior scattered the grazing heath-jacks as he rode. His progress was furious and passionate, for he had seen the three familiar figures in the distance. One moment there was no one and, the next, a woman and a man in Ima clothing, and a big red-coloured horse. Yet Leal did not lose his hold on the halter-rein of the horse he led.

They recognised him at once, greeted him gladly. When he had bowed to Gry and fastened her lost silver ring about her ankle, he embraced them all. They kissed each other again and again until, at length, they came to themselves out of their joyous confusion which lasted all day. Then Leal mounted Tref and Gry jumped up on Yarila's back. With great ceremony, Leal untied the bridle of Om Ren skin from his saddle-bow and handed it Nandje; but the Red Horse, though he bent his head toward the bridle willingly enough, no longer needed it. He had great love for Gry and loyalty to her father. Besides, Gry herself spoke out, saying, 'I promised him he need never wear bit or bridle again.'

The Red Horse bent his knee, assisting Nandje to mount. As soon as he was up and settled, the Horse bounded forward, taking his due, the lead. The other horses followed and the new Ima galloped off into the sunset which tinted them with hues of scarlet and orange, with blood and gold.

As for the rest of their lives – they, the Ima characters, must themselves decide how they recalled and reassembled the men of the tribe and, more importantly, whether Gry, her father's daughter, wedded Leal and, living happily ever after, bore him many strong sons and beautiful daughters or whether, obeying her supposed destiny, she gave Leal a chaste kiss and many blessings and then left him to live her shaman's life alone under Svarog, the sky; amongst the green grass and hills of the Plains.

THE END

Koschei Corbillion, in the
Library of the Palace of
Shadows, Date Unknown.

Unless I leave this wearisome prison and place of death and the dead I shall become one of them, frozen to a compliant state, deprived by apathy and exhaustion of my right to a life.

Parados's skills were mine, his words, his voice, his body. The library was becoming unreal without Helen, resembling a stage set or one of those inky Renaissance drawings of imagined studios and cells. Silence lapped, filling it up with negation. I looked about me, at my kingdom. Its sombre decor and dead light displeased me, the heavy carving of the table and twin thrones and, beyond the window (I'll create one, there! With leaded casements, naturally) – outside the open casements, the intricate, perplexing bastions and battlements of the rest of the Palace. The place was shabby. A corpse-moth, escaped no doubt from Yama's collection, crawled on the skull in the chandelier. The armies of books mocked me, regimented shelf by shelf. A thin sliver of the ebony which veneered the wall between their ranks hung down; I eased it away with my forefinger. The sheet tore. I pulled it free, and another. The panels were made of paper and I kept on pulling until the wall was bare and taut. I pushed my finger through the wall, caught hold and tugged until it collapsed and dragged the palace walls with it, black shadow folding into glaring white. The whole structure snapped together and lay, a twisted snake of paper, a folded fan upon the Asphodel Meadows.

The River Lethe was a pencilled line. I took a rubber from my pocket and erased it. I walked across the smooth, grey ground until I was close to the horizon; from it, I could easily reach the sky where dark stars blotted the page. Again, I reached out, caught a falling star which flared to life and light as I held on. It was attached to the sky. The airy sheet ripped and I clawed at it with my fingers, making a rent big enough to step through.

I was in the Memory Palace, walking quickly away from the shadows of fear, turning in my tracks to see which way I'd come out of the dark; but the wall behind me was solid and only a small dislocation in the starry pattern on it gave a clue. I recognised my surroundings slowly: such a time, an age, several lifetimes, since I had been there. This was the upper room, in Sehol and my memory both, where Friendship and I used to sit long of winter evenings and play at draughts and nine men's morris before a roaring fire. The grate was empty, swept clean, except for a piece of paper. I snatched it up, but it was only a forgotten wrapper from a sweetmeat and 'Succulent' I read and 'Jujubes by Appointment to the Archmage Koschei'. I dropped it to lie and be a memory again, passed on, out of the chamber and so, by a corridor of Castle Lorne, a corner of the Library and a red pavement I remembered only as I crossed it: the tiled floor of the colonnade on the south side of Martial Square, in Tanter. I walked into that dusty attic where once I had stood with Parados and watched him stare, amazed, at the music box of my design in which was imprisoned the carolling head of the boy, Christopher Young – Parados himself, in his young days.

The box was there still but I forbore to open it. I never could stand the boy's repetitive voice, which flowed from parted lips in a pure and high stream. Instead, I opened my own mouth, sang twice up and down the scale of C and was satisfied: a strong, pleasing tenor. Indeed, I had his voice and, smiling, went to the unglazed window for one last glimpse of sweet Nemione. There she was, and always will be, musing in the window above the Cloister, the night sky gathered above and about her to make a felicitous contrast with her gown and flowers, green and white, the whole picture a masterpiece of chiaroscuro drenched in candlelight.

I had to climb down the stair, the Stair it was becoming or even the STAIR Parados feared so much, dreaming of it many times each month, visiting it in a repeated, obsessive nightmare. My body stiffened at the mere thought of it. Yet descend, I must. I opened the little door at the stairhead and looked down. That was a mistake. Immediately the prospect of bare treads and yawning well made my head spin. I closed my eyes until the dizziness faded, opened them and swam in reeling, undirectional space once more. I shut my eyelids tight, felt for the rail, remembered there was none and shuffled like an old man sideways till I felt the wall. Only then could I begin the descent, my reluctant feet testing each step, my right hand scraping and grasping at the rough stone of the wall, turn and turn about.

When my forehead hit the door, I shouted aloud. Remembering, opened it and went down again and down until by all gods, strange and familiar, I found the bottom of the endless stair, opened the last door and stepped out of the cupboard into the bedroom. This, his in mine, his childhood in my Memory Palace, had ever been an enigma to me. I looked at the bed and the big cupboards, opened one and found it full of boxes spilling over with toys, little motor lorries and cars, horse-drawn carriages, soldiers, cap-guns, cricket stumps, a bat. A low chest by the curtained window held babies' clothes, neatly folded and stacked in piles. I picked a garment up, a cotton thing the length of my forearm, embroidered across the tiny chest with chains of daisies and ferny fronds. The curtain was thick, soft to the touch. I closed the chest upon the baby garments, knelt upon its smooth-worn top, lifted a corner of the curtain.

All this was new to me. Never before had I looked through his eyes at his possessions and now, at a piece of his life. In a wide street outside the window, people were passing to and fro, some carrying wicker baskets as if they had been to market, others riding bicycles. A brown horse plodded slowly on, drawing a cart on which stood sacks of carrots and potatoes and some boxes and baskets full of parcels containing, for I could see the blood-stains, cuts and joints of meat. I smiled, and almost lifted my hand in salute for I recognised my old friend Georg Deaner, the horse-butcher of Espmoss, though the legend painted on the cart was:

High-Class Butcher Sirloins and Steaks
Sausages and Pies
We Kill Our Own.
Proprietors George and Martha Peacock

The cart passed by and two figures rounded a nearby corner, walking companionably from another street. She was plain-faced enough, but had a pretty figure and a prettier smile when she looked down at him, her blond-haired, blue-eyed son, who was perhaps five years old and held a toy aeroplane by one of its wings. Catherine Young, I surmised, and her first-born, Christopher Guy. I let the curtain drop. Some coins lay on the dressing table, half-crowns and shillings, pence. I pocketed them, ran down the carpeted stair and out by the front door of the house.

The street had given place to another location. I saw grey stones, arcades, a small central garden; but this was not the Cloister at Espmoss. This was his place and his temple, the cathedral of St Edmund the King in Caster, the city of his birth and youth. The door was not the one I had closed behind me, being tall and iron-strapped, of dark and heavy oak. I opened it and saw a great, vaulted room in which were rows of narrow, low-backed benches and many statues and windows of coloured and painted glass: the cathedral itself. Sweet voices sang, scaling and bringing light to those bleak heights which only boys can reach.

'O sing unto the Lord a new song.'

Softly, I closed the door, stepped over the stone carved with the single word, '*Miserere*', 'Have pity', and left the cloister for the teeming city. Motor vehicles, fumes, and loud noises polluted its gracious streets, but the citizens smiled, for it was a fine, sunny day, and they all wore clean and brightly-coloured clothes and, to judge by the many bags each carried, had money in their pockets and to spend. Several young men and maidens whose hair was dressed in felted ringlets smiled at me. I stayed to greet them and give them good-day. I asked them how I should travel to Maidford Halse.

'Take the bus, mate,' said their leader: he wore a badge of rank with a forked stick printed on it and the legend on his knapsack was 'Holy Glastonbury', which I know to be a place of miracles and signs. 'That way, you can't miss it.' (Here, he laughed at his little joke.) 'It's green and yellow, number 106, goes at two o'clock. Good luck.'

His companion, the most well-favoured of the maidens, pressed some coins into my hand.

'Bless you,' she said, 'and don't spend it all on the purple poison.'

They all laughed.

I came to the bus which waited for me beside a canopied island. 106, for Maidford H, Thrup and Eden. These English place names confuse me. A man, the captain of this motor carriage, climbed into it and sat in the seat behind the wheel. He began to take money from the passengers. I proffered a handful of coins, from which he selected two circular pounds and a septagon of silver metal. He grinned at me.

'Good party, was it?' he said.

He started the engine as I walked to an empty seat near the back. Some street-urchins sat near me, whispering and nudging each other. Their shaven heads and ugly clothing showed them to be people of low class, very like the porters and street-sweepers of Pargur; therefore, I ignored them and watched the city passing by and then the green and fruitful fields in which (not hard for me who had been a mage and a cleric) I saw a great abundance of sacred places, hills and buried fanes, holy stones standing alone in consecrated groves, burial mounds and ruined castles. As I had written in my Journal, Albion is an 'old land full of loose, unharnessed magic which jealously guards its ancient secrets and its long-held reputation for perfidy'. Disarmed as I was, my magic taken from me and myself turned solitary into a new world, I yet intended to discover the first assertion and conquer Parados's demonstration of the second, namely his libellous treatment of me.

One of the urchins spoke to me.

'Been on the tiles, Granddad?' he said.

I gave him such a look as would have withered his testicles and shrunk his Generative Organ to the size of a snail's horn, had I not lost my Powers.

We travelled about one hour and came to the town of Badbury where a clock struck three. There, the bus seemed to take new energy and hurried forth upon a narrow road. High hedges concealed the view so that when we turned from this unsatisfactory highway to another with a steep incline, I was startled by my first sight of Karemarn Hill, that antique mound and hallowed site of witchcraft which broods eternally over the village of Maidford.

The Midland Counties bus set Koschei down on the village green. The place, its smooth-mown grass, its hoary oak and new, sustainable forest-wood bench seemed to him both familiar and very strange. The middle-aged (though healthy) body he inhabited knew very well where it was, and took control insofar as it at once set off in long strides toward the church. He was lucky that, at three-thirty, children have been collected from the Infant and Junior school and are at home with their mothers while everyone else, commuters and agricultural workers, still toils. He met no one. If he had, there would have been an immediate sensation of gossip, phone calls and the Press, for he – this tall, grey-haired frame which belonged to Parados – had been absent seven years.

He passed the church and walked through his own – or Guy Parados's – gateway. The old rectory which was his home looked charming in the sunlight, the stone clean, the paintwork fresh, the lawn and flowerbeds neat. The cedar tree had not escaped the modern fashion for an authentic, history-filled environment which looks new-built, and had lost its untidy, lower branches to the tree-surgeon's chainsaw. A Volvo with a 1996 registration plate was parked near the house door.

Two golden dogs, a venerable Labrador and his younger son, ran to greet Koschei. The old dog fawned, licking his hand, while the young one was irrepressible, barking excitedly and jumping up. Tails wagged. The ex-magician raised his hand to knock the door, and thought better of it, smiling to see that the knocker was a cast representation of himself in his glory days and high hat. He gripped the door knob and turned it. Already she was hastening along the hall and he met her a foot inside.

'Yes?' she said, the old response to her husband's querying 'Jilly?', gasped and put both hands to her mouth as if she would suppress a scream.

Time stood still. Koschei was familiar with this phenomenon when he was in magic's debt. Now, he struggled and felt conflicting emotions as the body directed: grief, embarrassment, joy, guilt. He spoke her name, but without the question mark.

'Jilly.'

Clearly she struggled too. At last, she spoke.

'Where have you been?' she accused.

(Where? Himself, or the Parados she could see? How to begin, how to explain? If he could not, he would not be admitted further, that was clear.)

'I was in Lyon for a while,' he said, 'and afterwards in M – Marseilles. I went to India.'

'India? So far – without telling me? You're mad!'

Someone was approaching from the back parts of the house, a tall and powerful man of Parados's age, who laid protective hands on Jilly's shoulders and peered at him through gold-rimmed spectacles.

'Perry,' she said. 'It's Guy.'

'I see,' he said, 'but what the fuck? – seven years –'

'It must be; all of that.' She stepped forward suddenly and lunged at his unshaven cheek. He felt the thin-lipped and saliva-free chafe of a wifely kiss. 'You had better come in.'

The man, Perry, also came forward and stuck out his right hand, which Koschei grasped and shook as heartily as he could.

'Well, you haven't lost your batsman's grip,' said Perry. 'But,' his voice grew confidential, 'but, where in hell did you disappear to?'

Koschei grinned. He could not help himself. It added to the impression he was giving of a psychotic drunk who has belatedly remembered he has a home, a wife, a profession, and a large family. The facts he needed came to him: this was Guy Parados's closest friend, the stained-glass artist Heathcote Perry who, because of his awkward Christian name and an English habit begun at school, was always known and addressed by his surname. They had been boys together and young men; they had lived within a hundred yards of each other for more than thirty years.

'But really, Jilly would be glad of an explanation. So would I. On the other hand – look, do you need a doctor or something?'

'I need nothing but rest,' said Koschei. 'Or perhaps, stimulation. No doctor, thank you. I am not ill.'

'You look as though you've been living under a hedge,' said his wife, twisting her wedding ring. 'The stains on your suit; and whatever happened to your hair?'

(Alecto, Koschei thought.)

'I will explain,' he said.

(As soon as I've invented a story.)

The dogs' tails were wagging again. They both looked up and there, leaping down the staircase, was a blond-haired boy of twelve or thirteen, a newer version of the child, Chris Young, whom Koschei had seen from the window of the Memory Palace. He rushed at Koschei and hurled himself into his arms, speaking one word over and over, 'Dad, Dad, Dad.'

It was remarkable, the compassionate way by which the boy took over, sending Perry to the kitchen for tea and toast and his mother to look out fresh clothes.

'We'll be in the study,' he said. 'He'll soon feel at home there and I'll show him the latest developments. Come on, Dad, upstairs.

You're not too tired for me to show you something, are you? Something exciting!'

He fell into their economical way of speaking.

'No, not at all.'

Ben prattled, that was the word for it:

'There, here we are. Sit in your chair, I'll switch it on. Abracadabra! Isn't it great?'

'It' was an engine, the kind they called a computer though its functions were more than mathematical. The glass window, or screen of it, was flooded with light and colour; an unseen orchestra played.

'Wait a minute –'

The boy hit several of the keys on the raked board before them.

'WELCOME HOME!' the computer said, with a voice like that of Parados himself, and the words scampered across the screen. The boy was jabbering again.

'Sorry it's not very good, no time for fancy text and pictures. But we have to get on the Net. That's it and now we want Shoal – I call it trawling not surfing 'cos the thing's so slow. Come on, come on. Now I have to type in "Truth". You know, Dad, you don't look too bad in that suit, like a mad professor. Mum found your Professor Branestawms in the attic. I've read them all – they're a bit dated, but not bad. Have you heard Professor Unwin on the radio, thiserl combumberlol's a buggeraloo?'

He burst into peals of laughter.

'I can't remember your name,' said Koschei.

'What?' The boy's eyes filled suddenly with fear and concern.

'Oh, I only said "Good old Ben."' (and thank the gods for Parados's memory.)

'Here it comes. Isn't it great, aren't you proud? Dirk and Micromansion did it while you were away – straight from that last bit in Lilith's Castle. Buh – boom!'

The castle floats on a sea of darkness, its golden walls and towers of lapis lazuli miracles or dreams come true. Yet, look again, and you see the rocky chasm which surrounds it and lies

358

close beneath the walls, the strong drawbridge which crosses it and, toiling over the uneven floor of the deep chasm, the small figure of a golden-haired knight, armed and wearing a silver breastplate, long boots of leather which reach halfway up his thighs and, in the collar of his white, ruffled shirt, a pin shaped like a cockerel's feather; and this, too, is gold.

Koschei exclaimed, 'By the Dark Lord himself! 'Tis very like. 'Tis the Castle itself, the very Donjon of Lilith and the Fortress of the Gypsies. Aurel is there, at the end of his journey from the Ocean's shore and the beginning of his adventure with the Enchantments.'

'You talk just like your book,' said the boy. 'You should do that at conventions – dress up as well. Look now, the title's coming up.'

The castle vanished into the machine and its screen turned blue. For an instant, the bright colour made him think of Gry and her beloved Plains. He wondered how she did, felt the boy nudge his arm, and read

The Castle of Truth

Koschei watched and listened. The machine was singing to him now in the vertiginous soprano he had locked in the musical box, sweetly singing, one glistening drop extracted from the honey of the cathedral choir.

> 'And let me set free, with the sword of my youth,
> From the castle of darkness, the power of the truth.'

The music died away. Though he hated it, and hated all it stood for, he longed to hear it again; but Ben was speaking and a new version of the castle's picture, in which snowclouds had gathered, the lengthening shadows of late afternoon lay black upon the stones and a flock of doves flew home to roost, was painting itself on the screen.

'Did you notice the tiny figure in the chasm just now?' said the boy. 'That's Aurel. He's got to get into the castle or you can't begin. And Magpie has, too. That's his page, his assistant, you know – they changed the story a bit. I usually play Magpie, he's a bit of a magician. We'll have to share the mouse, of course.'

(The mouse?)

Ben moved the small grey box which lay under his hand and a mailed fist wandered over the screen.

'When you want to make them do something, click,' he said. 'Anyway, you know – I'll show you how to get in though, it'll be much quicker!'

Koschei took a bite of the buttered toast Perry had silently placed at his elbow. He sipped his tea.

'OK,' he said, pleased with himself and his growing facility with the modern English language.

Ben pulled up a chair for himself and began to manipulate the mouse.

'You make them climb the chasm walls, Aurel first – there he goes. Magpie next. Under the bridge, then no one sees them. They keep a good lookout in that castle, I can tell you.'

'Then why do they not see Aurel and Magpie standing beside the bridge?'

'Look carefully. Line of sight. The bridgework conceals them.'

'Not very clever of the architect. In Sehol we had clear sightlines all round.'

'Yes, Dad – but it's not real, and what would be the point of a game that nobody could start playing? Guess what they have to do next?'

'Magpie scales the castle and lets Aurel in? He uses some simple magic to deceive the guards? Aurel pretends to come with a message for Darklis Faa?'

'No! It's not a novel – it's a computer game. They're quite limited. This is what you don't do: see, if you make them climb, they come to an overhang – whee, there goes an arrow –'

'So now the guards know someone is trying to enter?'

'It's a computer game, Dad. I told you. The program says

something like "if x gets to y then z happens" and z's an arrow. Just pretend the archer's a bit thick. If I move Aurel forward towards the gates – mind the arrow – he just walks into them, whoa! and would knock himself out. That finishes the game and you must start again. Plus, if he makes a noise –'

'How?'

'He farts at random.'

'The devil he does! Not Aurel.'

'Why not? Everyone does.'

'Not Aurel, I know him . . .'

'ANYWAY, DAD, what you have to do is find some food for him – there we go, he has some bread and cheese in his wallet – and then he stops farting. BUT *if* he makes a noise the Green Wolves – you know, the outlaw soldiers – come out and get him. And the game ends. *So* what you do is make them wait – you move on the clock with this menu here, like that – and it becomes dark and then, wait for it, the postern gate opens and out comes Old Angela.'

She held a dark-lantern in one trembling, age-warped, hand and touched Aurel's sleeve with the other.

'St Agnes' Eve – ah, bitter chill it is!' she said.

'It's out of copyright,' Ben explained. 'That's how they could mess about with it and make a joke of that quote.'

'A writer will use anything to get an effect,' remarked Koschei.

'We shall have snow before night falls,' said the old woman.

Aurel was sorry to see her shake so, for he remembered her untiring and vigorous and with great moral strength and purpose when she was Polnisha's Abbess in his home town of Flaxberry and he went to the nuns to exchange pieces of his mother's drawn-threadwork for vegetables at their garden gate. He wanted to ask her what had made her leave her calling, but forbore; he did not like to annoy someone so frail with excessive questions. Besides, Mother Angela still kept her gridelin habit with its white linen wimple and its silk stole and, though it

361

was worn and threadbare, the sight of it made him deferential and wary.

Angela herself had no such reservations. She drew him swiftly inside and beckoned Magpie to follow; retired with them into a dark cell some way from the gates.

'This is one of the Beadsman's haunts,' she whispered, 'but he's at evensong in the chapel. You are changed, Aurel: no longer a grubby boy, but a fine young man who looks as though he's used to the best bed and the bloodiest beefsteak, for all he's a hardy soldier. What's this scratched on your breastplate – 'Parados'? Is that a souvenir of your days with the paladin?'

'I serve him, even now,' Aurel replied.

'Better than serving Shereef Roland I've no doubt! He's a jealous master. None dare cross him. But you've not put yourself in peril to listen to my babbling, Master Wayfarer. You may get your wish and your heart's desire yet, for the young lady's at home.'

'Where is she?' Aurel spoke lightly but could not hide the eagerness in his voice. 'With her jealous guardian, I don't doubt – I believe he would marry her himself, had he not promised . . . where is she, Mother, where is Lilith?'

'You must follow me, though I cannot show you all the way. Quietly now, and do not chatter, Magpie!'

They walked the castle's undercrofts and service tunnels in near-darkness, for Angela kept the lantern hooded and they had only a weak yellow glimmer to help their feet on steps. As she had predicted, snow fell, drifting in at the unglazed windows and whitening their shoulders whenever they crossed a courtyard. Small flowers grew in the Physic Garden, up to their necks in snow and, 'Agnes's flowers,' whispered Angela as they hurried into the shelter of the hoarding atop the wall.

The old woman raised a quavering finger to point.

'Lo!' said she. 'That is where you must seek her, Aurel Wayfarer, and here, our ways must part. Come, boy, with me, for lovers despise a Peeping Tom.'

Aurel, who had been looking where she pointed, up into the whirling snow at a high, conical roof that topped a round tower, turned to speak; but Angela and Magpie had gone. Through the studded door, he thought, and laid a hand on it to push, grasped the ring. The door was locked and fast. He turned back to the tower which floated in a sea of snow-speckled night and was as blue as his own keen eyes and as tall as his aspirations and desires.

'Excelsior,' he muttered. 'You must fight for yourself, Aurel.'

Thou shalt be the first of witches known

Her fair face was reflected below the inscription, in the Mirror of Dreams. Now, smiling absently, she watched herself move through the orchard and pick an apple here, a cherry there, Chatainier, Fortune, Nonesuch Charm; Bleeding Heart, Bounty, take a bite here and a nip there, and place them fresh and whole in her basket. A pleasant hour. She bathed in milk and called one of the gypsy women to anoint her with oil of neroli, all in her Mirror and her dreams. Winging over the burnt distances of Malthassa, she sought and viewed the Ima thronging home; mutable, dismantled Pargur; further now, the white-cliffed stronghold of Albion, its water meadows and satanic mills, its teeming towns and quiet, legend-girt villages; and so, alighting from her dove-drawn chariot, watched Koschei and the boy staring at her and, below them in the taut-environed house, the embraces of a pair of lovers. Old they were, three times her green age, but nonetheless she felt a tendresse for them and wished to see, to kiss! her dream lover. She had followed the daytime rituals, combed her hair backwards, drunk a distillation of his sweat (obtained by Myomancy) in wine and matched the ram lamb's pizzle with the ewe lamb's purse. Uneasy suddenly, she wished to see her own face and figure to make sure she was the chaste and sensual creature of her truelove's dreams. She waited patiently. The dreams cleared in their own long time and she saw herself, splendid and voluptuous yet a maid entire, the privileged condition she had enjoyed since her mother changed her shape from gaunt Fish Child to this lovely accord. She stroked her corn-yellow hair: that favoured her mother, Nemione; she gazed deep into her green and sparkling eyes which favoured no one but herself and were the one remaining mark of her old, watery life. Her gown was ivory silk of Flaxberry Abbey, her petticoats and shift finest lawn of Flaxberry town and she wore, for luck, a tasselled red riband about her left wrist; her white shoulders were half-covered by her swansdown wrap. She leaned forward and kissed her reflection on its full and luscious crimson lips, leaned back and took up her comb of horn of unicorn, the gift of her guardian, Roland Hautdesert, which she had helped him gain when the unicorn laid its trusting head in her lap and Roland killed it swift and compassionate by one thrust to the heart with Durendal. She drew the teeth of the comb through her hair, and laid it by. The circlet of apple blossom was her final ornament. She set it low on her serene and matchless brow.

They all revere and love me, she thought: Old Angela, the Beadsman, Uncle Roland, every chal, chi and chabo, every rai and rawnie of the gypsy tribe; and sweetest Aurel that I see in my Mirror and long to touch. And this is well and good, for I am the daughter by enchantment of the virgin sorceress, Nemione Baldwin, and the great archmage, Valdine of Pargur, no lesser, whom Koschei slew before he came to power and forced me to submit to his desires – but I was in another body and in another time who now wait yearning here. It does not signify. Now show me my dear man.

He rose in her Mirror of Dreams as a star does into the night sky, alone and handsome, armed and valiant at the foot of her Tower of Love; and she, Lilith, rose from her seat and went, looking neither to right nor left, nor behind her, to her bed, Aurel's image bright in her eyes. She dropped her wrap, stepped out of her gown and lay supine on the coverlet which was embroidered like a meadow with daisies, buttercups and soft, yellow heads of lady's bedstraw. Her two familiars, the lion dog, Leo, and the monkey, Halfman, moved aside and lay down again; she did not see them, her gaze fixed on Aurel, but Leo licked her hand and Halfman took off his plumed cap and laid it carefully on the back of the dog. They curled tight and slept. Lilith reposed in her vision.

A supper of manchet bread, peaches and wine lay untasted on a stool near the bedhead. Though a rich fragrance stole from the fruit no hint of hunger or thirst entered Lilith's dream. She stirred languidly, touched her left breast and her thigh. He was there, ardent in her mind; he was not there in the flesh.

'This is a dull pastime,' she said, 'I will summon him,' rose again, moved to her Mirror and looked once more upon her peerless beauty.

'Go now, sweet Likeness,' she said, 'and bring my love to me.'

The semblance rose up like a swimmer in water and stepped from the mirror. Lilith watched it lovingly but only moved when it stood by the window and was ready to launch itself into the night. She cast a veil over it. Then her Likeness floated from the window with its yellow hair spread out in a train.

'Trap him, my Faithful,' Lilith said. 'Snare him in the

Sweet Toils of Love'

The snow fell with the sound of lovers' sighs and there was an intensity in it which betokened a larger body such as a scritch owl, harpy or winged horse. Aurel strained ears and eyes. He felt constrained, standing there not knowing which way to go; fettered, as if his soul was in someone else's grip and as if that grip was the clenched fingers of a mailed fist. The hold turned him swiftly about and he beheld the thing he had sensed, a veiled figure gliding towards the ground which, now, as he watched and laid a wary hand on the hilt of Joyeuse, approached him, pulled at the gauzy fabric which covered it and showed a hand, an arm, a face and breast the colour of Agnes's flowers.

'Lilith!' He breathed the word, exhaled it, soft and tender as his love for her; as gentle as the tower was hard.

She was crowned with a bridal wreath and a red riband was

tied about her right wrist. Her hair trailed over the pavement, swept aside the snow. She looked into his face.

'Step on my hair,' she said, 'and I will carry you to the place where dreams and reality are one.'

They rose as one and she brought him through an open casement into an arras-hung room at the tower-top.

'This lovey-dovey magic is boring,' said Ben Young. 'I'm going to bed.'

'Very well. But shall I play Magpie also?'

'You don't know where he is. I'll show you in the morning and, if I were you, I'd have a good look round this room. Never mind Lilith, she's very vain.'

Inspired, Koschei laid his mailed fist upon the door of Lilith's room. It opened and he clicked the mouse, again, again, descending the spiral stairs. Aurel stood motionless, stranded by the shift-clad Lilith and the veiled one and Magpie was nowhere to be found but, at the stair-foot, waited an old man bent and crabbed as Angela, whom he touched with his steel glove and propelled slowly onward along a wide, cobbled corridor and over an arcaded bridge, passing numerous pikemen and guards who saluted in the respectful way one uses to a priest.

At length burst in the argent revelry

The Beadsman took his customary seat beside the central fire and looked about him at the great hall, its beamed roof dark with encrusted smoke, its tables high and low. He saw a great rout of people crowding in, musicians blowing on silver trumpets, men-at-arms and lords; ladies, gypsy kings and queens; the Shereef Roland in his mail byrnie and red-and-white surcoat, his henchman Deon close behind. He observed the lustrous angel, Urdiv, standing quietly beneath the gallery, wings and hands folded. He recognised the sisters, Darklis and Lurania Faa, Supplista with her Muldobriar, Dorilia with Danku and his brother, Taiso, arm in arm with Seji. He watched the servants bring in the boar's head to a fanfare, serve the joints and hand the bread and wine. He noticed Deon's unsheathed sword and saw how Roland gripped his dagger as he cut his meat from the beeve's shank and how his dark eyes glinted in the candlelight which called up images of itself from every polished surface, the ladies' jewels, the gypsies' brass trinkets, the golden dishes, the red apples on the charger.

Roland took an apple and bit into it. He knew himself to be both clever and cunning, played his role as the son of a tragic love-match to the hilt, dressing in a mix of Christian and Saracen garb and enjoying the poetry and weapons of both. He suspected he was a stereotype, smiled in his beard and spoke to the Lady Malatest.

'Whence came these excellent apples?'

'Lilith gathered them in Verity Close; since autumn they have been in store.'

'Lilith.' He repeated the name as if it had a special savour for him. 'Lilith. And where is she?'

''Tis Agnes' Eve, my Lord. Your ward is practising the sacred rites all maidens delight in. She has observed the rituals and gone supperless to bed in hopes of a dream of her true love.'

'Nonsense! She has no lover – unless . . .' His eye searched the hall. 'Unless that country hob she danced with at the wassailing – no. Send for Angela, Lady. Lilith will leave her bed of dreams for her old nurse; and when she knows that I desire her presence in the Hall.'

The Beadsman, who had heard all this and seen how thinly-shrouded was the Shereef's anger, stood up. As an excuse for standing while the nobles sat, he raised his hands and voice in prayer, turned about and left as swiftly as his rheumatics allowed him. He found Urdiv outside, who openly declared, 'Roland makes difficulties where there are none.'

'Ay!' said the Beadsman, 'and men will murder on holy days. I am for the Love Tower – you?'

'I will – keep watch,' said the angel mildly, spread his barred wings and flew to the parapet of the donjon.

The Beadsman hurried across the bridge. Old Angela was hobbling towards him and, at her heels – from respect, not bodily weakness, he saw – walked a nimble and innocent-faced youth, a magician by his pied garb and bag of tricks. They halted to confer.

Beyond a mortal man impassion'd far

Both were lovely and loveable. Aurel did not know which way to turn but looked at one and then, with shaking hand to open mouth, the other. His face was red with embarrassment and desire. The beauty of that one was displayed; the other showed hers by concealing it. He noticed that the first wore a red riband on her left wrist; the second wore the favour on her right. Both of them were laughing at him.

'You must choose,' they said in unison.

Golden Aurel frowned, not knowing how much anger improved his handsome face.

'Not either, or – but both!' he offered and the two beauties laughed again.

He felt the mailed fist prod him and, without the prompt of association or memory, an idea leapt into his mind: it had to be the left, was sinister – did not this Lilith have the reputation of witch? Was she not the fair lady the gypsy-kind worshipped? It was the left.

'You, my Lady,' he said and took Lilith's hand.

She kissed him sweetly on the lips. Over her shoulder he saw the other woman, her double, walk up to a mirror in an ivory frame, raise her arms and dive into the glass which received her as fluidly as water does a swimmer. His arms were locked about his dear love, his hands straying over her warm back. Suddenly, she began to scream and beat him with fists upraised.

'Not again!' she cried. 'No, not again, Koschei! Find me a better fate, Parados!'

Someone was hammering on the door.

* * *

368

A panel appeared on the screen and obliterated Koschei's close-up view of Lilith.

> You have won 9775 points, traversed Five Levels, and been awarded the title of Apprentice Knight.

'You fool, Aurel, why couldn't you keep your hands to yourself?' he said and seemed to hear Aurel's reply, at the same time plaintive and irate.

'You were steering me, False Parados.'

Thunderbolts flew like crossbow bolts across the screen. He heard their heavy music, read the message:

END OF GAME

Night had fallen, as if some giant had cast a blanket over the world: he could not get out of the Fantasy idiom. Pricked with stars, he thought. I mean holes. The picture of the Castle of Truth had returned to the screen and begged the question, Resume or Retire? Parados's friend, Perry, was surely long gone to his own house. In this skin he, Koschei, must represent the husband of anxious-eyed, thick-waisted Jilly. He did not relish the idea, preferring dreams to flesh, the autoerotic stimulation of Aurel and Lilith's romantic games to reality. The Castle's blue and gold architecture filled the room with magical light and he went to the window to clear his head and to subdue his anxious thoughts and confused memories. He unlatched the leaded casement and leaned out.

Beyond the rose garden and the church, the Norman castle mound looked bigger than it was, worn down by nine hundred years of weather, rabbits and grazing sheep. The close it stood in was named for one of the old rectors of Maidford, John Humfrey. He verified these stray memories of Parados's by peering at the framed map which hung near the computer. It was a panoramic map, each cartographic feature embellished with perspective and

369

walls. This then, the old bailey of the castle (whose name was lost in unrecorded time) which was now the garden, had been named Verity's Close. Koschei smiled, amused. He raised a hand and said, 'I salute you, Parados!'

The phone on the desk rang suddenly, breaking apart the darkness and peace. He reached out and lifted the receiver; but it had already been taken up. By the wife, by Jilly, he thought, and listened silently while he pictured her alone in a wide bed; but not in silk like Lilith for she would wear some plainer kind of night-rail, a cotton gown perhaps or one of those upper-body garments he had worn the first time he escaped Malthassa, a T-shirt.

'By Christ, Jilly,' came Perry's voice, low and fervent. 'What shall we do? He's not there with you?'

'No – not yet anyway. In the study, playing the castle game.'

'Oh . . .' Perry sounded disappointed: perhaps he wanted a fight? 'My dear, it's up to you. The prodigal has returned!'

'At least I can divorce him now.'

'Come over to the cottage, come to me –'

'Don't be stupid. I can't leave Ben.'

'Guy's there.'

'I don't know him, Perry – he's a stranger to me. If he can vanish for seven years and then turn up without an explanation – what might he do next?'

'Perhaps you should lock your door?'

'Yes, I will. Come round after eight –'

'Ring me if there's trouble.'

'Of course. Goodnight, love.'

'Goodnight, Jillyflower.'

He would bath, that's what he would do, cleanse the good body Jilly despised. Find those clean clothes. Then he would resume the game.

This time, he hurried through the rooms he knew; the draughty corridors, the familiar procedures. He had awoken Ben who had protested mildly, flung on a Red Horse-patterned robe and plugged in a second mouse.

370

'I want you to play Aurel,' he said. 'I shall be Magpie and have better scope for my talents. I think he is more easily corrupted and I must make my impact on the game.'

'At least it's not school tomorrow,' said Ben. 'Crumbs! What's Aurel up to? – I've never seen him do that before: look, he's touching Lilith's bum!'

'Then move him.'

'And I'll give the poor girl some more clothes.'

The boy moved his emblem, a golden cockerel's feather, and touched it on the pile of discarded garments which at once, and without any intervening manipulation, clothed Lilith in her familiar ivory and swansdown.

'Come on, Aurel,' he said. 'Time to get some help,' and moved the little knight to unlock the door and admit a worried Beadsman, a youth in a white doublet and hose half-green, half-black, and a tall figure with furled and folded wings, who stooped beneath the ceiling and said, 'Good morrow, sire. We must venture forth and assail the mighty donjon. Have no fear for I, Urdiv the Lustrous Angel, am on your side.'

Somewhere in the castle or the churchyard, a clock struck four, and a rosy day dawned beyond the casement windows of the Tower of Love and the Old Rectory.

'But first,' said Lilith's guardian angel, 'we must pass through

The Fortress of the Gypsies'

Aurel, whose senses were still confused and whose body ached with unfulfilled desire, wiped his hot face on his sleeve. A small voice whispered in his ear: this was the first time since he had toiled up the gully that the lost soul had spoken.

'Is that you, Parados?' he said, inwardly. 'Have you moved yourself?'

'I have, but I think unwisely. I am crouched in the tunnel of your ear – from there I can peep at the action and leave your sight entirely alone.'

'That's noble.'

'Or foolish. Scratch in your ear – little finger, please! Do you feel me?'

'Mmm.' Aurel held his hand out before him, examined the tip of his little finger to which the tiny manikin which was Parados's soul had, for an instant, clung.

'You've been playing badly,' said Parados.

'I felt constrained. As if someone held me in check and then forced me forward where I did not want to be, or made me act as if I were a common lout and not a vigil-consecrated knight.'

'Koschei was controlling you. Never fear: he is Magpie now and you are in young Ben's hands. Trust him: he is my son. And keep a wary eye on Magpie.'

They hurried from Lilith's room, leaving the quiet and her two sleeping familiars behind them. The Beadsman knew a secret passage which brought them to a concealed balcony above the fortress's kitchen and there, some twenty feet below, sat Darklis and Lurania, conversing boldly in their canting tongue.

'Well – and deep as a thrice-transformed hag's cauldron the word is – *well!* Lilith has awoken the sherengro's displeasure.'

'Roland's good sense is tarnished with jealousy,' said Lurania. 'Besides, his word is the law and cannot be questioned.'

'Except by we gypsies, who run our own affairs. Am I not a queen?' Darklis stuffed her pipe with tobacco, lit it at the fire and drew a great lungful of fragrant smoke from its narrow stem.

'Aah! Now I shall see visions. Do you interpret them, Lurania dear, with your curtained sight. I see a flaming brand and the hot coal which ignited it. What are they?'

'That is Roland in the undercroft and Deon with him. They sniff at a cold trail.'

'I see a vase full of rare flowers of the field, a golden bachelor's bloom and a white brimmle close together, a hoary thistle with a yellow archangel. A robnest pecks at the bachelor. Who are these?'

'Easy to answer, Darklis dear. These are the members of the assaulting party (which includes one turncoat) and Lilith is with them. They have reached the balcony, huzzah!'

'You're on their side, Sister?'

'Mayhap. And you?'

'I cannot forget what a weak-kneed cockscomb Aurel is. Remember how he shilly-shallied at the cave and let his lady beg the dwarf for mercy. He was afraid, the wincing turd, the milk-fed baby – he should wear a white feather, not a golden! For his cowardice, I was forced into a parley with Erchon and had to offer him my precious gold (which I could ill afford to do). As you know, my bon-gossip, he is a bene cove and a pranking blade, a gentleman dwarf altogether. He declined my pretty coinage and we bargained otherwise – but from this ill-sorted affair came every following disaster, the Golden Head and Erchon immolated in the hellish fires, the destruction of my contract with the dwarf, our flight hence. This is Agnes' Eve when Erchon's debt is due, and cannot be paid, for the Head and he are molten droplets in continual flux. Were the Head here, right before us on this table – then would Roland and his poxy crew have good cause to unsheathe their swords for I, Darklis Faa, would know the future; I, Queen of the Gypsies, would know what's what and, gathering our Tribe about me, should declare myself the rightful Empress!

'So fie and bad cess to you, Sir Lurk-in-the-Bower. Show your pretty face and fight!'

Darklis looked directly at the hammer-beam which concealed the balcony.

'Show your face, pap-pigeon!' she shrieked and, descant to her noisy challenge, the raucous crowing of a cockerel rang out.

'See,' said Ben. 'The cockerel feather turns into the bird. He won't shut up till Aurel does something.'

'This seems to be a dead end and I (I confess) am confused.' Koshchei moved Magpie back and forth on the balcony, but could think of no way out.

'It's OK, the Beadsman always knows the way. Only the cockerel feather's warning Aurel of an ambush if they try to turn back.'

'The pursuit's so close?'

373

'Some of it. Let's see what Aurel will do; he ought to ignore Darklis, she's a red herring – oh, the twit!'

Aurel pulled away from the force which held him frozen with rage and shame. His mother had taught him to ignore the taunts of jealous schoolfellows and of the other prentices in the weaving-sheds where he had worked; the abbess had taught him patience, Parados forbearance and Hadrian how to keep faith with an ideal, yet hope, and how to abstain from worldly enticements. He knew he had broken the last rule and so, betrayed the old soldier's trust. It was Hadrian who, standing proxy for Parados, had dubbed him knight.

The cockfeather made him most aware: he stood on action's brink. The Beadsman was beckoning and holding open a door in the panelling; Lilith was reaching out to grasp his hand and pull him wherever she desired; Magpie prodded him in the arm. Only the angel was still and smiled impassively.

Aurel stepped forward and leaned over the balcony rail, his head close to the carved griffon on the end of the beam.

'I hear you,' he said.

Darklis spat dark tobacco juices on the floor.

'That's the coward's mark, shite-breeches,' she said and turned away.

Swiftly, Aurel drew Joyeuse from her scabbard. He ran along the passageway, back the way they'd hurried to the hidden refuge which had become a pillory.

Two waited for him, both burly, one with a leathern shield. He saw them clearly because of the feather. The man on the left had a weakness, one eye, but it was turned to him. First blow then.

After that, one-eye's cheek laid open and spurting, it was all limbs, sweat on the hilt and stinging; better to be blind? Blood won, and his lungs filling and emptying, the air too hot, too salty. Parados hissed in his ear, left, spin, on, directions; good, brave, press on, praise. Hadrian had told him that looting was wrong but he could not stop himself from shifting the two bodies so he could see what he had slain, and from feeling cast down because they were so unremarkable, that eyeless socket the only grotesque feature. Then the angel was embracing him and calling him chivalrous when he knew he had been foolhardy.

'What now?' Aurel asked him.

'Don't let go – that's the first thing you must do. We are flying and will soon – thus! – rise from the balcony and exit by the smoke-hole in the roof – I have you fast – and swift as thought or pleasant dream we cross the moat, avoid the unscaleable talus, the grim walls and keen-sighted archers of

The Donjon of Lilith

and – so – alight before the portal on the roof.'

Aurel, for one brief moment, saw the mountains moonlit and thought he saw the Altaish's highest peak. Which is curious, he thought, since Koschei is supposed to have destroyed Malthassa – though I well remember it and so do many more.

'Have no fear,' the angel said again. 'The others are gone before and, once inside, we occupy Lilith's territory and may rest until we are called upon to act.'

There was no interval between Urdiv's speech and the same instant, when Aurel found himself in a pleasant chamber with a fire and a table spread with good food and, best of all, Lilith, the angel and Magpie.

'But where is the Beadsman?' he said, wishing to tell the old priest he had sought the fight out of pride and so make confession to one qualified to hear it.

'We lost him in the portal, Dearest,' Lilith sighed. ''Tis an accident which often happens when time's laws are overborne.'

But Magpie, face pinched with mischief, said, 'You killed him, Aurel. His life is forfeit to your pride: the life of a holy man for two common guards.'

When they had all eaten sufficient of the cold fowl in aspic and the grapes and sweet cakes which were on the table, Lilith stepped forward. She made Aurel kneel before her by gently pushing on his shoulders, bent forward and kissed him on the brow.

'Now you are my suppliant!' she said and laughed merrily. 'You do not have to ask for my hand in marriage – not yet! – but you must carry out the tasks I set.

'If you cannot, we may go no further. Roland, in due time, will lay siege to the donjon and starve us out; you will be sent to the gallows and I to my Tower of Love; Magpie and Urdiv will disappear into God's machine – and all will be as it was with everything to conquer again.'

'I do not die, then – though I am hanged?'

'Effective characters never die. Listen well, my love. Your first task is to answer this riddle of mine: "How dost a shepherd hold water in a witch's sieve?"'

Aurel sat back on his heels, the better to look up at the beautiful lips which had spoken such an inanity. He stuck a finger in his left ear and tried to dislodge Parados who was whispering all kinds of drivel about eggshells and storms. He smiled so meltingly that Lilith's heart beat fast and she gave him a second kiss.

'Beloved,' said Aurel in his most sensual and persuasive tone of voice. 'I do not think it matters if he – or she, for that matter – who seeks to carry water in such a leaky vessel is a shepherd or a gravedigger, a king or a moneylender . . .'

'That is correct,' Lilith said, 'and . . .'

'And stuff and nonsense, Lady. Rubbish, moonshine, fiddle-faddle, Lilith!'

'But you must answer. The second task is to dip up water in my sieve – and here is the well, beneath this iris-broidered samite, and here the sieve!'

She gave him the sieve, which he turned over and over in his hand, examining it. It was made of wicker, he saw, closely woven but not so close it would keep water in.

'She uses it to make rain,' Parados told him.

'Shh!'

Lilith heard him and raised her eyebrows.

'Shall I call my familiars to aid you?'

'I must concentrate,' he said and, rising quickly to his feet, strode forward to grasp the cloth over the well. There was nothing to grasp: what had seemed an ornate wellhead underneath the cloth was air and magic. He lifted the cloth and for an instant was looking down a brick-lined well, the water a small silver disc one, two hundred feet below. It vanished, he whisked the cloth away and tore it in two with his teeth and free hand. He crushed the sieve in the other.

'Aiee!' wailed Lilith. 'He has destroyed the problem. Now the Wolves will come!'

He knew already, for the cursed bird crowed.

'No matter, they would have come later,' said Urdiv. 'On guard, Aurel, and make that magician work for you!'

Koschei, who knew that Wolves meant Green Wolves and that they were the renegade band of soldiery he had once belonged to, moved his mouse frenziedly.

If I am quick and dazzle the boy with sleight of hand, he will not know for whom I fight.

Ben looked at his father and saw the malice in his eyes. It alarmed him, but he thought, I s'pose he's very tired and maybe angry at the way Dirk and those software guys have messed up the story. Koschei was happy, if happy anyone may be who has come through Hell and is scarred with old evil and present ambition:

This is my chance to begin again at magic, with prestidigitation, with conjuration and figure-flinging –

This is my chance of fame, thought Magpie and, delving in his bag of tricks, pulled out a handful of wooden 3s, 5s and a 1, the Ace of them all, which were painted bright red, yellow and green like children's toys.

Asmodeus, I trust he knows the incantation!

'Tray, qwinkwey, en!' cried Magpie and flung his figures in the air.

The door of the quiet room burst open and a pack of men ran

in, the foremost crouching at the flank with scimitars levelled in deadly fashion. They found themselves abetted by nine young swordsmen, ten boys with catapults and a single warrior hefting a club with which he laid about him, smashing the furniture and fittings of the room and catching the angel a hard blow upon the wing-joint.

'It's gone wrong!' wailed Magpie; but Koschei, who had directed him, merely pushed him behind the open door and eagerly watched the fight.

'Anyone may employ a Green Wolf,' he said.

'I know, Dad. I've read all your books at least twice.'

'They are superlative fighters.'

'Yes, Dad; but they're not on our side.'

'Then you had better see if Aurel's success with the guardsmen was fluke or skill.'

Aurel went into battle with a cry of 'Parados!' He did not think much of his chances. The outcome, he was sure of it was: for himself, and within three minutes, the death that is no death; for Magpie, the dungeon; for Lilith, her guardian's displeasure followed by forgiveness and the Tower. He was sure the angel could look after himself.

Ben grabbed the mouse from Koschei's hand. There were tears in his eyes.

'No, no – they'll all be killed!'

Magpie was shrieking at him – hiding like a lily-liver behind the door.

'No, no – you'll all be killed! This way, the passage!'

The wall had opened up behind him. It was cowardice, but Aurel no longer cared. He caught Lilith by the gown and pulled. They were through, and the wall closed behind them. There was no sign of the angel though Aurel thought he heard the whistle of retreating wings.

'You little fool, you've spoiled a good fight.'

'No, I haven't, I've got us to the endgame. This is the Jerusalem Chamber – look! – this is truly

The place was immense, but finite and well-lit. The arches soared and the vaults were vast, but you could see both where they ended and where they began. There were windows, high up and inaccessible, unless you could fly; and there were no doors nor any visible means of exit.

It is a temple, Aurel thought, and tossed a memory of Flaxberry Abbey in the air where it flourished and glowed for an instant before he forgot it. It's the place Friendship and I were looking for.

It is my cathedral, thought Parados, peering from the porch of Aurel's ear. Both the one I dream of and the one I sang in when I was a boy. It is very like the Chapter House.

Aurel walked quietly about, touching a cold pillar here and a stone bench there, while he decided what to do. Lilith trailed behind him, her ivory finery an irrelevant impertinence in this austerity. Magpie crouched on the floor.

'You have deceived me, Ben,' said Koschei, 'been having me on. All this is new to you – you've never got this far, have you? Not even past the Sixth Level?'

'Not really – but I understand the principle.'

'Do you?'

Magpie looked up into the roof. If the ceiling was the floor and we could walk on it, what would we see? He laid his bag down for a pillow and stood on his head. That's it, hanging from the acanthus-leaf boss of the central vault – a thread of finest steel wire, the spinning of a metal spider, a filament of time. Forgetting his bag, his senses, every other thing, Magpie ran across the floor and up the wall, defying gravity, space and time itself for, in no time at all, he walked on the ceiling which was a floor to him. When he looked up he could see Aurel and Lilith pointing down at him.

There was a rosewood and glass case about the size of a chest, or coffin. He could not understand why it had been invisible from below but perhaps that was it: it was invisible, though solid. He bent to examine it, tried to prise off the lid which resisted him. The clock inside was unremarkable, a work of highest craftsmanship to be sure, with a verse engraved on its brass dial, the upright wire the sexton had forgot to cut after a repair, and a weighted pendulum which hung in another dimension. Through this, he could escape; perhaps return to Malthassa, restore it in Koschei's inimitable and baneful way to be a country of the dissolute, the lackadaisical, the chaotic unrestrained by time: what it had always been.

He read the verse,

> Who then to frail mortality shall trust
> But limns in water, or but writes in dust

He must be careful to hide his soul in a safe place, as Koschei had. Then he would be immortal. He reached for his bag of tricks: some spell or device from it would help him open up the clock case – and saw the bag, resting on the pavement high above him. No Bones of Divination, no Blue Bolts, no Everlasting Key, no Figures to fling and call up one strong warrior, two brawny porters, three young swordsmen . . . Then, he would be time's thief, and force the lock. He pulled his eared dagger from its sheath and slid it expertly between the rim of the glass door and the wooden case. One twist and time would be his!

The wood splintered. He thought it a shame to wreck such work but continued, rocking the narrow blade between the lock plates and into its heart. The lock parted with a soft 'clack!' and the loud and heavy noise of clockwork filled his ear. The clock struck ONE TWO THREE . . . he saw Aurel and Lilith covering their ears . . . FIVE SIX . . . in vain, he covered his own . . . EIGHT NINE. He was giddy, reeling with the noise, with the prospect of unlimited time to wreck as he willed, with the certainty that he would fall.

Like a cloth dummy or a puppet whose strings have snapped Magpie fell into the clock case which snapped shut and sealed tight upon its airless, eternally-regulated domain. The seconds, minutes and hours, whose regular march the magician had interrupted, began to hurry on.

Lilith looked up.

'It's very strange, that clock – that we never saw it.'

'You must accustom yourself to inexplicable events and weird sights if you are to be my bride.'

Lilith smiled, saying nothing, but remembering her origins, her parents, her familiars, her Likenesses, the depth and wealth of magic powers which she could call on if she chose.

'Time speeds on, golden Aurel,' she said. 'Let us make haste.'

Magpie protested in the trap he had made for himself. Aurel and Lilith shouted encouragement, but he only continued silently to yell. His mouth worked fast as a landed fish's. There was no one left, but the two of them; and they were caught as much as Magpie.

'But see,' said Lilith, 'He *is* trying to tell us: walk up the wall.'

'Can we do it? I am no magician and your powers are in eclipse.'

'With faith and courage, Love. Take my hand.'

At first, it was like walking in a hall of mirrors of illusion, the floor a series of ribbed bowls, the ceiling paved. They walked downwards. Aurel lost his nerve halfway.

'Close your eyes,' Lilith told him. 'I will lead you.'

'Are you not afraid?'

'No! I shall escape the Castle – and with you. Open your eyes: we are there and the vertigo is defeated. Here's poor Magpie.'

The young magician was fading fast, from lack of air inside the clock case.

'I shall save him,' Aurel declared.

'If you do that, you will break the clock. Besides, he's near the end and feels nothing – ah, 'tis so tragic! Look, his arms have become wings and his legs shrunk inward and upward. His mouth's a gaping beak – he breathes his last.'

The magpie, seen so close, was not black and white but had wings of glossy green and a blue patch on the crown of his head.

381

'He might almost be a stuffed bird in a collector's case,' said Lilith. 'Birds' souls fly free, you know, and in Malthassa may become stars.'

'Are we in Malthassa?'

'I do not know.'

'Then do you know how we get out? There's no door up here.'

'O, tish! Examine the stone boss. There's sure to be some device which will allow us to find our happy ending.'

Aurel pressed and pushed the carved acanthus leaves. The third try was lucky: the mechanism groaned a little before the mighty carving sank, revealing stairs down which they hurried to a small and sun-warmed courtyard. A shadow had draped itself across one corner of it, which hid a tunnel-mouth. Lilith ran now, full of joy and pulling Aurel with her.

'I shall not kiss you until I am free!'

The postern at the end of the tunnel was not locked. Bolts were its only defence and these, Aurel drew, and opened the gate. Expecting daylight, freedom, escape, they were not prepared for total darkness and confinement. Aurel blundered on, one, two steps forward. The only contact with reality was Lilith's cool hand, locked in his.

'Slowly, softly,' she whispered. 'I smell danger – wild animals, fear of the dark.'

His right hand was extended, some kind of guard or probe before him. He was thinking, I should draw Joyeuse and use that – when his hand met with coarse hair, a long and well-furred tail; next, hard, jutting horns; the pliant resistance of birchbark shaped and stitched. He was touching a shoe which, if his balance and orientation were still intact, floated level with his face. Something breathed on his neck, a gentle gust. He could smell rich sweat.

'Red Horse!' he exclaimed and felt a tail swish, but it was a woman's hair.

'Friendship!'

Then his feet were treading dry heathland, the floor of the

382

mine, the air on which he had floated to Peklo. He stumbled. Lilith held him up.

'We're inside,' she said. 'We could be here for ever.'

'Where are we?' He turned and gripped her tightly by the arms. 'Tell me if you know, Lilith, or be faithless and fickle like your mother!'

'She had her reasons – too complicated for simple minds.'

'Lilith!'

'We are within,' she told him. 'In his mind.'

'There must be a door – a window, eyes, a mouth. I shall find the way out!'

'I know that too. Reach out, just so. Can you feel wood? Then push – it is the door.'

The light was bleak, an early-morning drab, but it showed them the staircase which was short and plain, a domestic flight. They ran up and opened the little door at the top. Here was a library, small enough, the shelves fixed in regular stacks all round the room and overflowing with books. Aurel read some of the titles: The Bible; Shakespeare, the Complete Works; The Treasury of Song.

'Here are his favourites – see how well-thumbed they are,' said Lilith. 'He used to be a poet, you know, but gave up . . .'

She took one from the shelf. It was a slender duodecimo, green-covered, limp with age: some poet's life and memories trapped for ever in print. She glanced swiftly down a few of the pages. A bookmark lay between two of them.

'O Chatterton! how very sad thy fate,' she read 'O Solitude! if I must with thee dwell.'

A strong odour hung for a moment in the air, something chemical, something organic. She read a little more,

                      'the sweet converse of an innocent mind,
  'Whose words are images of thoughts refined,
    'Is my soul's pleasure . . .'

and Very True, she thought, while her mind ran on and on through worlds and universes. She moved the soiled and torn bookmark which kept the place to another page and smiled as she did so. It was fragile, old de-natured paper of a pale forget-me-not blue in the shape of a little man, one silhouette cut from a line joined by the hands and feet such as mothers make their children, or men in an idle, reflective moment.

'There's another door.' Aurel's voice interrupted her reverie. He's loud, impatient, she thought, A boy compared with me. She looked back as she followed him behind the velvet curtain, through the door. The books had gone to sleep. The room was full of dreams.

Aurel and Lilith stepped into an autumn forest where the leaves which remained on the trees were scarlet and gold and those which had fallen a deep russet hue.

'The colour of the Horse!' said Aurel.

'What?'

'Nothing – a memory, from before. Lilith – when I travelled alone in that world, after the Horse had died and Gry had gone to the Palace of Shadows, if I needed food or drink, it was there! Let's try it.'

'I would welcome a drink of fresh water.'

'And here is a pool – careful of the mud!'

Lilith did not care: she was thirsty. She was still holding the green-backed book of poems and laid it gently down as she knelt to drink from her cupped hands. Her gown was already dirty, from the fighting and the climb, and the down of her wrap was matted and torn. She ripped the lower part of it away.

'Your breastplate's getting tarnished, Aurel. Look in the water.'

Aurel studied his reflection briefly.

'I look like a gypsy,' he said.

'With flaxen hair? I am the gypsy – a little bit, at least, through my mother.'

'Wasn't she nivasha?'

'That's a story! Aurel – I've one last thing to do and you shall kiss me, and more.'

As Lilith gazed into the water she seemed to regain her peerless

384

beauty and her fine clothes. Her red riband glowed and her green eyes sparkled with life, and with mischief. She will conjure another of these reflections to tease and confuse me, Aurel thought, but all that happened was that two of the drowning leaves which lay upon the surface of the pool, floated into Lilith's hands. She breathed upon them and her two familiars were there, Leo the lion dog and Halfman the monkey.

'Will you take him? I must carry little Leo, who is a great comfort to me,' said Lilith.

'I will! For Friendship's sake.'

'We are more than friends.'

'That we are. I claim my kiss and shall bed you on a cushion of leaves.'

For Gry's sake, he thought, but did not voice his disloyalty which, in truth, was loyalty to Gry, his once and truest love. Laughing, he pulled Lilith to the ground and never noticed that the book had fallen open beside them and that a tiny soul rose up and walked across the open page. The soul of Parados slipped from his ear to welcome it with open arms and an embrace.

'We have been apart too long,' it whispered.

'Apart and warring. Let us unite and stand together against the world,' said the other.

The two souls held each other's weightless, ethereal bodies so close they melded, the essence and essential being of each flowing into the other until they were one. With one, last backward glance at the lovers, the soul jumped into the pool.

The screen was dark, a rich and even umber like still water. A pattern of leaves floated across it, again and again. He had felt the twinned soul enter him, a pang of black despair combined with boundless hope and expectation: he was one again, he was whole. He covered his fear and joy with words,

'What's happened?' he asked his son.

'The system's crashed. Memory overload – or maybe there's a bug in the software. I bet no one ever got this far!'

'To the end of the game?'

'Yes, Dad. To the very end.'

'Switch it off, will you? I'm going downstairs.'

'OK – I'm going back to bed!'

He stood up, stretched. Despite the lack of sleep he felt fitter, more alert than he had ever been. But Perry was downstairs – Jilly had asked him to return 'after eight'. It was some time since the church clock had struck nine.

They were in the kitchen drinking coffee, Jilly slumped over the table as if she and not he had been up all night. Perry's left hand rested on her shoulder while, with his right, he caressed her hair. They did not seem glad to see him but rearranged their postures and tried to smile; but the dogs thumped their tails and Pyewacket came forward to sniff his legs.

'Guy!' said Jilly, as if here were a distant acquaintance she'd met in the street.

'Coffee?' Perry offered.

Why not? He sat in the deep chair by the Aga, extended his legs and let them do their guilty best to make him welcome in his own house. Plenty of time to make up a good story – though he remembered little after France which had not been Malthassa. Except Pakistan and India, of course, and Turkey and Afghanistan before them. That wisent was an interesting creation: maybe he had been in Poland and seen the European bison there? But, if that were the case, he's possibly also been to the States and studied the Plains Indians – Gry, dear Gry. Or to Siberia and Kazakhstan? Gry, sweet Gry, whose Romany name was a variation on his own. Or to Ireland to see the original of Peklo tower? It did not matter. He had been to Hell and back.

'I suppose you obtained power of attorney?' he asked Jilly.

'I had to – it was very difficult.'

'Perhaps you would give me some of my own money?'

'Of course!' She blushed scarlet. He would be less kind to Perry.

'I trust Hilary's well?' he said. 'And the children?'

Perry, too, was blunt.

'How the fuck would I know? She took them with her when she left me – in '94.'

'I see! And you don't correspond?' He rose to his feet and bent over Jilly, enjoying his power to hurt. He was perfectly calm.

'I'll find myself another dwelling, Mrs Young, when I get my goods and money back.'

'My house –' Perry muttered.

'The old place? Well, well – we were friends when you bought it. Give me a key, and a pint of milk. I suppose you run to a jar of coffee? Stop fretting, sweetest Jillyflower. I don't own you – any more, any more than I have copyright on my pet name for you which Perry, with all else, has usurped.'

'Seven years!' she sobbed.

'"Till death us do part, according to God's holy ordinance" and all that shit. You were a Christian once, Jilly, and so was I. Didn't we marry in the cathedral?'

'A long time ago, before –'

'I began to write? Don't cry: all's fair in love and war.'

He sat down on Perry's unmade bed and opened the laptop. It started into life without a hitch. The empty screen was worse than a blank sheet of paper. He hit Shift and T and began.

The SpacedarknessSpacecoveringSpaceMalthassaSpacewasSpace-thickDeleteDarkness inhabited the land. Not a single star shone; nor had the moon been seen for an age [what character to use now, who was left alive?] and Colarix, the woodcutter, was blind to anything that passed in the perpetual night. The small flame of his penny candle was his sight.

Needing water, Colarix stepped out of the hovel, felt his way to the well and let down the bucket. It travelled slowly up again, slopping its liquid burden. The rusty gear creaked. The water, as he manhandled the heavy bucket, wet his feet and he saw, with a happy jolt, that he had also caught a luminous fish which lay like a bright star at the bottom of the bucket. A good supper! Colarix snatched at the fish in the water and saw it shatter in a thousand pieces, and reform itself as he withdrew his hand. There was no fish, nothing to feel, for he had caught a star indeed, a single, brilliant light whose parent shone above him and awoke the sky and the night to hope. He was an old man: there had been no such shining since his boyhood among the stacked logs and sawn-off tree boles. He watched the star settle itself above his smoking chimney and its child which, after all, had been only a reflection, disappear from his bucket.

Deeper in the forest, beneath the still and samovile-haunted trees, Aurel and Lilith woke in their bed of leaves and

Were they, then, to be his new hero and heroine? Disturbed by new imaginings and memories, Guy put the laptop aside and went to the window. Dusk was filling up the long village street and obscuring the neatly-mown Green; everyone inside, watching – but no, there was a pair of walkers: who? No one he remembered; but he had been absent so long. The street lamp outside the smithy dropped its orange light on their unsuspecting heads and Guy recognised Aurel – in jeans, to be sure, and a tarnished silvery blouson, his golden hair in dusty dreadlocks; Aurel, and Lilith, fair and moody in a fleece jacket and long, grimy skirt, oak leaves caught in her abundant hair. She cradled a Pekinese dog. The monkey clung to Aurel's arm. Guy pushed open the casement, leaned – and retired, closing the window firmly and latching it. No need to wave, no reason to hail them. They would come in anyway. He turned to the keyboard, back to the story, and typed, 'gazed into the velvet sky.'

He was content, happy perhaps, wifeless and childless, without distractions. This was his world. There were some regrets, the loss of his newfound son, the other children grown up and gone to their own lives, even Grace – but Benedict was only two minutes away, in his mother's house. He should have his own room here.

'I see a newborn star,' said Aurel.

'It represents our love –'

'No, 'tis actual, real. Malthassa wakes.'

Guy smiled to himself. He would go on but, for the paradise of it, for fun, he typed

THE END AND THE BEGINNING

Guy Kester Parados,
Verity's Cottage,
Maidford Halse,
June 24th 1997.

Leaving the computer open and ready, he rose and ran downstairs. The garden gate creaked, but he already had the door open. They were walking along the path, absurd and so young with their ragged clothing and their familiar animals. He stepped forward on to the threshold.

'Welcome!' he said.

Aurel was the first to embrace him. Struggling free, he gave his characteristic laugh, an upward bound of happy vigour and said,

'Parados! At last and whole again.'

He folded Lilith in his arms. After all, she was his as much as she was Aurel's. She tucked the little poetry book into his shirt pocket and favoured him with a deep and hungry look from her gypsy eyes, Nemione's, Helen's. She smiled at him.

Everville
Clive Barker

Five years ago, in his bestseller *The Great and Secret Show*, Clive Barker mesmerised millions of readers worldwide with an extraordinary vision of human passions and possibilities. Welcome to a new volume in that epic adventure. Welcome to *Everville*.

On a mountain peak, high above the city of Everville, a door stands open: a door that opens onto the shores of the dream-sea Quiddity. And there's not a soul below who'll not be changed by that fact . . .

Phoebe Cobb is about to forget her old life and go looking for her lost lover Joe Flicker in the world on the other side of that door; a strange, sensual wonderland the likes of which only Barker could make real.

Tesla Bombeck who knows what horrors lurk on the far side of Quiddity, must solve the mysteries of the city's past if she is to keep those horrors from crossing the threshold.

Harry D'Amour, who has tracked the ultimate evil across America, will find it conjuring atrocities in the sunlit streets of Everville.

Step into Everville's streets, and enter a world like no other . . .

'Clive Barker is so good I am almost tongue-tied. What Barker does makes the rest of us look like we've been asleep for the last ten years . . . His stories are compulsorily readable and original. He is an important, exciting and enormously saleable writer.'
Stephen King

ISBN 0 00 647225 7

The Thief of Always
Clive Barker

*A disturbing fable exploring childhood fears
and delights from the maestro of dark fantasy.*

Mr Hood's Holiday House has stood for a thousand years, welcoming countless children into its embrace. It is a place of miracles, a blissful round of treats and seasons, where every childish whim may be satisfied.

There is a price to be paid, of course, but young Harvey Swick, bored with his life and beguiled by Mr Hood's wonders, does not stop to consider the consequences. It is only when the House shows its darker face – when Harvey discovers the pitiful creatures that dwell in its shadow – that he comes to doubt Mr Hood's philanthropy.

The House and its mysterious architect are not about to release their captive without a battle, however. Mr Hood has ambitions for his new guest, for Harvey's soul burns brighter than any soul he has encountered in a thousand years . . .

'A dashingly produced fantasy with powerful drawings by the author'   *Daily Telegraph*

'Barker puts the dark side back into childhood fantasy . . . A welcome modern-day return to classic form, this fable lives up to the publishers' billing as a tale for all ages'
                                                              Publishers Weekly

ISBN 0 00 647311 3